P9-DNZ-667

AN AMERICAN PROPHET

AN
AMERICAN
PROPHET

BY
GERALD GREEN

DOUBLEDAY & COMPANY, INC.
GARDEN CITY, NEW YORK
1977

Library of Congress Cataloging in Publication Data

Green, Gerald.
An American Prophet.

I. Title.
PZ3.G8227Am   [PS3513.R4493]   813'.5'4
ISBN: 0-385-03709-0
Library of Congress Catalog Card Number 76-18348

Copyright © 1977 by GERALD GREEN
All Rights Reserved
Printed in the United States of America
BOOK DESIGN BY BENTE HAMANN

*A limited edition of this book
has been privately printed.*

To the memory of

JOSEPH WOOD KRUTCH

(1893–1970)

We must learn to re-awaken, and to keep ourselves awake, not by mechanical aids, but by an
infinite expectation of the dawn, which does not
forsake us, in our soundest sleep.

—Thoreau

AN AMERICAN PROPHET

1

———————————— ❊ ————————————

From behind a clump of prickly pear, a road runner flew onto the blacktop, and with comic determination began to race the right front tire of the jeep.

Daniel Vormund saw the feathery brown creature and smiled. He nudged the driver. "Ed, we've got company. That bird is contesting your right to Interstate Highway Ten."

"I saw him," Ed Bugler said. "They know this jeep."

Vormund's wife, Clara, seated in the rear of the rattling open vehicle, tucked an olive-drab blanket around Dan's narrow shoulders. In OD wool cap, woolen mackinaw, scarf, thick gloves, and long johns that peeked from beneath corduroy trousers, old Vormund seemed to have been outfitted from an army and navy store.

"Keep the wind out of your mouth, Dan," Clara said firmly. "Let Ed do the talking and you listen for a change. Oh, it's so cold. I shouldn't have let Ed talk you into this crazy expedition. And why so early?"

It was dark in the Arizona desert. The road runner, challenging the tire, was a blur of feathers and flying feet.

Vormund ignored his wife's admonitions. They had been married fifty-five years. She had been a nurse before their marriage.

Her profession had served her well, preparing her for a lifetime of ministering to an ailing hypochondriacal scholar.

"Got to start early to observe nature," Ed Bugler said. "When the wild things are waking up."

"Like fun," Clara Vormund said. She was seventy-nine. A small woman with a beautiful round face. Her white hair was thick and short and neatly combed. "I know why you and Dan sneaked off like this at five in the morning."

"Tell us, my love," Vormund said. He winked at Bugler: schoolboys putting one over on teacher.

"Because you'll be trespassing. Driving on land you have no right to be on. Ed's gotten the ranchers so mad at him—and you too, Daniel Dean Vormund—they won't let Institute people get near their land."

"Why, Clara," Bugler said, feigning injury, "you mean I'd sneak onto a man's land without permission? I'm hurt."

"Yes, and I don't mind hurting you. Dragging a sick man like Dan, aged eighty-one, coughing and sneezing, into the cold morning air."

"The sun will revive us," Vormund said. "Brother Sun, as St. Francis called him. Clara, we will soon be blessed by the white radiance of eternity."

Weary of his mad pursuit, the road runner darted off the blacktop, squawked irritably, vanished into a creosote bush.

"Good-by, friend," Vormund said. He peered into the desert darkness. Thoreau watching a turtledove disappear behind a cloud, he thought.

"Small crisis," Bugler announced. "We seem to be running out of gas."

"You were supposed to check the tank," Clara said.

"This gauge is busted. I was also supposed to fix it. Dan, you have to tell the Maybanks to get me some help. I can't do everything."

"There's no gas station between here and where we're going," Clara said. She was annoyed with Bugler. She loved him, and she knew how much he meant to Dan. But his casual way of life could be burdensome.

The fourth member of the group spoke for the first time. He was a stocky Indian in dusty Levi's. He was sleeping on the metal floor of the rear compartment. Stirring, his voice mashed with sleep, he said: "Guy at the Pima Trading Post, he keeps gas. No pump, but some gas."

"Sidewinder to the rescue," Bugler said.

The man on the floor sat up and rubbed his eyes. He was a Hopi of indeterminate age. Thick lenses clouded his eyes. A faded gray Stetson was jammed on his matted black hair.

"Aren't you cold, Sidewinder?" Clara Vormund asked. "In just that jacket?"

"No, ma'am."

"Did you have a nourishing breakfast?"

"No, ma'am. Just some grape soda."

"Ed Bugler should be ashamed of letting you start off the day that way."

The Indian laughed politely. He covered his mouth with a coppery hand. Old lady Vormund, always looking after people. As if the whole world was as old and as sick as Dan.

The Pima Trading Post was dark and deserted. Bugler asked the Hopi to awaken someone. Five gallons would be enough to get them to their destination.

Vormund's ears picked out the morning songs of desert birds. He was getting better. If he lived to be a hundred, he might know most of the birds of the dry land.

"Listen," the old man said softly. "Listen. A crissal thrasher."

Clara and Bugler turned their heads and tried to distinguish the sound or see the silhouette.

"I know he's there," Vormund said. "*There.* That warbling. *Pichoory. Pichoory.*"

Vormund's voice melded gently into the bird's morning song. *Pichoory . . . pichoory . . .*

Through binoculars Bugler sighted the thrasher—an elegant bird with a curved bill.

"Let's have a look at him, Ed," Vormund said. His hands trembled as he looked at the singing bird. What bird would be his last?

"I want to see him," Clara said. "Dan, isn't he beautiful?"

"All natural things are beautiful," Vormund said. "For nature is the art of God. I shouldn't be quoting this early. It's bad for the digestion."

Sidewinder came out of the darkened trading post with a six-teen-year-old Indian girl. She was fat and pock-marked, and had clever eyes. She carried a five-gallon gasoline can.

Sidewinder jammed a funnel into the gas tank. The girl grinned at Bugler. "Got a cigarette?" she asked.

"Sure. But only if you don't smoke while we're pouring gasoline."

"I know. Gimme a cigarette."

Bugler reached into the pocket of his gray Sears shirt and gave the girl two cigarettes. She let Sidewinder pour gasoline, retreated several yards, and lit up. Match flare illumined her squashed face.

"How is that cigarette, young lady?" Vormund asked. He liked Indians.

She exhaled fiercely through her nostrils. Smoke formed a nimbus around her head. "It tastes good like a cigarette *should*," she said.

Clara and Bugler laughed.

"Splendid," Vormund said. "I'm glad to see your education at the Indian School in Phoenix has been a liberal one."

The girl winked. "Yeah. You've come a long way, baby."

Bugler paid the girl. He drove to the highway again. *That Dan*, he was thinking. Only Daniel D. Vormund would talk to a Pima girl as if she were a professor's wife or a duchess. Last of the old Kentucky gentlemen, someone once called him.

"Dear?" Vormund said. "May I remove one of these blankets? I feel like Proust."

"Not until the sun is out."

Who was Proust? Bugler wondered. Never figure Dan Vormund in a million years. City man, professor, teacher, critic. All those honors and books and achievements. And he'd chosen, the last twenty years, to spend his time with road runners and cacti, and desert rats like Edward Earle Bugler. *I'm some companion,* Bugler mused. A man who got kicked out of high school in Hastings, Nebraska, for turning a skunk loose in assembly hall.

"We should be there by now, shouldn't we?" Clara asked.

"Prod Sidewinder," Bugler said. "It's one of these cattle paths, but I'm not sure which."

"He's asleep again."

"No I ain't, Mrs. Vormund." The Hopi got to his feet and

steadied himself against the cab. "Six paths after the trading post," he said.

"Six?" Bugler asked. "I thought it was five."

"Five or six."

"Oh, fine," Clara said. "Now we're lost."

Vormund reached back and took her hand. "Have faith in Ed. He has many defects of mind and many failings of character, but he is the best cactus finder in the world."

"Hold on, folks," Bugler said. "Over the ditch and into the desert."

Protesting with creaks and rattles, the jeep bounced over the shoulder, fell into the ditch, rose, and pointed its snout at the cattle guard.

"Open the gate, Sidewinder," Bugler said. "We're on our way."

"On private land," Clara said. "They'll shoot us one of these days."

"And what a thrill!" Vormund said. "Like the young Churchill, I'll hear bullets whistle over me and I'll come out a better man."

"At age eighty-one, Dan?" Bugler asked.

The jeep dug into the thick sand, winding its way between prickly pear, cholla, ocotillo. A touch of sun spread warmth and brought the dormant plants to life. Vormund saw a sparrow hawk take flight from a giant saguaro.

"Right turn by them big mesquites," Sidewinder said.

"It's farther than I thought," Clara said. "Dan, this jolting isn't good for your kidneys."

"My kidneys have never been healthier."

"Ed, did you bring enough water?" she asked.

"Clara, stop bothering Ed. If we run out of water, I'll draw it from a rock, like Moses. My only problem is, if a voice says I AM THAT I AM, what do I respond? I've never figured out what the Lord meant."

"Don't ask me," Bugler said. "They kicked me out of Sunday school right after they kicked me out of high school."

The jeep inched its way up an incline, the wheels struggling to bite into the sliding sand. Distantly the Santa Teresa Range changed color, as sunlight struck the brown-gray slopes.

"Oh, the mountains," Clara cried. "Dan, look at the colors. How they change."

"I see, Clara."

Bugler saw them also, but he said nothing. Clara and Dan were like that. They shared the natural world. Their love for each other intensified at the sight of a bird or a flower. He liked the wild things also, but in a different way. Bugler had slept in a coyote den, talked to raccoons, once helped a badger dig its way to freedom from a steel trap. Maybe the difference was that Dan saw God in birds and animals; Ed saw friends.

"How good the earth is," Vormund said. "Especially without man, present company excluded. Is it possible that the text of Genesis was garbled? Could it have been that God rested after the *fifth* day, before he created the great evildoer?"

"Old blasphemer," Clara said. "Be careful, Dan. You'll have to make your peace with God someday."

"I never knew He and I had quarreled."

What were they talking about now? Bugler wondered.

Clara had her huge woolen bag open and was offering vitamin pills to Sidewinder, Meritene to Dan, hot cocoa to everyone.

The jeep's bottom struck a rock. The metal frame shivered. Clara was thrown against the Hopi. "Steady there, ma'am," Sidewinder said. He helped her back to the bench.

"This is awful," she said. "Not for me so much, but for Dan."

He ignored her. "Ed, have you ever seen such a sunrise? You must forgive me for stealing words from my superiors. But at least I go to good sources. 'But look, the morn, in russet mantle clad, rises in the east.'"

"That's *Hamlet*, Ed," said Clara.

"You couldn't prove it by me." Bugler scowled. His leathery, square face, eyes squinting behind steel-rimmed glasses, surveyed the ragged foothills, the summits of the Santa Teresa Range. "Sidewinder, are you sure you weren't full of peyote when you saw those plants?"

"I never chew·peyote. That's for them in the Native American Church. I'm a Lutheran."

"I never knew you were," Clara Vormund said.

"Oh, I don't work at it."

"I wish he was a Christian Scientist," Bugler said. "Then he could *imagine* those cacti and I could stop driving."

"I knew it," Clara said. "We're lost."

The desert spread around them—silent, dusty, full of unseen life. Vormund loved it for its endurance, its sparseness. It proved that scarcity could be a blessing, that kangaroo rats were as courageous as men, and far more ingenious biologically. Birds, for that matter, were more joyous, more graceful.

The old man turned his seamed face to the sun. Like Thoreau, he conceded that he had never assisted the sun materially in its rising, but did not doubt that it was of the last importance to be present at it. . . .

"We got to be near," Bugler said. "Riding around for a half hour."

"We're not near it," Sidewinder said. "We're there." He took off his Stetson. His starch-fattened face turned toward a steep rise in the terrain. "Over that hill. There's a box canyon under it. They grow around it."

"Dan can never climb that hill," Clara said.

"Is there another way around?" Bugler asked.

The Indian shook his head. "Dry bed closes it off."

Vormund threw off the blanket and undid the top button of his mackinaw. He climbed out of the jeep. "Ed, we shall ascend the mountain and see the cactus. Clara, you can stay behind if you wish."

"No. I have to keep an eye on you." She let Sidewinder help her down the rear step.

Vormund, his shoes slipping in the sand, began to walk surprisingly fast.

"The old fire horse," Bugler said to Clara. "Dan claims he's half dead most of the time. His throat, his eyes, his chest. But tell him there's a rare bird somewhere, or a cactus he's never seen, and watch him take off."

Clara said nothing. She looked, with a joy that was reborn each morning of their lives, at her husband's slender stooped figure climbing the sandy hill. He had taken off his wool cap. A breeze fluttered the feathery white hairs on his crown.

Vormund stopped to catch his breath. "That sparrow hawk again, Clara," he said. "What a superb bird. Maybe the Holy Spirit was a hawk rather than a dove."

His wife laughed. "God will punish you, Dan. That funny

business about the fifth day. And now making the Holy Spirit a hawk."

The mountains were a vast mosaic of earthy colors. Grays and browns changed to lavenders, purples, greens.

At the crest of the hill, Vormund rested against Bugler's hard body for a moment. His legs were watery. Too fast going up the slope. The sun had deceived him, endowing him with temporary vigor, but unable to cure the accumulated ailments of eight decades.

"If you look sharp," Sidewinder said, as he helped Clara to the summit, "you might see them from here. Over yonder."

"Lord, I do see them," Vormund cried. "This is incredible."

About a hundred feet below them, on a particularly dry chunk of terrain, the ground was covered by a dull green tapestry. The cover was not continuous. Bald spots alternated in haphazard patterns with the green vegetation. The thick flattened cacti appeared to have driven the more common desert flora—cholla and saguaro and ocotillo—from their domain.

Vormund stumbled a few steps, then began to descend the slope. Once he almost fell, eliciting a warning cry from Clara and a muffled laugh from the Hopi. Then the old man straightened up and marched into the field of cactus. He planted his feet in the sand, like an explorer or a desert prophet. Opening his arms wide, he sought to embrace the plants.

"Look at him," Clara said. "Like Stanley finding Livingston. Or the first man on the moon."

"Don't be sure it isn't as important," Bugler said. "This is the first time anybody's seen a creeping devil in the United States. Boy, look at them."

"The creeping devil," Vormund intoned—as if addressing a lecture hall. "Behold it in all its glory. Sometimes called the caterpillar cactus."

"Mexicans," Sidewinder said. "Mexicans call it *oruga*. Means caterpillar."

Vormund remained with arms outstretched, as if seeking to protect the wild cacti, all the animals and birds and plants of the dry land.

"This is rich," Bugler said. "I got to get Dan's picture down there." He unlimbered a Pentax and took photographs of Vormund.

"Save your film," Vormund called. "This is a historic moment. What a laugh we'll have on the botanists, those experts who told us that no creeping devil grew in the United States."

The other members of the party walked down the slope toward the parklike area where the succulents grew. Sidewinder, less awed than Clara and Ed, squatted under a paloverde tree and lit a cigarette.

"A botanical milestone," Vormund said. "Look at the way they grow, Clara, hugging the ground, like spiked caterpillars, and forming a grand design. Natural forms are the most beautiful of all. No artist could duplicate such lines and curves."

The gray-green plants to which Vormund paid tribute were thick-trunked and wickedly spiked. Unlike a vertical cactus, they hugged the earth, twisting and turning, sometimes rising in small arches to leapfrog a neighbor. Some were a foot in diameter, armed with natural daggers, full of danger.

Ecstatic, Vormund walked among the plants. "Ed, are you aware what Dr. Butler, a clergyman contemporary of Shakespeare, said about the strawberry?"

Bugler was on one knee, inspecting a plant. "Not my department, Dan."

"He said that doubtless God could have invented a better berry, but doubtless God never did. Doubtless God could have invented a stranger cactus than these, but doubtless God never did."

Under the pressure of the sun, Vormund tottered. Clara was at his side. "You're getting dizzy."

"Unhand me, woman. I have never felt stronger."

"That ride in the cold wind. And now tramping around the desert. Dan, you are too old for these crazy adventures with Ed and Sidewinder. The Institute doesn't expect you to go on them."

Vormund ignored her. He turned away from the cacti and addressed the Hopi. "Sidewinder, you deserve the credit. Mr. Maybank will know about your discovery. If this cactus is a variant, we shall name it for you. *Machaerocereus eruca sidewinderii.*"

"I'd rather you got me a pickup truck."

"That too, Sidewinder." Vormund let Clara guide him to the shade of the paloverde tree. He sat on a stone next to the Hopi. "If the Institute's finances permit it, of course."

"Don't make promises to Sidewinder you can't keep," Clara reprimanded.

"It's okay, ma'am," the Indian said. "He'd get me one if he could."

Vormund let the sun warm his pate. He inhaled desert perfumes, and a whiff of Sidewinder's smoky Indian odor. He felt fulfilled, at peace with the earth. No scholar he had ever known had given him as much peace of mind as the Hopi. Thoreau knew a man who lived in a hollow tree and had regal manners.

Bugler wandered amid the plants, clicking off photographs, shaking his head in disbelief. Vormund watched him with drowsy eyes. There was never enough time to see of a world worth seeing. When they were younger, he and Clara had trudged through the museums and churches of Europe. They had loved every minute of their rubbernecking. But always, it seemed to Vormund, they had been cheated. There was never enough time. Not enough time to see, to contemplate.

But if man's creations took more time to comprehend than was ever allotted, what about God's works? What to make of these spectacular plants, unlike anything in the world? Nature's weavings? God's tapestries?

"You are infatuated with Nature," his friend Tyler Merritt once told him, "because Man can't take any credit. It's a negative approach, Dan. If Man isn't involved, you assume the forms and colors are superior and worthy of your admiration. How did you ever get so low an opinion of mankind?"

Vormund winked, and responded: "Introspection."

"Beats all, Dan," Bugler shouted. He was on his knees. "The rear end shrivels and the front sends the new shoots out. The roots run along the bottom."

"Be careful you don't get stabbed," Clara cautioned.

"My friend Edward Earle Bugler," Vormund said, "is impervious to pain and poison. Bitten by rattlesnakes, stung by scorpions, savaged by gila monsters, he survives."

"He'll get his comeuppance someday," Clara said. "His blood stream is full of poison. Dan, tell Ed to be careful the way he handles those thorns."

Vormund did not hear her. He had struggled to his feet and was shading his eyes. "Sidewinder, help me down the hill."

The Hopi aided the old man. Halfway down the incline Vormund broke from the Indian's arms and began to trot, as if fearful that the plants would vanish from view.

"What's he up to now?" Clara asked.

"Dan, they're not going anywhere. These plants'll be here forever." Bugler shook his head.

"Not the one I see."

Vormund was on all fours. He was doubled over, like a Moslem on a prayer rug, his head at ground level. "Ed, come quickly. This is beyond belief."

Bugler walked toward him.

"A flower, Ed. A perfect flower."

"Why is that so special?" Clara asked.

"Tell her, Ed."

Bugler paused on the other side of the cactus Vormund was studying. "No one's ever seen one, Clara. Nobody. No botanist has ever seen the *oruga* in bloom."

"We amateurs, Ed, will keep the world safe for scientists. Behold. Born to blush unseen and waste its sweetness on the desert air."

Bugler remained on his knees. "All I can figure, Dan, is that the botanists got to Baja at the wrong time of year. Or maybe the darn thing blooms every two or three years."

"Entirely possible," Vormund said. He bent closer to the pink flower. It was a perfect small bulb, streaked with dark red, the petals folded.

"Just look at those two, Sidewinder," Clara said.

"Yes, ma'am. They're sure happy." The Indian nestled in the shade of the paloverde. Nature people. A little loco, all of them. Better than ranchers, but loco. Ed and the professor and the old lady. He tried to act interested. But what was so great about a cactus?

Vormund was nose-to-nose with Bugler, the two of them trying (it seemed to Clara) to creep into the flower, like pollen-hungry bees.

"Clara, this is the kind of thrill that makes me grateful I've lived so long. Who would have believed when we struggled out of our beds this cold morning that we'd be rewarded?"

She smiled. There was a jewel in every day they spent together. The flight of a raven. Sunlight on a mountainside. She loved him more every day. The way Dan loved the natural world. *Should man, through his greed, vanish from the earth,* he had written, *lizards may yet run, flowers bloom, hawks soar.* . . .

"I wish we could see it in full bloom," Vormund said. "Maybe we could come back in a day or two."

"If you're up to it, Dan."

Bugler attached a close-up lens to his camera and bent low.

"Clara, look at our friend Ed. He reminds me of Dr. Johnson, who said he couldn't be a botanist because he would have to become a reptile. A reference to his nearsightedness. Ed makes a first-rate reptile."

"Some of my best friends are coral snakes," Bugler said.

Clara Vormund thought: Her husband was the only man in the world who, in the desolation of the Arizona desert, quoted Johnson, Gray, and Sir Thomas Browne to a Hopi Indian and a man who had been thrown out of high school.

With his corded hands, Bugler removed a chunk of creeping devil from the soil. The roots were bright orange. He and Sidewinder would transplant the specimen in the Institute's garden. It would be a wonder, like the boojum trees he and Vormund had brought from Baja.

"Don't cut yourself," Clara warned.

"I have already."

Sidewinder smiled. "Ed don't need no knife. He's better than any Indian. I seen him chase a fox out of his hole one night, so's he could sleep in it."

"But I invited him back the next day." Bugler severed the cactus section. His hands were bleeding, but he was oblivious. "Guess we can head back. Dan, you got all the pictures you need?"

Vormund nodded. Had he ever had a better friend than Ed Bugler? Ed was sixty-one and looked both older and younger. His square face sometimes looked ten years older—seamed, crosshatched, scarred. But his body was young and tough—long-limbed, big-boned. In the desert Ed did not walk or run, but *loped*—a loose stride that conquered mountains.

Sidewinder got up and dusted his threadbare Levi's. He turned to the west. His flattened nose sniffed the morning air.

"Guess we can go," Bugler said.

"I think so," Vormund said. "What a glorious day."

He waited for Ed to come toward him, marveling at the way

Bugler went forth into the wilderness. Like John the Baptist outfitted by Sears. A gray shirt and gray pants instead of a lion's hide. In the pockets were raisins, matches, two Band-Aids, a Sierra cup, and a folding tool that secreted knife, scissors, can opener, nail file, fork, spoon, and corkscrew. A ball-point pen and a notebook completed his kit. Thus equipped, he could live for days. Vormund, a sickly man, weakened by drafty lecture halls and New York winters, forever coughing, envied his friend. Bugler fondled tarantulas the way other men stroked gold ingots.

The four started up the incline. Vormund lingered, turning for a last look at the creeping devils.

"Come along," Clara said. "You can look at the photographs. I don't think we should come out here again. Ed, whose land is this?"

"I'm not sure." He cradled the cutting against his shirt. "It might be Duane Essler's."

"You mean you don't *know?*" she asked. "I'm wise to you, Ed. We're trespassing."

"Clara, it could be government land or it could be Essler's. Essler leases all the government land he can lay his hands on for a dollar an acre. Then he can kill all the predators he likes at government expense."

"But we shouldn't be trespassing. Why didn't you ask Mr. Essler's permission?"

"You kidding, Clara? All he'd have to hear is that the Desert Research Institute is poking around his land. He'd have the sheriff waiting for us."

"Essler's nuts," Sidewinder said. "Crazy man buyin' up land, rentin' land. So's he can run sheep. This ain't sheep country. Only Navajos are dumb enough to keep sheep."

Halfway up the slope Vormund turned and shaded his eyes to look at the cactus. "This area must be saved. It must be preserved."

Clara squeezed his arm. "You let the Maybanks handle that. They go to cocktail parties with the Esslers."

"I'm disturbed by what Sidewinder said," Vormund said. "I have visions of some snot-nosed ewe nibbling that flower."

"You stay out of it," she said. "You're too old to be picking fights."

"I'm not so sure. There's life in the old boy yet."

"Dan, no more committees, no more petitions."

"Why not? The legislators treat me gently, even if they reject my suggestions."

Bugler shook his head as he recalled Vormund's testimony two months ago before a state committee. The state senators began by chiding him. An easterner, a university man, a professor of *English*, presuming to lecture them on their own desert? But they'd grown friendlier when they heard Dan's Kentucky drawl. (The drawl got more countrified as the session went on. Dan knew when he had a good thing.)

Dan had told them that what Arizona needed were more *bad* roads, that if they refused to let the earth produce beauty it would not produce food. He had informed them that he opposed what they called "inevitable progress," because it wasn't inevitable and it wasn't always progress. ("We must assume Professor Vormund has his tongue in his cheek," the committee chairman said, laughing. "No, sir, I have never been more serious," Dan responded.)

"Dan," Clara said, "your arm is trembling. This was too much for you. Sidewinder, help him."

"Not exhaustion, dear, overstimulation. I'm like a man who has just come out of a prostate operation and is aroused by the sight of a buxom nurse. That's what that flower did to me."

The Hopi put an arm around Vormund's back, took the old man's left arm, and helped him climb the hill.

"Sidewinder, are you listening for something?" Vormund asked. "What do you hear? Tribal war drums?"

"No Hopi here. No drums."

"What, then?"

"Dogs."

"I don't hear anything," Clara said.

"It's dogs."

They climbed into the jeep. Although it was now hot, Clara wrapped a blanket around her husband. He sneezed. She dug deep into her bag for a vitamin pill and made him take it with a swig of cocoa.

"End to a perfect morning," Bugler said. He swung the jeep around and followed the cattle path back to the Interstate.

"I hear them also," Bugler said.

"I do too," Vormund said. "It sounds like a pack."

Bugler said: "Maybe Essler's using them to herd sheep."

Sidewinder shook his head. "He's huntin'." His nose twitched. "Maybe after a lion."

Bugler and Vormund stared across the burning land. They saw no movement—only scrub trees, cactus, sky, a few clouds, the mountains.

"The Lions Club of Senita must have given you specs with telescopic lenses," Bugler said. "I don't see a thing. Do you, Dan?"

"Nothing."

Bugler halted the jeep. "Wait a minute. A dust-up. That yellow plume."

The Hopi chuckled. "Yeah. A pickup. I can tell from the engine. It's a '72 Dodge."

"I don't believe him," Clara said. "Sidewinder is teasing you."

"No, ma'am. It's one of Essler's trucks. Comin' toward us. Goin' too fast, like he's chasin' somethin'."

"Let's go after him," Vormund said.

His wife's voice was firm. "No you don't, Ed. No looking for trouble."

"Ed, go on," Vormund said.

"Stopped," said Sidewinder. "He cut the engine. Out there, by them rocks. Listen to them dogs."

The barking was frenzied, angry. A powdery tan cloud was settling over the area, obscuring the vehicle. Bugler turned the jeep onto a narrow trail. He swerved off the track. They rose vertically, landing with a jolt on the hard seats.

"Short cut," Bugler said.

"Ed! Dan's *kidneys!*"

"Pay her no mind, Ed. After him."

The jeep thumped and groaned across the desert. The Hopi, balanced on bowed legs, pointed his head toward the dust cloud and the barking. "Huntin' hounds. Tear a wolf to pieces." He looked at Clara. "They cross them greyhounds with police dogs. One's for runnin', the other for killin'."

"Ed, stop at once!" she cried.

The raccoon had climbed into the upper branches of the palo-verde tree. Only Ed Bugler, Maybank thought, could get him down. And Ed was in the desert, chasing after some weird cactus with the Vormunds and Sidewinder. Maybank tried not to be angry. Today, a loose raccoon was a minor problem. The accountants had gone over the Institute's books that morning. They were broke. Unless Maybank could raise funds quickly, they would have to fire people.

"Try graham crackers," Maybank called to the two students who were trying to coax the raccoon down. One was blond and chubby, a zoology major, the other a looming football tackle. They worked part-time as keepers.

"He threw them back at us, Mr. Maybank," the zoology major said. "I never thought he'd run away."

"Put some jam on them," Maybank said. "God Almighty, we can't even get the mammals moved around."

He had asked the student-workers to move the raccoons into temporary pens. Bugler was making a trap window in the side of the fencing so animals could be photographed without the mesh showing. Big Mac, king of the raccoon colony, had refused to cooperate. He had slithered from the football player's gloved hands and scrambled into the paloverde. There he sat, hands working, nose twitching, his bespectacled face full of comic intelligence and contempt.

"It's a good thing you guys don't get overtime," Maybank said. "Look, you can't leave him there. Get a ladder. Use the pole but watch him when he falls. A raccoon can take your hand off in flight."

"We're sorry, Mr. Maybank," the football player said. He had a squeaky voice and he sounded humiliated.

Damn Bugler! He would have picked the animal up by the scruff of the neck (to Vormund's delight), talked to it, convinced it he wasn't worth biting, and dropped it into the wooden crate. But for all his talents with beasts, Bugler was a problem. There had always been something childish about Ed. No planning, no schedules. Jobs unfinished, chores forgotten. He knew wildlife, and he could camp in the middle of nowhere using his shirt as a tent and his nose to find water. But he was hardly a curator. The board members—except for Vormund, who adored Ed—had begun to hint that Bugler should be retired.

Maybank handed a broom to the football player and a rake to the zoologist. "Try these," he said. "Christ, the things I have to worry about."

"Phone call, Jack."

Maybank turned on long knock-kneed legs and squinted at his wife, Jenny. She was in the window of his yellow adobe office, looking dark and beautiful, holding the telephone toward him. "Mr. Fair. Long-distance from Los Angeles."

"I'll call back."

"It's urgent, Jack."

"Tell him I'm in conference with a raccoon."

"He's in conference with a raccoon," Jenny Maybank said to the telephone.

Maybank turned away. Everything was coming apart. He'd started the Desert Research Institute eight years ago with an inheritance from his father and income from a trust. The Maybanks were old Chicago money. Jenny, a Boston girl, had also been left some money. They had never, either of them, worked for any length of time at salaried jobs. With combined revenues, and with contacts among the beneficiaries of what Vormund called the "anonymous wealth" of Arizona, they had kept the Institute hobbling along.

Prodded by the broom, the raccoon tumbled from the tree. He sprinted for the open door. Maybank kicked the door with his sneakered foot. The athlete got a hand on the striped tail and lifted the animal off the ground.

"Good move," Maybank said. "Don't try to drop him in the box or he'll fake you out. Swing him over it. Like a pendulum. When he looks dizzy, drop him in."

"We'll try, sir," the football player squeaked.

"Jack! Mr. Fair says this is important. Can't the raccoon wait?"

Maybank walked across the Institute's inner court. The aviary needed cleaning. The coyote dens stank. Sidewinder had been neglecting the cactus garden. They were severely understaffed. He thought: We saved a lot of saguaro and five species of birds and Willard's rattlesnake, and maybe the masked bobwhite. More than most people do in a lifetime. And they'd brought Daniel Dean Vormund into the movement, gotten him to write for them, kept the old scholar happy puttering around badger holes, inspecting dune primroses.

"Please hang on," Maybank heard Jenny say. "Mr. Maybank is coming."

Buster, the Institute's pet bobcat, brushed against his legs. It rubbed its side whiskers on his shins, purred for attention. He picked it up and threw it over his shoulder.

Jenny watched Jack come toward her—on stiltlike legs, in ragged sneakers, frazzled chino shorts, a T-shirt laced with holes.

Maybank entered his office and put Buster on his desk. It crawled into an open drawer.

"Jack Maybank here," he said into the phone.

Jenny picked up an extension and listened.

"Mr. Maybank? The director of the Desert Research Institute?"

"The same."

"My name is Winston Fair, Mr. Maybank. I'm an attorney. I'm with Coggs, Toomey, Bright, and Levitow in Los Angeles."

"But you're none of them. You're Fair."

"I'm a member of the firm. One of the younger ones."

"What can I do for you?"

"Mr. Maybank, I hope you're sitting down. I hope you are calm and clearheaded this morning."

"Moderately so."

"Your secretary said something about a raccoon giving you problems. You weren't bitten or anything?"

"The raccoon is under control."

"Mr. Maybank, does the name Otto Denkerman mean anything to you?"

"I'm afraid not. Jenny?"

His wife shook her head.

"Excuse me, Mr. Maybank, but is your secretary monitoring this call?"

"My wife. Jennifer Maybank. She works here. Jen, say hello to Mr. Winfield Fair."

"How do, Mrs. Maybank. It's Winston, not Winfield."

"Hi."

Mr. Fair, who sounded young, and spoke in a crisp California manner, paused. There was something annoyingly offhand about these people. He had done some research on the Maybanks: people born with a status that gave them privileges.

"You have never heard of the Amalgamated Merchants Bank? Or Denkerman Realty?"

"Means nothing, Mr. Fair," Maybank said.

"I see. Two days ago, Mr. Denkerman died at his home in Pasadena. He was eighty-four."

"I'm sorry."

"Is your heart sound, Mr. Maybank?"

"I had an EKG a month ago. What is this?"

"Mr. Maybank, there was a filing of Otto Denkerman's will yesterday afternoon. I would have called you at once, but the lawyers needed a few hours to discuss it. Our firm represented Mr. Denkerman."

"A bequest? We sure need money."

"Yes, it is a bequest. By the way, I'm recording this conversation. I should have told you so at the start, and I apologize. You don't object, do you? If so, I'll cut it off and destroy the cassette."

"Not at all. My wife is scribbling furiously. Listen, I can put a coyote on the phone to howl. That'll drive some judge up the wall."

Winston Fair did not laugh. "Mr. Maybank, your organization, the Desert Research Institute, of Senita, Arizona, is the sole beneficiary of Mr. Denkerman's estate. The will is specific. There are small bequests to servants and there will be legal fees and the like, but the Desert Research Institute gets everything else."

"Why? I never met the man." He put his hand over the phone. "Jenny, hire a gardener. Buy more fencing. Get Sidewinder a pickup."

"Evidently he knew about your organization. Do you publish a magazine?"

"That's flattering. It's a biweekly newsletter about conservation. *The Road Runner Gazette.*" Figures danced in Maybank's head. Fifty thousand dollars? He and Jenny could stop pestering rich friends for a thousand here, five hundred there, to keep the DRI going.

"Mr. Denkerman was a subscriber to your publication. He saved all of them. He marked many of the articles and even made marginal comments."

"Then he *was* a member. A subscription costs seven and a half dollars a year and gives you a membership card. He might have visited us. But I don't recall anyone with that name."

"Mr. Denkerman was a recluse. He stayed inside his house in

Pasadena or at his ranch in the San Fernando Valley. Incidentally, he kept a private zoo."

Jenny broke in. "Mr. Fair, could you drop the other shoe? How much are we getting?"

"Of course, Mrs. Maybank." Fair recalled some data on her. Social Register. Boston. Wellesley. Discreet money.

"I'm not being greedy," Jenny said. "But—"

"Sure you are," Maybank said. "My wife is spaced out today, Mr. Fair. She's our bookkeeper and she's been auditing our books, a thankless job."

"You won't have to worry about debts much longer." An unctuous note crept into the lawyer's voice.

"Really?" Maybank asked. He looked out his window to the pens. Big Mac had escaped again. It had struggled free of the athlete's grasp and again scrambled into the tree. As a boy in Oak Park, Maybank had kept pet raccoons. They got to be like women—at his neck, his face, his hands, licking, nibbling.

"Mr. Maybank, the estimate is that the Denkerman bequest will be in excess of fifteen million dollars."

"You jest," Jenny shouted.

"I've never been more serious. Taking into account taxes, legal fees, and so on, your Institute will be richer by fifteen million dollars."

"Why?" Jack asked. "He had no wife? No kids?"

"Mr. Denkerman was a bachelor. There were no heirs, only some distant relatives. It seems his one abiding passion was wildlife. He took his conservation very seriously."

"But why us?" Maybank asked. In his young manhood, he had been taught never to discuss money, prices, wages. His father was a vest-and-chain lawyer, educated at Brown, a descendant of the Greenes and Wards of Rhode Island. They made a great deal of money but they never talked about it.

"It puzzles us. There are bigger groups—the Audubon Society, the Sierra Club. He read their materials but he didn't leave them anything."

Maybank was grinning. "Otto Denkerman! Jen, can you top that? Mr. Denkerman has given us fifteen million. What do we do now?"

"Fix the plumbing."

"What after that?"

"Buy state legislators the way the ranchers do. Jack, you've got to hire a PR man. A lobbyist. We'll show them who's in charge."

"I hope you'll forgive me," Fair broke in. "But I'm sure you realize the money is not *yours,* nor does it belong to any individual. It is a bequest to your Institute, a tax-free educational corporation. The money will be administered by us as Mr. Denkerman's attorneys. Eventually a special master will have to be appointed to keep an eye on you."

"We'll welcome him," Maybank said. "We'd only spend it in one place anyway."

"Mr. Fair," Jenny said. "I don't understand this. You mentioned our newsletter. You said Mr. Denkerman liked animals and kept a zoo. But has anyone figured out why *us?*"

"Well, there is one clue—"

"He came here and saw the bobwhites?" Jack asked. "He liked our rattlesnakes?"

Outside they had given up on the raccoon. It remained in the tree, a furry saboteur ruining the morning's work. Ed Bugler would have to sweet-talk it into the box.

"He liked what we said about the desert?" Jen tried.

"In a way." Fair paused. "Who is Daniel D. Vormund?"

Jen and Jack exchanged winks. Mr. Winston Fair may have been a legal hotshot. But not to know Dan's name?

"Professor Vormund. He's on our Board of Directors. He writes on conservation for us, at no charge."

"I have a stack of back issues of your newsletter here. In every one, Mr. Denkerman outlined in red some of Vormund's writings. And added comments. Here's one called 'Planting a Saguaro.' And in Mr. Denkerman's writing—*fine, fine, what must be said.* 'Kangaroo Rats and Me,' by Daniel D. Vormund. Mr. Denkerman scrawled next to it—*my sentiments exactly.* And one entitled 'Lessons from a Cactus Wren.' His comment is, *this man knows.*"

Jenny guffawed. "I guess he never read any of Dan's *books.* He'd have left us *fifty* million."

"Vormund obviously made an impression on him. And Mr. Denkerman was not impressed with most people. He once loosed a lion into a meeting of business associates."

Maybank tickled Buster's tufted ears. The bobcat stretched—a spotted marvel of grace, strength, and beauty. "He had good taste. Better lions than businessmen. No offense, Mr. Fair."

"On Mr. Denkerman's night table they found this last issue of your newsletter. It was open to Vormund's article."

"I have it here," Jack said. "'The Road Runner, the Quail, and the Hunter.'"

"He had written alongside it, *I am sorry I never met this man, but it is too late now. He understands everything I have thought for years.*"

"Mr. Fair," Jack asked, "are you sure he left no bequest to Professor Vormund?"

"None. He isn't mentioned in the will. Just the Institute."

"Excuse us a second, Mr. Fair," Maybank said. He looked across the desk. "Did you ever hear Dan mention Denkerman? Did they ever correspond?"

"Not that I know of. Clara discourages correspondents."

"Crazy," Maybank said. "What do we do now, Mr. Fair?"

"Don't mention this to anyone except your lawyer. I'll come out in a day or two and go through the papers. Mr. Maybank, have *your* lawyer present. These things get complicated."

"I bet."

"It's possible the press may get wind of this. The will is a public matter once it's filed. If any reporter calls you, refer them to me."

Maybank hung up. The bobcat rolled over on its back and poked at him with its forepaws, waiting for him to tickle its belly. "Roundheels," Maybank said. "Buster, as of now you are a rich cat and you and everyone else around this dump had better shape up."

Jenny was slumped in her chair. Her dark angular face was surfeited with confusion. "It boggles the mind, Maybank. What do we do with *fifteen million dollars?* Buy up coyotes so no one can kill them?"

Maybank scratched the bobcat's neck. "We'll start with the state legislature. Get them off that bill to shoot predators from an airplane. Mr. Denkerman may help us save the bald eagle."

Hot wind whistled through the jeep. Vormund bounced and rolled on the seat but he did not mind the rough handling. Clara, intent on her own safety, had stopped hovering over him and he was grateful.

The barking was mixed with snarling savage noises.

"Dogs got him," Sidewinder said.

Bugler asked: "What's your guess?"

"Coyote."

The blanket fell from the old man's shoulders. Clara hustled across the bench and secured it again. The Hopi smothered a smile. *Wraps him up like a taco.*

"There. The pickup." Sidewinder pointed. "Around the saguaros."

"I see it," Bugler said.

The jeep lurched, foundered, righted itself.

"Ed!" Clara cried. "This is terrible!"

"Lay on, Macduff," Vormund cried. "Once more into the imminent deadly breach!"

The jeep came to a halt in a flat area. It seemed almost a natural arena.

"What I said. A '72 Dodge. That motor."

A hundred yards from them a pale blue truck had stopped. On its bed a white wooden box had been mounted. Four snouts protruded from a slit in its side. The dogs were barking, whining, pleading for release.

A stout man in a Stetson leaned out of the cab and yanked a metal lever. A side of the wooden box clattered open and the dogs leaped from the truck. They were thick-chested, long-legged beasts with pointed snouts.

"I don't like this," Vormund said.

"Let's leave," his wife said.

The dogs sprinted across the sand to an outcropping of rocks. At the base of the rocks was a narrow aperture. The dogs clawed at it and howled.

"Old coyote ran to cover," Sidewinder said. "Figured he couldn't outrun a truck all day."

"He could lick those dogs one at a time," Bugler said. "But not four to one. Clara, you and Dan shouldn't watch this."

"I not only will watch, I'll do something about it," Vormund said. He lowered a shaky leg over the side of the jeep. Sidewinder saw the white flash of the old man's long johns and thought: some tough guy, eighty-one and wearing long under-wear.

The heavy man was lolling against the door of the truck. He called no orders to the dogs. Apparently, they knew their job. They kept circling the rocks, pawing at the earth, shoving their muzzles into the hole.

There was a flash of gray fur from the rocks. Unexpectedly, the coyote had flown from its cover. Why? Vormund wondered. Was it a simple act of courage? To go out fighting, rather than be burned out with a brush fire? Racing low to the ground, the coyote flew past one astonished dog, turned to snap at another, ran into the jaws of a third. Abruptly the coyote rose high in the air, a furry rocket, its nose pointing skyward. It seemed to Vormund as graceful a natural move as he had ever seen, more aes-thetically perfect than any entrechat.

At the peak of its flight, the coyote whirled in the air, fell to earth in a gray bundle, changed direction, ran between two dogs.

"Make him call the dogs off, Ed," Vormund said.

"No use, Dan."

"Then I will."

"No, you don't," Clara said. She tugged at her husband's coat. "You stay put, Dan."

The old man was walking purposefully across the sand. "You, there. You, sir. Call those dogs off. This isn't fair."

Was the man smiling? Vormund stopped. He was terrified, but he was determined to show no fear. For a moment he felt that the coyote was a surrogate victim, dying for him. Were the dogs not intent on killing it, they might turn on him. The imaginary kinship thrilled him.

Wary now, the dogs backed the coyote against a saguaro. They ringed the animal, hurling themselves at its scrawny throat and spindly legs. The beast seemed to have shrunk in size, offer-ing as small a target as possible. Lips curled, teeth bared, it hissed and snapped at its tormentors.

The largest of the dogs, a brindle, charged the coyote's rear and dug its teeth into a hind leg. At once the others swarmed over the struggling animal. Thrashing, flailing, the coyote battled on. One of the dogs found the soft fur of the belly and dug its teeth in. Another anchored its teeth in the neck. The fourth grabbed an ear.

"If I had a gun, I'd kill them," Vormund said.

Clara was weeping. "Dan, get in the jeep and let's go home. It's just an old coyote."

"A dumb one," Sidewinder said. He sounded unsympathetic.

"It isn't new, Dan," Bugler said. "They'll kill a coyote any way they can. Poison 'em, burn 'em, shoot 'em, hunt 'em. Let's go."

Still the dogs could not kill the coyote. It squirmed, wriggled, snapped with bared teeth, but would not die.

"Hey, mister," Bugler called. "Shoot the animal. Don't let them torture it. It's half dead."

The man said nothing.

"It's a bitch," the Hopi said. He was chewing on a brittle bush leaf. "Maybe she ain't so dumb. She got cubs somewhere. Led them the other way to save the cubs. Them coyote mothers sooner'd die than give cubs away."

Bugler folded his arms and waited. He was drenched with that sense of defeat and despair he always experienced in the presence of human predators. The coyote was on its back, kicking, snarling, refusing to die.

"Don't you have a gun?" Ed shouted.

"Don't need it," the man said. "The dogs'll finish her."

"This isn't fair," Ed shouted. He walked forward a few steps.

"Stay back, mister. Them dogs'll kill a man as soon as they'll kill a coyote."

"Ed!" Clara screamed. "Come here!"

Bugler called out: "The animal's darn near dead. Finish it off."

"We're from the Desert Research Institute," Clara shouted. "We'll report you."

"You're trespassin'," the man yelled. "I seen your jeep this morning. Get back, lady."

Vormund wavered in the sun. He put a hand to his freckled pate. Ah, the feebleness of old age. He had never been strong, combative, physical. Classrooms and dim offices, libraries and lecture halls. Poor co-ordination, weak lungs, asthma, chest problems all his life. Too many absences from class. Van Doren and Weaver filling in for him, while he sniffled and coughed at home, and Clara applied hot poultices.

Ignoring Clara's shouts, he picked up a stone. With two hands, he held it over his head. ("Like Frost's old stone age savage in 'Mending Wall,'" he told the Maybanks later). Vormund walked toward the dogs.

"I'll kill one of them," he called to the man.

"Dan! *Dan!*" Clara ran after him, clutching at his wool mackinaw.

"Away, woman. This is man's work."

"Come on, Dan," Bugler pleaded. He loped alongside his friend. "Keep the dogs away, mister. He's only fooling."

The coyote lay on its back, throat exposed. The traditional attitude of surrender. It was begging for its life. In the wild, wolves and foxes and coyotes spared the supplicant.

"Crazy old man," the man at the pickup said. He was confounded. Never had he been challenged by such an army—a white-haired old loony carrying a rock over his head, an old woman in a green coat, a guy in a gray work suit. Only the Indian had any brains. He had remained at the jeep.

"Boys, get off 'er!" the man called. He whistled shrilly. Tearing at the coyote's throat and belly, the dogs raised bloodied muzzles. They perked their ears, listened again for the whistle, and scampered to the truck. With pats and caresses from their master, they leaped into the wooden crate.

Incredibly, the coyote was on its feet. Crouching, bloodied, froth foaming at its jaws, it looked at the approaching man.

"It's not dead yet," Vormund said. He dropped the stone.

The stout man bent low, circling the snapping beast. With a sudden move, he grabbed its gray tail and yanked the animal off its feet. Bugler was astonished at how small it was. It had held four savage dogs at bay, refused to die, was still fighting for its life.

Struggling, the coyote tried to anchor its forepaws in the sand. Once, twice, the man stomped his boot on the skull. Bones cracked. Blood and brains spurted from the furry mask.

"Won't kill no more sheep," the man said.

"You should be ashamed of yourself," Clara yelled at him.

"Get his license number, Ed," Vormund said. "I can't see anything. Sidewinder, you know him?"

But the Hopi did not move. He knew better than to get mixed up with white men.

The man threw the lever and locked the dogs in the wooden

box. He did not look at the intruders as he climbed into the cab. "Those dogs don't know any better," Clara called. "But you should. You're a human being."

The truck roared off, vanishing in a plume of dust.

"Yes, a human being," Vormund said. "That's precisely that fellow's problem."

"Well," Bugler said, "that's that. Sorry you had to see it, Dan, but you weren't born yesterday. They kill coyotes."

"And not a thing we could do about it," Clara said.

"I'm not so sure," Vormund said. He lifted up his camera. "I took photos. Someone will answer for this brutality."

Sidewinder snickered. Someone answer? Sure, sure. He knew the ranchers better than old Vormund. Better to drink your grape soda and shut up.

Joe Fusaro, the Institute's lawyer, shoved a Xerox'd clipping from the Los Angeles *Times* across Maybank's desk. "Read it and laugh, or sing a song, or dance," Fusaro said. "Courtesy of the Senita Public Library."

Maybank cleared a space on his desk. Jenny leaned over his shoulder. She stroked his bald dome.

OTTO DENKERMAN, 84

Otto Denkerman, a real estate and banking pioneer in Los Angeles, died at his home, 226 Utter Drive, Pasadena, yesterday, after a brief illness. He was 84 and left no family.

Mr. Denkerman owned large tracts of land in the San Fernando Valley and in northern California in the Feather River area. He was a founder of the Amalgamated Merchants Bank and the Pasadena Investment Group. Mr. Denkerman sold most of his interests in 1954, and became a recluse, retiring for long periods to his ranch in the San Fernando Valley.

He maintained a private zoo on his ranch, although few people were allowed to see it. Among the exotic specimens were said to be a white elephant and a snow leopard.

Fusaro was a short, sallow, impatient man. A native of Stoneham, Massachusetts, he had come to Arizona for his asthma. "There you go, Jack. That's how fortunes are made."

"His or ours?"

"Both. A certified California screwball. A prime example of—what does Vormund call these characters with fortunes stashed away?"

"Anonymous wealth. Joe, what do we do now?"

"Laugh all the way to the bank."

Jenny shook her head. "And to think that our little newsletter did it."

"Not *The Road Runner Gazette*, Jen. Vormund's writing. I'll say this for crazy Otto, he knew class when he saw it. Joe, would you believe it? He scrawled next to Dan's last article—*a man who says what I have believed all my life*. And gives us fifteen million dollars."

"I gave Mr. Fair a buzz," Fusaro said. "He says not to start counting money. There may be static."

"Who from?" Maybank asked.

"He isn't sure. You don't think people are going to let that loot go to protect armadillos, do you?"

Jenny looked at the obituary. "What do we care? We'll settle with anyone who wants a *little* bit. My God, Joe, there's money there for everyone."

"They may not want a *little* bit," Fusaro said. "Fair wasn't telling me everything. He's coming out day after tomorrow. Don't go buying any canyons or throwing parties for the Bureau of Land Management."

Outside, the jeep clattered into silence. Maybank looked into the parking lot. Sidewinder was helping Vormund out of the front seat. The old man wobbled, straightened up, looked into the sun. Strange habit Dan had. Staring into the sun.

"The cactus hunters are back," Jenny said. "Joe, can we tell them?"

"No. Nobody."

"Ed? Our curator?" She looked at Bugler as he guided Clara toward the ramada.

"Christ, no," Fusaro laughed. "Bugler doesn't understand money. All he needs is a Sears shirt every two years. And don't tell Dan or Clara. Let's wait until Fair spells it out. Nothing to the papers. A good thing our local journals are so hot on chili recipes, or some reporter would dig this out. Once it's out, every nut in the state will be on your doorstep."

Maybank nodded. It would be a burden. A few hours ago he had been worrying about the DRI going broke. His annuities, his wife's, the money they raised, were not enough. Now they would be set *forever*.

He walked into the courtyard. Bugler entered first, holding a foot-long chunk of cactus. Maybank saw at once that it was a creeping devil, a rare find. Behind Bugler, Vormund walked with Clara. She led him to a bench under the ramada. Beneath the benches, desert tortoises munched wilted lettuce.

Vormund looked drained, too weary to walk another step. Clara was brushing his wispy white hair, talking softly to him. *Wife, nurse, companion, lover, audience.* Talk about devotion! Maybank, approaching them, saw that if Vormund's body drooped, his face looked determined. He was a handsome man— lean features, clear blue eyes with a wise light in them. And gentle. He was a man, Clara told the Maybanks, who had never inflicted pain, could not abide seeing it inflicted.

Someone must have hurt Dan when he was young, she told Jenny one evening. *I don't know who it was, or how, but that's why he can't stand anyone, any living thing, being hurt.*

"How did it go?" Maybank asked.

Bugler held up the cactus specimen. "Sidewinder was right, Jack. An *oruga*, right here in Arizona. First time anyone's ever seen it."

Vormund fanned his florid face with the wool cap. "Jack, that land must be protected. If California saved the bristlecone pine, we can do the same for the creeping devil."

Maybank seemed unsettled. "How much land?" he asked.

Bugler scratched his head. "I'll have to go back with a surveying rig, Jack. There's twenty acres of *orugas*, but an awful lot of land will have to be preserved to maintain an eco-system. We'll need a botanist to look the place over."

Clara pointed to Sidewinder. He was dozing against the adobe wall of Maybank's office. The bobcat slept in his arms. "And don't forget Sidewinder. He found them." With her lips she formed the words: *pickup truck.*

Maybank thought of Otto Denkerman's millions. Surely Mr. Fair would not object to a pickup truck being part of the first expenditure. Wasn't that a condition? That they start spending money?

"It was a beautiful day," Vormund said shakily. "But it was ruined by something we saw later. I'm too exhausted to talk about it."

"The jeep break down?" Maybank asked.

Bugler frowned. "We saw a rancher turn dogs loose on a coyote bitch. They tore the poor thing to shreds. I tried to tell Dan. There's no law says they can't kill coyotes any way they want."

"Jack, we have to get more involved. We have to get after some legislators." Vormund's face was scarlet. "He crushed that animal's skull with his boot. It was fighting for its life."

Maybank folded his arms. "Coyotes are a lost cause, Dan. Nobody makes any mileage fighting for coyotes. We're better off concentrating on broad programs—"

The old man's eyes flashed. "Maybe that's the trouble. We're all too polite. I left the university because I was fed up with committees and study groups. If I can't defend a coyote, what good am I?"

"That's enough," Clara said. "You're trembling all over. I'm driving you home. It's time for your Meritene."

Bugler smothered a laugh. Old mother hen. She was an Italian, born in Verona, and when she got upset vowels attached themselves to the ends of her words. Or else she used too many prepositions, or the wrong ones. He remembered when they'd camped in Grace Canyon some years ago. It had turned bitter cold. Clara awakened Dan with hot cocoa and an extra blanket. "Now, Dan," she'd said, "now, Dan, you lie down and I'll put something over on you."

Maybank sat next to the Vormunds beneath the ramada. The old man kept insisting on a new campaign—a battle to end poisoning on public lands, new laws to prohibit the introduction of toxicants, laws against aerial hunting and dogs . . .

Maybank kept shaking his head. Didn't Dan know that a state legislator was about to introduce a bill making it legal to kill *any* predator from an airplane with *any* kind of weapon, including grenades and napalm?

"Then we have to fight him also," Vormund said.

"Now, stop," Clara cried. "You worried all those years at Columbia that nothing you ever taught did anyone any good, so now you want to be a hero."

He ignored her. "Jack, we're doing this the wrong way with our newsletter and our reports in triplicate. We have to *act*. Those youngsters who get down in front of bulldozers may have the right idea."

Maybank stared at his ragged sneakers. "Dan, are you really ready for this?"

Clara clapped her hands. "No! You should have seen him today! He picked up a rock and was going to walk right into those dogs and stop them!"

Vormund winked at Maybank. "I did. It was great fun. Like an old stone age savage."

Maybank put his hand on Vormund's knee. He could feel the delicate shivers. Parkinsonism.

"I have photographs," Vormund said. He held up his camera. "I took pictures while those dogs and that ranch hand were killing the coyote. I want them printed. Jenny can call that editor who's sweet on her."

"You want us to take them on?" Maybank said.

"Why not?"

Bugler, lounging against an adobe arch, laughed. "You should have seen Dan with that rock in his hand. I'm glad he didn't get to those dogs or that cowboy. He'd have annihilated them."

"Don't encourage him," Clara said.

"I've dragged my heels too long," Vormund said. "I'm sick of being a desk soldier."

Maybank took the camera. The vision of Daniel D. Vormund, rock in hand, walking into battle, moved him. To please the old man, he'd send the photos out.

Clara helped her husband to his feet. Dan blinked at the sun, patted her hand, and walked away. He turned once. "The land, Jack. Ed's creeping devils. We must find out who owns it and buy it. Maybe you can talk to Mr. Essler."

Clara shook her head, followed her husband.

Maybank watched them walk to their Plymouth. He glanced at Bugler, tempted to mention the bequest, the inundation of money that would let them battle coyote killers, buy land, save birds. As he thought about it, Jenny and Joe Fusaro came out of the office. They were talking, Fusaro sawing the air with energetic hands.

Maybank spoke to Bugler: "Big Mac won't get in his box. He's had two college boys stymied all morning. Could you go into your act?"

"Jack, you should have asked me." He walked toward the enclosure, chuckling when he saw the raccoon in the paloverde tree. Too bad Dan hadn't been around. He'd have added it to his usual pitch to the Lions, or Chamber of Commerce, or Garden Club. *Ladies and gentlemen, in my fourscore years, I have learned more from jack rabbits than from university presidents, more from blue jays than from board chairmen. Next time you shoot a dove or trap a fox, reflect that you may be destroying a creature every bit as good as you, and in some ways better.*

Bugler produced a palmful of raisins from his shirt pocket. He held them up to the raccoon. "Hey, it's me, Edward Earle Bugler. Don't you know me?"

The cunning eyes gleamed. The bushy tail flicked one way, then the other. The round furry body descended. On its hind legs, the raccoon picked a raisin at a time from Bugler's hand. It stared at Bugler with innocent love. In seconds he had picked up the raccoon like a sack of turnips and carried it to its pen.

"A genius," Jenny said. "But a lousy curator."

Her husband nodded. "He keeps Dan happy. Next time the board tells me to can him, I'll bring up Denkerman's money. We can keep Ed around for Dan's morale, if nothing else."

Host, a licensed pilot who enjoyed taking the controls of the corporation's Aero-Commander for an hour or so, sat dismally in his seat. He slumped in the cushioned luxury and stared through wrap-around sunglasses at the Gucci case on the table. Correspondence. Interoffice memos. Sales reports. Cash flow. He had read nothing since their take-off a half hour ago from Burbank. Normally he plodded through his work, a deliberate, meticulous worker, making notes, writing suggestions to subordinates. Short, direct, humorless notes. But today he had no stomach for the bits and pieces that made Host-Labarre function.

Across the open saddle-brown lid of the case, his wife's beautiful face stared at him. She too wore dark wrap-around glasses. Corinne smiled at him—a meager rearrangement of the muscles around her heavy lips. There was a flash of capped ivory teeth, each a rare pearl, a dimpling in the smooth tan cheeks. But her eyes did not smile. Her flesh, Host thought, was of the same rich texture as the attaché case. Her seamless skin, unmarred features, and blank expression seemed of a piece with the luggage.

With her diamond solitaire she tapped against an empty tumbler. The Filipino steward materialized from the galley where he had been reading *Penthouse*.

"Thirds?" Host asked. "So early?"

"We'll make it a halfy." She gave the glass to the steward. "Light on the vodka, Manuel."

"More ice, ma'am?"

"Lots of ice. From the *rear* ice-cube machine. Not the one in front. One has to be careful where one gets one's ice."

Host's square head ducked a fraction of an inch. Corinne was off again. The comment about the ice machine warned him. And the drinking before noon. His father, James Wayland Host, founder of Host-Labarre, was a fair-minded, vigorous man, proud of his success, but never a braggart. But he had a weakness about ice-cube machines. There were *two* on the plane, one up front for the crew, one in the galley. He boasted about the machines to his friends at the country club. "We may operate the only private plane with *two* ice-cube machines," he would say to awed golfers.

"Alcohol is bad in the Arizona sun," Host said. "It's hotter out there than in LA, Corinne. The sun ferments it in your gut. How will you be able to play tennis?"

"I'll manage. I always do."

"You were warned."

She took a glass from the Filipino and sipped at the vodka. She did everything with precision and grace. A well-functioning woman, perfectly formed, forever envied. And bright. People assumed Corinne was a numskull with her interminable tennis and golf and partying. But there was a shrewd mind at work. Pop Host had warned him about her when they were married eight years ago. "She'll want to write poetry or listen to colored men play jazz," he said. "Something unstable there."

It was impossible to discern any weakness by looking at her. Raymond Host chose to believe that her instabilities were minor. Her origins were obscure. Father dead when she was a child. A

— 3 3 —

piano teacher mother, one of the shabby genteel of Arcadia, California. A scholarship to Pomona. Good grades, the campus beauty—adored, a girl who was managing editor of the newspaper *and* home-coming queen. Host was certain that he loved her very much. One had to be grateful for such women. Fatless, narrow-waisted, with swelling hips and thighs and hard breasts, she had the kind of body that age and alcohol could not conquer. At fifty, when he was paunchy and slow and bald (athletes tended to deteriorate), Corinne would be charging the net. Strong, tanned, with her golden hair flying behind her.

"Make that the last," Host said. He had a husky buried voice. To strangers, he sounded brusque, impolite. The truth was he was a courteous young man. His father had taught him that whenever he was tempted to lose his temper, manifest anger, or curse, he must first ask: *Will this benefit me?* "You will discover, Raymond," James W. Host said, "that the answer will always be *no*. If it does not benefit you, don't do it. Control. Reserve. Civility. Useful traits of character. You will get your way in the long run without outbursts because you are Raymond Host."

"*Last?* Forever?" Corinne asked. "Raymond, you sound like Pop."

"He wouldn't have said anything. He would have taken the glass away."

"I suppose he would have."

Host looked at her wide red mouth. The temptation to devour it, suffocate it with kisses, feel it caressing his body, sometimes mingled with the desire to smash it with his fist. He had never struck her. His father's wisdom: Never lose your temper unless you are convinced it will benefit you.

"You wanted to say something else," Host said. "About Pop."

"What makes you think so?"

"When you get that smirk on your face. He'd have taken the glass away from you because he's more of a man than I am? Is that it?"

"Ray, please. Not at ten thousand feet. Can't we talk about tennis? What club can we play at?"

"Any club you want." He did not say it jokingly. The Host name opened doors. Those who slithered around the feet of the very rich knew their name and knew their motto: *We Process*

— 34 —

the Desert. There were Host-Labarre developments, tracts, condominiums, shopping centers, factories, public buildings, power plants, all over the Southwest.

"I need competition," she said. She put the empty glass down. She did not tap her diamond against it for a refill. "Damn, we've beaten everyone at the club. I had to drag you into the husband-and-wife doubles."

"I get unnerved when I play with you. I'd hate it if you lost."

"But you don't mind losing?"

"It's only tennis."

She was about to say something about James Wayland Host and caught herself. Pop did not accept losing. Neither at tennis, or golf, or land speculation, or home building. Did her husband, she wondered, lack that compulsion to have it all, because it had been done for him by tougher older men?

Did she misjudge him? Colors were intense in her husband's blunted face, but they seemed less indicative of passion than artifice—fake hues smeared on a placid monochrome surface. Host's hair was beach-boy blond, suggesting a surfer. (He had tried the sport briefly and found it tiresome, as he did most games. He played excellent golf and tennis but had trouble taking them seriously. At Stanford, a career as a running back ended when he broke an ankle and refused to look at a football again. "A waste of time," he told his father, who wondered briefly about Raymond's manliness.) Host's face was preternaturally red—hypertension and sun combining to endow him with a florid, choleric look. Under stress, carmine splotches daubed his cheeks and his neck. All the features were flat, square, and hard. His eyes were a subdued green. The face gave nothing, asked nothing. But it spoke of suppressed strength, answers unfound. He did not like to be touched.

She envisioned him sometimes as the brooding head counselor of a Christian Endeavor Boys Camp—full of athletic skills, good at any game, strong and rough on the field, secretly reading poetry at night.

"What's this trip all about?" she asked.

"You don't really care, do you?"

"Maybe I do. You and Pop, so secretive. You run the company like it's the CIA."

A grudging smile turned Host's lips. The square features

turned handsome. Women stared at him as often as men ogled Corinne. He looked indifferent, drawing his head back into his muscular shoulders. Host had a size 18 neck. The ruddy head seemed to vanish into the corded column, until the upper part of his body suggested a rose marble pillar. When Corinne saw him withdraw in that manner—under the impertinent prodding of a headwaiter or the importuning of a subordinate—she knew he would grow silent, wandering in some private place she could not comprehend.

"Just a routine trip," Host said. "Pop wants me to look at land he's interested in. And we've got that new high rise."

"Isn't that in Phoenix?"

"We'll look at it on the way back."

A poor dissembler, Ray. The old man did it artfully, and called it business acumen, the application of intelligence to the task of creating wealth, jobs, places to live and work. Corinne abandoned any effort to draw him out. She had to be careful not to provoke them. Talking, drinking, playing tennis, traveling, he was cheerful in a flat unemotional way. Annoyed, he would slump in his seat, his green eyes dulled, his head turning into a red stone.

The jet dropped swiftly in the desert wind. Below they could see rows of tract housing. Each neat box with its auxiliary turquoise pool. The plane's shadow, a black smear, passed over the homes swiftly. "I think they're ours," Host said. "Four or five years old."

"Everything's ours. Yours, anyway."

"People have to live. We help them."

"They're ugly."

"Better than what they had before."

We Process the Desert. In California, Arizona, New Mexico, Host-Labarre's bulldozers and payloaders shaved and shaped the earth, felled saguaros, diverted stream beds, built mountains, sunk wells, seeded topsoil, created lakes, sent up houses, apartments, shopping centers, office buildings, power stations. Populations trebled, cities rose, civilization triumphed.

"When did you become such a critic?" Host asked her. His voice was not hostile. He was merely in search of information.

"I'm not. All those people down there, making babies, cooking steaks, smashing up their cars, worrying about the stock market. Their kids will grow up and do the same thing."

"Pop and I don't want to change the world. We give them a decent place to live. We don't owe anyone apologies."

"I didn't say you did."

"And we don't apologize. *You* don't have any complaints. You're better off than living in Arcadia, with your mother waiting for piano students."

"I know, Ray, I know." She meant it, but it sounded hollow. "We're in the three Mercedes category now. Let's see if I have it right. In Los Angeles, psychiatrists have *one* Mercedes, TV producers *two*, and the *really* important people have three. Or two Mercedes and a Porsche."

"I shouldn't have let you have that drink."

"Sorry, Ray. I get this urge to beat on Host-Labarre every now and then. There's nothing you people can't do. You *never* fail. Everyone else fails, some time or other, at something or another. My mother's piano playing. My writing. Richard Nixon's presidency. The Edsel. Small liberal arts colleges go out of business. The whales are vanishing. But you and Host-Labarre never lose. Why?"

"We're smarter and better."

"That's not enough."

"It's the national creed, Corinne. Winning is the only thing. We not only win, we excel. The rest is easy."

"The national *greed*. Why do you have to do so much? Earn so much?"

Host slammed the lid of the attaché case closed. "To keep us in Hollywood Hills in a twenty-three-room house. And the children in boarding schools. And let you collect sculpture. A lot of reasons. Besides, it's all we know, and we're good at it. Our stock pays dividends and our houses last."

She brushed back her blond hair and turned her head. "I guess that's enough."

"Yes, it is. And we give to charities. To the Baptists and Lutherans. The old man takes care of them every year. Not to mention the YMCA and the Girl Scouts and the March of Dimes. It's all programmed."

They could see the hazed skyline of Senita City. Austere towers rose from the ragged lower buildings, the winding freeways, the lofty gasoline and motel signs. There seemed to be a miasmic fog over the place. Ten years ago, Host could recall, he had come here with his father and loved the clear, bright, dry air. Now it was as sickeningly imprisoned by smog as Los Angeles.

The soiled city made him think of Corinne's remark about national greed. A coarse way of putting it, but there was some truth to it. But why call it greed? It was a cruel and dishonest way of describing hard work, honest gain, achievement. His father understood this better than anyone. James W. Host often quoted Lyndon Johnson—*If a fellow can't get half a loaf, he'll settle for a lot less, maybe even a slice of bread.* Someone had to do the slicing and doling out. Government, yes. But also far-seeing, intelligent, naturally superior men like the Hosts.

"It's uglier than your houses," Corinne said. "That awful haze."

"We'll figure some way to clean it up."

"Ray, you can't summon up the wind. You're like Owen Glendower in one of the Henry plays. He could summon up monsters from the deep, but there was no guarantee they'd come."

At Pomona they had predicted a writing career for Corinne. But she was too beautiful, too dazzling, for any newspaper office. A distraction. She was inevitably drawn to wealth, power, the rulers of Southern California. She came to the Hosts like a paramecium ruled by a tropism, wiggling toward the light.

"I still don't understand this trip," Corinne said.

"I'm not sure I do either." Ray Host yawned and stretched mightily. Chest, deltoids, and biceps stretched the cotton lisle shirt. The Brooks Brothers sheep on the breast inflated. He was tired. He had been up a good deal of the night with the architects reviewing a botched shopping plaza. Someone would have to be taken care of, some city official, some inspector. A close call. Host himself would not get involved. An underling. A hint here. An envelope there.

Suddenly Raymond felt the need to be active, involved, to make decisions, affect lives, control the future. An only child, a loner for many years, given to silence and solitude, his father had drilled into him the need for moving forward. When they had argued over whether he should marry Corinne, Raymond's insistence won the old man's approval. "I was waiting for you to stand your ground," James Wayland Host said. "Marry her. The bloodlines look good, even if she's impoverished. We'll buy her mother a new piano."

"I'll land the plane. Hang on, Corinne."

"No bumps, Ray. No tricks."

"I'm not the tricky type. At the controls, or in business."

"Or in bed."

Scarlet splotches bloomed on Host's cheeks. The green eyes were invisible behind the wrap-around glasses. "Can it, Corinne."

"Sorry. One more drink? To celebrate the arrival in Senita City?"

"No." He moved his stocky body toward the cockpit and opened the door. "George," he said to the pilot, "I'll take her in if I may."

"Sure thing, Mr. Host."

Corinne smiled. Always polite, low-keyed. It was better than coming on as a hearty handshake type. The Hosts made a fetish of melting into the background, talking little, divulging nothing. They were never late for appointments, returned gifts from business associates, would not let themselves be entertained by suppliers, real estate agents, lawyers, or anyone connected with their work.

"Ray, before you put on your space helmet, tell me why in God's name we are here in Senita City on a Tuesday afternoon in April."

"Later."

"Then let me have another drink." She lifted the smoked glasses. Her face was clear, unlined, alert, intelligent. She seemed more beautiful to Host every time he saw her.

"Just one."

He slammed the cockpit door, hearing as he did Corinne's diamond pecking at the glass.

Vormund loved the view of the Santa Teresa Mountains from the patio of his home in the foothills. Exhausted, depressed, bedeviled with the infirmities of old age—*I'm not only a hypochondriac*, he insisted to his friends, *I'm also a very ill man*—he never failed to find sustenance from the peaked, ridged, arid mountains that rose five miles from his patio.

He would sit in the shade of the pleached ocotillo wands and muse about the fascination mountains had for men. Once he had written of mountains: *Jesus went up, Mohammed fled, Buddha sat down.* Buddha had the right idea. Not under a ramada, of course, but a Bo tree. Ideas, definitions, classifications, skittered through Vormund's mind. What was a Bo tree? One more thing to look up. As a boy in Kentucky he had been a tireless collector. Rock hound, bug hunter, keeper of a small private zoo. And left it all for words, letters, art. How appropriate that in the last twenty years of his life he should come back to nature.

"Don't you want to take a nap?" Clara asked. She brought him his lunch—a foaming glass of Meritene.

"No thank you, Clara. This Meritene is delicious. A good vintage. We must write to the pharmaceutical house that concocts it."

Clara kissed his forehead. "Poor Dan. Picking up rocks to fight dogs, at your age."

"I was proud of myself. Clara, do you realize that in my entire boyhood I never started a fight and lost the few I had? Was I a coward?"

"No, darling. You were frail and civilized."

"I always feared pain, having had so much as a child. Scarlet fever, diphtheria, mumps, measles, even what my mother later suspected was a mild case of infantile paralysis."

"How lucky you married a nurse."

"I've often congratulated myself on my good judgment."

Clara busied herself dusting the redwood table, the sunbleached canvas chairs. "But I was never your intellectual equal. Did that bother you?"

"Certainly not. Just being around me for fifty-five years has endowed you with the equivalent of a Ph.D."

It was an old joke. They conversed like veteran vaudevillians, ready for the straight line, timing the punch line.

"I wish you'd sleep."

"I'm all gingered up by that fuss I started. Those photographs may get me involved. Clara, we haven't backed a cause since we supported Roosevelt in 1932."

"You once volunteered to ask Nicholas Murray Butler for raises for the junior faculty."

"Did I? That's funny. I don't recall it. Maybe because it was so unlike me." Vormund shut his eyes. It was sublimely peaceful. The house was compact, warmly furnished, loaded with books, records, the aromas of Clara's kitchen. (Lavish soups and stews went forth to succor sickly neighbors, but never the master of the house, who abhorred onions, garlic, and spices.)

"You don't want to take any calls?"

"No. I have an appointment with a toad."

"Late for every commencement, even when you got your honorary degree. But the *toad* can't be kept waiting."

"He's every bit as important to me as the academic senate. His manners are better. Clara, might I have some music? *Rosenkavalier* perhaps. Something suggesting passion spent."

"Speak for yourself, Daniel."

French horns wafted across the sun-baked patio. In the potent heat of afternoon, even the hummingbirds rested, disdaining the vials of red sugar water Clara had fastened to the eaves.

An enormous scorpion skittered across the sandy garden in front of the stone patio. "Hello, old-timer," Vormund said. People hated them and perhaps with good reason. But Vormund found scorpions a source of joy. A biological success by any standards. In business three hundred million years, give or take a few, longer than any dinosaur ever managed to stay alive. Man was an *arriviste* compared to a scorpion. But man possessed much more deadly weapons than the barb in the scorpion's tail. And used them indiscriminately, gleefully.

Pessimism was Vormund's companion. He tried to subdue it, live happily, divest himself of mean thoughts. In the kitchen he could hear Clara singing an Italian song, fussing with her dishes. How could he have managed without her? Forever ill, despondent, feeble, he had needed her sunny presence to get him from day to day. He was full of Nordic gloom and fatalism—Hanseatic Germans on his father's side, dour Scottish Lowlanders on his mother's. The families had met and united in, of all places, Kentucky. He needed the Mediterranean warmth that Clara brought to him. Just as he needed the desert sun, perhaps took more of it than was good for him. There were liverish spots on his hands and forehead. Dr. Mark had warned him that they might lead to skin problems. "At my age," he told the doctor, "I prefer cancer to bronchitis."

After a few false starts Vormund raised himself from the canvas chair. "It is the time of the toad," he whispered.

In the shade of the adobe wall that marked the edge of the garden was a small pool. Twenty years ago, when they purchased the house, Clara had built it, working on her knees like a Sicilian mason. He had supervised.

Vormund paused a foot from the lip of the pool. A greenish-yellow toad poked its head over the rim of the water.

Vormund removed his hat. "On schedule, as usual. *Scaphiopus couchi,* or as you are more commonly known, Couch's spadefoot. I know all about you, my friend. Not a true toad, but an impostor. With your cat eyes, wartless, and a set of teeth. Any real toad would disown you."

Yellow eyes blinked at him. The spadefoot set his front feet on the edge of the pool and waited. Vormund studied him a moment—green and yellow blotches, vertical pupils. Another old-timer. Not in the league with a scorpion, but old enough to merit respect. Toads, frogs, and spadefoots had been around long before the lemuroids, man's ancestors.

The spadefoot inched forward. Does he know me by now? Vormund wondered. Back in New York, at Columbia and in editorial offices, they probably regarded him as half mad, an eccentric who communed with frogs and birds. But his best friend, Tyler Merritt, understood. Tyler had never gotten over Vormund holding a peeper in his hand at the Merritt farm in Massachusetts, and whispering, *My friend, we're in this together.*

From his pocket Vormund took out a scrap of dried beef tied to a string. It was a daily ritual.

The flat head bobbed forward, gobbled the meat, gulped it down in froggy rhythms.

"Beatrix Potter would approve," Vormund said. "You did that as neatly as Mr. Jeremy Fisher."

Satisfied, the spadefoot left the string dangling in Vormund's hand, gulped again as if to thank him, then vanished beneath the scummy waters. Vormund waited. He cherished the loneliness of his home, his garden, the hot stretch of desert, the mountains. The highway was sufficiently far away so that the noise of cars and trucks was muffled. In this dry world, hummingbirds and toads ruled.

He returned to the chair. A conditioned toad wasn't much, but it helped. A reminder of his kinship with the nonhuman world. Some years ago he and Clara had trained a young coyote bitch to come to the garden and share the morning's garbage with rabbits and quail. They had called her Soprano, because of her high-pitched howl. One day it ate its free lunch, turned, and stared ruefully at the old couple. Clara knew at once.

"She's never coming back, Dan," she said. "She's saying goodby and we'll never see her again."

There had been a finality about the coyote's glance, a kind of graduate student's *Weltschmerz*. Gray tail flashing, the lean body darted between prickly pears and chollas, and vanished. For months Vormund listened for its wail, then admitted she was gone forever. More and more the coyotes avoided the outskirts of the city. Although a young biology teacher had told him that now, hunted, poisoned, and killed in increasing numbers, they were coming back to Senita, foraging in garbage cans, stealing from vegetable gardens.

He dozed in the ragged deck chair. Too much had happened that morning—the vision of the creeping devils, the savage dogs, his untypical reaction. Never a man of violence, he had tempted it, and was now disturbed. Worse, he had bragged to the Maybanks and in front of Clara—but was that right and proper? *An old stone age savage . . .*

The faint whirring of wings made him open his eyes. A hummingbird, one he had not seen before, flitted around the vials. Hummingbirds gave him trouble. Too small, too fast. Despite his bird guides and binoculars, they taunted him. It was far easier to place a quote from Dryden than to identify a hummingbird. It served him right, he thought, for insisting on having a foot in both worlds. Dryden ran through his head.

> In Saturn's reign at nature's early birth
> There was that thing called chastity on earth . . .

Vormund squinted at the tiny bird, making furious pinwheels around the glass bottle, dipping its beak into the red liquid.

"Either Anna's or Allen's hummingbird," he said. But he was too weary to look for the guide or to call to Clara to get it for him. She was singing again, as joyful as the vivid bird.

"I'm sorry I don't know your name and pedigree," Vormund

said, "but you're welcome here. Bring your friends and relatives."

At length he slept. In his sleep he heard the coyote bitch, calling to him across the desert. And what a song! What a heavenly sound! Unlike anything in the world. They heard it less and less around Senita, and perhaps, if man had his way, they would never hear it again. But it could not be forgotten. It was as memorable as a couplet by Pope or a Rossini overture.

2

—— ✳ ————————

"Who the hell is D. D. Vormund?" Ballstead asked.

Fassman, a news writer for a Los Angeles television station, bobbed his long head as if dodging a left jab. He placed the opened newspaper on Ballstead's desk. Ballstead was his boss, news director of the station. Ballstead was thin and ulcerous and hated television. In his youth he had been a police reporter, later a city editor in Kansas City. He hungered for print, for columns of words. He was forever frustrated by darting images on 16-millimeter film, a sense of stories undeveloped and unexplained.

"Daniel D. Vormund, Tom," Fassman said. "A great name in American letters."

Ballstead stared at the newspaper page in front of him. The Senita *Pantagraph*. Marvelous name. The bureau tried to cover part of the Southwest in addition to Southern California. "There's more to this part of the world," he told his reporters and deskmen, "than freeways, the space program, and UCLA basketball."

"Look at the photographs," Fassman said. "Great if we could get film of it. Those dogs, Tom. They're as big as lions. And that miserable coyote. Look at this one, with the guy crushing the head with his boot."

Ballstead read the article. It was not much more than a few

paragraphs of copy to accompany four black-and-white photographs of a coyote hunt.

ONE RANCHER'S TECHNIQUE
FOR PREDATOR CONTROL

There was a line of italics under the last photograph. *Pictures by D. D. Vormund.*

Trained dogs make short work of coyote in these photographs taken by Desert Research Institute team in the Santa Teresa foothills. Rancher, whose livestock was threatened by coyote predators, used hunting hounds—and his boot—to finish off marauding animal. Score: Rancher 1, Coyote 0.

"So?" Ballstead asked.

"I'd like to go out there and see if there's a film piece for us." Fassman sat down. Over six feet tall, unwieldy, he became a shapeless cord-suited lump in the chair. He had a long-nosed, heavy-lipped face and apologetic gray eyes. His hair was cut in campus style of the forties—short, trimmed around the ears.

The news director ran a hand over his face. "Alan, didn't we do a story on shooting eagles in Wyoming? And that sadist in Utah who pops at wolves from a chopper? What's so different about a rancher turning dogs on a coyote?"

"Vormund is involved."

Ballstead cocked his head. "I don't know. He isn't a household word."

Fassman agreed and nodded amiably. He looked into the smog-choked street outside of Ballstead's window. Modern man was suffocating in his own stench, adoring the noxious gases he breathed daily, his own flatulent gift to civilization. Gritty, poisonous, foul, the blanket lay on the city like a biblical plague, a warning from a disgusted Jehovah. D. D. Vormund would understand. He had often been quoted on his analogue of modern man's state—locked inside a powerful car, careening along at seventy miles per hour, incapable of a single thought, a solitary creative, compassionate, constructive act, because it was all he could do to control the monster.

"Vormund was my teacher at Columbia," Fassman said.

"Old school tie."

Fassman laughed. "Columbia doesn't go in for postgraduate sentiment. And never with an independent soul like Daniel Dean Vormund."

"What did he teach?"

"English literature."

Ballstead cocked his head the other way. "Now I make the connection. I read him at Kansas State. And I'm older than you. *The Elizabethan Drama*. What's he doing saving coyotes?"

"More than Elizabethans. Samuel Johnson. Pope. Restoration comedy. He wrote fifteen books on literature before he chucked it all and went out to . . . to . . . keep an appointment with a cactus wren. I was in his class the day he gave his last lecture. Those were his words."

"I know who you're talking about. I read *The European Achievement* when I was a sophomore. And *Modern Dangers*. Wasn't he a lefto of some kind?"

Fassman held his flabby hands up. "Just the opposite. Vormund hated what he saw of the Soviet Union in the thirties, and he said so, and wrote about it. And the commissars never forgave him."

"You might have something here," Ballstead said. "I'm not sure what. Academics aren't brilliant on the electric box. They're like all writers—they need space, time, print. Not flickering shadows."

"I don't promise a thing. But if someone like Vormund is taking on the powers, the people who run things, ranchers, hunters, developers, it might be a story."

"He might not want to be pushed into a fight."

"Maybe not a fight. Just a statement of what he believes."

Ballstead swiveled in his chair. He glowered at the thickening yellow poison over the city. "You could use a change of pace, right?"

Fassman's docile face reflected some mild misery, like an old bruise, a recurrent ache. Ballstead knew. Two weeks ago, Fassman's wife, a girl from Great Neck, New York, had thrown him out of their $90,000 Spanish-style stucco house in Westwood Village, which her father had bought for them. Wendi was fed up with his vagueness, his refusal to make a career for himself in journalism, the way he let others trample on him, beat him out of the choice assignments, the producers' jobs.

Fassman missed his sons, aged twelve and nine, missed the sprawling luxurious house, the comforts of Wendi's warm body. But he was a defeatist at heart, a man prepared to accept the worst, grateful that it wasn't more awful. After all, he still had a job. Wendi wanted no money from him. Her dad in Great Neck, a stationery tycoon, kept her in everything she needed, and would provide for the boys' schooling. Only one aspect of the breakup troubled Fassman. An *actor* had moved into the Westwood house. A bearded, booted, guitar-playing rustic, aged twenty-six. This was an insult so grievous that he refused to talk about it.

"I'd like to get out for a few days," Fassman said. "I'd like to see what Vormund's up to. He's written some great books on conservation. He was twenty years ahead of his time."

"It'll end up a close-up shot of a man talking."

"Pretty good talk."

"Maybe too good. Who cares out here?" Ballstead was sorry he said it. But he was sick of letters from the gun lobby, the hunters, the developers. Small sympathy for coyotes. Why should there be? They were wild, they ate an occasional sheep, they were an affront. *Kill 'em.*

"What bugs me," Fassman said, "is the way the caption writer made a gag about the thing. Sort of on the hunter's side. Vormund's made to look a fool."

"You'll have me in tears. Go on, draw a couple of hundred bucks and go to Arizona."

"Thanks, Tom." Fassman got up. "If I could only get across a small idea of the kind of man Vormund is. People might respond. He really made you understand poetry."

"Alan, don't you know they're closing down humanities departments all over the country? Keats and forty cents gets you a container of yogurt. No wonder Vormund switched to protecting badgers. There's no hope for the written word, kid. I spoke on the ethics of journalism at Valley Community College last week and I was outdrawn three to one by a man lecturing on body and fender work."

"I'll give myself three days to survey it. If it's a bust, what have we lost?"

"Don't get snake-bit. Those ecology nuts have a way of cuddling up to rattlesnakes and gila monsters."

When the newsman had left, Ballstead studied the photographs of the hunt. Rotten odds. A truck, a man, four dogs against a small animal. Man was a brute and a killer, and worst of all, he rigged the game. It didn't surprise Ballstead. He'd known all that since he was a reporter covering city hall in St. Joseph.

Maybank and his wife, dining in the kitchen, looked at each other when the phone rang for the fourth time.

"Take it off the hook," Maybank said.

"No, I won't let them terrorize me." Jenny went to the wall phone and picked it up. "Hello? Who are you, you cowardly son of a bitch?" She returned it to the hook. "The usual heroic gun lover. Hung up, no response."

Jack Maybank shook his bald head and took the phone off. "Enough," he said. "Nothing important can happen today. When Denkerman's millions come our way, I'll get an answering service. Or hire a private eye to find out whose those lunatics are."

"It was the pictures," Jenny said.

"Maybe we shouldn't have indulged Dan. I spent a half hour arguing with the city editor to run them. Funny, the way the guy hedged the whole thing."

"Hedged? He made the dogs and that shit-kicker the heroes! And *still* we get calls."

Maybank picked up a plate of lukewarm canned spaghetti, a slice of supermarket white bread, a half-finished glass of Seven-Up. The Maybanks, born to wealth and status, ate on a level only marginally higher than that of the Western Shoshones. They explained to their children, who hungered for steaks and desserts, that food was a distraction, and that they should be grateful for having parents who were unhampered by long hours in the kitchen, fussing over recipes demanding shallots and heavy cream.

"I hope Dan and Clara aren't getting any of these nut calls," Jenny said. She stacked dishes in the sink and ran warm water over them. Their house was luxurious but in disrepair. Appliances worked poorly or not at all. At the moment the dishwasher was flooding the kitchen floor.

"*People* don't bother Dan," Maybank said. He stoked his pipe, lit up, listened to the noise of his sons playing one-on-one in the driveway.

"There's only one Vormund in the phone book," Jenny said. She followed her husband to the patio. They sank into lounge chairs.

"Dan and Clara often take the phone off the hook," Maybank said. "They're in bed by eight-thirty and up at four to make sure that the birds are getting their nourishment. That's the big event around there, feeding the birds. Second big event is the evening garbage feast for the animals. Nobody'll bother Dan."

"Why was he so insistent on our publicizing that business?" she asked. "It's no secret that people murder coyotes."

"Don't ask me. I love him, but I don't always understand him."

Jenny flicked cigarette ashes onto the flagstones. Lights winked on the mountainside. Tract housing created jewel-like patterns on the purple-black ranges. The houses were better at night. During the day, the matchboxes gave the range a littered look. "I think I do. Dan's what? Eighty-one. He's been complaining his life was a waste."

"He's led five lives, all of them good."

"I know. And you know. And his friends know. It was after Columbia gave him some award. Alexander Hamilton Memorial, some such thing. He was too sick to go to New York. When they sent it to him, he sat in his study turning it over in his hand, wondering if he'd done anything to deserve it."

"Does that make it obligatory for him to take on ranchers and hunters?"

"Clara told me that all those years he spent teaching, he started every day convinced he had absolutely nothing to tell his students, and he doubted any of them ever learned a worthwhile thing from him."

"Clara told you that?" Maybank always sensed a chasm between himself and Vormund's earlier life as teacher, critic, and literary man. He had known him only as an observer of hummingbirds, a man who could wax ecstatic over an ocotillo flower.

"That's one of the reasons he quit teaching. He wondered if his books meant anything."

"I don't get it. What are they supposed to mean?"

Jenny shook her long black hair. "Maybank, you're dense. Dan was never a political man, but he was *concerned,* he was worried about people, and the country, and how things went. Nothing that's happened in the last twenty-five years has given him much hope. People making too many babies. Idiotic wars. Cities that are death traps. Crooked politicians. And the great god technology. It made him ill, and he began to think he hadn't done enough."

Maybank rubbed his eyes. "What was he supposed to do? For goodness' sake, he was writing about poets, that kind of stuff. That doesn't change the world."

"Exactly. Clara says he goes into these deep funks wondering if maybe he misspent his life. So—I hate to put it this way—before he dies, maybe he can do something to stop us from going off the brink."

"And that's why he wants us to take on every gun toter in the state?" Maybank asked. "He'll put the Institute out of business."

"We should listen to him, Jack. He's given the Institute whatever reputation it has. Even if it means we lose a donor here and there." She guffawed. "Donor, *wow.* Who needs any of them any more? I keep forgetting Otto."

"Don't remind me." Maybank heard frogs burping, night insects buzzing.

"Fifteen million, Jack. I'll remind you." She clapped her hands. "Let's buy the land where Ed and Dan and Sidewinder saw the cactus. You'll have trouble spending all that money."

"I'll think of something. Get rid of those slums we work in. A new lab. New pens. And we need a *real* curator. I love Ed Bugler, but he drives me up the wall. We'll give him another title—chief of field work. Turn him loose with his masked bobwhites."

"How about the Daniel Vormund Refuge for predators?" Jenny tossed a cigarette onto the patio, watched it glow, smoke, vanish. "It's loony, Jack. Here we are struggling along, passing the hat at luncheons, barely able to pay our bills, and along comes Denkerman."

"And because he read some of Dan's articles."

"And Dan thinks he's a failure?"

Maybank laughed. "It's what my father always said. In America, the right things get done eventually, but only for the wrong reasons."

"Your father said that?" Her recollection of John Maybank, Sr., was of a dour lawyer, an expert in bond issues and arbitrage, whose only interest outside of his stupefyingly dull work was Brown football.

"I know what's bothering Vormund," Maybank said. "It's deeper than the death of the desert and the murder of animals. He's part of the human family, and he's sore at his relatives."

Jenny got up. She walked toward her husband, who was seated on the brick wall at the edge of their garden. She embraced him. They kissed—tongues probing, lips biting softly. She breathed deeply and looked at the star-heavy sky.

"Orion is watching," she said. Jack was squeezing her breasts.

"Who?"

"You earth-bound biologist. Orion, the hunter. There he is, right over us. The pinhead. The big shoulders. Three stars in his belt. Quick—what star is his right shoulder?"

"Don't ask me. All I know is Cassiopeia."

"Betelgeuse. His left shoulder is Bellatrix and his left foot is Rigel. I don't know what his right foot is."

"Mine's asleep."

"Wake it up. This is the happy hour, as they say at the Ramada Inn. Jack, what squares we are! We're getting fifteen million dollars and we don't even get drunk."

"I wish we could give the money to Dan." She lay her face against his shoulder. "I have the feeling the money will never get here. Someone'll take it away. We've always had enough, so we don't know how to approach it. What if Winston Fair is a practical joker?"

Bugler knelt amid a dozen varieties of cactus—pincushions, barrels, prickly pear, fishhooks, chollas—and began to dig out the creeping devil. He had planted it two days ago, but the location bothered him. He wanted it in the highest and driest part of the garden.

Sidewinder, with a rake and a clippers, was tidying up the area. Somnolent, silent, he clipped dead chunks from the Santa Rita prickly pear, the organ-pipe cactus, the senita. He had disappeared again yesterday just when Bugler had wanted him to help with the animal pens. "Where'd you go?" Ed had asked. "Out. Lookin'."

The sun bounced off the Hopi's thick glasses, turning his eyes into sightless glass orbs. The Stetson was pushed over his squashed face. Bugler had not bawled him out for vanishing. What good would it do? But I should have, Ed thought. Oblivious to the pricks, he set the creeping devil into a new hole, extended the long roots, scooped dry sand over them. Maybank was after him to run a tighter ship. Get work out of people. Finish projects. They were going broke.

They want to get rid of me, Bugler thought. He resolved to get organized, keep a list of jobs that had to be done, stop running into the desert with Dan and Clara on expeditions. He made his mind up. Only one thing would get him to take Dan out again and that would be the trogon.

"You ever see a trogon, let me know," Bugler said.

"Yeah. I know."

"Know what it looks like?"

"Sure. Red breast. Green head and wings."

"That's it. Find me a trogon, Sidewinder, and all is forgiven."

The Hopi grunted, made a pile of the cuttings from the prickly pear and the organ pipe. That was a bird you saw once in a lifetime, if you were lucky. No chance. They *thought* they were going to see it once. Ed and the professor, two old crazies, riding out for a week, getting the wife angry over it. Freezing inside a blind, looking through binoculars for hours. And nothing. No trogon.

A long white convertible with its top down emerged from a cloud of dust like a whale exploding foam over the ocean surface. It bounced along the dirt road outside the botanical area and stopped. Sidewinder looked at it. *Lincoln Continental Mark III.* The big one.

A man and a woman dressed in white tennis clothes were inside. They were tanned, spotless, the kind of people Sidewinder avoided. At the Institute everyone dressed as bad as an Indian. The Maybanks, *boy!* In their dirty chinos, no shoes. Even an Indian knew enough to wear boots in the desert.

The man got out of the car. He was box-chested, square-headed, a blond and ruddy young man. His chest made two blocks inside the knitted shirt. Behind wrap-around glasses, he surveyed the plantings and the adobe buildings beyond. The woman remained inside the car. She rested her blond head against the tan leather back rest. She seemed to be dozing.

"Hi," Ray Host said to Bugler. "I think we're lost."

Bugler looked up from his work. He used the back of his trowel to tamp sand around the creeping devil. "That's not hard out here. What are you looking for?"

"The Pima Racquet Club."

Bugler squinted at the young man. "I'm not much on tennis. Is it a new place?"

"I guess so. It's on Ocotillo Road."

"Oh, the old Bernstein ranch. Used to catch salamanders there." Bugler got up. "You *are* lost. But it's not hard to find."

Host studied him. A rawboned man, with a weathered face, huge hands, splayfeet. A work suit stained with sweat and dirt. Pepper-and-salt hair, rimless glasses.

"Get back on the Interstate," Ed said. "As if you were going back to Senita. Go two exits past the one that says City Center, that's Ocotillo Road. Take Ocotillo north and you'll get to it. Does that sound right, Sidewinder?"

"Yeah." The Indian did not look up.

"Thank you," Host said. He lifted the dark glasses. Squinting in the light, he scanned the garden, the fences, the one-story buildings.

"Beautiful location," Host said. Like his father, Host understood land. The hills, the talus of fallen rocks, the slow rise of the desert. How they could *process* this place! No cheap tracts. Custom-built homes, starting at $150,000. In front of him he saw the native stone and brick dwellings rise—pools, cabanas, patios, barbecues, fantastic landscaping, using wild native trees and shrubs.

"I saw a sign back there," the young man said. "Is this part of the . . . what do you call it? Research Station?"

"Desert Research Institute," Bugler said.

"Government operation?"

"Heck, no. Private and broke."

Host bit the temple piece of his glasses.

From the car, lounging on the hot leather, one arm stretched out, Corinne said, "You're a poor liar, Ray. You need Pop for this."

Host lingered at the fence. "What kind of research?"

"A little bit of everything. Our aim is to preserve the desert as it is—wild and free, as one of my colleagues says."

"You do experiments, and so on?"

"Right. This is the botanical section. We do a lot of work with predators. Lions, coyotes. Breeding habits, range. We try to encourage endangered species. Ever hear of the masked bobwhite quail?"

"I don't think we have," Corinne called from the car. She lit a cigarette and tossed the match into the desert.

"Right, ma'am," Bugler said. He smiled innocently. "Most people haven't. Anyway, it's one of our projects."

The woman mashed the cigarette against an ashtray, then threw it out of the car also. Sidewinder shook his head. None of his business.

"Sounds interesting," Host said.

"We try. We've a study on water conservancy going on. Not too optimistic, but somebody's got to be a pessimist, I guess."

"Ray, can we get going?" the woman asked.

Bugler went on. "We've revived ten varieties of desert plants people thought were finished. Just by keeping rodents out of that acreage there." He indicated a fenced area. "People kill predators and the rodents multiply, and that's the end of a lot of vegetation. You keep poisoning foxes and badgers and coyotes, and the rats and mice and rabbits overrun the desert."

"How about poisoning rodents also?" Host asked seriously.

"You can try. But they're not meat eaters. Means you have to poison the whole earth, every piece of vegetation. Don't think it isn't being tried. Know what happens?"

Host shook his head.

"It's what Dan Vormund says. If the earth can't produce beauty, it won't produce food either."

Host thanked Bugler and turned to leave. He paused and spoke again. "Can I get some more information? Anything the Institute has published?"

"Stop by the yellow house. The first one off the road down there. Mr. Maybank might be in. We have a newsletter. There's a dandy issue I helped get up last year on trapping."

"For or against?" Corinne asked.

Bugler took an instant to realize he was being baited. "I think you know where we stand. If you ever saw a fox bite his foot off to get out of a trap . . ."

Sidewinder swept twigs and branches into another pile.

Host tried to assemble his thoughts. Who were these people? How did they come to possess what seemed to be such valuable land? Why all this fuss over rodents and desert plants? Where did the money come from?

"Who runs it? How are you funded?" Host tried to smile.

"You ought to talk to Jack Maybank. It's his baby. Or as he puts it, his delinquent child, the way it takes up his time and money."

"I think you're doing terrific work."

Under her breath, Corinne said: *Liar*. Ray had still not told her why they were in Arizona. Depend on the Hosts, father and son, to work secretly, with a minimum of memoranda, letters, phone calls.

"It's a tough battle," Bugler said. "Most everyone is against us. If you're interested, you can become a member of the Institute for seven fifty a year. Gets you *The Road Runner Gazette* and any special bulletins."

"It sounds like a bargain, Ray," Corinne said. "When have we last bought something that cost seven fifty?"

Bugler said: "We need every penny. The unions are on our back. They say we're killing the construction industry. The ranchers hate us. The hunters hate us. The developers and power plant people say we're saboteurs. Up at the state house, they claim we're crazy. They listen to us now and then, but that's mostly because of Vormund."

"Who?"

"Dan Vormund. He writes for our newspaper. He's kind of our guiding light."

Sidewinder muttered to his pile of sweepings: "And cold all the time. Sick a whole lot, too."

"If you're interested in conservation, you should meet him. By the way, I'm Edward Bugler, the curator. This fellow is Sidewinder Sid, our maintenance man."

"My name's Host."

"Nice meeting you. Drop by again."

Host thanked Bugler. The giant tires bit into the dirt road.

— 56 —

The car turned like a battleship executing a mid-ocean maneuver and sped toward the Interstate.

Bugler and the Hopi were showered with dust. The Indian squatted, studying with dim eyes the progress of a pinacate battle. When he poked it with a stick, the bug reared on its hind legs and made a tiny *pop!* releasing a foul spray. One of Vormund's favorite critters. Called it the six-legged skunk.

"They wasn't lost," Sidewinder said.

"No?"

"That guy was looking for this place."

"How can you be sure?"

Sidewinder rubbed his squashed nose. "People like that don't get lost. They was looking for us."

"Badly handled," Corinne said.

"I don't think so."

A hot white streak, the Lincoln blazed down the Interstate. It seemed to be fleeing the hideous works of man that bordered the six-lane blacktop. The landscape had been obliterated by signs, towers, and buildings of such determined ugliness as to deaden outrage, stifle protest.

"That *sincere* face," Corinne said. "What were you after?"

Host had not told her why he had been sent to Arizona. More and more, he kept the details of corporate business from her.

"It's complicated, Corinne. If I tell you now, it might affect my serve. You want me to play well, don't you?"

"You went looking for that place. You knew something about it."

"Yes, yes."

"Why don't you tell me? You want to buy their land. Another Host-Labarre enterprise. Golden City? Senior Citizen Sun Glades?"

Host said nothing. He was a slow-moving man. Was it her drinking? His own failings? But what had he done wrong? He was sober, faithful, reasonably attentive, a good father. Reluctantly, he concluded that her excessive beauty gave her prior rights to nastiness. Lately it was getting out of hand. If he did not love her so much—just the sight of her standing at net, bent low, her perfect backside frilled with white panties—made him tremble. His father must have sensed something when he met

— 57 —

her. "Too beautiful," James W. Host said. "And by no means stupid. She has everything and that may be a problem." Ray, aged twenty-two, had replied: "Except money." The old man then said that her poverty would make her an even greater problem. *"She'll want it."*

"Aren't you ashamed of yourself?" Corinne asked. "Picking on that desert tramp and an Indian? Trying to gouge information from them because you're so interested in nature?"

"Cut it out."

"Desert Research Institute?" she mocked. "Yes, we're all for saving the prickly pear."

"I said cut it out."

"God, how I'd love to see Host-Labarre land on its corporate ass once. Just *once*. You people rule the world. You have it all your own way. What I can't figure out is, you don't sit around a secret room and scheme. You don't have any philosophy or rules of operation or guidebook. You just *know* how to get it all. I'd like to warn those conservationists what they're in for."

How she could drink, play tennis, bait him, in this oven, was beyond him. Host loved her even more for her capacity to endure, remain lovely, astonish strangers, even when semidrunk.

"It has nothing to do with their land."

"What, then?"

"It's complicated. If I tell you . . ."

"I won't bother you again, Ray, honestly. I won't snitch to anyone."

Host turned off the Interstate at the Ocotillo exit, then headed north as Bugler had instructed. They passed through a shabby business district, old stucco homes. They spoke to him of tuberculosis and arthritis. On a three-block stretch he counted three osteopaths, a naturopath, two physical therapists, and five MDs. A place to die. Maybe the animals deserved the dry land as much as the people. Humans seemed to use it as a way station on the way to what his father's clerical friends called "the great adventure."

"The Desert Research Institute," she persisted. "Why are you after them?"

"I think they're a fake."

"Oh?"

"One of these letterhead outfits that raises money for fake causes."

"Why does that concern you? You saw the buildings and the land. And a man planting a cactus."

"Those buildings are relics of an old army post. They can't be doing anything worthwhile."

"Who appointed you—or the great J. W. Host, for that matter —as an authority on fund-raising? Ray, you're playing some shifty game and it's not like you."

Host stroked her bare knee. He could not get angry with her. Not for any length of time. Corinne was sharp, bright. She saw through his father. The careful speech, the elbow-rubbing with Baptists and others of the anointed, the silences, the anonymity, the shibboleths of integrity and honor. All of these hid a shrewd and calculating mind. A mind so subtle, so insightful, that the most cunning manipulators, land speculators, stock swindlers, and assorted rascals that infested the Los Angeles area were left denuded and stunned if they dared challenge him. But Ray was all surface. His character was as palpable as the square scarlet face and the curling yellow hair.

"It's a weird story," he said. Host wheeled the car into a parking lot. He picked up two tennis bags and a half-dozen rackets, and walked with her to the fortresslike beige walls and green canvas awnings.

"I'm listening."

"Ever hear any of us mention Otto Denkerman?"

"No."

"He was my mother's second cousin."

Fassman left his valise unpacked. He collapsed on the motel bed and began to read the afternoon newspaper. He was a newspaper freak, a magazine junkie. At his Westwood home (from which he had been ejected by gorgeous Wendi) he spent a drowsy Sunday reading everything the voluminous Los Angeles *Times* chose to print. When he had finished the *Times*, he read shopping throwaways, obscure magazines. Was it his sense of incompleteness about broadcast news that impelled him to wallow in print? He wondered. There was more permanence to a newspaper than to a TV broadcast—seen briefly, forgotten, lost. Department of Wind, Air, Gas, and Shadows he called it. And tearful Wendi would shout at him: "But you don't try. You could be a *producer*."

He hadn't been destined for authority. Too formless. Clumsy at office politics. Letting his unspoken contempt for the work manifest itself to important people. Once he had enraged an executive producer by asserting that people watched his program for the *commercials*. "It's true," Fassman blundered on. "Your audience consists largely of arthritis and rheumatism sufferers, shut-ins, geriatric cases, paraplegics. They like the commercials best. You could show old newsreels for the program, so long as you keep running Arrid and Drāno and Johnson foot powder commercials." Fassman was replaced by a Radcliffe girl with enormous breasts.

Immediately Fassman liked the local newspaper, the Senita *Pantagraph*. It was breezy and sharply edited. The ink stained his hands, but he forgave them. A sense of lost chances engloomed him. Would he have been happier on a newspaper?

The newspaper was crammed with news about "retirees," PTA parties, women's clubs, ranching and growing, new housing developments, high school sports. Lingering over the sports pages, Fassman was gratified to see photographs of the Cuff twins, Roosevelt and Wilson, ebony string beans. "The first pair of twins ever to make the all-state basketball team in Arizona history," the caption bragged. Fassman was happy for them.

On the front page of the second news section (he recalled enough of his journalism school training to know that it was the *split page*) he saw a six-column headline:

RANCHERS INSIST ON RIGHT TO KILL COYOTES

Association Protests Dog Hunt Photos

Fassman sat up and tore the page out of the paper. It was a long article, with a jump to an inner page, and he clipped that also. With a red ball-point pen, he marked sections as he read it.

Local ranchers today voiced strong protests against the *Pantagraph*'s publication of photographs of a coyote hunt involving the use of dogs, and particularly to remarks attributed to Daniel D. Vormund and other members of the Desert Research Institute of Senita City.

"Why not show photographs of ewes, lambs, and calves, disemboweled, with their throats slit by savage coyotes?" asked Duane Essler, President of the Santa Teresa Ranchers Association. "It would make a lot more sense than trying to arouse public sympathy for vermin."

Mr. Essler, owner of the Toilsome Ranch, said he spoke for several hundred members of the Association in protesting the prominence given to the photographs.

Mr. Essler said he backed the pending bill in the state legislature to permit the shooting of coyotes, lions, wolves, and other predators from airplanes. His brother, Wayne Essler, state senator from Hessenden, is cosponsoring the bill, which would permit the use of automatic and semiautomatic weapons, as well as grenades, napalm, and fire bombs, to control predator density.

"They're insane," Fassman said. "They're out of their minds." And who was to stop them? Daniel D. Vormund, who coughed his way through New York winters, and complained of asthma, ulcers, and arthritis? So timid had Vormund been that he had even shied away from smart-ass students. It was no contest. Fassman envisioned his old mentor, D. D. Vormund, that frail bookish man, walking down main street at high noon, ready to meet the gunmen.

There were more protests in the letters-to-the-editor column. One rancher bragged that he would go out and kill ten coyotes with his dogs. "I breed these dogs myself. They are part greyhound for speed, and part Irish wolfhound for killer instinct, and they will handle any coyote from here to Oregon."

Fassman pushed his feet into his loafers and stood up. He would wander around looking for a Mexican restaurant and bloat himself with chili, tacos, enchiladas, guacamole. Arizona, for some reason, served the best Mexican food in the world. Maybe it was the air, the altitude. Cheap, too. He never cheated on the company expense account, ate moderately, used inexpensive hotels, rented compacts. But he missed Wendi—so attractive with her lavish black hair, barbered nose, contact lenses. It would have been fun in Arizona, right now, the two of them getting smashed on Mexican beer, falling into bed for a long night of sex. All gone. She had her actor. He had nothing.

It was better once, he thought. *When I was an undergraduate.* He could lick the world, make a name, use all that education to construct a rewarding career. He leafed through the phone book, found a listing under Clara Vormund, and dialed the number. He had never met Vormund's wife, but he had read about her. The old man had written about her with great affection. *I doubt that I would have lived this long, accomplished what I have, enjoyed so many things, without her. I hope I've reciprocated in some small degree.*

"Who is it?" a woman's voice asked.

"Is this Professor Vormund's residence?"

"Yes. But he's asleep. You woke us up." She sounded annoyed.

"I'm terribly sorry." Fassman looked at his watch. It was a quarter to nine.

"I can't disturb him now. Can you call tomorrow? Leave your name."

"This is Alan Fassman. Is this Mrs. Vormund?"

"Yes."

"I was a student of Professor Vormund's at Columbia many years ago. I was at his last lecture."

"He isn't feeling well. Even if he were awake, I'm not sure he'd see you. It isn't personal, young man, it's just that he doesn't like to encourage visitors. I don't either. He gets tired."

"I understand, Mrs. Vormund. But, tomorrow perhaps . . . ?"

"Call in the morning. Any time after five A.M."

"Five . . . ?"

"We're up at four-thirty to see the birds. That's why we go to bed early. I hear him telling me to get back to bed. Call again, young man. Good night."

Mumbling apologies, Fassman hung up. Who could blame Vormund for retiring early so that he could spend the dawn hours with his birds? In New York, he had been continually ill, coughing, his voice clotted, his eyes tearing. His friends and colleagues—Weaver, Van Doren—often filled in for him. There were giants on the earth in those days.

Fassman fell to the bed, covered his face, and turned out the light. The loss of time, of good experiences, of places and people he had loved, filled him with a bottomless sorrow. The world should have been frozen in the fifties, when he had been an undergraduate. Spring on Morningside Heights. Had he ever loved another place so much? Even as a commuter, a brief-case-lugging obscurity from the Bronx, a pharmacist's son on a partial scholarship, a world removed from the super-bright boys who ran the *Spectator* and the *Jester*, light-years from the thick-necked jocks with Italian and Polish names, he had loved the place.

A warm breezy morning in spring. The end of the academic year. And Vormund, looking as if his chest were in pain, standing at the lectern, in an orange-brown tweed suit. It was his last class. He was leaving Columbia, New York, the East. He would spend his remaining years in the desert, write no more about his idols, Johnson, Pope, Dryden. His health demanded it. He had lost his appetite for the works of man.

The long sloping room in Hamilton Hall was packed, Fassman remembered. The class was Elizabethan Drama 103-104, but scores of students had heard about Vormund's farewell, and they had crammed into the aisles, on the window ledges, on the steps. Fassman, seated in the front row, had been surprised by the show of respect. D. D. Vormund had never been a campus character. He disdained student-faculty softball games, turned down invitations to smokers and literary society meetings. After class he could be seen hurrying across 116th Street to the subway. He walked in a quick shuffle, head down, as if reluctant to be stopped by some student seeking his opinions on a new novel.

But they were there in vast numbers—commuters, jocks, radicals, campus savants, student board members. A cold unsentimental place, Columbia, even the undergraduate college, with its losing teams and shabby dormitories and fiercely competitive premeds. But for one moment on a spring day, something had dazzled them, brought them into a musty hall to honor D. D. Vormund.

"I'm not sure why you're here," he began, in the firm voice, heavily tinged with the accents of his native Kentucky. "Perhaps you are thanking me for my leisurely marking habits."

They laughed. Vormund was a notorious granter of A's. B plus from him meant poor work. A C would have been failing in any other class. He threw A's and A minuses around with a lavish hand.

"I owe all of you an explanation, since I have earned the reputation of an indiscriminating marker. Mr. Little, I am informed, advises his players who are having academic problems to take courses with that fellow Vormund. It is guaranteed to bring their averages up. Let me explain my liberality. After twenty years on this campus, I have concluded that none of you ever learned much from me, certainly nothing worthwhile, nothing that will help you earn your way in the world, achieve status and success. So since you have learned nothing, and I have taught you little, it is much easier to give you all high grades than low grades. No one is hurt by it, and some of you may be helped."

There was applause, puzzled laughter. Fassman could recall looking at Herb Cohen, the premed who sat next to him, the two of them raising eyebrows, not certain whether Vormund was fooling or not.

"The other afternoon," he went on, "something occurred that convinced me I am making the right decision in going West while I am still ambulant and clearheaded. Most of you know that I do not encourage postclass visitors. But in this instance, the visitor was a pretty Barnard girl, who had an urgent question for me. She was doing a paper on Theodore Dreiser. Could I please give her some anecdotes since, as she so indelicately phrased it, she had heard that I was *alive* when he was writing. At that moment, I realized I had overstayed my hours on Morningside Heights."

He went on to talk about his decision to give up teaching. He was forsaking Racine for ravens, Bosswell for barn owls, Shakespeare for chuckawallas. "I'm going West not to make money, or build cities, but for clean air, solitude, and the company of wild creatures and wild vistas. I thank all of you for coming here this afternoon, and wish you well. Now, gentlemen, if you will excuse me, I have an appointment with a cactus wren."

They rose, cheering, applauding. Vormund did not linger, picked up his black hat, clapped it on his head, and was gone. Fassman never saw him again. But he had read the books that came out of his desert experience. He may have left literature, but it had not left him. Dune primroses reminded him of Ophelia. The croak of a frog summoned up visions of Aristophanes. When he descended into Supai Canyon, he thought of Virgil going into hell, and when he climbed Mount Lemon, he wrote about Peveril of the Peak.

In the sodium-lit parking lot, Fassman had to wait a few minutes while teen-age galoots used the area as a speedway, roaring mindlessly in desperate circles. No escape. Vormund had seen it coming—the brainless obsession with machines, the triumph of technology that in the long run offered nothing, devoured the earth, created ugliness and despair.

And yet, as Fassman settled into his rented Vega (and promptly flooded the engine in his eagerness to escape the hot rods), Vormund had retained, as his writings manifested, a remarkable zest for life. If man had betrayed him, there were still rabbits and hawks. *A pessimist with a zest for life.* Had not Vormund used these words to describe Dr. Johnson? And were they not (Fassman thought) applicable now to Vormund himself, despairing of man and his works, yet full of wonder at the sight of a piñon jay?

The Maybanks would be sore at him, Ed Bugler knew, but he could not resist another trip to the *orugas.* His excuse to Maybank—left in a note on Jack's desk at 5 A.M.—was that he wanted to survey the area and try to calculate how much land they would need for a preserve. Actually, Bugler wanted to clip off another chunk of creeping devil for Dan. Vormund looked drained after the first trip. No, it was more than fatigue. He was lapsing into one of his periods of despair. A hunk of the crazy cactus for his own garden (where grew the boojum tree Ed had brought him from Baja) would cheer him up.

But Maybank would be angry. They were behind on the new pens. The raccoons were a problem. The peccaries were trying to burrow out. The badger was off his feed, poking his snout around, baring his teeth. Only Ed could get him to eat, tempting him with a mouse or a lizard. The underwater conservancy experiment was falling apart (nobody but Ed understood the valves and pumps), and the college kid who had started the breeding program to revive the masked bobwhite had quit.

Bugler was supposed to keep the place running, but Maybank refused to get him first-rate help (so Ed reasoned). The trouble was, Ed concluded, we're all amateurs. The Maybanks were social, full of that airy self-mocking attitude that came with being *eastern.* They'd started the DRI as a hobby, and now that it was seriously involved in issues, they were over their heads.

Not that I'm much help, Bugler thought. He spun the jeep from the Interstate, put the vehicle into four-wheel drive, and bounced across the desert. Dan had made the difference. The DRI was his hangout, his corner drugstore. It got him out of the house, away from Clara's medications and heating pads and ice bags, away from the telephone with old students and reporters pestering him, and into the company he liked best—animals and birds. And by spending so much time at the DRI, he had, in some mysterious way, got them going again. You looked at Dan, listened to him, and it was like one of the Pima or Navajo wise men telling you what you knew was the truth.

At first light Bugler saw that in two days since he had visited the area, the desert flowers had doubled in profusion and brightness. Seas of marigolds, goldpoppies, sand verbenas, and purplemat undulated before him. He stopped the jeep, unloaded his camera, and clicked off a roll of color film. You could never have enough of the desert in bloom.

It was late April, and something Vormund had once quoted on one of their expeditions—could it have been last year when they tried to find the trogon?—buzzed in Bugler's head. *April is the cruellest month.* Some poet said it. A fellow Dan had known when he wrote for the intellectual magazines, even before he went to Columbia. What did it mean? Ed was an unlearned man. He wasn't sure. Something about being born again. Life renewing. But why cruel? Being born was joyful. Fledglings in the nest. Mamma bear and the cubs. It was beyond Bugler.

He'd invited Dan to come along on this trip. "No you don't, Edward Earle Bugler," Clara said. "Dan is in bed this minute and his back hurts. It's that jeep you drive and the way you drive it. He'll stay in bed today, and I'll make him some redbush tea."

Redbush tea! Or rose hips. Or sassafras. Or ginseng. The way Clara looked after the old man! When they rode down Grand Canyon on muleback (without Clara), she later accused the cowboy of deliberately—why?—putting Dan on the fattest mule, thereby causing Dan's prostate to act up. "My prostate has never been peppier," Vormund protested. "Ed took excellent care of me, and besides he showed me a new species of Kaibab squirrel."

But why did that fellow insist April was cruel? Bugler had rarely seen anything as lovely as the carpet of yellow, white, and purple flowers stitched to the desert floor as if by a giant worker in needlepoint. Nothing man created could equal it, no formal garden, no planting, no orchard.

A mile beyond the cattle guard, Bugler halted the jeep and studied the map he had drawn. He had brought with him a surveyor's level and cross, and a horizontal compass, and hoped to estimate the amount of land they would need as a preserve. Maybank could find out whose land it was (Essler's?) and start the ball rolling.

The air was spicy and cool. Back in the jeep, jouncing along the cattle trail, Bugler observed that desert birds were nesting furiously. They darted by him with bits of brush and twigs in their beaks—a cactus wren to the security of a cholla, a gila woodpecker to the loftiest hole in a saguaro. Quail skittered away from the jeep's tires, plump hens followed by squads of chicks.

Somewhere there was screaming. It sounded like children being tortured, high piercing wails, creatures absorbing more pain than could be imagined. Bugler shivered and shook his head. He knew what the sound was. And he understood why April was a cruel month. You were born again, the poet said, but you suffered pain and torment. The howls of protest and fear. Someone was *denning*. In the spring ranchers and growers and the men from the wildlife bureau killed coyote pups in the den. Fast. Efficient. Six and seven at one blow, the way the story had it.

A noise unlike anything in the world. Once you heard it you never forgot. Like a woman begging not to be strangled, a child running from a whip. The wails lingered, echoed, started again. *Christ*, Bugler prayed, *end it, end it, burn them fast, burn them dead, so they can't shriek any more. . . .*

Once Ed had seen it done. A warden had invited him along to prove that it was fast and relatively painless. "It kills quickly," the man said. "Better than cyanide or a trap. They die in a hurry and they never know what hit them."

The man tossed a gas cartridge into the den. Sulphur and phosphorus burst into thick smoky flame and stank like all the marsh gas in the world. They could peer in and see it flaming, spouting sparks and fire and smoke. Choking, suffocating, the pups fled toward the opening of the den, plunged into the fiery mixture, and were roasted. They screamed a long time. Bugler remembered the charred stench and the blistered black lumps of hair and flesh. Popped eyes, open jaws.

Someone was denning not far from where he was. Someone was shoving cartridges into dens. The wails diminished, but the stink lingered. Bugler could envision the scene—flames and smoke pouring from the mouth of the cave, the pups consumed by the heat. And the coyote mother standing a hundred feet away, hidden by grass or a cactus.

The day's adventure soured. Turning his head to the left, he saw a plume of black smoke rise from the desert floor. It was tableland, bright with flowers and red-rock boulders, a good place for a coyote to raise the brood. The odor was stronger.

"Not my business," Ed said. He had a date with his *orugas*. He wheeled the jeep up the hillside to the slope which led to the field of cacti. To his delight, he found the single pink-red bloom open. It was a handsome flower—full-petaled, deep pink, with bloodlike red streaks. "Almost too beautiful for an ugly cactus like you," he said. "No, that's a rotten notion. Dan would bawl me out."

Bugler set up his instruments and began to take measurements of the area. He was an indifferent surveyor and a poor mathematician, but all he wanted was a rough idea. Maybe a thousand acres? To make sure they kept the right mix of vegetation, rodents, predators. You would need the foxes and coyotes and hawks to thin out the rats and mice.

Preoccupied with his work, Bugler did not hear the truck. His jeep was parked out of sight, a hundred yards from the creeping devils. Intent on his work, alone, a part of the natural scheme, Bugler could not be distracted. He no longer saw the black plume or smelled the burned flesh.

A half hour passed. Bugler ascended the ridge again, leaving the *orugas*. Dan was right. What California did for the bristlecone pines, they would do for the creeping devils. Keep a small corner of the earth green.

At the crest of the hill, Bugler's nose, as sensitive as a badger's, sniffed the charred aroma. He heard no more wailing. The smoky plume in the distance had dissipated in the desert air. Why was it so close to home? Your nose could trick you in the desert.

A dust plume told him that a truck was somewhere in the distance. Whose? The rancher who had turned the dogs loose the other day? A government agent, wondering what Ed was doing out so far? But it was moving away. The feather was getting smaller.

As he approached the jeep the odor grew stronger. "What the heck," Ed asked. He was balancing a load—surveying instruments, a chunk of *oruga* for Dan's garden. He was glad the vehicle was riding away from him. Some rancher might not like his visits. Bugler could not abide confrontations or angry words. No animal acted that way. If they snarled, they had a reason for it. Kids (whom Bugler hated most of all) tormented caged ocelots and kit foxes for the hell of it. Ocelots and foxes never did. They hunted and killed to live.

In back of the jeep were fresh tire tracks. And the pointed toes and heels of cowboy boots. Someone had visited his jeep. The stink came from the back of the vehicle.

He threw back the canvas flap and saw the burned pup.

"I'll be darned," he said.

It was a chubby doglike animal, still hot, still giving off wisps of smoke from its encounter with the gas cartridge. In death its legs were curled beneath the body. The jaw was open in a final scream. Most of the hair had been scorched away. The flesh was blistered and full of cracks. Dried rills of blood on the black flaking flesh.

Bugler stared, shook his head in sorrow, and got behind the wheel.

Otto Denkerman's lawyer, Mr. Winston Fair of Los Angeles, was a lean Californian with a tennis-tanned face, curly black hair, and alarming white teeth. He seemed a bit lavish for a recluse like Denkerman (Joe Fusaro thought), and the Maybanks had the notion he was a specialist of some kind who had moved in once the provisions of the will were made known. Stuffy older types had probably humored Denkerman in his dotage, not young hotshots like Mr. Fair.

But it soon became apparent that Mr. Fair had indeed been at Denkerman's side when the will was drawn up.

"Our senior partner, Mr. Keen, did most of the talking," Fair said. "I just listened in astonishment."

They were seated in the Maybanks' living room. Jack had chosen not to hold the meeting at the Institute.

"God Almighty," Fusaro said, as he read the document. "This is no notation scrawled on the back of an envelope. It's a *will*. Witnessed, signed, notarized. The works."

Mr. Fair flashed his formidable teeth. "You know our firm, Mr. Fusaro."

"I sure do. Bet you never had anything like this before."

"It staggered us. Of course, no attempt was made to dissuade Mr. Denkerman. He was a rather fearsome old gentleman."

"Fearsome?" Jenny asked. "He sounds like a pussycat."

Fair fished more documents from his brief case. "Pussycat, that's appropriate. Did you know he kept lions on his ranch? At least a half dozen. They sometimes had the run of his house. Mr. Keen was at a meeting at the ranch some years ago when a lioness strolled in."

"Like a Dreyfus Fund commercial," Fusaro said.

"Denkerman had an elephant that was trained to squirt guests with water."

"Good thing he didn't train his pigeons. Or that elephants don't fly." Fusaro was getting the sensation that Denkerman was a *pazzo*, a crazy. Sooner or later all of this would come out. The will would be broken. Mental incompetence, undue influence . . .

"Get a load of this, Jack," Fusaro said. "'It is my desire that all of my estate, all incomes, all real properties, moneys, funds, real estate, possessions, be utilized to the fullest to save the wild creatures of the American desert from destruction. Pain and suffering among animals and birds, and the threat of extinction by man and man's devices, are to be fought relentlessly. Killing must be stopped. Endangered species protected. Predators must be preserved. I wish that land be set aside for the protection of desert wildlife, that they may flourish and reproduce, and be free of the threat of torment, persecution, and death at the hands of men.' There's a lot more, two pages of it."

"Read on, Mr. Fusaro," Fair said.

"The money is to be spent as dispensed. A million bucks every year for fifteen years, or as long as the estate keeps producing money. On the installment plan."

"Good," Maybank said. "We won't be tempted to spend it all on candy."

Fair had doubts about these lanky people. They wore old chino shirts and frazzled shorts. The woman was barefoot. Extremely good-looking in a large-featured way, she had not combed her hair or done her nails. The house was large and beautifully situated, but it looked as if it had not been cleaned in weeks.

"It staggers me," Maybank said. "Mr. Denkerman was never here. He didn't know us. All from *The Road Runner Gazette?*"

"You know what I told you on the phone. He'd marked the articles by Mr. Vormund." He paused. "Ah, would it be possible to see Mr. Vormund while I'm here?"

Jenny and Jack looked at one another. Maybank spoke. "He's usually tired and out of sorts. He doesn't encourage visitors. He's eighty-one."

"Maybe when he feels better," Jenny said.

Fusaro chuckled to himself. Fair would have a long wait. Vormund never felt better, only worse.

"We'll break the news to Dan gently," Maybank said. "Don't you think that's right, Joe?"

"Yeah. The old guy doesn't get any of this, but his words did it. What did Dan earn all his life?"

Jenny made a lateral gesture with her hand. "Dan wouldn't give a damn. He never knew anything about money. He and Clara never wanted for a thing."

"What do we do now, Winston?" Fusaro asked.

"We have to file for probate. That will be done at once."

"And then?"

"There will be challenges." Fair dazzled them with his teeth. "There always are."

"What kind of challenges?" Fusaro asked.

"Distant relatives. But where they are, and what their intentions are, we don't know. It's too soon."

"On what basis?"

The Maybanks were looking at one another as if they were Eskimos stranded in a Watusi village. They were out of their element. Although Jack's father had been a successful lawyer, a gray eminence who had counseled meat packers and railroads, and Jenny's family were prosperous shoe manufacturers, neither understood anything about money.

"Incompetence," Fair said. "That Mr. Denkerman was out of

— 71 —

his mind and didn't know what he was doing. That probably won't get far. Mr. Keen and I were present when the will was drawn up. He had absolutely no record of treatment for mental ailments. A bit eccentric, but aware of what he was doing and why he was doing it."

"So that's out," Fusaro said.

"Then there's undue influence. I hardly see how anyone can claim you people brainwashed him. You never met him. He knew you only through the newsletter."

"God Almighty," Maybank said. "There's justice in the world. Dan writes about—what was that last piece?"

"'The Road Runner, the Quail, and the Hunter,'" Jenny said.

"Fifteen hundred words of Dan's copy," Maybank said. "Ever see how fast he writes when he's made his mind up about an article? Fast as he can type."

"Okay," Fusaro said. "He was competent and the DRI didn't cast a spell over him. What else?"

"Someone might charge that your institute is a fake, a fundraising outfit that existed only for the purpose of bilking people like Otto Denkerman of their money."

"Some case," Maybank said. "If we are frauds, we're lousy ones. All the jury would have to do is look at my office and they'd know we're the world's worst fund-raisers."

"I meant no implication," Fair said quickly. "I know you are honest. But when vast sums of money are involved, people will try anything."

"What do you know about the relatives?" Fusaro asked cautiously.

"Very little. There's some relationship to a Los Angeles family, but from what we've learned they're even wealthier than Mr. Denkerman. I can't see them contesting the estate."

"Don't be so sure." Fusaro scowled. "Them as has gits."

"What's their name?" Maybank asked.

"It's the Host family. Not Mr. Host, but his wife, who is deceased. She was a second cousin of Mr. Denkerman."

"Host?" Maybank asked. "The developers? The people who tore up Senita Valley for a senior citizens community?"

"And bulldozed everything else from here to the California border," Jenny said. "What would they want with a puny fifteen million?"

Fusaro blew wind through his lips, a Boston street noise. "Hold your wallet, Jenny. Count the silver. Those are the kind who grab anything that's loose. Host-Labarre. *We Process the Desert.* Look out they don't try to process your inheritance."

"I hardly think so, Mr. Fusaro," Fair said. "They aren't that kind of people."

"Yeah? How do you think they got it all?"

The following morning Fassman found himself pleading with Mrs. Vormund to let him visit her husband. It was a little past eight. The newsman was sleepy, bloated with the beer and enchiladas of the previous night. But the Vormund household sounded full of activity. The old lady could be heard asking Vormund if he wanted a visitor; a door slammed; music filtered through the phone.

"I'm afraid he isn't up to guests," she said firmly.

"But I came all the way from Los Angeles to see him . . ."

"I am sorry, young man, that you made the trip, but my husband needs his rest."

"Perhaps this afternoon . . ."

"He takes a nap. Why don't you write him a letter and ask him a few questions?" She was polite but emphatic.

Fassman stared at the dead phone. Story of my life, he thought. Jobs undone, books unwritten, love unrequited. He could not go back to Los Angeles and tell Ballstead that he did not even get to see Vormund.

With a rare show of determination, Fassman drove out to the Vormund house. He realized, as he cruised down the hideous highway of garish signs and outlandish buildings, lunatic creations fashioned by demented craftsmen, negations of sense and orderliness, that he was seeking Vormund less for any television program than for his own salvation. The world had never seemed as good as it had when he sat in Vormund's class and heard him read from Shakespeare. That was all there was to it. He had to see him again, hear his voice.

At a doughnut stand, Fassman let the greasy dough and the strong coffee form a clot in his stomach. He ate slowly, sadly, thinking of undergraduate breakfasts wolfed in drugstores, of 9 A.M. classes in Hamilton Hall, and Vormund's farewell. *I have an appointment with a cactus wren.*

"Got an allergy?" the girl asked. Tears were rimming Fassman's eyes.

"No. Just the dust."

The dust of the past, he thought. Places and people remembered, memories of pain and pleasure and growing up. Was he, like Fitzgerald, doomed to find his life after college an anticlimax?

Driving down the main street of Senita, another memory surfaced. He knew what had prompted it. Hamburgers. The city was a vast hamburger. McDonald's, Big Boy, Hardee's, Carroll's. A vast sizzling griddle. Instead of people, Senita was inhabited by patties of ground round. But why was he making a connection with Vormund?

At a stop light he remembered Wimpy. Wimpy of the comic strips, Wimpy the hamburger freak. Once a year Vormund gave a lecture on Ben Jonson in which he compared the playwright's characters to Wimpy. Volpone, all cunning, Mosca greedy, Epicene silent. People ruled by one overwhelming trait. "If you can appreciate Wimpy," Vormund told the class, "you can appreciate Ben Jonson." The *Spectator* hailed the event annually:

SPRING OFFICIAL ON MORNINGSIDE;

VORMUND'S WIMPY RETURNS

Fassman studied the map of the city that the rental agency had given him. It was a simple gridiron plan, except for some developments in the hills. Vormund lived in a remote area, east of Senita proper. At a billboard advertising an exterminator's services, with a giant moving cockroach (it won the ugly prize, Fassman decided), he turned left.

The road changed from blacktop to gravel to dirt. He realized he was well into the desert. Distantly, Fassman could see boxlike housing marching up the side of a mountain. Vegetation had been chopped away as if with a giant chain saw. Over the city and its suburbs a heavy miasma of gas fumes and dust had settled. It could not have been this way when Vormund and his wife moved here. The old man had written enthusiastically about the limpid air and the solitude.

A dirt road led to Vormund's home. The newsman calculated that he was about five miles from the city. The homes and the attendant landscaping looked slightly eccentric, suggesting artists, teachers, university people. He felt he could have lived there. Written, raised children, made love to Wendi.

Beyond the last street, the desert unfolded, dry and hot and green-brown. No wonder Vormund had chosen the house. It was isolated, yet there were neighbors. The city was a ten-minute ride away. In a setting of ocotillo and organ-pipe cactus, under the shade of a huge paloverde, he saw a tilted black mailbox and the name D. D. VORMUND.

For a moment Fassman had the sense of a grand beginning. Thoreau borrowing an ax from a neighbor. Melville, in *White-Jacket*, throwing a piece of sailcloth to the deck and cutting himself a sailor's coat. He, Alan Fassman, of Westwood Village, California (by way of the Bronx), sighting a mailbox in the desert. Self-dramatization did not help. He had come uninvited and there was a good chance he would leave unfulfilled.

Fassman drove the car inside a mesh fence and stopped alongside a carport in which an old Plymouth was parked. The area around the carport was stacked with gardening tools, terra-cotta planters, adobe bricks, a coiled hose. Vormund had written about his abhorrence of physical labor. No doubt Clara Vormund was the avid gardener.

Hesitant, he rang the bell alongside a screen door that looked into a kitchen.

A short, round, white-haired woman came to the door. She had lively dark eyes, a firm chin, and a full mouth. "Yes?" she asked.

"Mrs. Vormund?"

"Yes."

"I'm Alan Fassman. The professor's former student. I called this morning . . ."

"I told you not to come. He isn't well."

"I thought perhaps a few minutes. You see, I'm with a television news organization . . ."

"You are a persistent young man."

"A few minutes. I heard about Professor Vormund's interest in the coyote business. Of course, I've read his books on the desert, *Desert Idyll* and *Dry World*, and I—"

Spare and stooped, Vormund's figure materialized behind his wife. Fassman tried to see the aristocratic thin face, but the screen impeded him. He appeared, through the blur of the wire netting, old and frail.

"Young man," Vormund said, "I make it a practice never to talk to former students or door-to-door salesmen."

"I'm sorry. I made this trip from Los Angeles after I heard about your run-in with the ranchers."

"You say you're a journalist?"

Fassman mentioned his station. The couple huddled, whispered. Clara opened the door. "But only to state your case, and then leave. What did you say your name was?"

"Fassman. Alan Fassman."

Vormund came forward and shook his hand. "No, I don't remember you. I don't remember any of them. They came, heard me lecture, and I passed them all. We'll sit on the patio. Some of the birds are still feeding."

He had aged, and yet in old age there was something strong and vital in him. Fassman remembered him as hollow-chested, pale. Now he seemed more erect, the sun tan and freckles endowing him with the desert's tenacity. The lean features were the same, but they seemed more assertive, more ready to confront the world.

"You see, Mr. Fassman," Clara said, "that's why I say no to people who come here. Once they're in the door, my husband can't refuse them."

"I won't stay long. Do many people call?"

She dismissed them with a sharp Italian slap at the air. "Every day. Students. People who read his books. They want Professor Vormund to assure them the land can be saved."

"And do you?" Fassman asked Vormund.

"Not of late. Come along. You can partake of my limitless wisdom and leave."

They walked into the baking morning air. Fassman saw the untrammeled view of the mountains and the way the Vormunds had camouflaged the neighboring houses with trees and a low wall.

"Mrs. Vormund is kind to let me stay," Fassman said. "I feel I know her. You once told a story about courting her in Greenwich Village. Wasn't it something about a Swede?"

The old man smiled. The same alert, intelligent face. High forehead, knowing eyes. "What moved me to tell it to an English class I can't imagine. Perhaps to illustrate some point about persistence in writers. I courted Mrs. Vormund for months in Greenwich Village. It was at the première of a Eugene O'Neill play." He paused and put his hands to his eyes. "God, how long ago."

"You helped discover him."

"In a sense. I never doubted his genius. What a beautiful man. Difficult, conceited, but beautiful. In any case, there was Clara, Italian, lovely, vivacious, and there was I, a string bean of a graduate student from Kentucky, redheaded, six feet tall, and weighing 124 pounds. She was elegant, dark, and graceful as only a Veronese can be. Three times I called at her apartment on Barrow Street and three times she ordered me out, the last time with a saucepan. But I did not admit defeat. I knocked at the door again and said, 'My dear Miss Pandolfo, I feel like the Swede who kept getting thrown out of a bar. After the fourth time, he told the bouncer, 'I think I'm getting the idea—you don't want me here.' She laughed, asked me in for tea, and we were married three months later."

He had told it the way he had lectured—perfect sentences, paragraphs, a pleasant cadence.

"I hope I'm not interrupting your work." Fassman pointed to a portable typewriter on a table in the living room. The table stood in front of what seemed an endless bookcase that reached to the ceiling and covered two walls.

"No. That's an advantage of the golden years. Or senility, as I prefer to call it. My time is too much my own. I thank God I have the desert." Vormund thrust his face to the sun, like an old Inca sun-worshiper meeting his deity. "So you were my student, Mr.—?"

"Fassman."

"I once tried to remember names, but every time I remembered the name of a student I forgot the name of a poet."

"I took two courses with you. Elizabethan Drama and the Comparative Literature seminar."

Vormund opened his eyes. He smiled. Not all his memories of New York were grim. "Do you recall my final examination?"

The newsman laughed. "I've never forgotten it. 'Question one: What were the three works discussed in this course that you found the least rewarding? Question two: To what failings in your own character do you attribute your choices?'"

"I used to enjoy watching their faces when they read the second part. But it didn't matter. I'd pass them anyway, and most of them with A's."

A troop of Gambel's quail strutted from under a mesquite bush and headed for some potato peelings that Clara had set out. Mother and chicks pecked at the treats.

"Gambel's quail," Vormund said. "I wrote about them recently. You see what a tumble I've taken from critiques on Restoration comedy."

"Wrote about them? Where?"

"A newsletter that our local conservation group puts out."

"The Desert Research Institute?"

"You know about us?"

Fassman fished in his attaché case and extracted the photographs of the coyote hunt and the letters of response. "That's how I came here."

"That dreadful business with the dogs." His face became grave.

"What did you have to say about Gambel's quail?"

"It was called 'The Road Runner, the Quail, and the Hunter.' I happen to like road runners as much as quail. But the hunters are determined to wipe them out on the grounds that the road runner eats baby quail and quail eggs, thus leaving less quail for them to shoot. I argued that the road runner and the quail seem to have been getting along for millennia, but that man, the greatest killer of all, will probably succeed in wiping both of them out before he's finished."

"I'll bet you got some letters on that."

"Not too much of a reaction. Not many people read our newsletter. They tend to agree with me."

Fassman held up the clippings from the Senita *Pantagraph*. "And these?"

Vormund sighed. "Oh, I expected that. They regard me as a harmless eccentric in these parts. Or else they think I'm joshing them."

"I see. The reason I came here was because of these photos you took. And the whole question of predators and why we need them."

"To publicize it on your news programs? To use me as a spokesman?"

"Yes. I'd like you to speak out. Many people remember you and your books, Professor. People are curious about the way you left literature for a career as a protector of foxes and snakes."

Vormund placed trembling fingers to his parched mouth. Clara came from the house with coffee for the guest and a large glass of a foamy white liquid for her husband.

"My morning infusion of Meritene. Care to try some?"

"No thanks."

"I eat very little. You'd be surprised how much nutrition there is in this. And it tastes rather nice."

Clara turned to the visitor, who was watching as Vormund drained half the drink with manifest pleasure. "And I'm such a great cook," she said. "But he won't touch garlic, onions, oregano, anything. I have to cook soups for the neighbors."

Vormund patted his lips with a handkerchief. "Most of whom are senile, bedridden, and incompetent. My Lady Bountiful keeps them alive with minestrones and marinara sauces. What's that awful thing you do with rice?"

His wife opened her dark eyes and bent her head forward. A beauty when she was young, Fassman saw. A woman who surely would make a skinny student from Kentucky keep coming back. "*Risi e bisi,* and don't joke about my cooking just because *you* stopped eating."

A pair of Arizona cardinals swooped into a cactus in the garden, surveyed the ground, flitted down to peck at bird seed.

"Don't you ever miss the plays, or the new books, or lecturing?"

"Unequivocally, no. Do you remember a story I told about Thomas Wolfe? My fellow southerner. That great roaring rhetorical hulk. Mrs. Vormund and I were at a dinner Wolfe hosted at some spiffy restaurant after he had received a royalty check from Scribner's. At one point he got to his feet—"

"And he was an enormous man," Clara interrupted.

"—and he bellowed, 'I want *more,* more of everything,' more lobster, more champagne, more violins, and more women!'"

"That sounds like him," Fassman said.

"There was a small starved left-wing writer named Abe Golub sitting next to me, a kind of hanger-on at these literary orgies. Abe nudged me and said, 'Dan, I wish that Tom would realize that in my own small way I'm every bit as Rabelaisian as he is.'"

Fassman laughed. It was a perfectly told story—pauses, emphasis, a punch line.

"That's how I see modern art—the writer on his feet bellowing for more, more, *more*. Braggarts, egomaniacs, flaunting their genitals in public, defining their art as a form of sexual adventure, a competition in which male members are measured with slide rules. I'm no prude, and I enjoy sex, and I have never turned away from a pretty face or a shapely leg. But these people will get us all killed with their incessant public orgasms. If you get everyone constantly coupling, talking about it, seeking it, demanding new and wilder variations, no one will be left to pick up the garbage."

"The old pessimist," his wife said.

"I see what you're getting at," Fassman said. "There's a world to be saved that goes beyond any writer's bed."

"Exactly. These egomaniacal navel watchers, worshipers of their own precious flesh, boasters about their endless climaxes, will succeed only in making art an extension of their genitals. It may be fun for a while, but in the long run it will destroy us. Sex is not much of a spectator sport. It's only the participation that's valid."

"But that isn't why you stopped teaching."

"That among other reasons. Things seemed to be getting nastier all the time. I turned to owls because there was too much hate among men, and I was too old to work at reforming them."

"This conversation is getting too intellectual for me," Clara said. "Young man, don't tire Dan out. Ask a few more questions, and then go. I'm not being impolite but I have to worry about him."

"I'll leave soon."

Vormund held out a palsied hand. "No, no, young man. It does me good to polemicize like this every now and then. The rabbits with whom I converse don't seem to understand much of what I'm saying."

The screen door closed. The two men were alone in the heat-laden silence.

"Do you get into politics down here?" Fassman asked. He was feeling more and more like the young Boswell.

"Goodness, no. I have no time for that. My last political adventure was in 1934, when Nicholas Murray Butler, with much reluctance, appointed me chairman of the English Department. 'And may I ask where you stand politically?' the great stuffed shirt asked. 'In the English Department,' I said, 'I am considered the house reactionary, because I dislike the Soviet Union and think that communism is as bad as fascism.' Butler thought that one over, and responded, 'That still gives you too much latitude.' "

Fassman had heard the story but he laughed again.

"Can I convince you that a television program on what you believe would do some good?" Fassman said, after a pause to let Vormund drain his Meritene. A white creamy mustache rimmed his upper lip.

"I'm not up to it. I have a small attention span these days. I prefer to watch a frog, or a hawk or a mountainside. The works of man don't mean much to me."

"I understand."

"A case in point," the old man said. "An editor sent me a novel some years ago by a young writer. I read it, and apart from a great deal of self-pity and morbid self-justifications—it was autobiographical—there were three climactic moments. Item, the hero inveigles a seventeen-year-old girl into masturbating with a cucumber. Item, the hero confesses to a psychiatrist that he leaves traces of his semen in soap dishes. Item, the hero beats his wife with a poker until she defecates in her underpants, and then is furious with her for soiling his apartment. All of this written with great wit and vitality, an obvious appeal to the reader to *sympathize* with the narrator."

"I know the book."

"I put it aside, and I made no judgment, other than that of realizing how out of step with the times I am. The book sold well and was nominated for literary prizes. Now you understand why I prefer the company of coyotes?"

"Perfectly."

"The most daring thing a young writer could do would be to write a book in which affection, honor, decency, joy, and regular habits predominated. It would shock the critics out of their seats."

Clara came out and gathered up the cup and glass. "I was listening. None of what you say is helping Mr. Feinstein's television program. But I guess that's your way of saying you don't want to do it."

"I don't mind," Fassman said. "I wasn't sure of what I wanted when I came out here."

What was Fassman seeking? More than a coyote. More than an old man determined to defend the wilderness from the despoiler. It had been a selfish errand. Son looking for father? Novitiate looking for a wise man? To sit at Vormund's feet again and assure himself there had been a better time in his life, that there were still men of sense and decency in the world? But Vormund was old and exhausted.

"You once wrote about how difficult it was to convince people of the value of experiencing joy by just watching the natural world."

"Difficult? Well-nigh impossible. That was in *Desert Idyll.* I also said the only values Americans cherished any longer were power and amusement."

"You still believe it?"

"I am convinced of it. Slaughtering the animals and birds, overbreeding our own kind, overgrazing, overeating, draining the watersheds, fouling the air. In whatever celestial woodlands the Almighty reserves for lions and wolves, a vast happy howling will shake the firmament on that day when the last parched acre of Arizona refuses to grow one more head of lettuce."

"But you do succeed sometimes. I read how you and a man named Bugler saved the birds on an island. You did an article on it."

"A sop now and then. Go to the northern part of the state and see what the power plants are doing to the land. It is dead. Plants, animals, water, sky. Ruined. And they cannot be stopped."

"They can if you let people like me help you."

"Mr. Fassman, you are young and hopeful. I won't abandon the fight, but I reserve the right to be my pessimistic self."

A road runner with a lizard's tail dangling from its bill poked its head through the prickly pear, glared at them insolently, ran away. Vormund smiled and followed its crazy passage. It seemed to Fassman he showed more interest in the bird than in Fassman's proposals.

"An interview?" Fassman tried. "On the coyote dispute perhaps? And some of your concepts on living with the land. Some of the things you've written about? I could get a film crew here . . ."

"And our phone would ring with angry ranchers and hunters. Coyotes are dangerous ground, Mr. Fassman. They arouse passions, rages, unreasoning frenzies. There is one rancher who traps them, cuts off their lower jaw, and lets them die of thirst and starvation. Another skins them alive. Another ignites them with gasoline and cheers as they die, racing in circles."

The newsman leaned forward. "But that's what we want to show. That's dramatic. If I could get films of that sort of thing . . . and perhaps some commentary by you . . ."

"Fat chance," Clara said. "No rancher is going to stage that for you. They shoot them from airplanes and burn them in their dens."

Vormund slapped his hands together. "But the coyote survives. The lions and wolves and eagles may be going, but not my gray friend, *Canis latrans*. Burn him, poison him, shoot him, trap him. He's out there raising cubs, catching mice, howling at his gratitude to a god unknown."

The voice was clear, rich with the Kentucky drawl. Fassman heard the voice reading from Marlowe. *And burned the topless towers of Ilium* . . .

"If only you'd say that for my camera," he said.

"I've never been a fighter. The other day I did something dreadful. Picked up a rock and threatened a man and four dogs. What devil possessed me? Perhaps I serve the cause better writing about road runners."

"Think about it. We could help."

Ed Bugler loped into view. Vormund introduced Fassman to him.

"Oh, an old student of Dan's," Bugler said. He winked at Clara. "Dan must be getting soft. Ex-students are usually in the same category as real estate developers."

"I thought it was door-to-door salesmen," Fassman said.

Bugler slapped his thigh. "Dan's been doing a job on you. Welcome to the desert. You from out here?"

Fassman explained that he was a television newsman and was interested in a story on the fight between ranchers, hunters, and developers (everyone it seemed) and the conservationists.

— 83 —

Vormund's eyes flickered with a solution—he could get rid of the young man, and perhaps help him at the same time. "Ed, take Mr. Fassman to the Institute, and let him see what we're up to. Maybe he'll be inspired."

"Glad to."

"And look out Ed's rattlers don't bite you." Clara was on her hands and knees in the garden, turning the earth at the roots of the boojum tree.

"Look at the woman work," Vormund said. "Gentlemen, you see the secret of this marriage. My wife's enduring strength, my own terrifying intellect."

Bugler was holding something in a brown burlap sack. He opened it and revealed a foot-long section of the creeping devil. "While you're at it, Clara, add this one to the potato patch."

Vormund got up. "Ed, you rascal. You went back there. For me."

"I figured Essler wouldn't miss one more."

Puzzled by their ecstasy over a spiked cactus with orange roots, Fassman looked to Bugler for help.

"Caterpillar cactus, or the creeping devil. We found 'em a few days ago. A botanical milestone. Maybe you could do a TV program on them."

Fassman nodded, said nothing. He could see himself confronting Ballstead's sour face, informing him he had shot a thousand feet of color film on a cactus. Clara took the plant from Bugler and looked for a patch of sand.

Vormund, Fassman noticed, was an enthusiastic straw boss. He hovered over his kneeling wife, made suggestions, and criticized her gardening, but made no effort to assist in the labor.

"They're some team," Bugler said. "Clara works and Dan thinks."

"Clara has the harder job," the old man said. "Gardening isn't like literary criticism, where you can say any damned thing you please and get away with it. Nature has standards. Critics have none. There is my platitude for the morning." He walked toward Fassman and took his hand. "It was nice talking to you, Mr.—"

"Fassman. Class of '54."

"You're in good hands with Ed. He's taught me more than any critic or editor. Good-by."

For a moment Vormund held Fassman's hand. The grip was

full of the sun's warmth. Fantasizing, Fassman indulged in self-flattery. He was young Boswell, meeting Dr. Johnson in Tom Davies' bookshop. Johnson's gracious words printed themselves in Fassman's mind. *Give me your hand, I have taken a liking to you.*

In Bugler's jeep, speeding toward the Institute, Ed talked about the battle over the coyotes. It had become a mania with ranchers. They dreamed about armies of coyotes marching over the hills to eat their sheep and calves. They faked statistics, claimed that any ewe that died of disease or hunger had been killed by a coyote. The federal government was relaxing the ban on toxicants. Soon the West would be soaked in 1080, cyanide, all the synthetics that killed not only coyotes, but badgers, ferrets, foxes, birds, domestic dogs, and careless humans.

"It's going to get rough," Bugler said.

"Vormund said he got so mad he wanted to throw a rock the other day."

"What a sight he was. Old Dan, spoiling for a fight. Who's usually so sick he can't stay up for the TV news. Did he turn you down?"

"Not entirely. You're supposed to brief me. Then I'm supposed to get some ideas."

"What do you want to know?"

"What's the worst single thing you can think of?"

"What's happening to the lion. They're going. I give them five years. There won't be a lion left. Anyone can kill a lion if he even *thinks* it's killing stock. They shoot or trap or poison any lion they see, and nobody can stop them. They're supposed to file a report, and give evidence, and show the carcass of the stock the lion killed . . ."

"But?"

"They never do. The ranchers are buddies with the wildlife people and the Bureau of Land Management. The rule out here is when you see a lion, *kill it.*"

Fassman shaded his eyes from the blinding sun. Was any sun, anywhere, so hot, so pervasive? Vormund had written some years ago: *Man's first impulse on seeing another man, not of his race, or a creature not of his kind, is kill it. Of all living creatures on earth, man is the most dangerous, to others and his own kind.*

That Meritene-sipping old man, with his feathery white hair and thin wise face! How could he take on the rulers of the earth? And what right had Fassman to involve him?

"Didn't you say something about his testifying before committees?"

Bugler nodded. "People respect Dan. Most of them, anyway. But Dan got them riled up a few months back on the lion hearings. I got him some data. No proof on any of the slaughtered lions. No reports filed. It was a record year for sheep and cattle, and these stockmen were claiming the lions were eating them out of their livelihood. That was baloney and Dan proved it."

"What happened?"

"The people on the legislative committee were polite enough. Dan's got quality. He can say things they hate to hear, but they listen. Dan just about called the ranchers a bunch of liars. He had evidence that I had collected that they'd killed more than forty lions around Grace Canyon in a year. They said they'd killed nine."

They bounced onto a curving dirt road. A weathered brown sign read: DESERT RESEARCH INSTITUTE. Appropriately two slender brown birds with curved bills roosted on it.

"Thrashers," Bugler said. "Maybe a couple of Bendire's. Dan would know. For a city man, he sure took to western birds. Darn if he didn't pick out a crissal thrasher the other morning when we went out to see the *orugas*."

"You were going to say something else about the hearings?"

"Oh. As we're leaving, two big bums in jeans push Dan against the wall and step on his feet. Said they didn't intend to starve because communists like Vormund were trying to protect lions. I tell you it was crazy. Clara shrieked and went for one, and before Maybank and I could turn, they'd slapped Dan twice, and ran off. Nobody knows who they were."

They got out of the jeep. Fassman shuddered. To do this to so gentle a man?

"Did the police do anything? Could you identify them?"

"Jack Maybank and I took after them, but they'd beat it out the building and they were gone. Later, Essler—he's the head of the ranchers' association and owns darn near everything around here—came up and apologized to Dan. He said they weren't any of his people and if he found out, he'd see they were arrested."

"You believe him?"

"Duane Essler? I guess so. People like him hate what Dan and me are trying to do, but they respect Dan."

Bugler reached into the back of the jeep and took out the charred corpse of the pup. "What . . . ?" Fassman asked. The stench clogged his nostrils.

"Coyote pup."

"What happened?"

"Denning."

"Burned?"

"They roast them alive. Use a gas cartridge. They get a whole den at once. Someone left this in the jeep. A kind of warning, I suppose."

Under the pounding sun, Fassman reeled. Law of club and fang? What was Vormund doing fighting these barbarians? Fassman drowned in guilt. He had no business coming out here, trying to force an issue over some rancher's savage dogs and an unlucky coyote.

As they approached the yellow buildings, a potbellied, round-faced Indian in denims walked toward them. He carried a rake on one shoulder.

"Mr. Maybank is sore at you, Ed."

"When isn't he?"

"Says you was supposed to clean out the snake cages."

"What's the matter? Am I the only one around here knows how to handle rattlers? Just because I've been bit seven times?"

Sidewinder laughed. "That's what he said. Before him and Mrs. Maybank went to play tennis."

"Goody for them. Sidewinder, this is Alan Fassman. He was one of Dan's students way back."

The Hopi touched the brim of his hat. "Hi." Then he dismissed Fassman. His clouded eyes looked at the burned pup. "Where'd you get that?"

"Fellah left it in the jeep. I smelled them burning and I heard the screams. I was out at the *orugas*. The guy left it as a present for us."

The Indian did not seem moved. "Yeah, them cartridges burn them good. It sizzles the blood."

"Sidewinder isn't much on sympathy," Bugler said. "He's a

Hopi, and their trade-mark is sincerity. If he were a Pima, he'd pretend he was sorry and sympathize with us nature lovers."

"I ain't no nature lover. I'm paid for my work."

Bugler winked at Fassman. Some secret shared? White men acknowledging mysterious red man? He walked with the bandy-legged Indian and Bugler to the office building. Beyond, he could see wire cages, planted areas, peeling buildings. It did not appear a place that could be much of a threat to the real estate and ranching interests.

"You got any more trips for me?" asked Sidewinder.

"I better stay close to home. Maybank thinks I go running off to avoid work. Maybe he's right."

The Hopi laughed again, covering rotted teeth with his fore-arm. Fassman did not know how to communicate with him. His New York guilt—for everything, dear God—suffocated him in the presence of Indians and Chicanos. So he settled for studying Sidewinder's puffed face with the squashed nose and lumpy cheeks.

"I hear they got Grace Canyon covered with lion traps," Side-winder said. "Whole canyon is one big trap. Some Hualapai told me they was going to clean every lion out by the end of the year."

"Grace Canyon?" Bugler asked. "There isn't any cattle grazed for miles around there." He scratched his pepper-and-salt brush. "We try to put one fire out, another starts. Doesn't sound like a winning game, does it?"

Fassman shook his head. He felt sorry for these outnumbered friends of the lions.

"Grace Canyon," Bugler said. He was smiling. It gratified Fassman that Bugler did not stay depressed long. He jumped from one aspect of nature to another, and like Vormund could find pleasure in the wake of pain, joy on the heels of misery. "Grace Canyon is where I took Dan to see the trogon. Say, that would be a great expedition. We could tell Maybank we're going to look for traps and we might see the trogon."

Fassman followed Bugler into the office. It was dim and cool. Shades were drawn against the fierce heat and light. The Hopi wandered off, rake at shoulder arms, to the cactus garden.

"What's a trogon?" the newsman asked. "It sounds like science fiction."

"Darn near." He led Fassman down a corridor redolent of Lysol and into a large gray room. The walls were lined with cages holding snakes, lizards, and salamanders. Immediately Fassman heard the sinister *click-click-click* of rattles. He prayed that Bugler would not ask him to help clean the cages.

"Snake of some kind?" Fassman asked.

"A trogon is a bird. *What* a bird." He put the charred corpse into a box. The stench must have aroused the snakes. The rattling grew louder and angrier. "The *coppery-tailed* trogon. There's a bird for you." Bugler strode to a cage, plunged a calloused hand in, and grabbed a diamondback by the rear of its triangular head.

"You've seen it? In that canyon?"

"No. That was the pity of it." Bugler carried the snake to a large wooden pen in the middle of the floor and set it down. It coiled, shook its rattles, and struck at the wooden side. Fassman tried to embed himself in the wall.

"Why?"

"I promised Dan I'd find it for him. But we were too late." He grabbed another rattlesnake by its head—Fassman was horrified to see how long, thick, and powerful it was—and carried it, thrashing, to the pen.

"A trogon, eh?" he asked.

"I promised Dan. Before he gets too sick to make any more trips, by God, I am going to show him a coppery-tailed trogon."

A short smiling man in a purple golf shirt and lavender slacks approached the Maybanks after they took a table on the dining terrace of the Pima Racquet and Golf Club.

"Mr. Maybank?" he asked. He had a pear-shaped head—narrow at the top, widening into a fleshy jaw. His eyes were pale amber and merry. The smile seemed to have been sprayed on.

"Yes. Jack Maybank."

"Duane Essler. We met a few weeks ago at the United Fund Drive cocktail party. Out at the Bernstein place."

"Oh yes." Maybank had no recollection of meeting the man. But he knew Duane Essler. He recalled Vormund and Bugler mentioning the Essler ranch. Something about an appeal to save the land around the cactus, a question as to whose land it was.

"This is my wife, Jenny. Jenny, Mr. Essler."

"*Duane* will do fine." He hesitated a moment. "May I join you? Buy you a drink?"

"Yes to the first question," Maybank said. "No to the second. We're playing tennis after we have a bite."

The grin seemed to split Mr. Essler's upside-down pear of a face. He had black, slicked-down hair, moist and thin, with patches of pink scalp peeking through the wet strands. It was parted in the middle, a geometrically perfect division.

"You folks are members here?" he asked—as if surprised to find the Maybanks at the club.

"Just for tennis," Jenny said. "We hate golf."

"To each his own," Essler said. He winked at her—a suggestion of locker room lechery. Essler studied her long legs and the clean dark face as if he were appraising a quarter horse.

Essler knew breeding stock. This was some of the finest. But why were they dressed like hippie bums? Maybank, he knew, was the head of that research group. Rumored to have inherited money. But he wore raggedy-ass shorts and an old button-down shirt. The woman had on a kind of pillowcase with a string around the middle. Neither wore socks. Their sneakers were gray with age, garnished with holes. Essler, who was on the bylaws committee, decided to talk to the pro about them.

Jenny nudged her husband's foot. She was telling him—talk to this man, ask him about the land. Jack tended to be wary of making the first move. When the time was right, he'd have Joe Fusaro call Essler about the land.

"Reason I horned in," Essler said, "is some of your people have been hacking around my land. Just thought I'd mention it."

"Your land?" Maybank asked.

"We thought it was public land," Jenny said. She shoved aside a half-finished tuna-fish sandwich. She could see where the conversation was leading.

"It's *all* mine. For ten miles past the Pima Trading Post off the Interstate. I tend to be lax about leaving gates open and letting people in."

"Like hunters," Maybank said.

Essler held his hands open. "One helps the other. If the hunters will help me get grazing rights to public land, I'll let them shoot varmints on mine. Jack, you know how it goes."

"I sure do. So do the masked bobwhites. The hunters killed them all. Those that overgrazing didn't eliminate."

"Don't look at me. I'm more of a conservationist than a lot of you dickeybirders. But some things are clear to me, and should be to you. First, if you want to go jeeping on my land, *ask*. And second, don't go making trouble by running photographs about us killing predators."

Jenny brushed back her dark hair. Her chin went up slightly. "So you were the one who stomped the coyote to death. And your dogs?"

"One of my ranch hands. He's got a right to do that. If you'd have identified him, I could have helped him sue you." Essler's voice was as warm as when he had joined them. "But I don't work that way. Live and let live."

"You must be joking," Jenny said.

"Oh, sure, sure." Suddenly he pinched her elbow. "Now that I see how lovely Mrs. Maybank is, I certainly wouldn't want her as an adversary."

Maybank's eyes rolled upward and looked at the green-and-white awning.

"I think Mr. Essler wants some kind of assurance that our jeep won't go back to his land," Jenny said.

"I wish you folks would call me Duane."

"Duane, Duane," Jenny said. "Go away, come again another day."

Essler took a second to catch the pun, then guffawed. Three men in brightly colored golf clothes and peaked caps appeared at the edge of the terrace. One called to him. "Hey, Honcho. Let's get it together."

Essler waved at them. "I can accommodate with anyone. If you want to go on my land, ask. And after you've trespassed, don't go slandering my ranch hands as killers. You know how we stockmen are, Jack. We'll kill anything if it hurts our stock."

"I've told our people the place is off limits."

Essler shook his pear-shaped face. "They didn't hear too clear, Jack. One fellow was back this morning. Surveying. What's he doing putting a survey on my property?"

"You sure it was our jeep?" Jenny asked.

"He was observed. His license plate was noted. I could make a case against him. And you."

"I . . . ah . . . actually I'm supposed to talk to you about that land," Maybank floundered. "I was going to call you."

"We can discuss this like friends. Come on up to the ranch for a little booze and steaks, and the missus and I will extend the hand of friendship."

"It's your cactus we're after," Jenny said. "Not your booze."

Essler's laugh boomed across the terrace. A fat man in a green shirt and yellow slacks lumbered across the room. "Duane, buddy, time's a-wastin'. Our partners will drink up their golf time if you don't stop flirting with that lovely lady."

"Stay loose, Duke. Cactus, you say? I must have a couple of million. What can you people want with a cactus?"

"The flat ones. The ones the Mexicans call *orugas.*" Jack tried lamely. "We want to save them."

"For what?"

"For everybody. Mr. Essler, they're a botanical rarity. Maybe we can discuss some way of saving the land, keeping it a preserve."

Essler, at the urging of his friend, got up. "I get it. The surveying gear. Like you folks did with the saguaros. Keep them off limits. Heck, if you want favors from me, why'd you take off on us for killing a coyote now and then?"

"Sorry," Maybank said.

Essler leaned over the table. He was small and thin, but a bit top-heavy with his odd head. "I went to college *also.* I know about the balance of nature and all that stuff. But livestock is business. You folks stand in the way of progress. Progress, hell. *Food.*" He grabbed Jenny's forearm again—the swift move of a hunter—and pinched. "*Duane, Duane, go away. Jee-sus,* that is cute. It has made my day."

Essler spun on ripple-soled white shoes and darted away. He left the terrace with the members of his foursome. Departing, one man turned and fixed a sirloin of a face on Jenny. He clucked approvingly. "New?" the Maybanks heard him ask Essler. "Institute people," Essler said loudly. "You know. Love me, love my badger."

Jenny covered her eyes. "Mr. Essler has ruined my tennis."

"Cut it out, Jen."

"You were no help."

Maybank rotated his head as if it were caged. "I know, I

wasn't firm enough. But we were in the wrong. We were trespassing. I'll strangle Bugler one of these days. He kept assuring me those plants were on public lands and it wouldn't matter if they took a stroll. Not only are we illegally on his range but we have to antagonize him by running those photographs."

"Dan asked you to. You agreed."

"Yes, and am I sorry." Maybank frowned. "Let's play tennis. I can't eat any more cottage cheese."

"My wife took off about a month ago," Bugler said casually. "That's why the house is a mess."

He had invited Fassman to his home, a tiny adobe building at the edge of the Institute. They sat in the bare living room, sipping Mexican beer from cans. Buster the bobcat had followed Bugler to the house, climbed into a rocking chair, and dozed off.

"I'm sorry," Fassman said. "I have the opposite problem. Mine threw me out."

"I bet mine had a better reason."

"Mine didn't have *any*. She just decided she'd had enough of me. She was away from the house six nights a week—yoga, TM, physical therapy, art classes."

Bugler's eyes were fixed on a chart of western birds on the wall. "Yeah, they get notions. I like women. Much better than I do kids. I've been married four times. Noreen, the last one, I liked her best."

"You said she had a good reason?"

"I suppose so." Bugler's rangy figure got up, found two more beers in the refrigerator and opened them. "You know I don't own a thing in the world except this Sears outfit, one more like it, and some desert boots? Everything you see here is the property of the Institute."

"I'd say you earn whatever they give you."

"Maybank says I'm disorganized." For the first time since Fassman had been with Bugler, a sorrowful look crossed the weathered face. The man had the quality of a dignified wild animal—an old badger, a wise wolf.

"Tell me why your wife left."

"I had these rare rattlesnakes. Ridge-nosed rattlers, or Willards, as they're sometimes called. This fellow in San Diego wanted to look at them and I decided to ship them by parcel post. It's illegal, sending venomous reptiles through the mails, but I figured in the interest of science I could stretch a point. So I oiled the rattles."

"Oiled?" Fassman, giddy with too much sun, heat, and beer, had a mad vision of Bugler squirting oil from a railroad engineer's can onto the snakes' rattles.

"I'd done it before. It muffles the rattles. Can't hear that *click-click*. Those Willards were lovely. Pale red-brown with white crossbars. I squirted some 3-in-One oil on the rattles and boxed them, and left them on the kitchen table. Then Noreen came home. It was her birthday, and I'd forgotten."

"Understandable, she being your fourth wife."

"Noreen is a delicate sort. She took the lid off that box—it looked like a florist's box, and she assumed it was her present. She got one look at those rattlesnakes and ran screaming across the desert as if she'd seen the Holy Ghost."

"Or a pair of rattlesnakes with oiled rattles."

"I guess that might scare some people."

"It would scare the hell out of me. Just watching you pick up those snakes and toss them around. How do you avoid getting bit?"

"I don't." He extended his huge hands toward Fassman. They were scarred, lumped, covered with white strips and silvery streaks, old stitches, burns, gouges. "I have been bitten by every known critter in this area. I have a natural resistance built up inside me, although Clara says I'm full of poisons and I'll die someday from an overbalance in the blood."

"You look healthy to me."

"I manage." Bugler leaned back in his chair. "I miss Noreen. She was a good-looking woman with fine bearing, much better educated than me. But she didn't understand *animals* the way I'd like her to. The way Dan and Clara do."

Fassman sipped his beer and studied the big-boned man in the faded work suit. An original. Bugler had never outgrown that boyish love for turtles and raccoons. There was always a kid like that in the neighborhood. One who collected snakes, trapped chipmunks, raised families of white mice, built ant colonies, repaired the damaged wings of fledglings.

"What do you figure you'll do with Dan?" Bugler asked.

"I have no idea. He doesn't seem eager to pursue this. Can't say I blame him."

"Dan's done his share. Books. Articles. Of course, if you got him on a TV show talking about predators, it might make an impact. He might even like it. Dan's quite a performer when he wants to be."

"He was one of the best lecturers I ever heard."

"The old Kentucky orator. Clara teases him sometimes."

Memories sobered Fassman. Vormund pacing in front of an English class and reading Dryden's translation of Juvenal.

> *In Saturn's reign at nature's early birth*
> > *There was that thing called chastity on earth*
> *When in a narrow cave, their common shade,*
> > *The sheep, the shepherds and their Gods were laid . . .*

And here was Fassman in this rude house, the house of the man who defended raccoons from evil children, and had helped a badger out of a trap. Another devotee of D. D. Vormund. The old man had an indefinable quality, as both Bugler and Fassman knew. Mexicans and Indians sensed it. They saw the light in Vormund.

More verses flitted inside Fassman's sun-dazed head.

> *For when the world was bucksome, fresh and young,*
> > *Her sons were undebauch'd and therefore strong . . .*

Fassman watched Bugler stroke the cat's arching back. He wondered if Vormund ever read Dryden's gloss on Juvenal any more. Was the world never again to know that "bucksome, fresh and young" time? Was man irretrievably debauched? The old man's writings had been gloomier in the past few years.

"Say," Bugler said, "I'm no TV expert, but—"

"Don't let it stop you."

"Suppose you got your cameras, and you went out with me and Dan and we looked for the trogon—"

"Two guys sitting in a blind and waiting for a bird they'll never see?"

"Hey! What if we go out and look at those lion traps Sidewinder was talking about? Let me tell you, a lion caught in those steel jaws is a dreadful thing to see. That would wake people up."

Fassman felt his eyes closing. The sun, the heat, the isolation of Vormund's people, were grinding him down. He'd read recently that the conservation movement was doomed. No one wanted it. Americans would happily suffocate in their metal cars, ruin the last stream with chemicals. They would do it, and enjoy what they were doing, and bray that it was *progress*.

The phone rang. Bugler dropped Buster and went into the unkempt kitchen.

"Jack, glad you called . . . this young fellow from the television, Fassman, wants to do a story . . ."

Fassman wanted him to stop. No, no story. Vormund wasn't interested. Nor was a world of labor unions, corporate greed, indifferent government, hunters and killers. *Outraged nature will assert itself,* Vormund had written, *and catastrophe will follow.* . . . The death of the seas? The destruction of the ozone? The reduction of the earth to an infertile slag heap?

"I'm sorry, Jack," he heard Bugler saying. "I should have told you. Essler, huh? You spoke to him?"

Bugler was being chewed out. *Reamed out.* It embarrassed Fassman to have to listen to Ed mumble apologies. Evidently he had been riding around private lands and taking specimens.

"I thought it was public land. That's what Sidewinder said. Dan thought . . ."

Invoking Vormund's name. They all did. And who could blame them? Battlers for lost causes, they needed a tribal god, a guardian of the temple.

"But those cacti, Jack. They have to be saved. Essler should listen to reason. Maybe if Dan spoke to him."

Fassman felt something tickling his bare arm. He thought at first that it was the spotted cat, which had made one brush against Fassman's leg, then decided the visitor was not keen on intimacy. The newsman looked down and saw an enormous tarantula crawling up his forearm. It had come to the table silently, on eight hairy feet, and was looking for companionship.

"Holy Jesus Christ," Fassman gasped. He raised a shivering left hand, and with an inept move (wondering how fast a tarantula could bite, how soon it would kill him, and what antidote Bugler kept in the house) brushed the spider from his arm to the table top. Its thick legs arched. It raised its fat double-sac of a body, feelers twitching as if insulted.

"Jesus Christ," Fassman cried. "Ed. Ed. There's a monster loose in here. Christ, get in here."

"Hold on, Jack, I got a crisis," Bugler said.

Fassman was pressed against the Audubon chart on the wall. He was convinced the tarantula was ready to charge. "That thing," he said.

"That's Bert. He's a pet."

"Some goddamn pet. He was all over me."

"If you'd have given him a fly or a moth, he'd have gone off. He wants affection."

"I don't carry flies or moths on me. That black bastard wanted to eat me."

Bugler scooped the tarantula from the table. He ladled it from one hand to another. The spider's hairy legs arched as they made contact with human flesh. Bugler manipulated the creature the way Fassman's son handled a metal toy called a Slinky. Right hand, left hand, right hand, left hand.

"I know this is a stupid question," Fassman said, "but what if he decides to bite you?"

"Never. He likes to be fondled. And if he did bite, it's no worse than a bee sting. Don't ever kill one, Alan. Bert keeps the house free of cockroaches."

As soon as Duane Essler had left with his golf party, the tennis professional approached the Maybanks. Rackets under arm, they were walking to the patio overlooking the courts. The sun was at its peak, pouring gobbets of heat onto the tennis courts. Yet it did not deter Arizonans. They owned the sun. They did not fear it.

The pro, Simmons, flaunted a prep-school oiliness—half syco-phant, half smart-ass—that got on the Maybanks' nerves. The last time Simmons had spoken to them was to ask them to wear regulation tennis clothing. They had ignored him. "They're white, aren't they?" Jenny snapped. "What do you want, a fashion show?" He had since avoided the Maybanks. Who were they anyway?

"Hi," Simmons said. He was prematurely gray and bronze-skinned. "Care for a little mixed doubles? There's a couple waiting for a game."

"Are they any good?" Jenny asked.

Simmons gulped. The Maybanks were regarded as class B duffers. "They look terrific. Tournament players." He bent his head close to Jack. "The Hosts."

"What are they hosting today?" asked Jenny.

"That's their name. Mr. Ray Host. Host-Labarre."

"*Those people,*" Jenny sneered. "The ones who ruined Santa Teresa Canyon."

Ray and Corinne Host got up when they saw the pro approach with their opponents. Host, his blockish face aflame with sun and health, looked blankly at the Maybanks. *No socks? Sneakers with holes?*

"Mr. and Mrs. Host, Mr. and Mrs. Maybank," Simmons said. "The Hosts are from Los Angeles. Don't be too tough on 'em, Mr. Maybank. They're guests and we'd like 'em back."

"Hi," Jenny said. She intoned the monosyllable in a fluty eastern seaboard manner. It was not lost on Corinne—rounder, softer, blonde, a complete Californian. Departing, the pro studied Corinne Host's thighs, ass, legs. A pouter. He had seen her down two vodka gimlets at lunch, tapping on the empties with a diamond the size of a Dunlop ball. Something to be pursued there, Simmons told himself, even though her husband had the look of a man who could kill you as easily as pay your salary.

"Are you folks vacationing?" Jenny asked Corinne.

"Sort of."

"Business and pleasure," Ray Host said.

"The pro said you were Californians," Jenny said. It was painful for her to be hospitable. Host-Labarre was, in many ways, *the enemy.* She had seen the polished California faces. Crammed with money, strength, a sense of owning all creation. Both looked as if they had been fitted into their tennis garb—creamy white, creaseless. The man's shirt appeared to have been painted on his square chest, drawn around his columnar neck. The woman wore frilly panties under a pale blue dress. She had on earrings and a dark blue velvet bow.

"Yes," Corinne said. "Do you know Hollywood Hills?" She named a country club and acted surprised when Jenny said she had never heard of it.

The couples parted at the net. Bouncing fresh yellow balls,

Host muttered to his wife, "Did you catch their name? Mayfield?"

"Maybank."

Host bounced a ball a few times. Jenny was fishing inside a tattered musette bag. Jack was tying a decomposing sneaker.

"Maybank. That's a break."

"Why?"

"I think he runs that research outfit."

"Show him who's in charge. Right, Ray?"

"Push will come to shove soon enough," Host said. "We might as well get an edge and beat them at tennis. They look awful. Maybe we should let them win a game or two."

Corinne shook her blond mane. Ray was faking. The killer instinct was not natural to him.

Host put the balls in play and they rallied for a few seconds. "They're hopeless," he said. "He hits the backhand with his elbow over his head."

Corinne bent low for a drive from Jenny, hit it back solidly, enjoying the thwack of the ball against the gut. "She isn't bad. Any woman who says Hi the way she does has had lessons."

"They're awful," Ray said.

"You could play one set and say you have a headache. I told you it would be okay if you hit with the pro."

"No. Even if the tennis is a drag"—Host ran to a soft lob that Jack hit to him and crashed down on it, like a coyote pouncing on a mouse—"I want to know the man a little before I call Pop."

"Ah. The victim can be measured."

"Ready?" Host called.

"Sure," Maybank called indifferently. He was having trouble with his sneaker lace again. Or was the shoe coming apart?

"Guests first," Jenny cried. "California rules."

Host served at half his normal strength. He won his game in four quick points. Once Maybank missed the serve altogether. The woman managed to return one serve, but Corinne put it away at net.

"Drat," Jenny said.

They changed sides. Maybank served. Gangly, ill-co-ordinated, sliding in his sneakers, his serve was a sliced butterfly. The Hosts slammed it deep four times, and led 2–0.

Maybank's ground strokes were hardly better than his serve.

He did not know how properly to stand on a court. Dangling his racket, failing to crouch, his head looked as if it sought a classroom. The Hosts led 3–0 on Corinne's serve.

"You've got good strokes," Host said, as he passed Jenny when they changed sides. He did not talk to Maybank. Host was not wroth, but his sense of orderliness was offended.

Losing concentration, convinced the afternoon would be a waste, Host let the next game slip away from him. The Maybank woman, with two perfectly placed lobs over Corinne's head, won her serve. The score was 3–1.

Host yawned, wondered about the dark-haired woman in the ragged tennis outfit, and promptly double-faulted.

"Wait longer between serves, Ray," Corinne said.

Host served four aces and they led 4–1. They changed sides again. Maybank seemed to be tottering. His knock-kneed legs were rubbery. The courts were dry, kicking up powdery clouds.

"You feel okay?" Jenny asked him.

"Yeah, fine."

"Turn it on, tiger. Make believe you're playing for Princeton."

"Jesus," Maybank muttered, as they passed the Hosts, "that *would* turn my stomach."

The Hosts heard them bantering. "They sound goofy," Host said.

"I told you. It's that *eastern* crap. They make a downer out of everything."

Host awaited Maybank's serve and smashed the dying ball into the next court. Before he and Corinne realized what was happening, Maybank had won his serve, plopping fluttering balls into the forecourt, making winners at net with the wood of his racket. At game point, Jenny poached, stabbed at a volley from Corinne, and drove it to her opponent's feet. Corinne flailed at the ball, missed, and went down. Host helped her up.

"Come on," he said. "Win your serve."

"I can't stand these pitty-pat players. They set my timing off."

The Hosts began to hit harder. They charged the net, blasted second serves as hard as the first. Under the punishing sun, they darted and leaped, ran forward, sideways, strained, stretched. And they kept losing.

Down 5–4, Ray Host watched Maybank unwind his clumsy body as he served. Corinne slammed the serve to the base line.

Jenny raced back (she seemed to do all the running, letting her husband amble about deep in the court) and lofted another deep lob.

"Out," Corinne called.

"Out?" Jenny asked. "It was a foot in."

"It was in," Host said.

"Play it over if you want," Maybank shouted. "It's only tennis."

Host drew his head inward. "It was *in*. Not by a foot, but in."

"Oh, hell, play it over," Maybank said.

"Godfrey Daniel," Jenny said. "The man is giving us the point, Maybank. The ball was way in. It's thirty-love."

"What did she say?" Host asked his wife.

"That it was in."

"But whose name did she mention?"

"It sounded like Fred Daniel."

Confounded, the Hosts smashed two of Maybank's feeble serves out of the court. Incredibly they had lost the first set, 6–4.

"It's beyond belief," Host said. "How'd they do it?"

Jenny held the racket between her thighs, cupped her hands, and called across the net: "Stay for one?"

Host squinted at his wife. Her attempt to cheat on a ball that was inside the court upset him. He did not cheat.

"I've had enough," Host said.

"Yeah," Maybank said. "The sun is tough if you're not used to it."

"They're from Los Angeles, Jack. They get the same kind of sun we do."

The Hosts were standing as if rooted to the green surface.

"Let's play them again," Corinne said. "Ray, that was ludicrous. We can beat them 6–0."

"It's not my kind of game. I'm not a doubles player."

They walked toward the bench where they had left their bags. Host seemed relieved. He no longer had to debase himself by playing against inept opponents. (Yet how *did* they win?) Corinne looked at him. She knew his relief was not feigned or hypocritical.

"You folks were too good for us," Host said.

"Lucky," Jenny said.

"Hell yes," Maybank added. "You could beat us any day of the week. You arrive today?"

"Yes," Corinne said. "We flew in from California."

"Ah," Maybank goggled at her curved buttocks. He admired the absolute beauty of the slow glide from cheek to thigh. "On the new Western flight?"

"Company plane," Host said. "Can we buy you a drink?"

Corinne smiled at Jenny. "Losers buy, isn't that it?"

"I wouldn't know. But a lemonade wouldn't be bad right now."

"You can't buy," Maybank said. "It's our club and only we can sign."

The pro approached them. He would have liked to be invited to the postgame drink. The Hosts were worth knowing. The Maybanks he could take or leave. Freaks, university types, not the usual Pima members.

"Mr. Host has membership privileges," Simmons said. "He can buy at the bar or the restaurant, Mr. Maybank. We've got an exchange agreement with his club in Beverly Hills."

The Hosts drank vodka gimlets. Jack sipped a Tecate beer, Jenny lemonade. Conversation was minimal. The Maybanks did not—for all the Host power—regard them as anything more than rich Angelenos. The Maybanks breathed *East*—from their ratty tennis clothing, their sneaky game, their inside jokes, their superior air. It distressed Corinne.

There was another reason for the abrupt failure of small talk, Corinne understood. Ray was looking for an opening. He was poor at these errands. Direct, plain-spoken, he had no stomach for the job Pop had saddled him with. He had told her about Otto Denkerman's lunatic will. He had been instructed to dig out all he could about the beneficiaries of the bequest. James W. Host would not tolerate such a wastage of funds that could be used for . . . *for what?* Ray had stumbled as he told Corinne about Pop's cold anger. For what? she kept asking. Growth. Progress. Expansion. Jobs. Ray had rattled on, talking into the hot wind that whipped around the convertible. *Greed,* she had said. Ray did not get angry. He hunched his shoulders, as if the desert wind had chilled him. "Yes, greed," he said, moments later. "It's what keeps everything going."

Corinne watched him. He was running out of comments about the weather and country clubs. There was this strange ambivalence in him. He had it all. The company plane, the palatial house, the yacht, eventually the Host-Labarre empire. Yet he always seemed to be standing outside of them.

"What line of work are you in?" he asked Maybank.

"Research."

"With the university?"

"No." Maybank looked edgy. Corinne could tell that he was not impressed with Host-Labarre. He had a bulging forehead, wispy hair. She had, while an undergraduate at Pomona, been in love with such a detached academic presence, a wispy scholar of Malayo-Polynesian languages.

"Scientific?" Host asked. The words seemed to issue unfinished from his throat.

"In a way."

Corinne could not let him flounder forever. "Are you in research also, Jenny?"

Jenny sucked noisily at the dregs of the lemonade. "Jack is the head of a research foundation. We're into conservation."

"It's called the Desert Research Institute," Maybank said. "We're trying to save the desert."

"That's a big order," Corinne said.

"Almost as tough as processing the desert," Jenny said. She stared at Host.

"You know who we are," Host said. He smiled at Jenny.

"Who doesn't?"

"Got me tabbed as the enemy?" Host asked. "You beat me at tennis. Maybe you can beat me at whatever it is you people work at."

Corinne tapped her ring against the glass. The waiter appeared. She was the only one who wanted a second drink.

"Don't look at it that way," Maybank said. "I don't know if you're any worse than anyone else who wants to carve up the desert. Some outfits have pretty good programs. We're just trying to hold the line in a few areas."

"Like the Sierra Club? Or the Friends of the Earth?"

"We're much smaller."

Jonny laughed. "And we don't have any Dave Brower to make waves for us. We're low profile."

"You have a man named Vormund who works with you, don't you? He's pretty well known."

The worst of liars, Corinne thought.

"He isn't that active. He's on our board. Do you know his books?"

"I may have seen an article of his somewhere."

Jenny was suspicious. "We sell some of his books at the Institute," she said. "You can order them by mail. Jack, what kind of a director are you? Sell Mr. and Mrs. Host membership cards. They can read *The Road Runner Gazette*. All about the battle to save the black-footed ferret."

"If you're interested," Jack said, "I can send you the applications. It's deductible."

Host smiled uneasily. Like his wife, he was having trouble with these people. They had beaten him on the tennis court by appearing not to care one way or the other. The woman with her "Drats" and "Godfrey Daniels" had upset him. But Maybank was even worse.

"You heard about Daniel Vormund through an article?" Jenny asked.

He would not tell them that Pop's lawyers had learned about Denkerman's affection for Vormund's writings. They even knew about the red-lined articles. Corinne saw the disarray on Ray's face. Any moment, she suspected he would blurt it out—*I know about Vormund because my father sent me here to break a will.*

She was almost tempted to throw it at them. Let them know they were in for a battle. Let them understand that by the time Host-Labarre's lawyers got through with them, there would not be enough money left to plant a prickly pear.

"You are privately supported?" Host asked. "We get into foundation work ourselves. . . ."

Jenny darted a look at Jack. Church work? She seemed to be saying: These two? This square-headed jock, and his California Sunkist wife, made of brown-and-white candy?

Maybank spoke. "Jen and I started it. We rattle the tin cup."

Jenny got up and gestured to her husband. "Look out that Fearless Jack Maybank here doesn't try to put the arm on you before you leave Arizona."

"I'd like to know more about your operation. If we process so much of the desert, maybe we should be restoring some of it."

Corinne smiled. "Corporate image."

Maybank assembled his weedy legs and picked up the rackets.

"Your money's as good as the quarters we get from school kids who collect tin cans and bottles."

Host frowned. Joking?

Jenny rescued them. "Jack isn't kidding. Some junior high school biology teacher ran a drive for us a month ago. We had every kid in Senita City salvaging cans and papers and bottles and giving us the pennies."

"They raised two hundred and fourteen bucks," Maybank said proudly.

"Wonderful," Host said.

"Maybe you'd like to come to the Institute tomorrow for lunch?" Maybank asked. "We have a routine for likely donors— handle a rattlesnake, show them the coyotes mean no harm. Maybe I can talk Vormund into showing up."

"That would be fine," Host said. He wondered what kind of a man, through the magic of a few words, could raise fifteen million dollars.

The couples parted in the parking lot. Duane Essler, mildly drunk, waved at the Maybanks. "No sweat, Jack. We'll work it out. I hope I didn't ruin your tennis."

"Nothing could," Jenny said.

The Maybanks watched Essler staring at the Hosts' Continental as if he knew it or knew them, then climbed into their dented VW squareback. It coughed, violating the torpid air.

"Something fishy," Jenny said.

"Essler? He's okay. We can work something out with him."

"Those two golden retrievers."

"I didn't notice anything."

"They heard about Dan, and they hadn't. Couldn't recall any of his books, never read *The Road Runner Gazette*. Why did they mention him?"

"Beats me." Maybank caught a glimpse of the Continental zooming onto the Interstate. "They're interested in what we're doing."

"People that rich aren't interested in the likes of us, or the plight of the masked bobwhite. Maybe he isn't even Raymond Host. Maybe he's a chiseler. The kind Fusaro warned us about."

"Jesus, Jen." Maybank laughed. "No way. Not those two."

"Watch yourself at all times, Maybank. Maybe Fusaro should be there tomorrow."

Speeding to their hotel, the Hosts reflected on their chance meeting with the heirs to the Denkerman fortune.

"All that poor-mouthing about passing the cup for donations," Corinne said. "Kids raising pennies with scrap drives."

"I didn't expect him to mention that they just came into fifteen million. They're the types who find money embarrassing."

"But the way they *dress!* And *act!* It's so low-keyed you could puke. Not even a hint that they've just come into a fortune."

"It isn't their money."

"When you and Pop get through with them, it won't be."

"I didn't mean that, Corinne. I meant that it belongs to the Institute."

Corinne stretched her neck against the rest, lifted her arms. "How in God's name did they beat us? They were terrible. You lost your temper. You quit halfway through when they kept returning everything."

"I had an off day."

She did not care who got Otto Denkerman's money. But increasingly she resented the way in which the Hosts made the world jig to their tunes. Secretly she hoped that the Maybanks, in the same threadbare yet effective way, would defeat the attack on the millions intended to save badgers and foxes.

3

———————— ❈ ————————

"Dan would have loved this trip," Bugler said. "He always loved Grace Canyon. Especially McGregor's grave."

Fassman was seated in the jeep next to Bugler. They had started before dawn. Bugler, acting on Sidewinder's tip, wanted to inspect the lion traps the Hopi had described. He had invited Fassman to come along. The TV newsman was reluctant to call Vormund again.

Bugler, eager for excuses to get away from his chores, had left Sidewinder and the students to clean the botanical area, and had taken off. He had failed to ask Maybank's permission but it did not seem to bother him.

They drove into higher ground. Grassland and cottonwoods replaced the desert shrubs. The air was chill and bracing. Soon they could see red-rock cliffs jutting against a crystalline blue sky.

"Redwall," Bugler said. "Dan wrote about it somewhere. The ancient sea that washed over the desert. I'm no geology expert. Dan isn't either, but he makes it more exciting than any geologist."

"What's McGregor's grave?"

"Some naturalist who lived to be ninety-three. He had this cabin in Grace Canyon and they buried him there. He was a scout for the Museum of Natural History in New York. Dan knows the whole story. McGregor fought at Gettysburg and Antietam, that kind of thing. There's a grave at the head of the canyon with a marker. Spooky, but beautiful."

Fassman, shivering, turned up the collar of his Windbreaker. They were traveling southeast, into a range of mountains higher than the Santa Teresas that ringed Senita City. The highway rose like a slowly ascending graph. The sun, at a left oblique angle to them, painted long cold shadows on the brown earth and greening meadows. Barbed-wire fencing was continuous, marking the compartments man had imposed on the grasslands. Good ranching country, Bugler explained—mountain streams, lush pasture. A lot of it was public land, leased for a tiny cost.

"I'm not clear on the purpose of this trip," Fassman said. Bugler had awakened him at 4 A.M. at the motel. It had been dark and windy when they left. Black coffee sloshed around his stomach. Bugler assured them they would be able to stop for a bite somewhere, but there appeared no sign of a town or any habitation along the road.

"The lion traps."

"What about them?"

"Sidewinder saw them along the canyon ridges and the canyon floor. Someone wants to kill a lot of lions."

"They can, can't they?"

Bugler explained. In spite of the lion being classified as big game, one per year to any hunter who paid a dollar for a license, the animal was being exterminated by stockmen through an ambiguous law. People described as "livestock operators" were allowed to take "such measures as necessary to prevent further damage" to kill lions who preyed on their stock.

"It's no loophole," Bugler explained. "It's a barn door. It says *such* bear or mountain lion—which means a specific animal. But they can kill anything that moves. Up north, they took twenty-two lions in the last two months—shooting and trapping. They're supposed to file a Stock-Killing Report. No chance. They didn't file *one* up there. No evidence, nothing. The state lets them get away with it. I doubt there are more than four thousand mountain lions left in the country, and you better see one soon or you'll *never* see one."

Fassman tried to summon up sympathy for the vanishing predator.

"Dan goes batty over this one. He did a series in the newsletter. I told you how he testified and those louts attacked him. I told Dan that traps don't discriminate. They'll trap *any* lion who walks by. Lions are stupid. Much dumber than coyotes. They aren't put off by a man's scent."

"Maybe they're more trusting."

"I doubt it. Just a lower order of intelligence. I like lions, but they're no match for a number four and a half wolf trap with a twelve-foot chain loaded with brush hooks. You'll see what those contraptions look like."

Bugler slowed down at a dirt road. His sense of direction amazed Fassman. All the terrain looked alike, all the dirt roads were replicas of each other. "This looks about right," he said.

"About?"

He looked sideways at Fassman. "All you educated people are alike. It took me five years to convince Dan I knew where I was going in the desert without a map. You get a sense of where you are after a while."

Which, Fassman thought, is not a bad thing to have.

They drove toward the sun. Hawks and ravens circled above them in search of breakfast.

"This indiscriminate trapping," Bugler said. "We figure we can make an issue of it. If a calf has been killed by a lion—and damned few are—and a hunter takes off after it with dogs, he can track the cat and kill it. But that's too much trouble. It's easier to carpet an area with traps and catch any lion, not to mention a lot of what they call *trash*—skunks, badgers, ferrets."

"Anything that lives."

"That's the idea. Dan and I figure we can ask them to write a new law or strengthen the old one. Force them to fill out reports. Let's see the *evidence* of lion kills. Make them stop covering up and trying to murder every lion in the state. Cougars have rights too."

"Not many people agree with you."

Bugler passed a calloused hand over his forehead. "Dan says it's a national frenzy. He once was going to do a piece comparing the way we kill wildlife to the Vietnam business. A national compulsion to murder."

"Why didn't he?"

"Jack Maybank said it was too political for the Institute. Clara was against it and Dan dropped it. He says he isn't political any more. He's sick of mankind arguing over this and that, when nothing will matter the way he's destroying the earth."

They came to a grove of thick cottonwoods, glinting gold and silver in the morning light. A spuming clear stream ran through the clusters of trees. Small birds flitted in the branches.

"The canyon's a ten-minute walk," Bugler said. "You mind?"

"No. It's beautiful. Do you just drive in and park here like this? Won't you get in trouble with the rancher?"

"No one cares. It's leased anyway."

"But we have no right here."

"Maybe Essler runs some cattle through here. But what are we doing so terrible?"

"Ed, you're trying to put the guy out of business. To stop him from trapping and shooting and poisoning, all those things that make his life worthwhile."

Bugler seemed oblivious. He walked ahead in loping steps. His rawboned body was invigorated by the crackling morning air.

"Grace Canyon's a phenomenon," he said. "You should see it a month from now. *Birds!* They come up from Mexico, get as far as the canyon wall, and stay there. What colors! Warblers, orioles, cardinals, every kind of western bird known. It's the place I dragged Dan to try to see the trogon. McGregor's grave is on top of that knoll."

The path steepened. Junipers and piñon pines clung to the rocky heights. Fassman wondered how any man, experiencing such beauty, could ever settle for anything less.

"It's a small canyon," Bugler said. "But it's a beauty."

"I hear the stream."

Bugler smiled. "That's right. McGregor went to bed every night listening to it. The music of God, he called it. There are some remains of his cabin beyond those junipers. Hey, look at that flock circling and wheeling over there."

"What are they?"

Bugler shaded his eyes. "Mountain bluebirds. Thousands of them around here. The insects start coming out, and the bluebirds know it."

Fassman inhaled the air. It was like a draft of pure oxygen to an asthma sufferer in a stratoliner. But it was more. It reminded him of possibilities. *To delight in the variety of nature,* Vormund had written. But few would accept his advice. He argued for the appreciation of "useless" plants and animals. The earth, Thoreau said, was more beautiful than useful. But *use* was the national religion—Fassman felt—next to football. And that made Vormund and Bugler and their friends heretics, blasphemers, enemies of revealed faith.

They moved higher and turned into a grove of junipers. Soon they entered a clearing. Through the tracery of evergreens, Fassman could see the reddish cliffs of the miniature canyon. Scarred, jagged-edged, dotted with stubborn shrubbery, they were marvels of design. Natural forms, full of harmonious proportions. *Learn for the ancients a just esteem, to copy nature is to copy them.* . . . Words read in a classroom leaped across the years, endowed him with a luminous awareness of the manner in which Vormund had bridged his two worlds.

"There it is," Bugler said.

A rectangular mound rested in the midst of the clearing. It was covered with a golden-brown mantle of oak leaves and pine needles. At one end was a cairn of stones, and wedged into it, a brass plaque. Had Vormund entertained thoughts of his own mortality on visits to the lonely canyon?

"A little scary," Fassman said.

"Dan thinks this is a joyful place. Read the inscription."

Fassman knelt in the damp compost.

MYLES T. McGREGOR

SOLDIER, WRITER, NATURALIST

(1845–1936)

Beneath this, in letters three times the size, was a sign:

FAGEL & MALLET
FUNERAL DIRECTORS—SENITA, ARIZONA

"What taste," the newsman said. "Right on the man's grave."

"It tickled Dan every time he saw it. He wrote about it in the newsletter. Something about McGregor being remembered because the morticians used his grave to let people who needed their services know where to find them. He said it proved you couldn't stop the power of advertising."

At the edge of the clearing was a pile of warped gray boards. "His cabin?"

"What's left of it. He wrote once that he observed twenty-two different lions in the canyon one year—knew them by their pug marks and got to recognize their voices."

They started down the canyon side. The cliff wall was covered with hardy shrubs and early-blooming wild flowers. In the grassy areas blue harebells and western yarrow were beginning to blossom.

As they walked—Fassman stumbling, unable to keep up with Bugler's comfortable lope—the naturalist expanded his theory of why lions were easy to trap. They were solitary hunters who traveled a great deal, but followed the same route, made a scratch or scrape in the dirt or the base of a tree and sprayed it with scent. Once the rancher or trapper found the "scrape" with the strong odor, he set his traps on a trail leading to or from the marker.

"If Sidewinder is right, I'll be able to show you how it works. Watch out you don't step on something black and shiny. I don't want to be responsible for trapping a television reporter."

"Thanks a lot. Do you have a knife to cut my foot off?"

"I'll let you gnaw yourself out."

Fassman, clumsy and overweight, had given up exercise years ago despite Wendi's prods that he get out and play tennis. He always lost and people didn't care to play with him. Soon he was gulping for air. A fire had started in his chest. "Slow down, Ed," he pleaded.

Bugler stopped. He was on all fours. "By golly, this is it. Some cat's been through here. Get a whiff of that scratch at the bottom of the piñon. Squirted all over it."

Fassman got to one knee and moved his face to the place where the bark had been scratched away. A musky odor assailed him—memories of cat pee in tenement halls. Only stronger and wilder.

"That's the scratch," Bugler said. "Every lion in the area will squirt at it. A community sniffer."

"Why?"

"Lions are strange. No coyote would do that. A coyote would leave a fake scent somewhere, maybe rub a dead skunk against a tree stump, to fool you."

"I don't believe that."

"Hold it," Bugler said. "We're at the edge of the trap line."

"How can you tell?"

"Look at that oak tree. The one that's fallen down."

"What about it?"

"It didn't fall naturally. It's been power-sawed. Look at the way it lies."

"I don't see anything special."

"It makes a funnel away from the scrape. Lion comes by his scrape mark, takes a leak, and keeps walking. The log keeps him against the canyon wall. He follows the funnel and gets trapped."

"Doesn't the lion realize something is fishy?"

"Dumb, dumb." Bugler sounded as if he wished he could hold adult education classes for cougars. "You could set traps this way forever, and if there were lions left, they'd keep coming back."

Bugler halted at the fallen tree and sat down.

"What now?" Fassman asked.

"Looking for the holes. Stay a few steps behind me. You land in one of those traps, we'll have more to worry about than Essler."

"You look for trouble, don't you?"

"Follow me. Stay close to the rock face. So long as the ground feels firm, you're okay."

Bugler preceded him, probing the earth with his hiking boot. Halfway down the fallen oak he stopped. "There's one of them," he said.

"I don't see anything." Fassman, on blundering feet, recoiled.

"It's camouflaged. See that pile of brush?"

Fassman nodded.

"Look close. You can see the pan. A black metal disk with a V on it."

Fassman inched forward. "It doesn't look too big. I mean, big enough to trap a lion."

"It's the steel jaws do it, not the pan." Bugler walked agilely along the fallen tree. He stopped when he was a foot from the trap, squatted, and picked up a long branch with which he touched the trigger.

"Ed, don't. You'll set it off."

"It isn't that easy to set off. This fellow knows what he's doing. I poke it, but it won't spring. There's something stuck under the pan—maybe a twig or a hunk of foam rubber. That keeps skunks or raccoons from springing it. It's got to be a heavy animal, and he's got to take a big step on it. That lion's paw will be deep in the hole when the jaws clamp on him."

Bugler swept the twigs and leaves away. Fassman walked along the oak and squatted beside him. With the scraps cleared from the hole, he could see the spread steel jaws, the tensed spring. Coiled beneath them was the enormous chain.

"Fellow didn't miss a trick," Bugler said. "Ever see cactus up this high?"

"I haven't noticed any."

"Except around the hole. Look again."

"Prickly pear?"

"Not growing naturally. Thrown around it. A lion hates cactus thorns. The trapper not only funnels him toward the trap hole, he puts cactus around it—hell, I've seen broken glass—and the cat walks onto the pan."

"Nothing left to chance."

"But no guarantee they ever get the lion they claim is killing. It's a rigged wheel. That's what gets people like Dan and me sore."

Like Columbia football, Fassman thought. Year after year of losing teams, unable to recruit jocks the way Harvard and Dartmouth do.

"Let's move ahead," Bugler said. "Sidewinder says he saw them all the way to the crest of the canyon." He took photographs of the exposed trap, brushed the twigs and leaves back on, and strode ahead, clinging to the red face of the canyon wall, balancing himself against the trees.

A dead cypress had been placed beyond the oak to continue the funnel through which the lions were directed. A hundred feet beyond the first trap Bugler spotted a second. It eluded Fassman completely. He was too weary to concentrate his senses. The vivid beauty of the canyon, the showers of bluebirds, the obstreperous ravens, the whisper of mountain wind, filled him with joy, dulled the pain, rendered his exhaustion sensual. "I don't . . . oh, yes. That pile of cactus. There's the pan sticking out. Clever."

Bugler walked along the tree. Beyond, dead limbs had been piled to continue the passageway. They counted two more traps, all secreted in holes, with the debris-hidden jaws at ground level.

"Four or five of them will use the same run. That scrape gets them. Even a bear's got more sense. There's a fellow up north claims he trapped fifty lions along one run in the last ten years."

The canyon wall turned sharply left, following the snow-swollen stream, gurgling and boiling a hundred feet below. Fassman periodically caught glimpses of it—clear, full of debris, magical rocks.

To almost everything except man, Vormund once wrote, *the stench of man is the vilest of odors, the sight of man the most terrifying of all sights.* . . . But the cougar had not learned this.

Bugler had stopped. "Alan, look at that."

"What . . . ?"

"That hole. Something dug its way out. Stand still. Whatever it was, it's around."

Bugler pointed ahead on the trail. There was a vast wound, almost ten feet across, in the earth. The soil and the natural cover —branches, growing plants, the cactus—had been scattered about. To one side, on the lowest rocks of the redwall, were streaks of dark blood.

"Tried to dig clear, chain and all," Bugler said.

"They . . . do this?" Fassman's voice congealed in his throat. His eyes went upward. Surely the cat was overhead, waiting, wounded.

"Pain and fear make animals do crazy things."

"Ed, he won't blame us, will he? Explain we're on his side. Besides, I'm Jewish."

Bugler took his glasses off and scanned the surrounding trees. "He can't have gotten far. Not with that chain and the hooks. They get hung up, or they climb a tree and starve, or die of thirst. If they're lucky someone finds them and shoots them."

"We should have brought a gun."

"I can't kill an animal when there's a chance of saving him." His eyes studied the trail of blood, the ravaged earth. "I once found a badger, no bigger than two feet long," Ed said. "The chain was anchored deep, and he started digging, with one foot in a leg-hold trap. Chewed up a place big enough for a fish pond. I helped him dig his way clear and then I forced open the trap."

"What do we do, Ed? Should I go to the jeep? Do you have a weapon? Maybe the first-aid kit?" Fassman sounded idiotic—an inept city man.

"Let's try to find him first." He knelt along the canyon side. "Yeah, he's dragging the chain. The hooks made scrapes on the stone."

They walked another fifty feet. Bugler heard it first—a hissing, spitting noise. "There he is," he said. "Beyond that clump of juniper. The chain hooks are locked around the roots. Don't move, Alan. He's holed up at the rear of the ledge. I see the tips of his ears. The bugger is probably half dead."

Fassman's eyes followed the hooks that were locked into the roots of the junipers. The drag chain snaked up the side of the canyon.

Bugler scampered up an outcropping of red rocks. He motioned to Fassman to follow him. They stood together, following the dangling chain. A trail of blood paralleled the loops.

"There it is," Ed whispered. "Poor thing is darn near dead. Look at him."

Fassman saw the flat hexagonal face first, a beige-gray tabby's head. The darker brown ears were flattened. The amber eyes were half closed. The blunt nose was caked with mucus and blood. It was breathing heavily, jaws slack. The lion pricked its ears when it saw the men. But it did not move.

"Would it . . . he . . . charge?"

"Can't move. By golly, I think it's a lioness. With cubs inside her, at that."

"I don't see any trap," Fassman said.

"She's lying on it. They do that sometimes. It drives them insane. Look at the right forepaw. It's a lump of blood and pus. The trap's to the rear. There, she's moving it."

Two black steel half-moons were visible, half covered by the lion's pale tufted belly. It seemed strange to Fassman that so small a contraption could immobilize so large and noble a creature. The predator was long-necked, small-headed, with thick foreparts, and heavy muscled legs. The recumbent tawny body, with its dark ridge down the spine, broadened and thickened to the rear. The elegant tail was draped over the edge of the rock. "Sometimes they chew their feet off," Ed said. "I guess this one couldn't bring herself to do it. Dying of thirst, maybe." He scratched his hair and squinted at the beast. "Nice kitty."

The cougar opened its jaws and hissed. To Fassman (or was he hallucinating?) it seemed like a friendly greeting.

"Could be the leg bone was broken," Bugler said. "I wish they'd come out and kill them, not leave them rot like this. Gangrene, starvation, hemorrhage."

"What do we do, Ed?"

"I'm not sure. Maybe set her loose."

"With what?"

"I'm working on that." He looked at Fassman's formless face. Classrooms, books, ideas, all sorts of fancy education. Not much help in the woods. But his heart was where it should be. "Feel brave?"

"I don't want to get clawed by a gangrenous lion, if that's what you have in mind."

"I'll work close up. Go back to the jeep. I'll stay here and talk to her. There's a tool chest and a crowbar in the back. Bring 'em. Also my Sierra cup. We'll see can we get her to drink."

"What will you be doing?"

"Calming her down."

Fassman stumbled down the canyon trail. The path was thick with pine needles and multicolored leaves. Gaudy birds darted around his head. He ran past McGregor's grave with its advertisement for the funeral parlor and sprinted toward the jeep. Who was it bragged of feasting with panthers? Wilde? Here in the Arizona mountains he had a friend who drank with lions. Something hummed above, sawed the mountain air. Overhead he saw a small plane.

Raymond Host insisted that they stop at a bookstore after the tennis match with the Maybanks. He found, to his surprise, that the leading store stocked many of Vormund's works, in both paperbound and hard-cover editions. Corinne studied the titles with him. He depended on her for advice in these areas. When they were first married, he had made her give him oral résumés of the best sellers she read. He had no time for frivolous reading. Pop demanded his mind, his time, his concentration.

"The boy's smarter than I am," he told the Board of Directors. "Give him three years and he'll stand the company on its ear." But he had not. Not yet anyway. Young Host seemed to do everything well, but he was not a self-starter, the old hands complained. He knew construction, land use, financing, sales. But he seemed to lose interest, pull back, let the old man make the decisions. Recently two West Coast banks had given Host-Labarre thirty-five million dollars with instructions that were not instructions at all. *Build,* they told Pop. *Whatever you decide to build is good enough for us.* Pop had asked Ray for recommendations. The request was still on Ray's desk in their suite of offices in Century Plaza.

"Take these," Corinne said. "*Desert Idyll. The Spirit of the Desert. The Precious Balance.* And look. These from when he taught English. *Elizabethan Drama. The Restoration Comedy.* He had his hand in everything." She glanced at one title page and was astounded to find that the book on Elizabethan drama had had six printings, the first in 1938. The full list of Vormund's works came to twenty-four titles.

"One of our regional authors," the elderly lady at the cash register said. "We're proud of him."

"You know him?" Corinne asked.

"No. But when he was sprier, Professor Vormund used to talk to the high school biology classes."

At the Senita Inn, they swam in the pool, returned to their suite, and sampled the champagne and fruit that the manager had left for them. Host-Labarre had bought the inn several years ago. Elegant, discreet—its only concession to the outside world was a tiny blue sign—it included a Rockefeller cottage, a Vanderbilt cottage, and a Baruch cottage.

"Baruch, what a laugh," Corinne said. Shaking her gleaming hair, she reclined on the chintz-covered bed, glancing at one of Vormund's desert books.

"What's so funny?"

"For years he was the only Jew they ever let in here. The Hollywood writers had a joke about him. Every morning, on his breakfast tray, under the rose, was a telegram from the B'nai

B'rith asking Mr. Baruch to explain why he continued to stay at such an anti-Semitic place as the Senita Inn."

Host pulled on a pair of jockey shorts. Naked, he was like a ruddy statue. "We changed that. The day Pop bought in he had the Kaplans out here. Give us *some* credit."

Corinne smiled. Agreed. The old man was not a villain. Anyone who dealt with him fairly would expect a decent return. There were lots of Jews in finance, building, land development. He liked to work with them, and they respected him.

Her eyes winced at the modest maple-and-print room. "I bet the Kaplans wondered why they ever wanted in after they saw this place."

Host settled into one of the narrow maple beds—Corinne was right in her analysis of the inn's determined plainness—and opened Vormund's *Desert Idyll*. What could the man have said so effectively, as to cause the late Otto Denkerman to give away fifteen million dollars?

One world? One earth would be more accurate. Unless we are prepared to share the earth with the wild creatures of field, mountain, desert, lake, and ocean, all living things, we will not inhabit it much longer.

Grim stuff, Host thought. He had heard it from the long-haired kids who picketed Bald Indian Power Plant, hustled petitions to protest Host-Labarre developments. But there seemed to be more to Vormund. Host was not stupid or insensitive. He realized there was some validity in the old man's warnings.

By what right, on whose instructions, has man arbitrarily divided plants into useful and useless categories? And who appointed him the judge over what animals are "domestic," designed for his personal use, or "trash" and fit only for extermination?

Corinne got up—naked, smooth, inviting. Host wanted her. They were compatible in bed, even when she was at her bitchiest. The union of their tanned young bodies, the superb end-products of California sun, sea, and diet, had a blessed perfection. He glanced up from the book, admiring, as if seeing it for the first time, the curve of neck, back, buttocks, thigh.

"Champagne?" she asked.

"I've had enough. And go easy, Corinne."

"Yummy." She drained a glass of champagne as if it were No-Cal ginger ale. "That tennis pro had a lech for me."

"Who can blame him?"

"It's funny. They know who you are. Terribly rich. Strong enough to kill them. And they look me over as if they aren't *afraid*. Don't you get sore when men do that?"

"I'm trying to read, Corinne."

"The unconquerable Hosts, *père et fils*. That tennis bum looked at me as if he knew something. You wouldn't fight for me, would you, Ray? Kill?"

"Can it. If some guy ever got serious, you'd beg for mercy and run. You'd scream if he put a hand under your skirt."

She poured another glass, sat down, naked, on a chintz-covered platform rocker, and cradled the glass in her hands. "Don't be so sure, Ray. Someday, someday." She sang tunelessly. *"Someday, sweetheart, you will be sorry. . . ."*

Pop was right, Host thought. *She wants to be wealthy and she doesn't want to.* She has it all now, and she wonders what it's all about. You had to be like Pop and his associates to savor money, make it work, handle it, know how to get more. You had to love it. Corinne alternated between sneers at wealth and a need for luxury. *She'll never be happy,* he thought. Someday she would have to take a vow of poverty, go off to a commune, let him support her with a monthly remittance. And she could write. Or paint. Or just live. She had threatened several times to run off to a farm commune in the San Bernardino Mountains. He had laughed at her, half fearful she would carry out her threat. "Let her," Pop advised. "She'll come home when she gets hungry."

When we demand unconditional surrender of a natural creature, such as an insect, we are, in effect, dooming ourselves. Drench the earth with poisons, kill the last moth and the last beetle, and we hasten our own rush to oblivion. We celebrate our victories over insect pests, little realizing that there are no winners, only losers, when we upset the delicate balance. . . .

"How's that book?" Corinne asked.

"Interesting."

"Worth fifteen million dollars?"

"I don't know. I'm not sure how it ends."

Reading, Host tried to sort out annoyances: Did they want Otto Denkerman's millions that badly? Why did trails keep leading to D. D. Vormund, a man neither of them knew?

Because man is a threat to every living thing, he is a threat to himself. And he is successful, frighteningly so. He wills the death of species, and they die. He is offended by plants, and they vanish. He wants nothing less than total victory.

It was a good thing, Host reflected, that Vormund had a limited audience, no wealth, no platform. A few eccentrics, some dickeybirders, listened and nodded shaggy heads. In the long run Vormund had to lose. Who could oppose total victory—over an enemy, an insect, or the desert, or the world?

His chest on fire, Fassman trotted up the canyon again with the tools Bugler requested, the Sierra cup, and an empty coffee can he had found in the jeep.

Bugler had climbed higher up the red-stone wall. To Fassman's astonishment, he was now on the same ledge as the cougar. Ed had sat down, his back against the escarpment. His bespectacled face was a yard away from the lion's panting mouth.

"Ed, for God's sake," Fassman called. His voice quavered. "No closer. She'll take your face off."

The lion seemed at peace. Every few seconds the bloodied lips peeled back, the long teeth were exposed, and it hissed at Bugler. Bugler did not move. He was talking to it.

"It's okay, Alan," he said. "We're getting acquainted. Leave the tools up here. Go down to the stream and fill the cup. Poor thing's dying of thirst."

Sliding in city shoes, Fassman stumbled to the brook at the base of the canyon. He was winded and scratched and his shirt was ripped by the time he reached the waters. A raven studied him with a contemptuous eye, croaked, took wing from a spruce.

Fassman filled the cup and the can. Spray from the pounding waters struck his face. It felt marvelous. A rather cowardly man, he experienced a surge of courage. Why? It was Ed Bugler conversing with the trapped beast, not him. But some of the bravery had taken hold. He was like a spectator at a prize fight, full of vicarious gumption.

It took him twice as long to climb the canyon. It seemed to have gotten steeper. Roots leaped from the ground and clutched at his feet. Branches slapped nastily at his face. Twigs poked at his defenseless eyes. How did Ed Bugler scramble up and down mountains and across deserts, oblivious to nature's barbs and darts? Each breath scorched Fassman's throat, constricted his heaving lungs. He staggered to the base of the ledge and rested his soaked back against a tree. He could hear Bugler's soothing voice.

"Nice kitty, good lion. Good girl. Got a bad paw, don't you, girl? Good girl . . ."

He's mad, Fassman thought, *mad as a March hare.*

"Nice kitty-kat. Yeah, you like it when I touch your ears. Those are fine ears, but you slick them back like you're scared."

There was a short savage roar. Fassman, unable to see the man and the beast, trembled. Crazy Bugler. Sleeper with coyotes, friend to badgers. He would lose a hand as he muttered words of love to the dying cat.

"Ed, be careful. Are you all right?"

"We're getting acquainted. Get the water up. I can't work on the trap until she knows I'm her friend. Hand it up if you don't want to come onto the ledge."

Fassman plodded up the rocky slope. At the lip of the escarpment, he was able to see them. The lion had not moved. Bugler had his left hand on the tawny head. He was stroking the space between the dark ears, kneading the fur, tweaking the back of the ears. The animal hissed from time to time and threw its head back feebly, as if to shake off the alien hand. But it did not snap at Bugler.

"You sure it won't . . . turn on you . . . take your hand off?"

"She understands. Nice puss. We'll get your leg out of that trap, won't we?" The beast opened its jaw and snarled fiercely. The long teeth flashed. Fassman leaped backward and water spilled from the can. Bugler had not removed his hand. "Nice girl, nice girl. You're upset. I'd be too, caught in one of them."

The pink tongue darted from the opened jaws, flicked a few times, retreated. The lion appeared to be surrendering. Weak, tortured, dying of thirst, it could not fathom the enemy who had come to it speaking softly, stroking its head.

"The water, Alan."

Fassman worked his way up the red stone and handed Bugler the Sierra cup and the can. Bugler took the cup of water and held it under the lion's nose.

"Go on, kitty." He sounded like a mother enticing a sullen child to try the strained pears. "It's good. Right from the creek."

The head tilted forward. The pink tongue emerged again and licked the water.

"Good girl," Bugler said. "Finish every drop. It's on the house."

Fassman wanted to applaud. In the newsroom, they would laugh at him when he would claim to have seen a trapped cougar drink from a man's hand.

The lion's mouth made a messy slurping noise. Fassman remembered a mongrel puppy he had owned briefly in the Bronx. It made the same kind of slushy noise when it drank. For a small dog, it stank terribly. It wet his mother's spotless floors, crapped on the rugs. His parents were not partial to dogs. They made him get rid of the dog and he had wept.

"She's reviving," Bugler said. "I've got her confidence. Give me a few weeks with her, she'd let me deliver her kittens. Alan, hand me the crowbar."

Bugler squatted next to the animal, patting its head, holding the cup beneath its snout. It shook its whiskers. The ropelike tail thrashed.

Fassman worked his way to the rear of the ledge. His pants were ripped at both knees. His left knee was bleeding. Schoolyard memories rattled inside his head. Leaping from the castiron fence at P.S. 179, scraping knees. What concatenation of events had brought him from the gray canyons of the East Bronx to this wild place? Vormund, of course.

"Can you pry that thing open?" Fassman gasped.

"I can try." Bugler moved back. He rubbed his chin and studied the way the leg-hold trap rested under the lion's leg. "She won't like it if I touch that paw. Got to move slowly."

"Can I help?" Fassman asked. One hand flattened against the face of the cliff, he minced toward Bugler. "I mean . . . is there any way we can get at it?"

"I'm trying to figure it out." Bugler studied the trap again. "Let's see."

Edging closer, Fassman's nose was assailed by an asphyxiating stench. He realized that it was the rotting, blood-crusted paw. There were crawling white dots on it. "Maggots?" he asked Bugler.

"Nature's antiseptic. They keep it clean. Dan says everything has its function in nature. You think you could get where I am and do what I was doing?"

"No. I'm scared shitless."

"Just keep the water under her nose. Talk to her. Never mind. I'll keep talking if it embarrasses you. I've enjoyed every animal I've ever talked to."

"It won't embarrass me, Ed. It'll scare the crap out of me. What if she decides to swat me with the good paw? Ed, I'm a city boy. She'll smell the fear coming out of my pores."

"Don't believe that. We all stink to a lion. Come on, change places. Squat down and fill the cup. You don't have to tickle her ears. I'll work on the trap."

Fassman asked himself: How will I show this on the expense account? And why did he not have a cameraman with him to record a story that could have dramatized everything in which Vormund believed? He moved closer and dropped to one knee.

Bugler said: "Don't jump if she snarls. She's too weak to do anything. Animals don't like sudden movements."

"With my luck that water will revive her."

"Not a chance. I hope she's strong enough to walk off once I can pry this thing loose."

Fassman inched toward the lion. His hands shivered as he held out the cup. The rasplike tongue darted out and lapped at the water. The amber eyes were half closed. Fassman tried to look into them. Boyhood myths rattled in his head. True or false: *An animal cannot look a man in the eye.* The cougar did not seem to care. The hissing seemed *pro forma,* a beast doing what was expected of it.

"More than one way to skin a cat," Bugler said. "Or get a lion out of a trap. We'll give it a try."

He maneuvered his body alongside the lion's. Once the curling tail struck at his back. "Whoa, girl," he said. "She's saying she likes me. She understands."

"You're imagining it. You said yourself cats are dumb. No loyalties, no affection. Look how dumb she was walking into the trap."

Bugler got to one knee. Slowly he moved the trap and the swollen paw a few inches. The lion let out an agonized roar. It thrust its flat head, teeth bared, at Bugler. Fassman dropped the cup and flew backward, scuttling like a legless beggar.

"Jesus, Ed. This is impossible."

"Nice kitty. That didn't hurt, did it? Now relax, drink your water, and pay no attention to what I am about to do."

Trembling, Fassman crept back. He stretched his arms, offering the metal cup. The lion averted its head, in a stately move that reminded him of the M-G-M lion's last nod before the screen went to the main title. *It knows, it knows,* Fassman thought. *It knows I'm frightened, an alien in these mountain fastnesses.*

"Easy there, puss," Bugler said. "Here goes nothing."

On one knee Bugler lifted the crowbar and inserted it into the locked half-moons of the trap. The lion snarled again. Fassman watched in horror. The beast raised its free forepaw as if to slash at Bugler, and then, as if realizing it had a friend, it lowered it, contenting itself with guttural growls.

"Good kitty," Bugler said. "I'm lucky and I'm not lucky."

"What do you mean?"

"The paw's jammed at the base of the trap. I need room to maneuver without hitting the sore part. I can't get a grip on the trap. I need some counter pressure. Now if I could move it out . . ."

"Don't look at me."

"When I lift the trap with the bar, grab at the chain and pull it. Be careful. If you pull it too far, you'll drag her paw with it. She might not like that. Pull it far enough out so I can ram the bar all the way to the ground and force it open."

"Must I?"

"Take hold of that link near your foot. The one above the brush hook. When I say three, pull it away from her."

Fassman forced himself forward. His hands seemed to be shaking an inch in each direction. The lioness bared its teeth.

"That's it," Bugler said. "Get a grip on it. One. Two. *Three.*"

Fassman pulled at the chain. The trap and the lion's festering paw moved with it. The animal roared. It was the most terrifying sound Fassman had ever heard in his life. It tried to slash at him with its free paw, but the gesture was halfhearted.

"Nice pussy. Don't swat your friends."

Fassman staggered to his feet. Bugler, his back and arms straining, jammed the crowbar into the locked half-moons, ramming the point into the rocky soil below the black pan. "Dammit, *give*," Bugler wheezed. His face was scarlet. The bristles on his long head seemed to vibrate. "The way they lock these damned things. Alan, I need help."

Fassman stumbled along the ledge. He avoided the lion and stood in back of Bugler.

"Now, the two of us. Grab the bar above my hands. And when I say three, bend backward with me."

"I'm not strong."

"But you're big. The weight may help. Ready?"

Grasping the metal bar, Fassman swallowed mountain air.

"On three. Once more. I never learned to count much above that."

"Yeah, but you know a lot of other things."

"Ready? One. Two. Three. *Bend*."

The two men strained against the bar. Fassman could feel Bugler's body tensing, each muscle bulging inside the shirt. *And what am I contributing?* he wondered. As ineffectual at opening a trap as he was at being a husband.

"Little more," Bugler grunted. "I see daylight."

"I'm straining my milk."

The lion whipped at Fassman's back with its tail. It seemed like a caress. It averted its flattened head. In profile it looked even smaller—a pointed narrow face, not much bigger than some of the cats that had roamed the alleys of the Bronx.

"Bend, Alan. Give us more."

"The skin's coming off my hands."

"*Unh . . . unh . . .* almost there. Now if she'll start moving the paw."

They braced their legs against the rocks and again on the count of three, pressed their weight against the jaws. This time Bugler got to both knees. His pepper-and-salt head almost nestled against the cat's flank.

"Ah, it's giving. Unh . . . *unh* . . . lean on it, Alan."

"I'm leaning."

"Open."

Fassman, feeling his heart turn to flame, his arms trembling with the exertion, glanced at the trap. It was almost an inch apart. Then two inches. The lion, if it were willing to squeeze its mutilated paw, could work itself free. But it seemed confused.

Bugler reached behind him with one free hand, keeping the rest of his weight on the bar, and found a flat red rock. He wedged it into the aperture between the metal semicircles. "Now we can operate," he said. "Alan, stand back. I'm letting her go. The rock'll keep the jaws apart."

"Androcles," Fassman gasped, "Daniel."

"Watch it. She may decide to get up. Odds are she'll run away or climb a tree."

Before Fassman knew what had happened, Bugler grabbed at the lion's leg and yanked it upward. The hexagonal head snapped at his hand, but he pulled away. Fassman slid down the ledge. He was convinced he would die.

The cougar's paw was free. Bloodied, swollen, maggoty, it was a black-purple lump. But it was free. With curious daintiness, the lion raised the infected foot and began to lick it.

"Like a tabby," Bugler said.

The two men stood twenty feet away, looking in wonder and gratitude at the liberated cat.

"Free, by golly," Bugler said. His chest was heaving.

"You did it. Now I know a man who freed a lion from a trap with his bare hands. From now on, you're Androcles."

Bugler moved forward a few steps. "Maybe you'll have your cubs, hey? Name one for Ed. And one for Alan."

The lion ignored him. Its tongue worked on the wounded paw, licking up dried blood, maggots, bits of flesh, smoothing, soothing, cleaning the gouge that the trap had inflicted.

"Glad we got to her," Bugler said. "They'll chew clear to the bone."

"Why doesn't she get up and take off?"

"Weak."

Fassman thought of Don Quixote's circus lion. Challenged by the Knight of the Mournful Countenance, it turned on its side and farted.

"Starving," Ed said. "Animals become morose. They give up.

– 127 –

Come on, puss. Give it a try. You can limp around. If you can't hunt, eat berries or roots."

"She doesn't have the strength. I don't feel like offering myself as a CARE package."

"We'll get some chow."

"How? Where?"

"There's a general store about a half hour away, other side of Fort Kachina."

"You think she'll wait for us?"

Bugler rubbed his chin. "If she's gone, it means she got her strength back and wandered off. If not, we'll bring her a meal."

"A third possibility."

"What?"

"Somebody came back and killed it," Fassman said.

"Maybe. Let's go. We can be back in little more than an hour."

Host read slowly. At first he was annoyed by Vormund's naïve notion that man must learn to love the nonhuman world or perish. It seemed a supreme arrogance. People who spent too much time in universities tended to nourish high-minded panaceas. They could not be made to understand that greed ruled the world. Getting and spending was *all*. Nature existed to be used, turned into measurable wealth. It was not just the Hosts, father and son, who believed thus, but damned near everybody in the world.

"He's deceiving himself," Host said to Corinne.

"Who?" Showered, her tan flesh glistening, she rested on the maple bed. Her hair formed a golden corona around her face. She glanced at him from time to time.

"Daniel Dean Vormund. He expects too much. If he ever had to run a construction site, or meet a payroll, or haggle with the government over specifications, he'd sing another tune."

"*Meet a payroll!* You sound like a Republican candidate before 1929."

"He's got good ideas, but they won't take. Listen to this. 'Laws, education, public programs in health, medicine, and housing, all these well-intentioned notions which are presumed to improve the state of man are doomed. They never accomplish what they set out to. Something is lacking. And that lack renders them powerless even as they are enacted. What is lacking is *love.*'"

"He sounds like a revivalist. A Maharishi or something. Love me, love you, love God."

"That's not what he means. 'I speak of the love for the natural community of land, rocks, rivers, earth, plants, and animals. We are part of that natural community. We must learn to love it and protect it, or we shall keep failing. No amount of low-cost housing, no free-trade program, no computers, no new concept in mass education can succeed, without this acknowledgment of the natural world. To live on this earth in good health, in a vigorous mental state, we must live with it. It cannot be endlessly exploited. In the long run, it is ourselves we exploit.'"

"He says it well," Corinne said. She turned to face him. Her hips and thighs formed a rising rounded curve. Was there an equation that would produce a graph in terms of x and y for such a curve? Probably not. Host wondered, could this be part of Vormund's analysis? No amount of mathematics wizardry could produce such an equation, plot such a line?

Host said: "We're as concerned as he is about education and housing and what he calls good public works. But if he thinks nature trips for blacks or bird watching for Chicanos is going to elevate them, he's more of an innocent than I imagine. I tell you what Vormund is. He's the oldest kind of conservative there is. He thinks that by getting people to love nature, they'll improve. Tell that to a ghetto kid on dope. Or a housewife with a leaky roof."

"Maybe he means the leaders of society have to think differently. Maybe Host-Labarre should set an example."

"If he does, he's even wronger."

"Denkerman agreed with him. Maybe that's what this comes down to. Cousin Otto saw something in Vormund. You and Pop, you want it all. More homes. More parking lots. Ray, it's a classic struggle."

"I don't think so. Everything's going for us. He's a dying species. I respect him. But he's licked."

"Then why doesn't he quit?"

"Eccentrics go on. But he should realize he's in the path of progress. There's nothing we can't do."

The telephone rang. Corinne lifted it and heard the cheerful tunes of James W. Host's secretary, Miss Vessels. She chatted briefly with her, then gave the phone to Ray.

Host put *Desert Idyll* down, almost with relief. It was easy to dismiss Vormund as a naïve dreamer, a man whose mission was doomed. Yet his gloomy prophesies seemed to hold germs of truth. When water holes for frogs vanished, who was to say that in a hundred years faucets would run dry?

"What have you learned?" James W. Host asked. He whispered on telephones.

"Not much, Pop."

"What kind of people are they?"

"They seem to be legitimate. We managed to play tennis with Maybank, the director of the Institute."

"How did that come about?" On guard at all times, a private person—ah, the headwaiters and salesmen who had learned how private he was!—Host did not trust quick friendships.

"Corinne and I went to the club and we were matched with them. They're not people who'd be involved in a confidence racket. I can't see the Maybanks hustling millionaires."

The whisper again. "What sort are they?"

"Inherited money. He's a biologist, and she sort of helps out."

"Did you get to the Institute? Are they what they claim to be?"

"It's a dump. How they'll ever spend fifteen million dollars, I can't imagine. The land is good. It's a wonder it hasn't been bought and developed. I'm sure there have been bids for it."

"Land hoarders. Don't be deceived by appearances, Raymond. They're sitting on that land, waiting for a killing. The Denkerman money will make them even more difficult to deal with."

On naked feet, Corinne walked into the bathroom. Gently, she took the phone from the hook and listened.

"I'm not sure I agree, Pop," Ray said. "The Maybanks aren't thieves. They didn't impress me as crafty."

"Then they are a front."

"I doubt it."

In the bathroom, Corinne shook her head. James W. Host at his insistent best.

"This Denkerman thing does not make sense. To me or anyone I've talked to. The lawyers tell me Denkerman was crazy as a loon—"

"That's not what they said a few days ago," Ray said.

A pause. James W. Host was trying to recall. He had a curious habit of discarding what he did not care to remember. But it was unusual for Raymond to contradict him. "Did they?"

"That's right. You told me so yourself. Denkerman's lawyers would swear to it. Pop, when you're that rich, crazy means eccentric, that's all."

There was a longer pause. "Raymond, that is your money. You are the legal heir through your mother."

Ray sighed. He could hear Corinne mocking him in the john. She was suffocating her giggles.

"Raymond? Is someone on the line?"

"No, just me."

"I cannot believe that a man as wealthy as Denkerman would lavish that sum on people he did not know. I'm not alone. There will be relatives and associates far less deserving than you who will make claims. And every conservation group, all the fools fighting progress—"

"It isn't always progress."

"You're joking. It is inevitable progress."

Corinne placed the phone to its cradle alongside the marble toilet and walked into the bedroom. She applauded noiselessly. "Give it to him, Ray," she said *sotto voce*. "Quote Vormund."

"Pop, some people disagree with you. It's not always progress and it sure as hell isn't inevitable."

"You sound like one of them."

"I didn't say I agree with them. But not everybody appreciates the way we screw up the desert."

"When you see fifteen million dollars in your own name, ready for investment, expansion, the creation of jobs and homes, you'll change your tune. You get that inheritance, Ray, and I'll give you your own subsidiary."

"I appreciate that, Pop. But I think this is a wild-goose chase."

"Money like that can't be allowed to lie fallow. If that Institute is as shabby as you say, the money will go down the drain."

Ray Host hesitated. Corinne was right. He was no good at this kind of thing.

"How long am I to stay here?"

"I would keep it an open-end arrangement. Don't breathe a word to anyone. Try a little harder. Talk to the bankers. They'll give you a line on these people. Don't talk to anyone from the media. Clear?"

"Yes, Pop." He moved his body toward Corinne. She was stretched out again—lithe, undulant, a composition of soft pink and tan curves, a form of unitary magnificence. Host craved her. Relief. Surcease. For all of Host's physical hardness, he tired easily, lost interest, did not finish things. The old man knew it. And he had sworn to break him of bad habits.

"What about this Vormund?" Host asked.

"What about him?"

"Have you seen him?"

Ray shook his head, glancing at Corinne, as if to plead for help. "We're meeting him tomorrow. The Maybanks invited us to lunch. Vormund is supposed to be there."

A hoarse croaking—James W. Host's substitute for laughter—clotted Ray's ear. "That was very good of you to arrange that."

"It was a break. I said I was interested in their work."

"I am convinced Vormund had secret dealings with Denkerman. Something is being hidden. To leave that sum of money for some articles about birds and lizards? Impossible. Listen to me, Raymond. I had investigators check on Vormund. The man flirted with radical movements in the thirties. He was on the board of left-wing publications. I don't know that he can be trusted. But people like that are naïve—"

"He's also eighty-one years old. He couldn't have been capable of concocting a plot to steal an inheritance."

"*Your* inheritance."

"All right. I'll talk to him." Ray paused. "Maybe this thing should be turned over to investigators, Pop. You know how I feel about these matters."

"You know how *I* feel. We are not an organization that goes around spying, snooping, wire-tapping. That has never been our way."

"Then why now?"

"Because it is your money. I want you to take the credit for breaking that will. I want you to be able to say you went out and fought for what was yours. Am I being unfair?"

"No. I'll know more tomorrow. I'll get a better look at the place. I'll talk to Vormund and the others."

"If they mention the bequest, you will, of course, profess ignorance of Mr. Denkerman."

"Do I know he's dead?"

"Yes. It was in the papers. Give my love to Corinne. Good-by, Raymond."

Host, in one continuous move, returned the phone to the hook and reached out for Corinne. "Baby," she said. "My Raymond. I hate his guts, Raymond."

"He loves me too much. He should have had four sons."

They kissed like adulterous lovers.

"Photographs got you in trouble once," Fassman said.

"We're supposed to get in trouble. Dan says it's about time."

Bugler and the newsman were speeding back to Grace Canyon in the jeep. At the general store, Bugler discovered they carried no meats or pet food. He settled for two dozen tins of corned beef, which he had the owner open. They dumped the contents into a plastic bag. Vigorous flies buzzed around the bag, taking nips at Fassman's neck and ears.

"Didn't you say the ranchers raised hell after the coyote pictures?"

"Yes, but that can't stop us. It's one of those fights you keep fighting."

Bugler had taken a roll of film of the lion in the leg-hold trap.

"You think that corned beef will revive her?"

"I hope so. After what that poor cat went through."

In the brilliant sky, Fassman again saw the monoplane. It looked small and frail, like the balsa wood models he made as a boy. He had won third prize in the Fordham Road Woolworth's Model Plane Contest. He had built a De Havilland Gypsy Moth.

They parked the car at the foot of the trail and climbed through stands of juniper and pine to McGregor's grave. It was midafternoon. The sun was hot and bright, but the mountain breeze made Fassman shiver. The colors were too intense—browns and reds and greens and blues, mosaics more inspiring than the masterpieces of Ravenna. No wonder Vormund had abandoned art for these wild places.

"McGregor hasn't moved," Fassman wheezed.

"The funeral director's sign neither. Wonder if the morticians ever got any business because of that ad."

Fassman followed Bugler's figure, always a step or two behind the gray work suit, the desert boots, the bobbing pepper-and-salt head. How little Ed needed! How satisfied he seemed with his brotherhood with animals and plants!

"She's gone," Bugler said.

"The lion . . ."

"What I was afraid of."

"How can you tell?" They were still a hundred feet from the ledge. Fassman could see the links and brush hooks tangled in the junipers.

"I can't smell her."

"You must be kidding."

"Lions have that ammonia stink. It's gone."

They clambered up the escarpment to the shelf of red rock on which the lion had waited to die.

"Good or bad?" Fassman asked.

"Good, I guess. I hope she's strong enough to catch something. She'll eat grass and leaves if she has to. The corned beef would have helped."

"Why not leave it for her?"

"Yeah." Bugler looked down at the fallen trees, the buried traps. "But not here. At the creek."

Fassman staggered behind Bugler to the stream. The naturalist found a sandy cove where the swift cold waters formed an eddy. It was a natural drinking area. He dumped the pink processed meat on a rock.

"It won't go to waste," Bugler said. "The raccoons or the coyotes will get it if she doesn't."

"A shame we can't see her again."

"I hope she's learned her lesson and stays away from scrape marks." He sounded morose, a teacher giving up on a student who refused to read.

"What now?" Fassman asked. He felt as if he wanted to spend hours in a hot bath, sleep for a week.

"Home."

"But . . . what next . . . about the traps?"

"I'll make out a report to Maybank. Maybe I'll ask Dan to do a piece for the newsletter with the photographs."

They walked past the grave, descended the narrow trail,

emerged to the plateau. The jeep sat in isolation amid the soaring red walls.

"See those two pillars?" Bugler asked. He pointed to two redstone pinnacles. "The Hualapai Indians say they're a chief and his wife."

"Turned to stone?"

"Yep. The people were ordered out because a flood was coming. But the chief and his squaw turned around for a look and they turned into a pair of pillars. Dan says it's not an Indian legend at all. The missionaries doused them in the Old Testament. It's probably a Hualapai version of Lot's wife."

The monoplane rose from the other side of Grace Canyon and began to descend. It flew over the "chief and his wife," equidistant between the gargoylelike rocks.

"He's low," Fassman said. "Who is he?"

"Lots of the ranchers keep planes."

"Jesus Christ, Ed." Fassman felt an old street fear in his bowels. Before the blow lands. As the rock is hurled. "He's coming at us, the crazy bastard. He's trying to land."

"He can't. Not in these rocks."

The snout of the plane grew larger, expanding in their field of vision like a spreading stain. They could see sunlight sparkling on the Plexiglas windshield. It was a propellor-driven plane with a long upper wing and supporting struts. The propellor spun—a whirring silvery circle. It was a small white plane decorated with dark blue stripes.

"Under the jeep," Bugler said. "He won't crash. He's trying to scare us." He loped ahead.

Fassman galumphed after Bugler. They crouched against the metal flank of the jeep.

Little puffs of sand arose in a ragged line, not twenty yards from the vehicle. The noises were faint, unmistakable. *Pop-pop. Pop-pop.*

"Ed, Jesus Christ. He's shooting at us."

"Not to hurt us. Scare us."

"Does it matter?"

"I think so."

The plane circled, dipped its long wing—Fassman saw his De Havilland Gypsy Moth, frail and shabby in the Woolworth window—and gained altitude.

"He was watching us," Fassman said.

"Probably saw the lion limping off. Maybe he shot her in the canyon. Or down at the stream."

Fassman climbed into the jeep. Harder and harder. Or was it pointless, useless, a battle that could not be won?

They saw the plane moving around them in widening circles. It seemed to be a warning. *I see you. I know you're there.* Fassman's mind, full of movie clutter, thought of Cary Grant in a Hitchcock film, pursued by a machine-gunning crop-duster. Or an old Marx Brothers routine. Chico and Groucho in a leaky rowboat that lands them on a naval gunnery target. Chico to Groucho: *Boss, I think they're shooting at you.*

"That guy," Fassman gulped. He struggled to locate his strangled voice. "That guy wasn't trying to kill us, was he?"

"Oh no. They stop at that." Bugler did not seem perturbed. He sounded like a man accustomed to being shot at. Or was it his kinship with beasts that made him accept the role of vermin? "You meet these fellows, they're the nicest people in the world. But the predator issue is driving them loony."

"Why?"

"You'd need Dan to explain it. I'm no philosopher. It's just they have to kill anything that doesn't look like them."

Clara dropped her husband at the Desert Research Institute with her usual warning. "Dan, you keep your hat on. This is the hottest day of the year. I don't want you getting too much sun."

"There is no such thing as too much sun. Too much sex, probably. Too much food, certainly. But I have never had enough sun."

Jenny Maybank came out of the office and took his arm. "Inside, Professor. Clara, you go on your errands. He's in good hands."

"I don't want him wandering off into the hills to look for some beetle or butterfly. He gets woozy and he doesn't know when to stop."

"He won't wander today. There's a beautiful girl coming to lunch. He can be the old roué for a few hours. I'll have Ed or that reporter drive him back."

"Reporter?" Vormund asked. "My former student, Fassman?"

"He's still looking for a story and he may have one. Wait till you hear! Ed freed a lion from a steel trap. And someone shot at them from a plane."

Vormund grimaced. Clara shook her head. "Did you tell the police?" she asked.

"Jack's hesitant. Ed was trespassing. And the rancher would claim the lion was killing stock. The authorities always believe them." She changed the subject. It was painful to keep talking of defeats. "Dan, let me show you how beautifully the creeping devil took to our garden. And Ed has some new snakes. One of them is your favorite—the rattlesnake with no rattles, the kind they find in Baja."

Clara kissed his cheek. "Don't get overstimulated."

"I'll try. A beautiful girl? Who is the ravisher? And was she brought here for my benefit? Clara, stop frowning. A modest orgy would be good for me. Old age hath yet its honor and its toil. Good-by, my love."

She walked off, forever worried that if she left him alone for ten minutes he would catch cold, stub a toe, aggravate his hernia.

Jenny led him toward the Institute. "A lady named Mrs. Host from Los Angeles," she said. "The construction people. Jack and I met them at the tennis club. Mr. Host said he was interested in our work and wanted to meet you. Very, very rich and social."

"I trust Jack will hint at our need for funds? I won't mind doing it. Let the fellow write a few checks before he leaves. If it will help, I'll recite Cardinal Wolsey's soliloquy. 'A long farewell, to all my greatness . . .'"

Vormund stared into the sunlight reflected on the hills beyond the buildings. Weather in the desert was always good, beneficent. Sun gave life, rain brought flowers, snow beauty. But rain or snow in the city meant clogged drains and garbage.

In the courtyard, under the ramada, Jenny had set a cold buffet—egg salad, sliced ham, bean salad, iced tea. Ed was there, talking to Jack Maybank (Jack looking hesitant as usual). Alan Fassman was listening, arms folded.

Jenny guided Vormund to the head of the table.

"Another reward for senility. I insist that the beauteous Mrs. Host be seated next to me. With Clara away, I may even play a bit of footsie."

Joe Fusaro came out of the office, greeted Vormund, and summoned Maybank. It seemed to Jenny they were on the phone incessantly. The Denkerman matter was taking all their time. Fusaro did his best, but he was hinting at the need for legal help. Word was out. There was a fortune available. Animal lovers were making claims. A woman who ran a cat shelter in Burbank was filing suit. She had a letter from the deceased praising her kindness. A man in Arcadia who ministered to injured birds had made inquiries, as had a veterinarian in Sherman Oaks.

Bobcat Buster rubbed against Vormund's calves, then climbed into his lap. Claws sheathed, tail twitching, it touched his cheek with a soft paw, demanding attention. Vormund tickled its ears. He could not resist animals. Years ago, he had been a guest on the "Today" program, after winning a literary prize. He had spent the morning talking to the chimpanzee.

Bugler and Fassman joined him. Ed told Vormund about the lion, the trap, the airplane.

"The darn thing looked like a toy," Fassman said. "An old-fashioned monoplane. But those bullets were real."

"I'm not surprised," said Vormund. "You were at the mercy of machines, like the lion."

"Dan loses me every now and then," Bugler said.

Fassman also looked confused.

"The machine, rather than man, is the measure of things. It's not an original notion with me. Emerson said it. 'Things are in the saddle and ride men hard.' Thoreau wrote about the tragic accident when the train took off to go nowhere."

"What has that got to do with killing animals?" Fassman asked.

"Wild animals refuse to acknowledge machines. A cow will go to the slaughterhouse. A sheep can be shorn with an electric tool. A dog will learn to ring a bell or get out of the way of a car. But a lion or a bear or a coyote is an affront to the new religion. It is not that they eat an occasional lamb. It is that they live, breed, and know joy with no need for machines. So they must be exterminated. Indeed for their own good."

"Would your theory explain Vietnam?" Fassman asked. "Primitives, poor people, reject machines also."

"I don't want to force the analogy. I imagine that primitive people are viewed as a variety of heretic. They get along without machines, so they must be put to the torch. The more complex a society gets, the more it demands sacrifice. The ancient Hebrews are supposed to have ended human sacrifice with Abraham. But they kept piling up eviscerated chickens and lambs. Today, we make hecatombs of coyotes and eagles. We murder the land itself. Mountains, rivers, desert—all sacrificed, disemboweled, by the gods of electricity, power, and so-called progress."

Fassman was watching the thin features, the sharp eyes, with a sense of loss. He should have brought the camera crew and let Vormund speak his mind.

"That's enough preachifying," Vormund said. "If there's a beautiful lady arriving, I'd best be gay and charming."

A couple in immaculate white tennis clothing was approaching. Jenny was leading them toward the ramada. Fassman had heard the Maybanks talking about them. He could smell California money. Eager, enlightened, educated types who wanted to meet the desert sage.

Vormund rose as they approached. His manner, Fassman observed, was southern courtly, but without the molasses accent. Kentuckians were a plainer breed. Vormund held the straw sombrero over his chest and greeted the Hosts as if he were the master of a plantation.

"Our apologies for coming all sweaty from tennis," Corinne said. "Ray had some fabulous singles with the pro."

Fassman pegged him: a lord of the earth. Wealth, strength, skill, and a wife who appeared to be edible, a hot quiche lorraine on legs.

Jenny made the introductions. The Hosts smiled at Vormund and nodded at Fassman.

"Ray did some homework," Corinne said brightly. "He was up most of last night reading *Desert Idyll.*"

"Was it sufficiently soporific?" Vormund asked.

"Not at all. My wife is right. It did keep me awake."

"I'm flattered. That's a great deal more homework than I ever seemed to get out of my students." Vormund looked at Fassman, who remained outside the ramada, hesitant in front of the golden Hosts. "I shouldn't say that. One of them is here."

Ray and Corinne Host seemed momentarily disoriented. They glanced at Fassman's ungainly figure. He had been introduced as a newsman from Los Angeles but now . . . ? It seemed to Fassman that in the protective shell of their limitless wealth, their youth, their beauty, they wanted the outside world to be categorized, graspable. But a newsman . . . and a former student?

"That's right," Fassman said. "Elizabethan Drama and Comparative Literature. That was at Columbia. A long time ago."

"How nice," Corinne said.

"He gave me an A in both courses."

"Which tells you nothing of his intellectual attainments," Vormund said. "I gave everyone except learning disabled football players an A."

"Are you . . ." Host struggled. "Are you here on a story? Or a visit for old time's sake?"

"A little of both."

They had made their analysis of him and decided he could be dismissed. They had come to pay homage to the philosopher, but a disciple could be ignored. The Hosts had seen rather quickly, Fassman realized, that he was of modest means, ill-favored, and that his speech betrayed a suspect New York origin.

"Actually I'm doing a survey," Fassman tried.

"Survey?" Corinne asked. Her voice was edged with contempt. "Where are your instruments?"

"Not that kind. For a TV story on conservation." With hierarchs like the Hosts Fassman had learned to be neutral and noncommittal.

"Alan seems to think," Vormund said, "that in my dotage I have hidden stories of wisdom to impart to people who would rather be watching 'I Love Lucy.' I've persuaded him otherwise."

At Jenny's urging, Corinne Host sat down next to the old man. She seemed revived, talkative. She had pegged them all—the Maybanks who had licked them at tennis, the mannerly ancient, the clumsy reporter, and the desert rat Bugler lingering at the edges. She squeezed Vormund's hand. His eyebrows arched. That was more like it.

"I think it would be fascinating to hear you interviewed," she said. And squeezed again.

"Do it again, my dear," Vormund said. "Or as Dr. Johnson told the actress, who at Garrick's urging had sat on his lap and kissed him, 'Once more, my sweet, and let us see who tires first.'"

"That's precious," Corinne said. "That's what I *mean*. I looked at the books you've written and I realized I'd read some when I was an English major at Pomona. I know we had to read the one on Fielding."

"Evidence of the good judgment of Pomona's English Department." Vormund was exuding charm. "I hope I won't offend you but I just thought of another Johnsonian comment regarding beautiful women."

"I'd love to hear it," she said.

"Garrick kept egging his bosomy beauties on the old man, until Johnson refused to come backstage any more. Davey, he said, the silk stockings and white boobies of your actresses arouse me too much. I've always liked that. *Boobies*."

Bugler, sidling up to Fassman, whispered behind his hand: "Dan's off the reservation. He wouldn't pull that stuff if Clara was around."

"Maybe that's why she didn't come to lunch."

"Maybe." Bugler retreated a few steps. Fassman followed. "Something's fishy. Those two were here yesterday in that big Lincoln. The man said he was lost. Now they're back."

"Californians are like that," Fassman whispered. "They probably want to buy the place."

"What shall it be?" Jenny asked. "Lunch or the two-dollar tour?"

Host had become silent, glancing at Vormund, seemingly unable to manage conversation. He was glad Corinne was at home in literature, could find common ground with him. "I'm not hungry," he said. "I'd love to see the animals."

"Ed," Jenny called. "Take over. You all know Mr. Bugler, our curator."

"Yes, indeed." Ed bowed stiffly. "We met the other day, when you were lost out here."

"Of course," Raymond Host said. "You helped us get back to town."

"I apologize that my husband can't show you the place," Jenny said, "but he seems to be on the phone all the time."

"Are the photographs still giving him trouble?" Vormund asked. "Refer some of the complaints to me."

Jenny hesitated. Sooner or later Dan would have to be told about the windfall. "Routine stuff. I should help him, but I'm a rotten secretary."

Ray Host's ruddy face was listening intently. He could guess what was keeping Maybank busy. They would need more than secretaries to handle imminent problems. Pop would see to that.

"Tour starts in the cactus garden," Bugler said. "We've got the best specimens in the state. Chollas, barrel, five kinds of prickly pear, saguaro, senita, organ pipe, fishhook, beaver tails—"

"I love to hear Ed when he gets going," Vormund laughed. "He sounds like my uncle who was a conductor on the Central of Kentucky."

Fassman looked at the Hosts' white-and-tan figures. They were spotless, perfectly formed, loaded with California sun, food, and vitamins. Yet they seemed intrusive in Bugler's garden, like statuary, decorations. In their earth-colored, dusty clothing, Jenny and Ed appeared more at home amid the gray-green succulents.

Fassman and Vormund did not join the tour. But they could hear Ed's voice.

"Ever been to Baja California?"

"We fly in," Corinne said.

"Ever see a boojum tree?" Ed asked. "Mexicans called them the *cirios*. That's one right there."

The Hosts did not seem impressed by the yard-high carrotlike growth covered with thorns and with a ridiculous tassel at its top. Vormund had gone into ecstasies over the strange plant.

"And next to it a creeping devil," Ed said. "That's the one we found the other day. No one believed they grew anywhere in Arizona. Dan says it's a botanical mystery."

Ray Host's square head was noncommittal. He had no way of responding to Bugler's enthusiasms about desert plants. "I really enjoyed his book. But almost too many ideas at once."

"Dan is like that," Bugler said. "It takes a little while to follow him. But what he's preaching is basic stuff. Let the land alone. Keep it wild."

The implacable sun was bothering Corinne. She was ravenously hungry. She needed something stronger than the iced tea she had seen on the redwood table. Could she hint to the Maybank woman that she craved a cold beer? Or a vodka tonic?

Bugler was talking about the destruction of natural cover, and how it would lower the water table. Soon it would be so low as to make drilling prohibitive.

"What happens then?" Host asked.

"You fellows may have to go easy on the building. You may

have to give the place back to Sidewinder's relatives. They use less water."

For the first time Host smiled. "We'll find a way."

"Dan says there's no such thing as a permanent victory over nature," Bugler said. "You keep breaking the chain of life, and after a while it won't support life. Yours or a lizard's."

Host nodded grudgingly. "I gathered that from his book. He's a pessimist, isn't he?"

"I suppose so."

Bugler knelt in front of the raccoon cages and fed bits of dried dog food to them. They took the food with cunning hands. The furry spectacles made them look like greedy schoolboys.

"Maybe we're intruding here," Corinne said. "I gathered that he doesn't encourage callers."

Bugler smiled up at her as the raccoons grabbed at his sleeve. "Dan likes good-looking women. The Indian girls at Supai were crazy about Dan. He treated them like ladies."

"I'm flattered."

"Don't be. When you get down to basics, Dan dislikes most people. He figures it's just as easy to be civil as it is to be nasty. He's kind of written off the human race."

Host's voice was blurry. "And he's a conservationist? He's the one who criticizes us for building homes and highways and supermarkets?"

"Dan doesn't turn up his nose at all progress. His wife talked him into an air-conditioned car. But he says it's got to stop somewhere."

Fassman watched them wander off—Bugler, Jenny, the young couple—into the aviary. Ed would surely show them his precious masked bobwhites.

The newsman walked up to Sidewinder. The Hopi was studying a pile of dead cacti. For what? Fassman wondered. An omen?

"Listen, Sidewinder," the newsman said. "I'm on your side, you know. I helped Ed with the lion."

"Sure."

"Maybe I could do a story on your people up north. Your customs. The fight to survive. Do you still have any of the old folkways? If I brought a camera, would you be willing to stage a war dance for me?"

The black eyes, distorted as if underwater, stared at Fassman. "Sure. If you tie a white man to a stake."

"Start thinking of ways to spend fifteen million dollars," Fusaro said. He was standing in Maybank's office, cradling the phone. Maybank was looking across the court at Vormund's solitary figure.

"Why so fast?"

"The nuts are after your money. Mr. Fair says we'd better be ready to defend our program."

Maybank closed his eyes and whistled. He and Jenny had been raised to ignore money. People of quality did not need it, hence they did not discuss it. Now they would wallow in it. Maybank thought of the appeals to rich friends, the fund-raising dinners, the teachers who ran scrap drives and car washes.

Fusaro hung up. "Everyone wants to see the will. Fair says the word in the legal community is that Denkerman did this to screw some relatives he hated, and that he wasn't that queer for road runners. You and Bugler and Dan better have some terrific programs for saving our feathered friends, such as the coppery-throated Trojan."

"Trogon, Joe, trogon. It's a coppery-tailed trogon."

Fusaro frowned. "I don't want you and the Institute euchred out of the money. I'm a Prince Street ginzo and my idea of wildlife is an Irishman from South Boston. But I believe in what you and Dan are doing. Otherwise you wouldn't get free legal services from me. But you'd better move. A year's worth of projects. Five years. You need buildings. Start thinking of buying land. How about that place where Bugler found those creeping things? Jack, the days are gone when you and Jenny could run this dump as if it were a hobby for you and your friends, or a place for Vormund to come afternoons and shmoos."

"I think we're more than that."

"Shape up, Jack," Fusaro said. "I've heard you moan about paying bills for fencing." The lawyer looked out the window and saw Vormund. The newsman—what the hell was he after?—was talking to him. "It's not enough to have D. D. Vormund around as resident sage. Or Ed Bugler wandering into canyons. You need a *program*."

"I'll sit down with Jen tonight and see how we can spend a

million a year. It shouldn't be too hard. We could buy Bugler another pair of pants from Sears."

"You'll have to do better than that. The executors will demand it, if only to save you from the clowns who want Denkerman's money."

"I'll try."

"When there's money like that lying around, it draws flies. I wouldn't be surprised if some of those relatives put private eyes on us."

"A magnificent-looking woman," Vormund said.

Fassman had joined him under the ramada. The Hosts were still touring the Institute. The newsman wondered what they would think of the shabby buildings, the forlorn cages. They did not seem to be people who could be awed. But perhaps their hearts were pure. Conservation was enjoying a vogue among rich Californians. Save the redwoods, revive the sea otters.

"In the tradition of the great American girl," Fassman said. "She has everything."

"La Fanciulla del West," Vormund said. In a cracked voice he hummed a few bars of Puccini.

"You never sang in class," Fassman said.

"I'm not sure I'm singing now. Alan, study the line from that young woman's neck to her ankle. There's nature for you. No machine could mill such a beauty."

"She reminds me of a James T. Farrell title. A World I Never Made."

"Ah, Farrell. I liked him." Vormund paused. "Is it proper for the two of us to stare at Mrs. Host so boldly?"

"It's harmless." He wanted to tell Vormund about his lost Wendi, his sons, the house in Westwood Village. Instead he reminisced. "I once knew a beautiful Barnard girl. Sort of a Jewish version of Mrs. Host. For three years I dated her, wrote love letters, phoned her. It dawned on me she had never once phoned me or written to me. Finally, a week before I graduated, she called. It was to tell me she was engaged to a crewman from Zeta Beta Tau at Penn."

"You seem to have survived."

"In a manner of speaking."

Outside the bird cages, Bugler was holding a hawk in one

hand and letting it beat its wings for the amusement of the Hosts. Fassman thought they looked interested.

"So you were shot at," Vormund said. "That was quite an adventure you and Ed had."

"Ed insists they didn't want to hit us, just scare us."

"Did they succeed?"

"I think so."

Vormund coughed. "I've often wondered how it feels to kill someone, or accept the notion of violent death. My parents were River Brethren, a peaceful sect. We could not fight or show anger. I was frail, bespectacled, and timid, and so I suffered innumerable drubbings. It was no great pleasure growing up. How splendid it was to attend the University of Kentucky, where I could read all day and never have to flex a muscle."

"If it's any consolation, Professor Vormund, I couldn't fight either. I took my lumps."

"But maybe we've missed part of life. Hitting and being hit. Tasting one's blood in one's mouth. Spitting out a tooth. The moment when one pulls a trigger and sees a living creature fall, bleed, die." He shook his head. "I always detested Hemingway not so much for his compulsion to shoot and kill, but for the *joy* he found in watching beasts die in agony. That description of the hyena eating its own guts . . ."

Fassman crossed his legs and squinted into the burning desert. The Hosts, Ed, and Jenny were approaching. "Why should it surprise you? You've been fighting it in your books for years."

"Is man truly a killer and torturer? I hate to think so. I had a student, before your time, a chubby Italian boy named Errico. One of Mr. Little's athletes. He became a marine officer, went off and killed scores of Japanese, came back to graduate school with a chestful of medals. He hadn't changed a bit—soft-eyed, rather sad. He said his experiences had not affected him one way or the other." Vormund tapped the table. "I rather envied him."

"Chow down," Jenny said. She sat the Hosts on either side of Vormund. Fassman rose to help Corinne over the redwood bench. His hand was sweaty and soft as he took her arm. Was he trembling? He feared that his weak Semitic mitt might leave a stain on such choice flesh. A line from Sandburg skittered through his head. *And the girls were golden girls. . . .*

Jenny sat next to Ray Host and began to pass the warmish

salads, tostadas, and tea. She shouted to the office: "Maybank! Our guests are waiting to hear how you saved the elegant tern from extinction!"

Host turned his head toward Vormund. "I can't tell when Mrs. Maybank is joking. Didn't I read that you did save some birds?"

" 'Twas a famous victory," Vormund replied. "Mr. Bugler and Jack and I tented on Cazadores Island for three days. Fishermen were egging the birds to death. The terns and gulls had lived on rather good terms for centuries. It was only when man showed up that the balance was tilted. The birds were smart enough to keep their egg-laying a few paces ahead of the egg-eating. But that wasn't good enough for man."

"But it seems such a minor issue," Corinne said. "A few terns more or less. Did you leave no tern unstoned?"

Jenny caught Host's eye. A California country club notion of humor. An old joke.

"Ed did the field work. He proved the loss in population. Jack wrote the report. Then we called on the Mexican equivalent of the Secretary of the Interior, and miraculously, they approved our proposal. Cazadores was declared the first bird sanctuary in Mexico. The terns and gulls are flourishing."

Jenny shoved the last of the warm chicken salad onto Raymond Host's plate. "Dan left out one thing. The Mexican Secretary of the Interior had been a student of Dan's. He didn't care much for birds, but he trotted out a copy of *Restoration Comedy* by D. D. Vormund and asked Dan to inscribe it."

"A charming man, Senõr Ugarte," Vormund said. "I had absolutely no recollection of him. He may have even confused me with Lionel Trilling."

Host was attentive. He understood the story, Fassman could see. The man of quality, Vormund, and the Mexican functionary. Class told.

Maybank and Fusaro emerged from the office.

"Join the party," Jenny shouted. "Bring lawyer Fusaro also."

Vormund, with an old man's sensitivity, suspected a problem. "What's Joe doing out here so much? I get nervous when I see him with that brief case."

"Trivia," Jenny said. "Taxes or something."

"I thought we didn't pay any," Vormund said.

Distracted, Maybank sat at the opposite end of the table. He appeared to have forgotten the Hosts.

"Wake up, Maybank," Jenny said. "Ask Mr. and Mrs. Host if they enjoyed the tour."

"Sorry. I have trouble keeping more than one thing at a time in my head."

"We're impressed by your work here," Host said. He sounded stiff. "Our corporation tries to do right by the environment when we can. We have a program to preserve natural settings. . . ."

The words, Fassman noted, were clogging the young man's hard palate. Millions on top of millions did not seem to render him articulate.

Corinne tapped her ring against the iced-tea glass. "Ray is saying that within Host-Labarre's means, they try to avoid total destruction of nature. Save a cactus here, a stream there."

Vormund's blue eyes came alive. "Why *limited?* Your corporation has a great deal of power."

"And a soul," Corinne taunted.

Turtlelike, Ray Host appeared to be drawing his head inward.

Bad blood here? Fassman asked himself. The wife was teasing him, holding up his end of the dialogue, and in a way not entirely pleasing to the heir. The woman was not only beautiful and desirable, but had a sharp mind and a wicked tongue. And how was blond, rugged, laconic Raymond in the sack? Fassman, starved for the silk of feminine flesh and the soft breath of love, found it punishing to be seated next to her.

"Soul?" asked Vormund. "But it is a lifeless entity. One of mankind's factitious excellencies, as John Stuart Mill termed religion."

"Get it down to earth, Dan," Jenny said. "You're losing the class."

"But it *is* artificial, a function of machines. What right does it have to a soul, or to wield power over flowers and rabbits?"

Host edged his head forward. "Corinne overstates the case. I attach no mystic importance to Host-Labarre, or General Motors, or the Soviet Ministry of Tractor Production. But they have a role to fulfill."

"Which is?" Jenny asked.

"More goods. More services. More jobs. A better life for people."

"Which people?" asked Vormund.

Host's head went into a peculiar, boxerlike movement, as if ducking away from a left hook. "The majority. If you put these issues to a vote, you'd lose. Homes win out over wolves. Everyone wants more and bigger power plants. Americans will spend ten dollars a gallon for gasoline before they give up on big cars."

"No argument there," Maybank said.

"So the majority prevails," Fassman added.

"The majority may be full of beans," Vormund said. "Majorities have supported the vilest tyrannies in history. Majorities have applauded mass murder, mass torture, lunacies, and arbitrary violence."

"We aren't like that," Host said. "You can't compare middle-income housing to a gas chamber."

Jenny nodded her head at Jack, as if to say, *Not bad, Mr. Host.* The young man was no fool. He was something more than a spoiled son of wealth.

"I concede that," Vormund said. "But for God's sake, why can't the land be left alone, at least the most beautiful parts? Can't we be free of rusting junk piles, slag heaps, rivers that are swamps, poisoned streams? And it is getting worse, not better. Must we level every mountain, chase every lion and bear into hiding, turn the desert into a checkerboard of kennel-like homes?"

"It's the way the world has to go," Corinne said. "We'll be fed by vitamin-enriched algae bubbling in vats, breathe filtered air under a plastic dome, and make love according to a schedule so the population bomb can keep ticking, but never go off."

"That last sounds pretty good," Fassman offered. "I'll volunteer."

Mrs. Host turned her head and studied Fassman's inoffensive face, as if affording him recognition for the first time. She seemed to be awarding him temporary membership (subject to cancellation) in the human race.

Fassman yearned to say something trenchant. Another Farrell title clanked in his head. *When Boyhood Dreams Come True.* The woman's odor was driving him up the nearest adobe wall—musky, oily, sweaty, some kind of perfume sold only in minuscule crystal vials in a Paris boutique. Ah, to eat her whole, skin, flesh, innards, explore the cunning openings, the hairy secrets.

"Would that be your idea of fun?" she asked. "Programmed sex?"

"As the Irishman said about the Vietnam War, it's better than no war at all," Fassman said.

"What does *that* mean?"

Like jesting Pilate, Corrine Host did not wait for an answer. Fassman decided to be quiet from now on. In front of luscious Corinne, he would be a talmudical scholar, pale and aloof. Let her come to his Mea Shearim and he would stone her.

Vormund noticed his ex-student's unease and began to tell a story. A few nights ago, at a small dinner party, the host had offered everyone a Mexican liqueur alleged to be aphrodisiac. "I'm normally temperate," the old man said, "but I sipped the stuff and announced that I didn't feel any more lecherous than usual. To which the hostess replied, 'I suppose that depends on what kind of base you start from.'"

Everyone but Host laughed.

"Mrs. Host, you're quite right," Vormund resumed. "We are moving into a mechanically controlled age. I'm not an intransigent opponent of technology. I like air conditioning, and we do live longer, and our lives are more comfortable. But for how long? Look at our cities and our rivers. We spray villages with DDT. The villagers live longer but will eventually starve, as food runs out."

Host almost smiled. "What would you do, Professor Vormund? Let those people in India and Africa die of disease?"

"I regret their misery," Vormund said. "But if science wants to help them, stop them from breeding. The earth will sustain only so many human mouths. India is a vast toilet. I ask that we stop to catch our breath. Maybe it's time to go backward."

"Progress won't allow it," Host said.

"Then progress is a whore." Vormund stroked Corinne Host's arm. "My apologies, Mrs. Host. Say, this talk is getting grim. Do any of you know the story of King Charles II's carriage careening through London?"

Fassman raised his hand.

"Ah, my ex-student. I'll tell it for the others." He turned to Corinne. Clearly she was the court favorite. "A mob began to stone the royal coach. It was rumored that the occupant was the Duchess of Bedford, one of Charles's mistresses. The Protestant whore!' the mob shouted, 'kill the Protestant whore!' The coach halted, the curtains parted. Nell Gwynne stuck her head out and said, 'Nay, good people, the *Catholic* whore.'"

Corinne Host laughed. She rewarded the old man with a squeeze of his papery hand. That, Fassman thought, should stop the trembling.

Fassman nodded at his old teacher. "The star of the greatest English Lit Department ever assembled. Krutch, Trilling, Weaver, Van Doren, Emmerich, Lyons, Clifford, and D. D. Vormund."

Vormund blinked. A shaft of sunlight pierced a space between the ocotillo wands and crossed his aged face, like a dab of war paint. "It will happen faster than any of us know. The earth will rebel. Despoiled, it will refuse to produce food. We'll be no better than the Pueblo Indians. The water holes dried up, and the earth could not produce beans and squash. But I'm not here to argue with you, Mr. Host. I'm sure you and your colleagues are men of good will. It's always men of good will who give us our biggest headaches. Why is that?"

Jack Maybank said: "Dan is our spiritual guide, so we let him think on the grand scale."

"I'm good at that. That and inspecting wild flowers."

"All we want to do is save the wilderness," Maybank went on. "Like that creeping devil you saw in our garden. There's a forest of them on some rancher's land, and we'd like to buy it. But it's a problem. First, money. Second, the ranchers don't like the precedent."

"Have you asked that fellow Essler?" Vormund interrupted. "Why don't we call the governor? I met the man once and he seemed to like me."

Amazing, Fassman thought. In his old age, Vormund had become something of an operator, a schemer.

"I might be able to help," Host said. "I know a little about land values."

"I bet you do," said Jenny.

Host ignored the hint of rudeness. "I've heard of the Essler holdings. Corinne, didn't Pop do business with him a year or so back?"

Bugler had walked up the ramada and was resting against a pole, holding the bobcat. "I think he may be the guy shot at me from an airplane," Ed said. "Blasted me and Alan when we were looking around Grace Canyon."

Host disregarded him. "I mean it," he said to Maybank. "Show me what you want from Essler and I can tell you what it's worth. There are lots of ways of buying land. If it's too far from town or too far from water, it may not be as expensive as you think." His eyes narrowed behind the wrap-arounds. "I might even get Host-Labarre into the act. These landowners know us and they want our good will."

"I don't know," Maybank said. "We have to be careful, being tax-exempt and so forth."

"Suit yourself. I know I could get you that land at the best price."

Corinne Host was staring at her husband in disbelief. The voice was the buried voice of Raymond Host, but the words were the words of his father, James Wayland Host. Ray was trying to play Pop's game—open poker, all the cards up but one. But what did he want? To infiltrate this ragged group of do-gooders, then expose them as frauds?

"Jack, this young man may be offering us a service. Let's take him up on it." Vormund looked pleased.

"We hate to get people too involved in our business," Jenny said. "The next thing you know you'll be helping Ed Bugler coax raccoons out of trees. We just like donations, not first-aid."

Something was out of whack, Fassman sensed, a general malaise touched off by Host's unexpected offer to show the Maybanks how to buy land, perhaps coffeehouse Mr. Essler out of acreage. The California princess was silent. She had wrapped her golden arms around her breasts and had closed her eyes.

"There are ways of doing this," Host went on. "We have a subsidiary that could make an offer to this man. We might suggest a lease with an option to buy."

Jenny shook her head. "Ray, we can't have Host-Labarre acting as a front for us. It isn't in keeping. We're innocents, and we can't destroy the image."

"Maybe it's about time," Vormund said. "I like the notion of having Mr. Host's organization on our side. What if we're adversaries in the long run? In the short term we can be cynical and cunning, and use his tactics. He doesn't seem to mind."

"Dan, what the devil's gotten into you?" Jenny asked.

"I'm not as pure as you think. Remember I spent a good part of my life scheming around faculty meetings."

"I hate to sound like the town drunk," Corinne said abruptly. "But I could use something stronger than iced tea."

Host coughed into his hand and turned his head away.

"Is there any beer in the refrigerator?" Maybank asked.

"It would help," Corinne said. "I'm parched."

"Ed used to keep some around for his Indian friends," Jenny said. "Do you think . . . ?"

"There's a general store a few miles down the road," Maybank said. "We could send Sidewinder for a six-pack."

Corinne spun her golden head. The mane flicked at Fassman's shoulder. "Albert? It is Albert, isn't it, newsman?"

"Alan."

"Alan, there's a plaid thermos in the front seat of our car. Could you fetch it for me?"

Fassman thought: They assume they can buy and sell the likes of me. And Vormund? Were they also trying to purchase him?

"Sure, Mrs. Host. The car's unlocked?"

"Yes. The way you'll unlock my heart if you bring me the thermos."

"Can it, Corinne," Host said.

"Ray, maybe someone else wants a martini. I may not be the only boozer in the crowd."

"It's my fault," Jenny said. "I should have offered something to drink. But we're all so straight here."

Vormund (the old boy was showing a facet he'd kept hidden at Columbia, Fassman realized) took Corinne's hand. She acted as if she enjoyed it—the Dean of Humanities having a whirl at the Home-coming Queen.

"You aren't a Christian Scientist, are you, my dear?" he asked.

"Ray and I aren't churchgoers. My father-in-law does penance for both of us."

"If you were, you could *imagine* your iced tea is a beer and be happy. Years ago I was giving a lecture at the Young Men's Hebrew Association. As I was about to begin, a man at the rear called out, 'Is there a Christian Scientist in the house?' A woman in the first row stood up and said, yes, she was a reader. The man shouted back, 'Would you mind changing places with me? There's a hell of a draft back here.'"

Fassman exploded in laughter. The Hosts managed belated smiles.

"I still want my drinkie," Corinne said. "Newsman . . . ?"

Fassman plodded through the lot to the Continental. The hot tan leather was like human flesh. Kin to the kissable skin that encased Corinne Host. He imagined her sprawled, half naked, on the rear seat, legs open, the honeycomb beckoning. An orthodox fetishist, Fassman entertained visions of the manner in which the adorable white lace bikini would come off.

"Mrs. Host," he called, "I can't seem to find the thermos."

She came to him across the sandy waste as a vision of all of California, bouncing on Adidas sneakers. Was the taurine husband turning to reprimand her?

"I'm woozy from this goddamn sun," she said, as she approached. "I forgot. It's in the trunk." She jangled her keys at Fassman.

"I'll open it."

"Thanks, newsman. Do you mind if I call you that? You are a newsman, aren't you?"

"I feel more like a newsboy or an errand boy." He fiddled with the lock. The trunk sprang open like the door to Ali Baba's treasure. "Actually I'm a writer. I sometimes produce special shows."

"How exciting."

Golf bags, luggage, rackets, dazzled Fassman's eyes. The price of one golf bag would have fed the Republic of Chad for a year. Fassman found the plaid thermos. Her delicate hands shook as she took it from him. Fassman slammed the trunk down.

As if cued by the mighty *thwatt!* of the trunk, she whispered: "I know a secret."

"I'm a bad person to tell it to. It might show up on the six o'clock news."

"I don't give a shit."

Mrs. Host opened the thermos. She sniffed the liquor with the undiluted joy of an alcoholic. "Full of things that are good, and good for you. Look, I wanted to be a writer also." She poured and drank from a red plastic cup. Gin fumes wafted through Fassman's nostrils and dulled his brain. "I was managing editor of my college papers," she said.

"I think you're marvelous, Mrs. Host. Beautiful, bright, clever.

You are too beautiful for one man alone, as Lorenz Hart once said."

"Want a drinkie?"

His bluff was called. "I'm not much on martinis. At least in parking lots at two in the afternoon."

"Then make yourself useful. Pour. I don't give a damn if my husband is staring at me."

"Mrs. Host, this isn't a tail-gate picnic. It isn't football season, and it's hot as hell."

"Shut up and pour me another."

She knows me, the newsman thought. *A kiss of her nipples. A touch of her buttocks. I would fall into a dead faint.*

The people at the lunch table were avoiding them, apparently out of concern for Host's feelings. Fassman could hear Jenny denouncing the ranchers' association for overgrazing.

"My husband is in Arizona to screw the Desert Research Institute out of fifteen million dollars," Corinne said.

"I beg your pardon?"

"Open your ears. Call your office in Los Angeles and ask them to check the will of a man named Otto Denkerman. That bunch over there, the Maybanks and Vormund, they got it. Fifteen million dollars."

"Fifteen mill—?"

"God, you're some help. Can't drink, can't hear. Isn't this what you people call a *scoop?* Shouldn't you be racing for a phone booth?"

"How do you know?"

"I know." She drained the martini as if it were spring water.

"I don't get it. Your husband is loaded. He's the heir to Host-Labarre."

"Christ, you are dense. Pour me another."

"No." Fassman screwed the red cap to the bottle. He envisioned himself as her kindly psychiatrist, a decent old friend. Never would he know her body. But he would save her. They would live to a dignified old age, performing good works among the Digger Indians. "Now tell me quickly why your husband is after this bequest. I know a little about professional drinkers, and they're usually professional liars."

"He's *related.*"

"Who?"

"Ray. He's some kind of cousin of the late Denkerman. I don't know the details, but all that polite chatter of his, that sudden interest in raccoons, is bullshit. And that overnight infatuation with Mr. Vormund is also bullshit."

"I don't believe you."

"That's why his father sent him here. The Hosts are after fifteen million dollars, and what the Hosts want, they *get*. Give me the thermos."

"No way." He was surprised at his own authority. He grasped her forearm (more muscled than his) and held her away from the car. "Yes, they get what they want. They got you."

"Don't get too friendly. You aren't one of us."

"No, but I have my sacred honor." He threw the thermos in the car and steered her toward the ramada. They arrived to find the guests laughing. The bobcat had dumped a live mouse on the table.

"Scram, Buster," Jenny said. "Take it away."

"No, no," Vormund laughed. "He wants to join the party. He's sharing his lunch with us."

Maybank reached across the table and picked up the purring cat, prey in his mouth, and threw both to the ground.

"You've hurt his feelings," Vormund said.

"He'll get over it. You spoil him, Dan."

"A real wildcat?" Host asked.

"Buster is domesticated," Vormund said. "But the instincts are there, as they are in any cat. He was being generous with his mouse. He was saying, you feed me, so I shall feed you. We join in the sacrament of eating."

As if encouraged by Vormund's praise, the bobcat dropped the mouse, let it crawl a few feet, then smacked it down with a paw. Then it tossed the mouse in the air. When the prey was at the height of its flight, Buster swatted it with the other paw.

Corinne Host gasped and covered her eyes.

"Like a kid playing one old cat," Fassman said.

Vormund got up slowly. He looked weary. The flirting with the lovely woman had helped, but it could not undo eighty-one years of ailments. He needed Clara, his eye drops, his bed. "Don't feel sorry for the mouse, Mrs. Host. Mice are born to be eaten. They are the universal lunch of the animal world. Hawks fly and coyotes run because of the decency of the mouse."

"I don't like it," she said. "It's cruel."

"Beat it, Buster," Maybank said. He shied a stone at the cat, who retreated to the shade of a cholla. The mouse's tail dangled from its jaws.

"That mouse personifies ultimate goodness," Vormund said. "We should not deprive him of his saintliness, any more than we should inhibit a martyr."

Bugler emerged from his laboratory with a set of contact proofs of the trapped lion. He loped toward the table and waited. Dan was performing.

"Ultimate goodness?" asked Host.

"What a life of sanctity the mouse leads! A brief passage on earth, nourishing himself with grain, so he may furnish a meal for other creatures! It leaves me with the conviction that perfect goodness can be attained only by those willing to take the consequences. In the mouse's case, dinner for a barn owl."

Buster gulped. The mouse vanished.

"His role is fulfilled." Vormund saluted the cat and the ingested mouse. "That mouse lost the world but saved its immortal soul."

"Dan, you don't believe a word of that," Jenny said.

"I do. To be purely good is to be purely exterminated."

Fassman nodded. "He must believe it. I read it in one of his books a long time ago."

"Evidence from an old student. My thanks, Alan."

The Hosts got up and shook hands. They thanked the Maybanks for lunch. Ray Host held Vormund's hand, seemed to want to ask him something, ducked his head. "Maybe . . . maybe . . ." He ducked again. "Maybe people like us can have a meeting of minds, a compromise. . . ."

"I'm ready. I'm not sure you are."

"Go easy on us," Host said.

"I didn't know I was so mean. In any case, leave a bit of the country for people like me."

Bugler walked up and showed Host a photograph—the lion held pinned by the steel trap, the bloody leg. "And for her, also."

At his motel Fassman phoned Tom Ballstead in the KGDF newsroom.

"Ready to come home?" Ballstead asked.

thought, perhaps I will have saved a few acres of wilderness or a family of badgers. No small accomplishment.

A car's heavy tires crunched in the driveway. "Who would be coming here so late?" Clara asked. "Do you want to run in to bed? I'll say you have a headache."

"Probably someone in need of your invigorating soup."

Clara got up in response to a knocking at the kitchen door. She found Raymond Host, in tennis clothing, standing there.

"Mrs. Vormund? I'm Mr. Host. I met your husband at the Institute today. Is he . . . ?"

"He's about to go to bed."

"Oh, then . . ."

Clara looked at him—handsome, rugged, thick-bodied. Dan had come back from lunch talking about a stunning young woman from Los Angeles. But he had said nothing about a man.

"I'll just be a minute. My wife sent me for some things at the drugstore, and since we're at the Senita Inn, I thought I might ask Professor Vormund to autograph this copy of *Desert Idyll*."

"If that's all, come in."

Host bowed stiffly. He seemed ill at ease—educated, good-looking, but a young man who kept his distance. He spoke with hesitancy, spacing his words.

Clara led him around to the patio. Then she excused herself. "You're Mr. . . . Forgive me, in my old age I have trouble with names."

"Host. Raymond Host."

"The man who processes the desert. I don't normally welcome visitors."

"I apologize. I thought perhaps you'd autograph *Desert Idyll* for me. I don't know how long we'll be in Senita."

"If it's still in print, it merits a signature. What shall I say? I'm not good at this sort of thing. Inscriptions remind me of mortuary verse. Besides, I hardly know you."

Fireflies darted in the dark. Across the desert, frogs and toads croaked. Vormund liked to think his friendly spadefoot joined in the nocturnal chorus.

"I found myself envying that man who was your student twenty years ago," Host said.

"Fassman?" It appeared odd to Vormund that someone as rich

and as potent as Host, possessed of such a wife, could envy Alan Fassman.

"He had a chance to learn from you. I had the feeling I would have enjoyed being in your classes."

"Don't feel you missed anything not going to school in New York. Apart from the Chinese restaurants, Morningside Heights was a bleak place. It took courage for me to spend so many years there."

Vormund maneuvered the book so that the flyleaf reflected light from the living room, and wrote:

> To Mr. Raymond Host, whose interest in preserving the natural world is of great importance, since he wields far more power than I do.
> —Daniel Dean Vormund.

"I'm sorry, I can't read your writing."

"Penmanship was never my strong suit."

Vormund took the book and read his words to the young man. "I'm flattered and grateful. Maybe I can try to live up to it."

Vormund looked about cautiously, as if to see whether his wife were checking up on him. "Sit down for a few minutes. It isn't quite my bedtime, and I'm not as feeble as everyone thinks. When I go into the desert or the mountains with Ed Bugler, I get along fine on water and soda crackers. Down in Baja, Ed finds me mangrove oysters. A unique man, Mr. Bugler."

"So are you."

"You barely know me. You read one of my books, and heard me perform at lunch, and you seem to feel you've found an oracle. Is that it?"

"You make sense."

"Careful, young man. Too much of my kind of sense will put you and your corporation out of business."

Host's red-gold head edged forward. In the semidarkness he could see the old man's fine-featured face. The mouth seemed to hang open slightly, as if the facial muscles had weakened. Every now and then his tongue flicked at his lips.

"More than Host-Labarre, Professor. You don't beat around the bush in that book. You don't give mankind much of a chance."

"Why should I? They will be machine-gunning coyotes, poisoning lions, polluting rivers, and overgrazing the pastureland until there is not a single wild creature left. At some point the earth will rebel."

Host folded his arms. They seemed to Vormund all-powerful. He was of that breed of American who could do anything he put his mind to. "I wish I could help."

"That puts you in a rather embarrassing position, doesn't it? The best way you and your people could help would be to file for bankruptcy."

"Maybe not so extreme a step. If I could convince Host-Labarre to . . ."

Host now realized he had not thought his mission to Vormund through clearly. At the Senita Inn he had had a painful argument with Corinne. It began when Pop had tried to reach him, left a telephone message for Ray to call back. As he reached for the phone, she had stopped him. Let him wait. Let him sweat, Corinne said. Why cheat these bird lovers of their money and their fun? To hell with Denkerman's money. Host had defended his father. She had gone to the bar where, with terrifying swiftness, she drank two double vodka gimlets.

Ravishing in an apricot suit, bathed, perfumed, hair brushed, skin glowing, she lit up the bar of the inn, like a flaming poinsettia in a wintry garden. Ancient Midases stared at her with lickerish glee. In his sweaty tennis clothing, Host watched her drinking in defiance of the inn's unwritten rules, looking like the highest-priced call girl in the world. Disgust overwhelmed him. He despaired of her ambivalence over their wealth. But he feared scenes and would not reprimand her publicly. Instead he had found himself looking up Vormund's address in the directory.

"As I said at lunch," Vormund said, "you can always subscribe to our newsletter or become a life member. Maybe some of your business associates would like to join the Institute."

Another planet, Ray Host thought. Vormund, erect in the faded chair, hands folded in his lap, was serious. A few subscriptions at $7.50 a head, a few life members at $100, and all would be right in the world. It would never occur to Vormund that Host-Labarre was capitalized at $456 million and that its growth potential was one of the highest-rated in the world. An energetic, imaginative, well-run, constantly expanding organization, *Business Week* called them. But Vormund's horizons were limited to a newsletter that cost $7.50 per annum.

"I keep peddling our ideas in my small persistent way," Vormund said. "It keeps me out of trouble."

"Your book aroused me. No one ever phrased it that way, made me see that maybe we're trifling with the earth itself."

"A convert a day isn't bad. I don't think Jesus did as well when he got started."

"He was a revolutionary also. That's what you are."

Vormund looked sideways at the young man. "Me? A revolutionary? I'm a conservative, young man. I always have been. I was black-listed by the literary commissars after I went to the Soviet Union and disliked it. I didn't want paradise provided for me by a Politburo. And I never had much use for Marx."

"But the ideas you preach. They'd stop progress. No technology, no machines."

"That isn't revolutionary. It's backward. I'm a primitive." Vormund laughed, a light dry sound. "Ah, these political trivialities. Conservative or liberal or radical, all we seek is *more*."

Host lingered, full of unanswered questions. Could so wise a man really believe that there could be too much progress, that machines were destructive? "I've bothered you enough, Professor Vormund. I'll get going."

"I enjoyed the visit. At my age any reader is welcome. All autographs given happily."

"My wife says I should read some of your earlier works on literature. The books you wrote before you came to the desert. She found some of them in print."

"I'm well aware of them. They furnish me with a tidy little income. About six thousand dollars a year, for doing nothing at all. Mrs. Vormund, who is a thrifty Veronese, says those royalties about fill our needs with a bit left over."

Vertigo swept over Raymond Host. *Six thousand dollars a year? More than enough?* Corinne could spend that in a week in New York City. A wrongness so vast as to leave him humiliated and isolated, drowned Host. Here was Daniel Dean Vormund, happy, full of talk, stories, memories, achievements. All the good words he had put to paper, all the students he had influenced, the pleasure he had given, the wisdom he had imparted. And now on a final doomed crusade, he defended the rights of badgers and foxes. The notion seized Host that he owed the man something. But what?

"It's been a privilege to know you," Host said stiffly. "Maybe I'll drop by next time my wife and I are in Senita. Perhaps to ask you to autograph another book."

Ghostly white in his tennis shirt and shorts, Host was anchored to the flagstones. He appeared to Vormund a chunky, monolithic form, as enduring as the supermarkets and high rises he built. In the fragrant darkness he did not leave. He remained as if he had forgotten something.

"I . . . I'd like to talk to you again. When you're not too tired."

"I can't be profligate with my time. I don't have much left."

Host asked: "Do you like to fly?"

"Fly? I love to. I rarely get the chance to look at the desert from above. My wife says the altitude is bad for my asthma."

"I'll take you up in our plane."

"That's very kind. But I'll have to get Clara's permission."

"She can come along."

A memory stirred Vormund. He perked up in the creaky chair and slapped his knee. "Do you know that I was the first commercial airplane passenger in the state of Kentucky? A barnstorming pilot came through Lexington during the First World War. The local paper offered a ride in his biplane for the best essay on the future of aviation. Being the city's brightest student, I won."

Host smiled. "Did you enjoy it?"

"Yes, but I had to fight for the reward. The pilot proved to be a chicken heart. He claimed the cloud cover was too heavy. Being a brash young fellow, I persisted and he took me up for six minutes. It made the front page. *Local Youth Braves Stormy Sky.* One of the last complimentary things they ever wrote about me."

Something about the anecdote made Host feel happier about the confrontation he knew must come with his father. Daniel Dean Vormund knew what he wanted. He knew how to get it. Qualities Pop could appreciate.

"Then you accept my invitation?"

"I'm delighted."

"Good. Why didn't the paper write anything complimentary about you?"

"The Scopes affair."

"Scopes?" Host was lost.

"The monkey trial. About teaching evolution in the Tennessee schools."

Vaguely, Host remembered something. A movie Corinne had taken him to? Darrow? Darwin? He needed Corinne for this kind of talk. He missed her. She would have loved to hear Vormund reminisce. Instead she was drinking herself into a stupor.

"I covered the trial for *The New Republic*. Naturally my articles opposed the fundamentalists who were a power in Kentucky. The local newspaper reprinted some quotes from my pieces and ran a headline over my photograph: WE ARE NOT PROUD OF HIM. So much for home town fame."

Vormund shut his eyes. What did the young man want? Host had wealth, power, physical endowments, a magnificent wife, anything he wanted. What could he offer this heir to a fortune?

"About that flight . . . perhaps later in the week," Vormund said.

"We'll only be here a few days." Host had planned to leave tomorrow. "The day after . . . ?"

"Perhaps. It would be interesting to see that area where the creeping devils grow."

"I'll stay until you feel up to it. They won't miss me in Los Angeles. The houses will get built if I'm gone a few days."

"Very well. The day after tomorrow, provided Clara agrees."

Clara appeared in the door to the patio. "It's cold, Dan. You must come in."

"I'm leaving, Mrs. Vormund," Host said. "I'm sorry I came unannounced."

"Please call next time. Dan needs his rest."

"I will. Good night, sir. Good night, Mrs. Vormund." Host walked away in an athlete's pigeon-toed stride. He turned. "I felt I had to talk to you. What you have to say . . ." The voice wavered, vanished. He sounded like a man unaccustomed to giving explanations, making excuses.

The roaring of the car engine dwindled. Frogs and insects resumed their dominion over the night. "That's better," Vormund said. "Someday the roar of one vast machine will drown out the last bird. I don't want to be around."

She led him to the house. "Old pessimist."

"Just a realist. Pleasant young man, despite his unfathomable wealth. But he's disconcertingly earnest. Like a lady Ph.D. candidate from Iowa."

"Newsman?"

"Who's this?" Fassman asked.

Watching a TV news program in his motel room, Fassman was roused by the phone. He knew the voice. The ice-cream princess, the honeypot Corinne Host. She sounded thick-tongued. Thrilled by the call, Fassman could not suppress images of her barrel-chested husband dismembering him for dallying with his golden girl.

"Mrs. Host." His voice was a lump of clay. Why was she after him? And where was she calling from? He sought clever suggestive words, failed. Wendi used to bait him wickedly: "What woman in her right mind would sleep with you if I didn't? What a total loss! *I'd love you more if you had the guts to cheat!*" He made a mental note to tell his wife that Corinne Host had once telephoned him.

"Meet me for a drinkie."

"Where are you?"

"I'm in the loathsome bar of this motel. May I order you something while you're on your way?"

Fassman mused: Were I a man, I would invite her here, to drink in the curtained, Lysol-redolent, dark confines of my modular nest. Disrobed, she would succumb to my cabalistic Hebrew power. Instead he agreed to meet her in the bar.

She was seated alone in a black vinyl booth, sipping a vodka gimlet. She wore an apricot suit and her hair was brushed high to reveal what Fassman could think of only as a noble brow. His knees turned to the consistency of lentil soup.

"Hi."

"Good evening, Mrs. Host."

"Stop that shitty formality. Corinne is my name. You're Alvin?"

"Alan."

"Alan, you can't let me drink alone."

"I can't drink alcohol this late at night. I'll get a migraine." He ordered a Diet Pepsi from the waitress.

Mrs. Host shook her head. "Making me feel guilty?"

"Not at all. I'd drink if I could. I have no feelings one way or the other about your boozing."

"That's better. That's much better." She nodded. A whiff of perfume from her hair set off pulsations in Fassman's crotch.

"Why did you come here? Where's your husband?"

"He ran off to the desert philosopher."

"Vormund? Why?"

"Who knows? Raymond gets attacks of integrity now and then. He wanted Vormund to autograph *Desert Idyll*."

Fassman tried to envision their meeting. What would Vormund have to say to the emperor of subdivisions? "People often feel that way about Vormund," Fassman said. "They read and they want to talk to him. Mabel Dodge Luhan once conned him into a meeting with a couple of mystics, a guy named Gurdjieff and some swami. Vormund sat in a room with them for an hour and all that the mystics wanted to discuss was their dentists."

Blankness filmed her face.

"I told it badly. Left out something."

"I'll have another gimlet."

"Your husband would say no. Maybe I should. Look, what if he finds you getting smashed with a horny Jewish writer? He looks like the kind who could strangle me for staring at your ankle. And I've stared at it and all the other choice parts."

"Ray's a pussycat. Oh, he could kill you. He can run, jump, hit, tear phone books apart. But he never, *never* fights, never even gets *angry*." She lowered her voice. "Pop took the fight out of him."

"Pop?"

"Ray's father, James Wayland Host. The master builder."

Fassman stared moodily at his Diet Pepsi. "As Victor McLaglen said to Una O'Connor in *The Informer*, 'I'm sorry for your troubles, Mrs. McPhillips.' "

"Don't pull that eastern trivia crap on me. Besides it was a different movie."

"*The Informer*. I've seen it seven times. It was always playing at the Thalia. Does this deballing by his father, this nullification of Raymond's pugnacity, affect his performance in the sack?"

"None of your business. He worships me. Do you have any idea how rich they are?"

"How rich?"

"You can't begin to guess, you idiot. Last year Host-Labarre put up a new city outside of Fort Lauderdale. A *city*. They did it for some shifty types, not the usual kind of ethical people Pop insists on. Anyway the deal was that for every day *under* schedule that the job was completed, Host-Labarre would get an extra ten thousand dollars. But they had to forfeit ten thousand a day for every day *over* schedule."

"And what happened?"

"Pop finished the city eighty days ahead of time."

"So they owed him eight hundred thousand dollars above the agreed price."

"And my father-in-law told them to keep it. *Keep eight hundred thousand dollars!* He said it might make better men out of them."

"I know how you feel. I once had a rich father-in-law."

Tak-tak-taking her diamond against the empty glass, she did not hear him. His troubles were not hers. The staccato noise brought the waitress.

At the circular bar two shave-headed men in western suits turned to see who had tapped on the glass. "New way of orderin' a drink," one said. And the other: "She could order me around with a shake of that tail."

"This is a puzzler," Fassman said. "They turned down darn near a million dollars from a client, but they're after *fifteen* million of that inheritance. The Hosts figure they don't mind conceding a few dollars if they win the big ones."

"It's Pop's way of shoving Raymond around. Forcing him to do something he hates."

"I see. It's the building of Raymond's character that's important."

"Don't be a smart-ass. I'm sorry I told you the story. I was sore at Ray and sore at my father-in-law. That's why I'm here." Her hand was on his thigh. "Have you told anyone? I shouldn't have talked to you. It isn't much of a story, is it?" Fassman shivered as she touched him.

"It's a hell of a story and I have told someone."

Little creases of worry etched her forehead. The lush mouth drooped. "You shit. Who?"

"My boss at the KGDF newsroom."

"What is he going to do?"

"I don't know. He was going to check on the Denkerman will. It's no secret."

"Oh, God." She drank the new gimlet. "Why worry? So it comes out now, or a month from now."

"Can't you stop them? I'll pay for the call. Get your boss on the phone and tell him it was a mistake."

"Corinne, I don't have much, but I have my integrity as a journalist. Don't smirk. I think I have a story here. How some of the richest people in California are trying to screw a decent bunch of bird watchers out of a lot of money."

She stopped stroking his leg. "You want to hurt me, don't you?"

"You want to hurt yourself. And maybe Raymond. There's some kind of bad vibes between you and the muscle man. Or between you and what do you call him, Daddy-O?"

"Pop."

"*Pop.* You people astonish me. Host. The Hosts. Lord God of Hosts. How much loot do they want? Why?"

"Don't be nasty. The Hosts are not the way you think they are. They're educated refined people. I'm a rat doing what I did. Alan, what can we do?"

"Nothing."

"Please." The stroking began again.

"I can ask the newsroom not to attribute the story to anyone if they use it."

"You mentioned *me?*"

"Of course I did. What kind of editor of the Pomona college newspaper were you? Haven't you ever heard of sources? What better source than the wife of the guy who's trying to break the bequest?"

She nibbled at the hard green cherry. Fassman wondered who grew them. Who bothered to pickle and bottle them for the Corinne Hosts of the world?

"They'll find out. They always do."

"You're afraid of them. That's why you're here. The story is bound to come out. The Hosts will be seen in all their naked greed. But why should it bother them?"

"They wouldn't want it to get out. Not so soon."

"Yeah, I see. That's why they sent Raymond snooping around here, making believe he loved Vormund."

"You'll call that man in LA? And keep me out of it?"

Fassman shrugged. Here it was. The grand conquest. He would brag to Wendi someday. "From my room."

"All right."

With a flourish, Fassman signed for the drinks. A nice expense account item—vodka gimlets for Mrs. Raymond Host, heir to half the world, boozer, potential beaver.

They walked across the grass to the motel's inner court. "Don't get too close to me until we're inside," Fassman said. "I might throw you to the turf and know you in the biblical sense."

"That would complicate matters, wouldn't it?"

Inside the boxlike room, Fassman clutched at her waist, but she eluded him. Suddenly she was brisk and businesslike. "Call him."

"He won't be in the office."

"Call him at home."

The network switchboard connected him to Ballstead. While Corinne sat primly in a fake antique chair, knees together, hands on apricot thighs, Fassman explained to his superior that for important reasons, Mrs. Host could not lend her name to the story on the fight over the will.

"Okay, if she insists," Ballstead growled. "I don't even know if it's been checked out. We'll keep her out of it unless someone gives us trouble. By the way, I think this dump of an apartment I own is a Host-Labarre production. Tell them the plumbing is lousy."

Fassman laughed and hung up. "See how easy that was?"

"Then I'm safe."

"That's what you think. I will now perform the act of love on your sunshine-nourished body. How shall we start?"

Her compact seated figure offered him no encouragement. Her eyes had turned flinty. "Forget it, newsman."

"Got what you wanted. As you always do. I'm glad the Maybanks beat your ass at tennis."

"Who told you that?"

"Jenny Maybank. She said she and Jack laughed all the way

home. They conned you and Ray into losing to them, a pair of pushers."

"It was Ray. He deliberately lost to infuriate me."

"Sure."

"That's right. It's his revenge on his father, and a slap at me."

So he goes off in search of Vormund, Fassman thought, the gentlest of men, a man who never fought anyone. "I have a terrific idea," he said. "Come to bed with me. I did you a favor, didn't I?"

"This is idiotic. Walk me to the parking lot."

He bent over, ashamed of the bend in his trousers, and grabbed her arms. She sat rigidly. He was inept at these maneuvers. The future loomed—massage parlors and hookers. Her perfume punctured his central nervous system. He had the sensation she was all apricot flesh through and through, her buttocks a simulacrum of the fruit.

"Get away."

A hard shove sent him wobbling toward the bed. "Okay, but don't laugh."

"I won't laugh. You're all right, Alan. But you aren't my dish of tea. You're another sufferer."

Fassman recalled a story in Bertrand Russell's autobiography. An afternoon of passion with Lady Ottoline Morrell, spiced by the possibility that her irate husband might appear while the philosopher lay coupled with the bluestocking. Reminiscing in his wintry years, Russell decided that he would have died happily at the hands of the cuckold, so incredibly sweet was the experience. He, Fassman, to kiss her breasts, her apertures, would have died in that hotel room for the sheer honor of it. Ray Host could mash him to a paste and he would succumb smiling.

"Maybe we should take the side exit," he said.

"The lobby is fine. Are you afraid someone will see us? Or they might think I'm a whore?"

"Who could afford you? Not even the Shah of Iran."

The lobby was full of displays, placards, card tables from which pamphlets were dispensed. Middle-aged men in dudish cowboy clothes slapped backs, laughed, talked in voices amplified by whiskey and beer.

They stopped to stare at Corinne. Their wives tended to be

cement-assed and saddle-sore. Fassman took her through the glass doors to the parking lot.

"Why not me?" he asked. "Why him?"

"You'll never understand money so big, so terrifying. I adore it."

He watched her get into a small car. It belonged to the manager of the Senita Inn, who had been only too eager to help out a Host. The world waited, happy to help out, to touch them.

Back in the lobby Fassman observed a half-dozen men standing around a cage on a bridge table. Inside was a coiled rattlesnake. Over the cage was a sign:

PUBLIC ENEMY NUMBER ONE

WANTED FOR KILLING

SHEEP, CATTLE, AND FOLKS

"Celebration of some kind?" Fassman asked a podgy man in a lavender suit. He was one of the men at the bar who had ogled Corinne.

"Rattlesnake Roundup. Jaycees' big money-raiser. Raises funds for the orphans and crippled chirrun. Want to buy a ticket?"

"How much?"

"Five bucks. All the beer you can drink, a free rattleburger, and admission to the roundup."

"I may be leaving tomorrow."

"Hang around. It's the day after tomorra. It's a real show, son. Watch them young'uns chase snakes across the desert."

Fassman studied the blue pasteboard the man thrust at him.

FIFTH ANNUAL RATTLESNAKE ROUNDUP

SPONSORS:

Senita Jaycees

Senita Ranchers and Hunters Association

Associated Gun Clubs, Doble County

Drive 'em, Kill 'em, Skin 'em, Eat 'em!

"It looks interesting," Fassman said.

"Keep your stub, son. You may win a snakeskin golf bag." He looked warily at Fassman. "You sound like one of them New York fellahs."

"Los Angeles."

"Same thing."

Fassman, sensing something that might interest Ballstead and save his Arizona trip from being a total loss, bought four tickets with a twenty-dollar bill. He would need a cameraman and a soundman. Ed Bugler would be interested.

"That's the spirit," the fat man said. "What line of bidniss you in?"

"I'm southwestern regional sales manager for the A. B. Dick Company."

"You tell 'em in Los Angeles, they always welcome out here." The man punched Fassman in the arm, then turned to three stringy women in their sixties. They wore cowgirl outfits—fringed, pocketed, sassy.

Fassman studied the reverse side of the tickets. There was a map giving instructions to the Essler Ranch, the site of the roundup. He tugged at the man's sleeve. "This Essler place. Is that the big ranch?"

"You know it, son."

"He's the big landowner, right?"

"Finest man in Doble County. But don't cross Duane Essler. His word is his bond, unless you get him riled up. As he tends to be these days. As we all are inclined to be."

"Why is that?"

"That conservation crowd. The dickey-birders. Ramming gun control on us. Trying to save coyotes and snakes and vermin that kills stock. They aim to put us out of bidniss."

"Are you a rancher?"

"Hell, no. I'm an insurance man. But I'm with them. Listen, young fellah. All a coyote is good for is to be killed. So's a lion or a bear, or anything that takes the bread out of a man's mouth."

"Eagles too? Our national emblem?"

"If they kill sheep."

Fassman thought: *trade before the flag, as ever.*

"It'll be an education for me," the newsman said.

"You sure you aren't from New York?" the man asked.

"Pure Los Angeles."

"Then you got something to *learn*." He bent his cropped head close to Fassman, who recoiled from the whiskey breath. "There's people in Senita should be treated the same way we treat coyotes. Anybody sticks up for a coyote deserves to get what a coyote gets or what a lion gets."

"You mean that?"

"Bullets and poison is too good for that crowd. And that includes that bunch over at the Institute. Duane Essler's caught them on his property three times." He pulled Fassman's shirt collar close. "Would you believe two of those sumbitches turned a lion loose from a trap on Essler's land?"

"I find that hard to believe."

"You better believe it. Mrs. Essler popped at 'em with a carbine from the plane to shake 'em up. Next time she says she won't miss."

"I can see why you people take this so seriously. But isn't the issue of predator control a complicated one—I mean, the balance of nature and so on . . . ?"

"Balance of nature?" he guffawed. "Son, the only balance those people understand is a load of bird shot. When you see a coyote or a lion, *kill it*. Same goes for some folks."

Minutes later Fassman phoned Ballstead again. The news director liked the rattlesnake roundup. He authorized him to call in a crew from Phoenix. Grumbling at a world he didn't care for (rather like Vormund, Fassman thought), the news director dismissed his reporter with bitter words: "Fake gunslingers. They can't kill Indians or gooks any more so they go after snakes."

4

---　❈　---

Host sat at the controls of the corporate jet. His tanned fore-arms (like Popeye's, Vormund thought, with a wistful memory of his friend Wimpy) appeared to be part of the infinitely complex control panel. Vormund sat in the copilot's seat. Host had sent the pilot to the rear of the plane, where he now dozed alongside the Filipino steward.

"I'm ignorant of flying tradition," Vormund said, "but isn't your pilot rather oddly dressed?" The man wore a vested checked suit, shirt, tie, and a cocoa-brown porkpie hat.

"My father lets them wear whatever they please, so long as it includes a shirt and tie."

"Them?"

"We employ six pilots. I don't want to sound as if I'm brag-ging, but those are the facts of corporate life. Distances are huge out here. A fleet of jets helps us get the jump on people."

Vormund, dazzled by the possibilities of industrial forces (*six pilots?*), looked back, past Clara and Mrs. Host, to the sleeping pilot. "He seems relaxed."

"He knows I can handle this without him. He's a former Ma-rine Corps colonel with a degree in engineering from USC. I can fly rings around him. It isn't that hard. I'm younger and I have better reflexes."

And what were the other pilots? Vormund wondered. Professors of aeronautics?

"I admire the way you make this machine obey you. In spite of my animus for machines, I like to fly."

"I'm glad. I wanted to make up for the autograph."

Vormund believed him. The young man spoke frankly, innocently. There seemed no side to him. And for reasons he could not divine, Host appeared to be trying to break down whatever barriers separated them—age, wealth, background.

"North over the Santa Teresa Mountains, is that all right?"

"I'm in your hands. It's all magnificent."

"Can you see your house?"

Vormund shaded his eyes and looked out of the curved plastic bubble. "I can. This is remarkable. I even see the frog pond and the garden wall." He called to his wife: "Clara, look out on the right. Our house. And Mrs. Munn's."

"I see, Dan."

"How clear the air is," Vormund said. "No smog out here, no wastes. And look at Mount Gatos. Every tree is visible."

"I read what you said about Mount Gatos. About thinking you were alone with God, like one of the prophets . . . what was it?"

"Waiting for eternal truths to be whispered into my ear. The ultimate answers. But all I heard was the chattering of the piñon jays."

Host smiled. "Did you mean . . . I think you meant . . ."

"Yes?"

"That the jays' singing was God's answer."

"That would get you an A on your final examination."

"That man who used to be your student—I heard him say getting an A from you was no great shakes."

"I suspect you'd have earned it."

Blushing, Host was silent. He guided the twin-engined plane higher. The desert unrolled beneath them, a carpet of yellow-beige, sprinkled with patches of green and darker brown. Here and there were daubs of spring flowers—fields of primroses, penstemon, daisies. The design, in form and color, was of an intensity that left Vormund mildly intoxicated. He could never convey the sensation to anyone, not in his writings, not even to Clara. It was not enough to call the desert beautiful, or awesome, or inspiring. It was all those things, and it was free of man's hand.

One had to return to nature for the purest of forms, the most gratifying colors. Art had come to a dead halt—geometry, the colors of death and disease and defeat, fakery, exegeses that explained nothing.

Behind the two men the wives conversed—Clara wary at first of the young woman, but soon warming to her. Clara made friends instantly. She was as comfortable with Antonio, their Mexican gardener, as she was with university presidents who visited Dan.

"It's kind of you to take us on this trip," she said. "I worry about Dan. I know I'm partly at fault, babying him, but it's all or nothing with him. Either he moons around the house, or else he's off on one of those wild trips with Ed and Sidewinder. I tell you, he gives me fits."

"He looks fine to me, Mrs. Vormund."

"My dear, you don't know the half of it. He walked off the plane in Arizona twenty-two years ago a step from the grave. He was almost in a wheel chair. That New York weather and dirt. Would you believe in six months, he was almost healthy? That's why Dan feels he owes a great deal to Arizona and wants to save the desert. It saved him, I can tell you."

"I think you helped, also."

"I know that." Her loud musical voice took away any hint of self-esteem. She was simply setting the record straight.

"How long have you been married?"

"Fifty-five years. What good years, my dear. And these years in the desert were the best. Do you know how shy that man was in New York? He never palled around with anyone, except Tyler Merritt. Hardly ever talked to the other professors or the editors he worked with. But, my goodness, out *here*. In a year, Dan was a regular cowboy, slapping people on the back, telling jokes to Indians and ranch hands. And some not very clean jokes."

"I'd love to hear some."

"Never to you. Dan is an old-fashioned gentleman. It's that Kentucky upbringing, and that strict German father."

"You sound as if you have been very happy."

Clara blew her nose strenuously. Was she getting sentimental? Corinne wondered. She seemed to Corinne a marvelously earthbound soul, full of good sense, vigor, a grasp on life.

"Happy, so happy. We never had children. I could not, but

Dan was my child. Tyler used to make fun of me, how I babied Dan. But what else could I do? Drops, pills, vitamins, injections, hot-water bags, ice packs, heating pads, God knows what else. When we went to Europe, I carried a medicine chest for him, and it was lucky I spoke Italian and French and he spoke German, so we could get service in drugstores. Dan always liked Switzerland because you could get any drug in the world."

Incredible, Corinne thought. It sounded like fifty-five years of practical nursing for a man half-invalid, half-hypochondriac. Yet they loved each other profoundly. Every now and then the old man would turn around and wave at her, draw her attention to some feature of the landscape. Would she and Ray wear as well after *ten* years?

She had her doubts. She feared for Ray. Something brittle in him. Something that someday might crack under his father's goading. Pop loved him too much, wanted too much for him. Like the Denkerman fortune. She suspected that she had infected Ray with some of her own ambivalence about wealth. In him was some buried inchoate force, something that tried to resist James Wayland Host, turn away a father's ambitions. But he kept it smothered. It took its toll in headaches, in bruising silences.

"What a beautiful young woman you are," Clara said. "You are like a painting, or a statue. You are blessed to be so lovely."

"That's kind of you, Mrs. Vormund. Looks are just a matter of genetics, biology. I don't think people deserve compliments for being attractive. What your husband has accomplished is much more admirable."

Clara laughed. "It's good to have both. Let me tell you, my Dan made a very handsome professor. He had an eye for the pretty lady Ph.D. candidate."

"He's still a handsome man."

Clara blew her nose again. "Yes, but we are old, my dear, so old. Still when Dan has a good day, he has that gallant air, with those sharp eyes and the way he holds his head." She leaned toward Corinne and took her sleeve, lowering her voice. "Listen, my dear, that's why I never worried about his straying from the straight and narrow. Sooner or later he'd get sick, coughing and headaches and what not, and he'd be back to his faithful nurse. He'd need the vaporizer more than he needed some lady student's sighs. Well, now we're old and we get our excitement from feeding the birds, and laughing at our rabbits and squirrels. Dan even has a pet frog that comes to be fed."

A descent from Shakespeare to a frog, Corinne thought. Not too strange. Aristophanes honored them with a play.

"I envy you, Mrs. Vormund."

"You? So young and lovely? With such a handsome husband, and your whole wonderful life ahead of you?"

"I envy something that you and your husband seem to have . . . some understanding. Things you share . . ."

"It's not hard to achieve, my dear. Believe me, it's easier with money. I know. I am a Veronese and we understand double-entry bookkeeping."

The plane lurched abruptly, then dropped several dozen feet, hurling them forward.

"Air pocket," Host said. "No problem."

The pilot did not even open his eyes. He knew about air currents over the windy desert. Once more the plane dipped and shuddered.

"Sorry," Host said to Vormund. "Did I frighten you?"

"Not at all. I look at those gauges and I know we're absolutely safe. Maybe I'm wrong to distrust technology so much."

"I read what you said about the powerful car bolting along at eighty miles per hour. With the driver locked in, unable to think or be creative, because all he can do is keep the monster under control. Your analogue for modern man and the modern world."

"I believe it. It's not one man in one plane that bothers me. It's an entire civilization trapped in a pounding destructive machine. Don't let me distract you. Your job is more important than my maunderings."

"You know my father opposed my learning to fly. He said it was a distraction."

"Learning shouldn't be snubbed. In my sixties I took a course in biology at the university so I could better understand the birds."

Host's head seemed to pull back again, that odd gesture of withdrawal. Beneath the plane the desert colors appeared to blend, like the patterns on a laundered Madras shirt. Vormund feasted on the shadings, the chiaroscuro effects, the rolling shadows caused by a vagrant cloud, the sunlit slopes and peaks. It appeared lifeless, a hot wasteland. But he knew that millions of lives were at work in the vegetation. There was a drama every second, hawk clutching snake, owl grabbing mouse, ants swarming over a beetle.

"My father would approve of what *you* did, but not what I did," Host said softly. "You wanted to help your writing. But my flying was pointless, since we have all the pilots we need. He said I'd do better learning more about marketing. The bottom line is always *sales*."

"Sales?"

"Sure. Those pennants you see flying over new tracts. It isn't terribly hard once you're as big as we are."

"What isn't?"

"Making a lot of money. Besides, if we get into trouble, the government will bail us out. Do you know we have *four* former cabinet officers on our Board of Directors?"

"Does your father let them wear anything they want to board meetings, so long as it includes a shirt and tie?"

"That's pretty much the case. One's a former governor. He calls Pop *Mr. Host* and me *Young Mr. Host*."

Vormund was getting an insight into real power. He had read articles about people like the Hosts and organizations like Host-Labarre, but he had never quite understood them or gotten them into focus. The Marine Corps colonels and the cabinet officers explained a great deal.

"Mr. Host, I am not surprised by what you tell me . . ."

"I wish you'd call me Ray."

"Fair enough. If you're comfortable calling me Dan, like everyone else out here, including Sidewinder. I'm no cabinet officer."

"And you're not on my payroll."

"No," Vormund said—and his eyes twinkled. "But I'm open to offers. Though I draw the line at wearing a tie."

"I'm afraid our table of organization couldn't fit you in. But it would be tempting. I can see you telling us to tear down a block of offices."

What does he want? Vormund wondered. Surely not a desire to turn me loose on his father and his high-salaried potentates, an act of filial revenge. Teasing the stern elders who "processed the desert"? Vormund could not see himself lecturing those puritanical men on the dangers inherent in overmechanization, the limits of the tortured earth.

"I think it would be fun if you joined the company," Host said. "Imagine what you could tell Pop and his board about the Bald Indian Power Plant."

"Are you involved in that monstrosity?"

"My father put the consortium together."

"I was not aware of that." He drew away a few inches and studied the young man's scarlet face. "Did you personally build that abomination?"

"A subsidiary handled it. It never would have come about without my father's intervention. It was too big for any single company. The government insisted it be done privately. Everyone was afraid of the environmentalists, the Indians, the professors. But Pop made it work."

"*Work?*" Vormund cried. "Have you seen it?"

"Several times."

"Then you know that it is a hell on earth, a stinking inferno that is ruining everything for miles around. It is an omen of our future. It should be bombed, plowed under, covered with topsoil, and planted with buffalo grass."

"But you haven't seen it. It does a great deal of good. It's *needed.*"

Vormund shook his head. "Jack Maybank and some ecology people sent a team up there a month ago. They say it's worse than anything anyone believed. Technology run wild. You're a pleasant young man. I might even be sociable to your father. So I'm sorry you were the ones who committed this atrocity."

Host did not appear insulted. "That power keeps homes lit and lets people raise families."

"For how long? Your tracts will come to resemble cliff dwellings. Arid, vacant, dead. Every square foot of desert you destroy brings us closer to the abyss."

"I don't believe it. My father says there's nothing in the world we can't do."

"You agree?"

"So far he's right."

"So far is not very far. Keep watching the water table. This assault on a fragile environment is relatively new, perhaps only thirty years old. What is thirty years in nature's scheme? A fraction of a second."

The plane circled the crest of the Santa Teresa Range, dipping a wing, almost as if to salute Mount Gatos, where Vormund had awaited an answer that never came.

"What the devil is that?" Vormund asked. He squinted through the plastic.

A long yellow cloud cut across a stretch of desert. As the wind shifted, Vormund and Host could see that it was a procession of automobiles. They were heading toward a parking area. Around this area vans and trucks were parked and temporary buildings had been erected.

"A fair of some kind," Host said.

"Can we go down and have a closer look?"

Host dipped the jet. They could see sunlight glinting on mirrors and windshields.

"You couldn't land here?" Vormund asked. "I'm curious. I imagine this is near the area where the *orugas* grow."

"I could land our smaller plane but not this one. Maybe we can see what it's all about."

A lesion, a stain, Vormund thought. He peered at the endless file of trucks and cars. They had no time to lose. Ranchers, boosters. They were a menace to the rare plants. Jack Maybank would have to see about buying the land and creating a refuge.

At seven in the morning Fassman and Bugler met the cameraman and soundman at the motel. The cameraman was named Merrill Apodaca. He was a squat brown man of indeterminate age with whom Fassman had covered a plane crash near Flagstaff. He grunted a great deal and immediately demanded that they have breakfast in the coffee shop. The soundman, a lean fellow named Downs, busied himself rewiring a tape recorder while Apodaca leisurely ate waffles, eggs, bacon, and grits.

Fassman, impatient to get to the roundup, did not complain about the delay. He watched Apodaca eat with noble dedication. Union members had to be allowed their perquisites. Among old-timers the rule was: Eat as much as you can, as often as you can.

Downs decided he was hungry too and ordered four fried eggs. The eating went on. Fassman sipped a fourth cup of coffee and looked at his watch. It would do no good to rush them.

"They won't start much action till noon or so," Bugler said. He had noted Fassman's jumpiness. "What buggers me is how they're going to get those snakes in the sun. A rattler is a nocturnal animal."

The soundman snorted: "If I get bit, the network better pay for everything, including a coffin."

"I've been bit," Bugler said. "It isn't all that bad."

Fassman suggested they leave the Institute jeep at the motel and take the cameraman's station wagon. Like most cameramen, Apodaca had brought far more equipment than he would need. There was barely room for Fassman and Bugler to cram into the rear seats.

At the exit from the motel lot, they saw Sidewinder. He was crouched at the foot of the motel sign, wearing his faded Stetson, frayed shirt, patched denims.

"Stop for our friendly Hopi," Fassman said.

"We don't take hitchhikers," Apodaca said. "Especially Indians."

"He's no Indian, he's a member of our staff," Bugler said.

Fassman laughed: "Consultant."

Bugler called through the window. "Did you ask Maybank's okay to come along?"

"He's meetin' with his lawyer. Miz Maybank gimme the day off."

"Jesus, there isn't any more *room* in here." Apodaca whined. A Hispanic of ancient lineage, he did not cherish Indians.

"Ride on the roof, if you let me. On the hood."

Fassman got out.

The Hopi crawled into the rear of the wagon. He cleared space between film magazines, tripods, reflectors, and auxiliary cameras and doubled up on his side. Then he said: "They say they are gonna kill a thousand snakes."

"There aren't that many in the county," Ed said.

Sidewinder shut his eyes and slept.

Bugler looked at Fassman. "I hope you get a story out of it. All this equipment and two men from Phoenix."

"Fucking snakes," Apodaca said. "The more they kill the better."

"I don't know," Bugler said. "They kill rats and mice."

"Yeah. So does rat poison."

It was not hard to find the signs to the road leading to the roundup. A cloud of tan dust hung over the road. Already jeeps, cars, trucks, even a few horse-and-wagons were turning off the Interstate toward the site.

"Hang out the KGDF news banner," Fassman said to Downs. "These people love press coverage. Might even get us a free lunch."

A man in a denim suit was checking passes and collecting tickets alongside a cattle guard. The ticket-taker saw the station flag and greeted them effusively. "Welcome, strangers. Where y'all from?"

"Los Angeles," Fassman said.

"Go right in. Free barbecue and beer up ahead for the press."

Bugler noticed the name plate on the man's spotless suit. ROY HUBSCHMID, ACCURATE VALVE CORPORATION, SENITA. The Jaycees were out in force today—polite young men.

Fassman waited while the crew assembled their equipment— the camera, the recorder, hand lights, extra magazines. Although he was in charge, he did not hesitate to do manual labor. Fassman had a healthy respect for technicians. They were often surly and they ate too much but they were professionals who rarely gave less than a hundred per cent. He shouldered a tripod, slung a power pack over one shoulder, and felt he was earning his way. (Like Vormund, he often had the sense that he was a nonfunctional member of a technological society, who should occasionally show respect for the machines that paid for everything.)

Bugler lugged a case of magazines and raw stock and the Bolex camera. Apodaca locked the station wagon and they strolled toward the sound of western music. About a hundred cars had arrived. Stands had been set up and were serving hot dogs, tacos, enchiladas, and chili. Vast quantities of beer and soft drinks were consumed. Women in buckskin jackets sold chances. Hawkers peddled balloons and pinwheels. The most popular item with children were rubberoid rattlesnakes that clicked when their tails were agitated.

The country music blared from a raised wooden platform. Three men in blue sequinned suits were playing a frisky cowboy tune. An elderly couple jigged in the sand.

Bugler shaded his eyes. More people were pouring into the area. The dirt road was clogged with a file of cars inching toward the roundup area. Horns honked. People shouted out good-naturedly, greeted one another.

"State cops," Sidewinder muttered. He was a step behind Bugler and Fassman. The Indian carried two hand lights, one slung on each shoulder. Fassman made a mental note to pay him out of his advance for the day's work. An interesting expense account item—*one Hopi Indian as bearer, ten dollars.*

"There's where they'll drive 'em in," Bugler said. He pointed to a corral to the left of the bandstand. Knots of people had gathered around it. Cinder blocks had been stacked to form a circular arena about fifty feet across. At the side of the arena, facing the desert, where a half-dozen men were poking around with rakes and hoes, there was an opening in the wall. Two lanes of blocks ran for about twenty feet. They formed a funnel, a conduit, to the corral.

A convoy of buses was jamming the road, raising clouds of choking dust. Schoolchildren began to debouch from the blue-and-white buses.

"Look at them fence posts out there," Sidewinder said. He pointed to a stretch of barbed-wire fencing.

"What the hell is that?" Apodaca asked. "I get it. Dead coyotes."

"It's a rancher's trick," Bugler said. "Supposed to scare away other coyotes. It doesn't."

The crew walked across the corral toward the fencing. It was a permanent structure, strung with barbed wire, demarking sections of the Essler property. About two dozen of the fence posts had been decorated with the disemboweled carcasses of coyotes.

"Sure stinks," Sidewinder said. "Even with the guts out."

Fassman tottered in the sun. It was like the crucifixion scene in *Spartacus.* Victims nailed to the wood, left to die in the sun on the Via Appia.

"Makes a nice shot," Apodaca said. "Lookin' right down that line. Downs, you bring the insect repellent? Flies are eating me alive."

Bugler was inspecting a carcass. "Tore the bladder out. See that hole? They rip the coyote's bladder out. Sometimes while it's still alive."

"Coyotes don't feel pain," the cameraman said. "I seen them bite their feet off to get out of a trap."

Ed said: "Maybe you ought to try it and see how much pain's involved." He walked down the line of dead animals. "All of them. The bladder cut out."

"Why?" Fassman asked.

Ed scowled at the people around the bandstand, eating tacos, drinking beer, buying toy snakes for their children. A great yellow cloud diffused over the area. In the desert white-jacketed young men carrying hoes, rakes, and shovels were being deployed.

Bugler sighed. "It means they're poisoning everywhere. They use the coyote's bladder to make a broth and they smear it on the M-44."

"M-44?" Fassman asked.

"The coyote-getter. The cyanide gun. They smear the stuff on the wick to attract the animals. It shoots off a cyanide cartridge into the coyote's mouth."

"What now?" Apodaca asked. "I got the crucifixion."

"Those kids getting off the buses," Fassman said. "Get some shots of them, okay?"

They trudged off. Sidewinder trailed them. He greeted a state trooper in a broad-brimmed hat.

"Sidewinder knows the cops. He was a marshal up at Second Mesa some years back." Bugler winked at Fassman. "There's more to that Indian than meets the eye."

Fassman and Bugler returned to the cinder block corral. Three sets of grandstands had been erected around it. "Like a bull ring," the newsman said.

An enormous trailer truck backed into the sandy area—knocking down prickly pears, chewing up chollas and ocotillos. There was a display on one side.

"For God's sake," Fassman said. "Get a load of that." He summoned the cameraman.

The silver flank of the trailer had been turned into a giant visual aid. At the top in blood red was the warning:

THE ONLY GOOD PREDATOR IS A DEAD ONE

WE MEAN BUSINESS!!!

"Gets right to the point," Fassman said. He and Bugler walked toward the van. A crowd was gathering to look at the exhibits below the statement of policy.

The pelts and skins of wild animals were nailed to the side. In his heat-hazed mind, Fassman kept thinking about a President who had asked the soldiers in Vietnam to "bring back the coonskin."

"More coyotes," Bugler said softly, as if mourning the passing of friends.

Three dead coyotes were nailed by their snouts to the side of the vehicle. They looked small and weak, not much bigger than mongrel dogs. Their limbs seemed atrophied.

Next to them was the pelt of a black bear. It was small and mangy. Then a half-dozen rattlesnake skins. Finally there was the pelt of a mountain lion. It was by far the most impressive of the dead animals. Its flattened head was propped forward, the amber eyes open, full of wrath. The legs were stretched out and hammered into the van, the tail pulled down and nailed fast.

"It's ours," Bugler said. "Look at the paw." Fassman moved closer to the van, sidling between two stout women who were clucking their approval. "That's how to handle 'em," one said. "I'd kill 'em all if I had my way."

The lion's right forepaw was blackened and deformed. Above the claws the newsman could see the gouge that the trap had inflicted. He remembered the way they had sweated on the canyon ledge as the beast snarled at them. They had labored in vain.

"I'd know her anyway," Bugler said. "Even without the wounded foot."

"You would?"

"You get to know animals. That looks like a bullet wound above the shoulder."

Fassman felt larger than life. Part of something worthwhile. If people wanted to kill you that badly, you probably were doing something good. He'd thought that way about his Jewishness for many years, although he was not observant and had never gone to Israel. If people had been so intent on killing Jews, Jews must have had something worthwhile going.

"We tried," Bugler said. "Dan would have been proud of us. But they got her anyway. They'll clean every mountain lion out of the canyon in a year."

"Quite a line-up," someone said. "Quite a rogues' gallery."

Fassman turned. A short man with a pear-shaped head and slicked black hair was grinning at him.

"Hi," Fassman said.

The man was wearing a cream-colored Stetson. It had to be specially made, Fassman thought, with a tiny crown to accommodate his small head. The man's jaw and cheeks were chipmunk-fat, the mouth wide and smiling. In his tight-fitting pearl-gray suit he might have been a promoter of country music.

"I see we have the media with us," the man said. He pointed to the cameraman and soundman. Apodaca was taking crotch shots—thighs, legs, pudenda of baton twirlers and pompon girls.

"Thought it might be an interesting story. I'm Alan Fassman. KGDF, Los Angeles."

"Duane Essler."

"You're the chairman, right? And this is your ranch? Maybe we can interview you later."

Essler took off his hat. "My pleasure. Isn't that Mr. Edward Bugler with you?"

Ed had been standing to one side—tall, broad-shouldered, his arms dangling at his side. In his gray Sears outfit he seemed out of place. He did not look festive. But he smiled. "Hello, Mr. Essler."

"From the Institute, right?"

"Correct."

Essler twirled his Stetson on his chest. "Spying on the bad ranchers?"

Behind them the Senita City High School Band was parading around the cinder block arena to the tune of "Get Me to the Church on Time."

"Just curious what happens at a rattlesnake roundup."

"You must know, Ed. A naturalist like you."

"I guess you beat up the desert to rouse 'em. Then you herd 'em into that corral and kill 'em."

"More or less." He winked at Fassman. "It gets a little gory. Might be you won't want to show it on the television. Knowing as how you media folks are squeamish."

Fassman rubbed his burning nose. "We can edit out anything that's too rough. You're right, though. People are having dinner then and they might not like seeing a snake getting shot."

"We don't shoot 'em. It's fast and painless the way it's done. Snakes have no feelings. Besides, they aren't good for a thing except killing people and stock. Poisonous trash."

Bugler looked pained. He tried to talk, could not find words. Too many people. Too much noise. Worst of all too many kids.

"Don't look so sad," Essler said. He put a hand inside Fassman's arm. "The media deserve first-class treatment. You and your crew be my guests at the barbecue. I always cook a steer at these wing-dings. Meet the folks you think are the enemy. I assure you they're the finest people around."

A big-bellied man in a mauve suit plodded up to Essler. "Beaters are getting out, Duane. About time for you to fire the starting gun."

"Sure thing, Mac. Give 'em a few more minutes to beat the rascals out."

"I don't get it," Bugler said, perplexed. "You think you can round up a couple of hundred snakes in an hour? That's impossible. Snakes hide during the day. There aren't that many left out here."

"We find the buggers," the man in mauve said. "Burn 'em, smoke 'em, beat 'em with sticks." He held up a gasoline can with a pliable spout. "A little fire and they wiggle out."

Bugler ran his hand over his brush cut. "Snakes feel pain, Mr. Essler. They have delicate skeletons. They die slowly."

The two stared at Bugler as if he were certifiably insane. Then the paunchy man exploded in laughter. "*Jee-sus!*" He waddled away.

"Ed, you folks won't quit, will you?" He winked at Fassman, trying to include him in his mockery of Bugler.

"We have to keep trying," Bugler said. "Snakes matter also."

"As much as lions?"

"Yes, as much. And coyotes also."

Essler jammed the hat on his head, folded his arms, and rocked on his high heels. *What heels!* Fassman thought. As high as the platforms of a Harlem pimp. "Ed, have you sprung any lions from traps lately? On private land in Grace Canyon?" He nudged Fassman in the short ribs.

"I did. That female nailed up on the side of the van."

"You admit it?"

"The beast was dying of starvation. If you set traps, you have an obligation to kill animals quickly so they aren't tortured. They die pretty horribly."

"Is that law on the books somewhere?"

Bugler turned his head away. Poor Ed. At home with wolves and eagles, tongue-tied with men. Fassman wanted to help him. But he was an alien in this dry place, packed with noisy children, Jaycees spewing burning gasoline. They could stomp on him as fast as they would kill a horned rattler.

"No, it isn't a law," Ed said. "It's an understanding among humane people. I'd like to see the report you submitted on that lion. How many calves did she kill?"

"Now, Ed. You and me, we're westerners."

"There's all kinds of westerners. And since when do you have to set twenty traps to catch one lion? You get a good hunter and he'll find the one's been killing stock. But you people want to kill them all."

"The world would be better without them, Ed. They were born to be killed. Like snakes."

"They have a place in the world."

Essler sighed. "I have no fight with you. I like Jack Maybank and his wife. Oh, I know how you people worship the ground Professor Vormund walks on. He's a gentleman. Don't you know I'm a trustee of the community college, and they had to ask my approval before Vormund was invited to speak? I said, let him spout off."

"Mr. Essler?" Fassman asked. "Would you mind if we filmed a debate between you and Mr. Bugler? A little give-and-take?"

"I do mind. I'll make a statement for you about the charitable work of the rattlesnake roundup. I'm sure Mr. Bugler doesn't want to get involved in a brawl on a festive day like this."

"Alan, forget it," Bugler said.

"You folks have trespassed on my property three times now," Essler said. "You had that jeep in the foothills looking at cactus, and you stole specimens. You might have asked."

"I thought it was public land."

"I lease it. The Bureau of Land Management has never had a complaint on how I use it."

"Sorry," Bugler said. "I should have found out."

"And you rode into Grace Canyon and messed with my traps. People get shot at for things like that."

Willful bravery inflamed Fassman. He had no delusions about himself—a passive man, fearful of getting hit. But he could not let Ed stand there and take the blows. "Mr. Essler," Fassman said, "people not only might get shot at, they did get shot at."

"That a fact?"

"Someone in a blue-and-white monoplane opened up on us."

"So *you* were the other hero." Essler's smile broadened.

"I invited him," Bugler said.

"Do you own a blue-and-white upper-wing plane?" Fassman tried to imitate Essler's grin. It seemed to help. They all smiled a great deal.

"As a matter of fact, I do. Actually it was Mrs. Essler took the shots at you. Labelle was madder than a wet hen. She's killed forty lions. Got that one up yonder—the one you fellows let loose."

"Time's wastin', Duane," the stout man named Mac called.

There were over a thousand people milling around the bandstand and the refreshment stands. Games of chance had been set up—wheels, baseballs, dart boards, and balloons. Wives of the Jaycees were selling kisses. Music blared competitively—the high school band, the country music group.

"God Almighty, this is dreadful," Bugler said. Essler was mounting the bandstand. He carried a bullhorn and had strapped a brace of six-shooters around his waist. Everyone cheered. Across the dusty desert, among the mesquite, the creosote, the saguaro, the chollas, several dozen men in white coats were wandering about. Some carried red gas cans. All carried hoes or rakes. Others bore canvas sacks.

"I wanna catch a snake," a towheaded child bawled.

"You let Daddy do it," a woman said. "It's too dangerous."

"I wanna catch a snake." He bolted for the open country. The woman wobbled after him on Wedgies. She wore a top-heavy pile of curlers under a pale blue scarf. She had a giantess' behind, sausage-tight in orange pedal pushers. Stumbling across the sand, she lunged for the boy, yanked at his arm, and pulled him away. "All I need is for you to get snake-bit."

Essler was delivering his opening remarks and introducing people—Jaycee officers, local officials, beauty queens, a cowboy singer.

Fassman sent Apodaca and the soundman to the bandstand. There were two crews from local stations filming the proceedings.

"Everyone benefits," Essler was shouting into the bullhorn. "The dollars you folks spend will help the Jaycees' hospital program. The desert will be rid of a lot of ornery varmints. Everyone will have a good ole time. Don't miss the raffle for the snakeskin golf bags. Don't miss the snake milking contest. That's another benefit to the community—we are going to collect venom from the snakes and turn it over to the medical society for use in production of antisnake venom. How about that for usin' everything but the squeal?"

"No rattleburgers, Duane?" a woman shouted.

"You bet, Wanda Sue. When the skinnin' and bonin' is over, I'll be the first man to eat a rattleburger and I just might top it off with some rattlesnake stew."

A troupe of men in gaudy western dress, the leader on a pinto pony carrying a banner reading SHERIFF'S POSSE, rode by, then circled the bandstand. Everyone cheered.

Bugler said: "They're not lawmen. The guy with the banner is Ward Slade, the president of the Senita Bank. He's Jack Maybank's buddy. The rest are businessmen."

The mounted men drew pistols.

"In just sixty seconds," Essler called out, "the great rattlesnake roundup gets under way. When I give the countdown, draw your guns, set up a hoop and a holler that'll spook those rattlers out of their holes, and fire away! Ready?"

They roared. The western band struck up a fanfare. Children were held up to see the fun. The posse drew guns. They looked to Fassman like men who chaired charity drives and ran school boards.

Sidewinder materialized. He had been wandering around the outskirts of the crowd. His eyes were clouded. *Yes, ma'am, I'm the Hopi who works out to the DRI.*

"Somethin' funny goin' on," Sidewinder murmured. He dug his boots in the sand.

"Like what?" Bugler asked.

"Hold it a second, Mr. Essler," Apodaca called. "Let me get a close-up before you give the countdown."

"Anything for the media," Essler shouted. "That's the media from Los Angeles. We're liable to be on Walter Cronkite tonight if we put on a good show."

"*Yowee!*" a posse member shouted.

"What's going on?" Bugler asked Sidewinder. "What'd you find out?"

"That state trooper I was talkin' with. He's part Indian. I know him from Second Mesa. He seen some trucks out here early."

"Doing what?" Ed asked.

"He wasn't sure."

Fassman could not catch the mutterings of the Indian.

The air exploded with gunshots. Besides the posse and Essler, a score of men had brought side arms to the roundup. Blank cartridges were discharged into the bright sky. Cordite burned Fassman's nostrils. Children clapped their hands to their ears. Women shrieked.

"In case anyone gets bit," Essler shouted, as the shooting subsided, "there's a first-aid tent just the other side of the rattleburger stand."

From three thousand feet the plane cast a cigar-shaped shadow over the desert. Host and Vormund could see a growing crowd around a bandstand and a corral, a huge parking area, a crush of vehicles. A fine amberish dust veiled the air.

"It's not more than a few miles to the place where Ed and I saw the creeping devils," Vormund said. "This upsets me terribly."

Host said nothing. The old man grieved for an obscure cactus that might be trampled underfoot, but had no understanding of the millions of human lives that were improved with the electricity flowing out of Bald Indian. Yet there was a perverse truth in Vormund's view of things, a long-range logic that made him something more than a nature crank.

"Maybe they've turned it into a tourist attraction already," Clara said.

"Quite possible," Vormund said. "They can burn the real specimens and replace them with plastic models that look just as good."

Below, people at the rattlesnake roundup waved at the low-flying plane. Why the corral? Vormund wondered. A rodeo? A fair? He was no friend to indigenous western sports, but out of respect for his adoptive home, he had not written about broncobusters and bulldoggers.

"*Orugas* or not, it's all going," Vormund said. "The desert won't be the same when they're finished. Beer cans, filth, litter, man's junk. I'm told the Mojave is a vast junk pile—motorcycles and jeeps are killing it off."

Host nosed the plane toward the Interstate. It was the same road from which Bugler had taken the Vormunds to the desert site, where they had seen the coyote baited by dogs and kicked to a pulp. To Vormund the animal's death seemed a harbinger of what was in store for the desert. He saw with a grieving eye the line of vehicles inching like some multifooted machine into the pristine sand.

"I don't like what I see," Vormund said. "Man's stench is the worst in the world, man's tread the heaviest. No self-respecting herd of elephants would destroy the natural cover in that fashion."

"Now, Dan," Clara said, "you've seen it before."

"Maybe it would be better if my father took over," Host said. "At least we'd put up neat cities."

"There is no such thing as a neat city any longer."

"Host-Labarre might create one."

"No thank you. None of your controlled environments for me. I'll take my air fresh and my flowers real."

Corinne leaned toward Clara. "May I confide in you?"

"You dear girl. You have just met me."

"It isn't much of a confidence, and maybe you suspect the same thing. My husband wants Professor Vormund's approval."

"Whatever for? With all your money? Excuse my bluntness, but it's the truth." Clara looked at the young woman's impossibly perfect face. Everything: health, looks, wealth, intelligence. Yet she was sometimes sullen, withdrawn. And why this information about her husband, that shy man who seemed so taken with Dan?

"He wants Professor Vormund to *approve* of him."

"Maybe he just likes what Dan said about nature. You know a lot of people respect Daniel D. Vormund, even if that terrible Mr. Mencken didn't."

Vormund's ears, catching the name, turned to the women. "Clara, Mencken and I got along famously. You just hated his cigars."

"And his beer, and his nasty comments about women."

Corinne Host brushed her hair back, envious of the lives they had led. Mencken. Dreiser. "I know Ray quite well, Mrs. Vormund. He suffers being the son of an emperor."

"He looks strong enough to bear up under it."

"It's not the money. It's what his father makes him do." She caught herself. Did the Vormunds know about the Denkerman matter? They had not mentioned it. None of the Institute people had. She had talked too much to Fassman. She had to be on guard.

"I must be frank with you," Clara said. "Dan does not go around handing out A's any more. He is not an easy man to know. Ask his colleagues in the English Department. And for the last twenty years, he's preferred the company of animals. So you should tell your husband not to expect too much."

"I think your husband should let Ray know."

"Know what?"

"That he can't be bought with plane rides."

"Oh, dear. Mr. Host knows that. He's not a foolish young man."

Host turned the plane in the sparkling air. They lost altitude rapidly, sailing over the swarming crowd and the vehicles. The automobiles and trucks created a glittering mosaic of synthetic colors.

"Appalling," Vormund said. "I wish the Institute were rich and powerful, so we could buy land, buy legislators, buy anything that had to be bought. Jack should have moved on this."

"What did you have in mind?" Host's red face looked appealingly at the old man. He was almost begging to be of help.

"We could have made an offer for the land. Ed Bugler knows how much we would need to save those plants. And if the state or federal government won't do it, we should."

"I might be able to help."

"You?" Vormund studied the thick neck, the blockish head. "Yes. You said something at lunch the other day about giving us advice."

"More than advice. Maybe I can buy the land."

"And donate it to us? That would be the grandest donation in our impecunious history."

"We could work something out."

"But that's quite the reverse of what you people are supposed to do. You do things with land. You don't let it remain there and attract birds."

Host blinked. His jaw widened. "Maybe we should make a gesture."

"A token?"

"Better than that. Set an example. It would not be a problem for us to purchase Mr. Essler's land or any other land you and your friends wanted."

There was no indecision in Ray Host's voice. Vormund noted it. The voice of uncountable, flourishing wealth.

Corinne's ears caught enough to know what Ray was doing. He wanted Vormund's favor. An examination paper returned with an A. Perhaps a notation: *extremely well done, you know the subject.*

"You know," she whispered to Clara, "I think my husband wants to *buy* yours."

"Dan is not for sale."

"Everyone is."

"But not Dan, my angel. He never was. Not to anyone. And not for any price."

A Jaycee wife in tight jeans was handing out circulars. They were single-sheet flyers with the heading:

LET THEM HEAR US LOUD AND CLEAR

Stockmen, sheepmen, ranchers, hunters! The environmentalists, dickey-birders, bleeding hearts, all the so-called conservationists must be stopped in their tracks.

Predators that take away the livelihood of honest men cannot be tolerated. We will rid the land of vermin, whether they be coyotes, lions, bears, snakes, or birds.

Let the crybabies who moan over a dead coyote see what one coyote can do to a herd of sheep—dozens of innocent lambs gutted and left to bleed to death. Or the way a lion will go through a herd, murdering the fattest calves.

"File for future reference," Fassman said to Bugler. He took a half-dozen copies.

The crowd ran to the sides of the enclosure. Others tumbled across the desert. They formed cheering groups around the snake-hunters. Fassman ran behind the crew. Dust clogged his nose and throat.

"First of the day!" a young man shouted. He had a five-foot rattler on the end of a hoe. Suspended like a loop of rope, the snake thrashed and squirmed.

"Stay away from its head!" someone shouted.

"Stand back."

Bugler said: "They don't kill 'em right away. They get them into that corral."

A mob, including many children, raced after the first catch. Dumped inside the hot arena, the snake appeared stupefied. It coiled halfheartedly, clicked its rattles.

"Goddamn bastard." A man in rubber boots and a butcher's coat moved around the snake. Four other men were bringing in snakes, pushing them with long poles against which the rattlers struck blindly, or carrying them looped. A fifth man held a sack aloft.

The man in boots pinioned a snake with a metal pole with a forked tip. Then he grabbed it behind the head and lifted it high. He let it sway back and forth. The crowd cheered.

"I wish they'd kill it," a girl shouted. "It's so ugly."

"They gonna milk it for the venom," a youth said.

The man was pressing the snake's jaws against a gauze-covered jar held by a Jaycee. "Milk, you bugger," the man said. "Spit it out, you sumbitch."

Bugler scowled. "Doesn't know what he's doing. That's no way to milk a snake. He's smashing its jaw. Why doesn't he just kill it?"

A fat woman dug Bugler in the ribs. "They kill them all at the end." She picked up a child. "Dwight, you want to see them kill the snakes? You want to eat a snakeburger?"

The man in rubber boots threw the milked snake against the cinder wall. It slithered toward the shade, coiled, waited.

Within fifteen minutes the corral was crawling with rattlers—beige sidewinders with characteristic horns, pink-gray diamondbacks, western rattlers blotched brown and black. They seemed passive, sliding to the shaded corners of the enclosure, struggling feebly when they were sorted out for milking.

"It doesn't make sense," Bugler said. "I've never seen so many westerns out here. Sidewinders, some diamondbacks. But a western rattler is rare."

As he spoke three more men brought in more snakes. Out in the desert Fassman could see fires flaring.

"Burning them out," Ed said. "You can't get a rattler to go out in this sun. They're spraying gasoline into the rocks."

The snakes glided toward one another. They formed a tangled heap in the shaded side of the corral. Bugler told Fassman they were half dead. Exposure to the sun, rough handling, shock. Soon none coiled or tried to strike. The beige of the sidewinders mingled in looped patterns with the darker brown of the westerns, the pink, almost pale violet of the diamondbacks.

"Do they feel pain?" Fassman asked foolishly. He led Apodaca and Downs to the edge of the corral. The cameraman framed the mass of looped reptiles in his view finder. *Jesus, what an assignment!*

"They don't," Duane Essler said. Flanked by two members of the posse, he walked up to Bugler and Fassman. "You fellows will make a thing about how we torture snakes. But it's a fact that a rattlesnake feels no pain."

"It's a fact that they do," Bugler said. "As much as you do."

"I bow to the man of science. They inflict death and suffering. The desert is a better place without them."

"But nobody uses this desert," Fassman said. "Why kill them for no purpose?"

"The rule out here is, you see a rattlesnake, kill it," the paunchy man said.

Bugler said: "Mr. Essler, I wish you'd have come to us on this. That man is torturing them. He doesn't know how to extract venom. I don't believe what you said about selling it for serum. That's bunk. The drug companies get all the venom they need from snake farms."

Two more Jaycees came plodding to the corral. One carried a sack in which a captive snake was wriggling. The other had a six-foot diamondback hanging from a rake.

"Let 'er rip," Essler said. "*Operation Good Snake!*"

A small boy, no more than eleven, wearing rubber boots and a white butcher's coat, was led to the corral. He carried a broad-bladed machete. He looked terrified.

Essler took the bullhorn and hopped nimbly onto the corral

wall. "I see a mess of rattlesnake stew and snakeburgers. The honor of killing the first varmint goes to Peter Essler, my grandson. Go on, Pete. Show 'em how the West was won."

With a hoe, the man in rubber boots pulled a sidewinder out of the heap of snakes. He draped it over an oak log.

"One good chop at the head, son."

The boy raised the machete and brought it down without any conviction. It missed the head by a foot and severed part of the body midway to the rattling tail. The snake was still moving.

"Give it here, son." The man slashed at the horned head and severed it from the quivering body. "That's number one."

As if enflamed by the sight of the carcass, four men ran into the stadium. The chief butcher began untangling snakes. He tried to keep a semblance of order, confining the beheadings to the oak trunk. He draped a snake over the log. At once it was cut in half by a Jaycee. He tripped as he slashed downward, fell into the heaped snakes. Women screamed.

"Get the fool out," Essler shouted. "All we need is for one of them to get bit."

The rattlers looked drugged. They lay heaped, plaited, brown-beige-gray patterns intermingling. Colors of the desert, Fassman thought, the colors Vormund celebrated in his works.

A half-dozen men were now flailing at snakes. Blood splotched their white coats. One man picked up a diamondback by the rattles and smashed its head against the cinder blocks. It did not die. Twitching, it tried to coil and strike.

"Show you, you bastard," the man said. He chopped its head off with one stroke of the machete.

"Anyone keeping score?" Essler shouted from the top of the corral. The crowd thickened around the killing ground. Men held tots on their shoulders. A young man slashed at a western rattler and cut off its tail. It turned, coiled, struck at his feet. He rose vertically in the air, howled, came down with both feet on the snake. With his high heels, he mashed its head into a pink pulp.

"That's the ticket," the stout man in mauve said. "The heads are soft."

"It's good the youngsters get to see this," one of the posse said. "Teach them how to handle snakes."

"See it, kill it. That's my rule."

"Son, when you run this on the TV," Essler shouted to Fassman, "give us a fair shake. It's you media people make us look bad."

Fassman feared Essler. He feared the posse. He feared the women in curlers and western skirts. He wanted to add—*we don't have to*, but he was trembling. This was worse than the lion. The eager men with machetes scared the daylights out of him. What would it take to have them turn on him, sever his apologetic head from his clumsy body?

"Call them big westerns 'coon-tails,' " a wrinkled ancient muttered to Bugler. "It's because the tail just this side of the rattles is got them black-and-white rings. Fight like all hell them coon-tails."

Two Indian women began gathering headless snakes. They nailed them to a board and skinned and gutted them with curved knives. The dressed meat was thrown into a pail of water for washing, then passed to a man wearing a chef's toque. A fire of dried mesquite wood smoked under a metal grille.

A tall woman in a sunshade pinched Fassman's arm. "Ever eat a snakeburger?"

"Not lately."

"Better than chicken. The poison's only in the mouth. It don't hurt the meat none."

More snakes were thrown into the corral. The hacking and cutting was indiscriminate. In spite of the booted man's attempt to keep it orderly the butchers waded into the slithery mass, slashing and flailing.

"They trucked 'em in," Sidewinder whispered to Bugler.

Ed was resting his arms on the top of the enclosure. "Trucked what in?"

The Hopi pushed the frazzled hat over his eyes. He wanted no one to hear. "Rattlers."

"Who trucked what?"

"People came in trucks. They was out on the foothills all morning turning snakes loose. That trooper told me."

"Essler?"

"People runnin' this. Them ain't local snakes. They brung 'em in from New Mexico, Texas, even from Baja. They been collectin' rattlers for three weeks for this here."

"No wonder they got so many," Bugler said. "That is the

worst thing I ever heard in my life. They're supposed to be killing snakes to clear the desert. So what do they do? They bring them in to kill them."

"Don't say I told you. Don't say the cop told me. You know how it is. Him bein' part Indian. They'll say we're lyin'."

"He's sure?"

"Seen the trucks this mornin'. Half dead most of them."

"Good God. Hey, Alan."

Fassman was talking to Apodaca and Downs. The cameraman was getting grumpy. He was sick to his stomach. He could not take much more of the blood, entrails, and bashed heads. Fassman told him to liven the coverage up. Snake fillets sizzling on the mesquite fire. Kids munching snake sandwiches. Beer foaming from kegs.

A shriek went up from the throng. A sidewinder had struck at a Jaycee's boots, sunk its fangs into the leather. "Missed me," the man gasped. The man in boots picked up the snake by its rattles and smashed its head against the blocks.

Bugler told Fassman about the imported snakes. Sidewinder stood alongside him, chewing on a strand of grass. He didn't care one way or the other. Snakes were snakes, dead or alive.

"I can't believe it," Fassman said. His dust-veiled eyes studied the crowd, the snakes, the cowboy band. Essler was advising people to save their ticket stubs for the drawing. He was on the bandstand again, flanked by his posse, calling encouragement to the butchers. "Get some of the youngsters in there," he shouted. "Teach 'em not to fear anything that walks, crawls, or flies. Go on, son. There isn't a rattlesnake alive can face up to a man. That's it. Bash him good."

Fassman turned to Bugler. "Ever hear of something called a citizen's arrest?"

"Yeah. Jenny Maybank pulled it once on a guy who was starving horses up at Las Minas."

"Feel brave?"

"Me? I can't figure any law's been broken."

"How about shipping snakes interstate?"

"I'm not sure. They'll deny it anyway."

"Listen to your friend Alan Fassman. It doesn't matter whether there's a law been broken or not. These assholes have to be taught a lesson. I've got a cameraman here. I'll put it on the news tonight. Show them up for the brutes they are. You go up there. I'll keep the crew under Essler's nose. Lay a hand on Essler and say you're making a citizen's arrest, that they shipped snakes into Arizona illegally and are torturing them."

"Alan, there are twenty state cops around here. Not one has made a move to object to anything that's going on. One of them even told Sidewinder he saw the trucks bringing the snakes in this morning. Who am I to stick my two cents in?"

Sidewinder kicked the sand. "Leave me out of it."

"You are Edward Earle Bugler, curator of the Desert Research Institute, friend to desert creatures. Dan Vormund would want you to do it. Not a thing can happen except that Essler will tell you to get lost. Grab him and make the arrest. I'll keep the cameras going. I'll write a script that will have America weeping for diamondbacks."

"But the cops . . ."

"All they can do is drag you off."

Bugler began to smile. Timid at first, wary of man and his institutions (how compare them to the social order of a quail family, the affection lavished on pups by a mother coyote?), he now saw possibilities. Maybank would not like it, for sure. He hated getting the Institute into fights. But Dan would have a good laugh.

"Go on," Fassman said. "If you don't, I will. But I'm the press. I can't start fights. You're the voice of the desert, Ed."

"I like the idea better and better."

A man in the corral was complaining that the snakes at the bottom of the heap were "no damn fun." Apparently they had died of suffocation and were to be spared beheading.

"Cut 'em up anyway," Essler shouted. "Kill 'em a few times over if necessary."

"What now?" Apodaca asked.

"Follow Mr. Bugler to the bandstand. He is about to make history."

"History?"

"Of sorts. Go on, Downs. Use the shotgun mike. I want the dialogue. Ready, Ed?"

Bugler loped through the crowd—kids with balloons, men quaffing beer, Indians imbibing soft drinks, women in print dresses. In two long strides Ed was on the bandstand. He seemed out of place in his sweat-stained gray Sears work outfit.

Bugler walked toward Essler's peppy figure. Essler looked at Bugler and welcomed him. "A guest of honor, folks. Mr. Bugler, one of our leading dickey-birders. No hard feelings, even if you and me are on opposite sides. At least we can agree on rattlesnakes, correct?"

The camera crew positioned themselves in front of Essler.

"Great," Fassman said. "A blow is about to be struck for every snake in America."

"I hate to do this," Bugler said loudly. He did not seem shy or confused. "Mr. Essler, I am here to make a citizen's arrest."

"You got to be joking."

The posse drew their guns and discharged them into the air. Children screamed. Women howled.

"Oh, brother," the fat man in the mauve suit yelled. "This is beautiful. Man's going to arrest Duane."

"I am not kidding, Mr. Essler," Bugler went on. He walked up to Essler and stood, rawboned, long-armed, a few feet away from him. "You are under arrest for the illegal interstate shipment of venomous reptiles and the inhumane treatment of said reptiles."

"Bugler, you got to be out of your skull."

One of the posse playfully leveled a six-shooter at Ed. "Reach, Bugler. You're covered."

Ed looked down at Fassman. "What do I do now?" he asked.

"Call the police," Fassman shouted. "Explain to them that a crime has been committed and you need their help."

A diamondback, revived in the cool shade, slithered out of the pile and crawled to the opening in the corral. People shrieked and scattered.

"Kill the bastard."

"Hack him good, Phil."

"Oh, Jesus, it's loose."

"Stand back. I got him. Watch his damn head. If he coils, run like hell."

There was a chorus of delighted oohs, ahs, then applause.

"Got the son of a bitch. Clean through the skull. Look at the size of him. I'll keep that bugger's skin for myself."

Bugler advanced toward Essler. The posse members grinned. A few of them—the banker, the accountant—knew Ed as a local character from the Institute. Harmless, a goofy sort of man, always carrying on about badgers. The *Pantagraph* had once written him up in a funny piece: "He's Slept with Skunks."

Around the bandstand four state policemen had assembled. One of them was Sidewinder's friend. They looked big, immaculate, and extremely competent. One wore yellow sergeant's stripes. "What's up, Mr. Essler?" he asked.

"Darned if I know, Marty. Mr. Bugler has a complaint."

"What is it, Mr. Bugler?" the sergeant asked.

"I'm making a citizen's arrest. Mr. Essler here is guilty of inhumane treatment of animals—"

"Snakes aren't animals," Essler said. "They're vermin."

"Furthermore, there is evidence those snakes were illegally transported across state lines for the purpose of killing them, which is a violation of some kind."

"It's the media," Essler said. "That fellow from Los Angeles. He's filming it, Marty. They staged it to make a fuss. You know, make the gun clubs and ranchers look like fools."

"Keep filming," Fassman said to Apodaca. "Get every word he says."

Downs, the soundman, pushed the rubber-sheathed microphone closer to Essler's pear-shaped head. The Stetson seemed to have fallen even lower over his narrow skull, so that only the mouth was visible.

"I ask for the assistance of the police," Ed said, "in enforcing the laws of the state. Those snakes were trucked in half dead. They're being tortured."

"Mr Bugler, you better come down," the sergeant said.

"He's crazy as a loon," a posse member shouted.

"Let's drag him off," another said. "Necktie party."

"Oh, he's a good sort," the banker said. "Ed, beat it, will you? We'll talk to Jack Maybank about this. Don't push Duane, huh?"

Bugler thought of the mangled snakes. The guts and blood staining the enclosure. The way they had been dragged in, dying of sun and thirst. He felt alone and miserable in a world that did not understand him. No wonder Dan Vormund talked to a toad every afternoon.

Ed walked two steps toward Essler and placed his right hand on the rancher's right forearm above the studded pearl-gray glove.

"Mr. Essler, you are under arrest." His bespectacled eyes appealed to the troopers. "You fellows give me a hand."

"Get your hands off me, Bugler."

"Any man who delights in torturing animals should be in jail. You not only organized this rotten affair, you killed that lion, and God knows how many others you shoot, most of them illegally. And your wife shot at me a few days ago."

Fassman, watching the crazy drama he had helped produce, addressed a trooper. "Aren't you fellows supposed to do something?"

The policeman's bland face looked at Fassman (clearly an intruder) and made a loco sign alongside his forehead—a turning of the right index finger at temple level.

"Hey, Marty," Essler called to the sergeant. "Get this guy off me. George, Fred, do something."

Ed's grip was like the steel traps Essler had set in Grace Canyon. As if in rigor mortis it had locked around Essler's arm. Would Essler, Fassman mused, try to bite his way out? Was he as brave as the cougars that ate their own flesh and bone to be free? Or the badger that had dug a pit big enough for an automobile in its frenzy to escape?

The man in mauve stepped forward.

"Look here, Bugler, I'm Mac Timmons, Mr. Essler's attorney. I know Mr. Maybank, and I know lots of people who support you birds at the Institute. This is not what they give money for. Let go."

"No," Ed said. "He's under arrest."

Timmons walked to the apron of the bandstand. People had gathered around the troopers and around Fassman's crew, not quite certain what was happening. A few munched snakeburgers. A rich stench roiled the air—snake guts, snake blood.

"Marty, we had a case like this up at the commune," Mac Timmons said. "Some of those hippie kids pulled a stunt like this. We had to jug them."

"Let go of Mr. Essler, Mr. Bugler," the sergeant said politely.

"No."

"I don't want to force you. Please let go."

"No. He's broken the law. He should be arrested."

The hand was the hand of an angry Jehovah, Fassman thought. Was Essler in pain? Did he understand the celestial wrath he had aroused? Fassman made a connection—Bugler as Vormund's agent, Vormund as the angel of God, or the Life Force. Essler was among those who denied the earth the right to produce beauty and joy. An agent of darkness. Was he thus condemned? One of the first who would suffer when the earth refused to grow wheat or bring forth water? Was Bugler merely a little early in his wrathful judgment?

Timmons gestured to the sergeant. "He's nuts, Marty. Get your men up here and make him let go of Mr. Essler. Bugler's the one committing a crime."

"Yes, sir, Mr. Timmons." He turned to the other officers. "Fred, Joe. Get up there and pull him off."

Fassman stumbled after the part-Indian officer. "Sir! I'm told you were a witness. You saw them bring the snakes in this morning."

"You were told wrong. One side, mister."

The officers trotted up the wooden stairs.

"Mr. Essler is preferring charges against this man," Mac Timmons said. "He charges him with assault, trespass, and false arrest. Arrest him."

"Let's go, Mr. Bugler," the sergeant said. "Let go of Mr. Essler and come along."

"We intend to ask for criminal prosecution," Timmons said. "I want the sheriff and the DA notified."

"But he's the one's murdering things," Bugler said. "I'm trying to point something out."

"Let go of him," a trooper said.

Ed shook his head sorrowfully. The ways of the world were beyond him. He saw the snout of the soundman's mike, the long lens of the camera. He did not blame Alan. It had sounded like a good idea. But what would Jack Maybank do? Fire him, maybe. He let his hand fall from Essler's wrist.

"You want him, Sergeant?" a trooper asked.

"County jail," the sergeant said. "Come on, Mr. Bugler. You can ask for a lawyer. You have all your rights."

"It's sort of silly," Ed said. "What did I do?"

Timmons caught the sergeant's eye. "Three counts. Assault, trespass, and false arrest. Mr. Essler and I will discuss how to handle it. Thank you, Marty."

"Alan," Bugler said wearily. "I guess you better call Maybank. Dan also."

People churned around Fassman and his crew. People saw two state policemen leading away a bespectacled man.

Essler and Timmons were laughing.

"What happened?" a woman asked.

"Some nut," a man answered. "Some nut tried to attack Mr. Essler. They're gonna put him away."

The woman nodded energetically. "Serves 'em right. Probably some crazy hippie."

A Klaxon razored the air with its *wah-wah-wah*. Fassman, wobbling under the sun, trying to keep a few paces behind Ed and the troopers, wondered if it was a police van.

Then he saw an orange-and-white ambulance, red lights flashing on its roof. The crowd parted as the ambulance bounced off the dirt track. It headed for the corral.

"Fellah got bit," a man said to Fassman.

"Bit?"

"Got too close to a big'un. Wasn't quite dead. Sunk its fangs right in his hand."

"Too bad."

"They skinned the bugger alive."

The newsman stumbled after his technicians. *Before they skin me alive.*

Twenty minutes later Fassman was calling Maybank from the Senita County jail and courthouse. He explained the problem: Ed Bugler had been arrested on Duane Essler's demand—assault, trespass, false arrest. Essler was sore as a boil. He knew about the fooling around with his lion traps. This was the last straw. Maybank—Fusaro was with him, discussing a meeting regarding the bequest—asked if Bugler had done anything to provoke Essler. It didn't sound like Ed. He disliked most people so heartily he couldn't be bothered arguing with them.

Fassman seemed to be muffling his voice. "Hard to explain, Jack," he said. "Ed tried to make a citizen's arrest."

"Has he lost his marbles?"

"I'll explain when you get here. Ed needs a lawyer. He'd like Vormund out here also."

Maybank told Fusaro what had happened.

The lawyer's eyebrows went up. "Trespass and false arrest?"
"And assault."

"Christ Almighty. We're worrying about fifteen million dollars
and your curator is out getting the ranchers sore. When are you
going to can him? You and Jenny have been discussing it ever
since he let the plant pathology lab burn down."

"I have a better reason now."

In Maybank's station wagon, speeding toward Vormund's
home, Fusaro began to worry. "Anyone out to show us up, Jack,
to prove we're a collection of cranks—they've got ammunition
now, thanks to Ed."

"Of all people Essler. He owns half the state legislators."

"Essler, hell. I can hear Denkerman's relatives bringing this in
as evidence. Do you, Mr. Maybank, believe that an organization
such as yours, whose officers go around committing criminal acts,
merits such a vast sum of money? If Mr. Denkerman were aware
of the true nature of your so-called Institute, do you think he
would have been so generous?"

"Cut it out, Joe."

"By the time they're through with us, they'll have us looking
like the Black Panthers."

Corinne pleaded fatigue and asked to be dropped at the Senita Inn before Host drove the Vormunds home. In some
undefined way she had found the flight discomfiting. The old
woman was wonderfully vivacious. Full of marvelous stories
about their early married years in Greenwich Village. Stories
spiced with famous names, all reduced to human proportions by
her realistic, humorous Italian eye and ear.

"Oh, Gene O'Neill," she said to Corinne, who had asked about
him. "Gene was so beautiful. In a magic way. Women and men
were attracted to him. He would sit quietly, not talking, very intense, and you *had* to look at him. If you didn't . . . he'd get
mad and get up. Beautiful, though."

She tapped Corinne's knee. "And listen, my dear. Dan had a
great deal to do with O'Neill's career. Dan was the first critic to
say this man was the great voice of the American theater. And
he kept saying so, even when the young critics were knocking
Gene. Dan was right, of course. As he always was."

O'Neill. Dreiser. Mencken. Trotsky. The names flowed easily from her. She was not flaunting past acquaintances, merely reminiscing. "I was an outsider," Clara said. "A little Italian girl with a funny accent. I was not an intellect like most of them. But Dan was. So they accepted me. Besides, they liked my cooking. Too bad I don't cook much any more. Dan's stomach. I think if we had had children, I would have cooked more. But poor Dan, it's Meritene and vitamins for him."

Corinne asked herself: What do I resent? She tried to put her finger on it. Perhaps it was that the Vormunds seemed to have had so much—on so little. He had never been rich. He had never known power, never possessed the strength to change things, move mountains, shift populations, divert rivers. Yet he had been a happy man, doing precisely what he wanted to do. And she had always been at his side, encouraging him, giving him his eye drops and cough medicine. Hadn't she heard the Maybank woman mutter something at lunch about Clara being "the iron lung" that had kept Vormund going?

Corinne had to get away from them for a while. They were, those two old people, unwitting donors of guilt. Poor was worse than rich. Very rich was better than rich. Astronomic, soaring, unassailable wealth, like the Hosts', best of all. Yet Corinne remained bitter, full of questions about who she was, who Ray was. And did they love each other? Enough? After fifty years could they possibly be as devoted as the Vormunds?

The fault was Ray's, she decided. She had increasing difficulty respecting him. For all the wealth, the potency, the great machines and vast enterprises, he was Pop's man, Pop's possession, another payloader or earth-mover. Vormund had never been anyone's man. No one gave him orders. He sat in the adobe house in the foothills, listening for lost coyotes and the morning birds, and he savored the world. Clara shared it with him. How had they achieved this? What right had they to such a dazzling capacity for making the best things in the world theirs? "We hear the wrens and the thrashers in the morning," Clara had said to her, "and we know it has to be a good day. Dan and I know it."

Their certainties disturbed Corinne. It was idiotic being jealous of a woman three times her age, but she felt shaky, full of a cold malaise, when she walked into the lobby of the Senita Inn.

Simmons, the tennis pro, was talking to two white-haired men.

They were old California money, people awed by the Hosts. All three men—the arrogant pro and the ancients with veined heads —ogled her gold hair, tan skin, superb figure. Simmons excused himself and walked toward Corinne.

"Mrs. Host. Hi, there. Mr. Host around?"

"Not for a while."

"Interested in a lesson?"

"No. I'm exhausted. We've had our plane out."

"May I buy you a drink?"

She detested his smarmy manner—a bootlicker to the wealthy. She could imagine with what meanness he treated the boys who rolled the courts.

"I'm tired. I'm going to my room."

"Then I'll bring it there. It's usually a vodka gimlet, right?"

Corinne looked at his dark insolent eyes. A cheap man. Easily bought, easily owned. Not at all like that fragile naturalist whom Ray was cultivating. She thought of Vormund, of how much joy he had given to readers, students, colleagues. Yes, unbuyable. The world seemed to split into two groups—those who could be purchased and those who never could. Unfortunately unbuyables were in short supply. No wonder Ray was intrigued with Daniel D. Vormund.

"A vodka gimlet," Corinne said. "On the rocks."

"Super. I'll be at your room in five minutes. I'll be so quick, the ice cubes won't have a chance to melt."

"I'm in the Vanderbilt cottage."

"I asked already. Could you leave the door open? I can make a grand entrance that way."

"Just knock. I will come to the door and take my drink, and then you can get back to your practice balls and your line markers. And if you dare to try to enter my room, you'll be fired, and the Hosts will see to it you never work anywhere in a five-state area. Understood?"

"The flight wasn't too tiring?" asked Host.

He and Vormund were on the patio. Clara had gone to prepare Dan's Meritene.

"Just a little. It was exciting."

Vormund covered his palsied right hand with his left. Too much exertion. Too many new sensations. The mob near the *orugas* upset him. The wild places were doomed. And what had his efforts availed? Damned little.

"Sorry about the bumps. The currents get tricky when you cruise below the mountains. But I haven't lost a plane or a passenger yet."

Vormund blinked and rested his head against the back of the chair. Opening his eyes, he gazed at Host's square solemn face. The young man was forever seeking recognition or at least an acknowledgment from Vormund that he had done well. Yet to Vormund, Host's wealth and power seemed more than adequate to equip a man with a fair quota of self-confidence. In his years in Arizona, Vormund had come to know many people of great wealth. In the desert they grew senile, sat on their money, cultivated either alcohol or a hobby. By and large they were quiet, self-effacing people, most of them bores or Johnny-One-Notes. But a heartening minority were creative and worthwhile. An old man, heir to a lead fortune, was a leading expert on termites. Vormund had read his articles. A trembling nonagenarian, once Wall Street's first man in arbitrage, delved into plant fossils. But the usual routine with these aged Croesuses (Croesi?) was golf, alcohol, right-wing politics, and if the glands permitted, a touch of adultery. What was that rhyme from Byron?

What men call gallantry, and gods adultr'y,
Is much more common where the climate's sultry.

Young Host was different. For one thing, he was far richer. There was something tentative, searching, in him. He was curious about new things, almost ashamed of his curiosity. Vormund, who had once given a series of lectures at Stanford, tried to draw him out about his undergraduate years. Did he know a certain professor, an old friend of Vormund's? Host shook his head sadly. No, he had not enjoyed those years. An only child, protected, gifted with athletic skills and a good mind, he was something of an enigma to the fraternity jocks who sought his favors. With blunt contempt, he rejected the social climbers, the fraternity potentates, the other rich boys. He was a loner who kept his dormitory door locked while he studied.

"I don't know you would have been happier back East," Vormund said. "Columbia was a marvelous place but it was always in trouble. Their teams lose. They verge on bankruptcy. There is always tension between administration and senior faculty, senior faculty and junior faculty, everyone and the fractious students. Today, one runs the risk of getting brained by falling plaster in a classroom, or mugged by the revolution of rising expectations."

Clara brought Vormund his Meritene and his pills. "Don't make fun of the old place. We had good friends there. New York was great fun for us, wasn't it, Dan?"

"I prefer my back yard."

"Tell Raymond that story about Irwin Edman. The time he had to go to dinner with Dr. Butler."

"I'm not sure he's interested."

"I am," Host said, "if you aren't too tired. Anything Mr. Vormund tells me . . . it's all new . . . I hear about people and concepts . . ." Choking, he stifled his embarrassment.

"Tell it, Dan."

Vormund obliged. It was a rambling story, not too funny. One had to have known Edman, that gnomelike, gentle philosopher, to appreciate it. It involved President Butler, Edman, and a visiting Anglican bishop. The point of the story was Edman's confusion over Butler and the bishop referring to other Anglican churchmen as "Canterbury" and "York" without their titles. Edman confessed later to Vormund he couldn't follow the conversation because he assumed "they were talking about cathedrals."

Host did not laugh.

"That's it, I'm afraid," Vormund said. "I didn't tell it well. Perhaps the salt has lost its savor."

Maybank's slouching figure, arms folded on his chest, was approaching from the carport.

"Dan, we've got an emergency. Hi, Clara. Hello, Mr. Host." He rubbed his head, fidgeted.

"Emergency?"

"Ed Bugler's in jail."

"Our Ed?"

Maybank thought: Here is the problem in firing Ed, who deserves to be fired, if only for the dumb stunt he had pulled. Dan Vormund adored Ed.

"It's some idiotic business," Maybank said. "Essler was running this rattlesnake roundup. Can you believe it? He had thousands of people out there killing snakes and eating rattleburgers.

— 212 —

Your former student Fassman was filming it and somehow Ed got involved. Ed got into a hazzle with Essler, as nearly as I can figure. They arrested Ed."

Vormund got up. It took a fraction of a second for his knees to articulate and support him. He rested his left hand on the redwood table. "What are we doing? Let's get Ed out of jail. Who can we call? I'm eager for a fight."

"No you don't," Clara said. "Jack, you keep Dan out of this. He's exhausted. Ed's a grown man, and so are you, and you have a lawyer."

Maybank looked chastised. "As a matter of fact, Clara, Ed asked for Dan. He said he wouldn't want him to miss the fun."

"Then I'm going. I haven't felt so much like a fight since George Jean Nathan attacked my appraisal of Eugene O'Neill." He slapped his hands. "Lead on, Jack. Watson, the game's afoot."

Host stepped forward. "May I come?" The hidden voice was a polite appeal to Vormund—and an assertion of the weight that the Hosts threw around.

Maybank replied: "Sure. I can't figure anything terrible happening. Joe Fusaro, our lawyer, is with me. He says maybe we can make a deal with Essler."

"I'll appeal to his nobler nature," Vormund said.

Host took the old man's arm and helped him toward the carport. "I have a feeling we can do better than that."

Vormund looked at the young man's square face. He was heartened to have him as an ally. He did not delude himself. It was the money that lent him power. It instilled fear, respect, awe. Against the Esslers of the world (no pikers themselves) one could use a Ray Host.

The four men—Vormund, Host, Maybank, and Fusaro—found Sidewinder asleep at the wheel of Fassman's station wagon. The vehicle was parked in the sun-scorched lot at the side of the Doble County courthouse, a new concrete building facing a statue of Abe Bernstein, the peddler who had founded Senita's first department store, bank, and stagecoach service.

All living things, human or animal, except the dozing Hopi, seemed to have vanished, obliterated by the savage light and merciless heat.

— 213 —

"Sidewinder, wake up," Maybank said. "What happened?"

The Indian's eyes blinked like a chuckawalla's. "Ed tried to grab that guy but the cops arrested him."

"Jesus," Fusaro murmured.

In the tiled lobby Fassman and his technicians were seated on benches. The newsman got up when he saw the men enter. Vormund looked angry. His crisscrossed face was twitching.

"Hi," Fassman said. "Ed's in the lockup until someone posts bond. It's only five hundred dollars. I'd have done it myself, except it would clean me out, and I may have more crises before this is over."

Fusaro's eyes were annoyed with the intruder. "What in hell got into Ed?"

"He tried to make a citizen's arrest of Essler."

"He *what?*"

"Marvelous!" Vormund cried. "That's what we need! Those youngsters are right who squat on highways. Where's Ed? I want to shake his hand."

Fusaro barked: "Is it proper to ask what led Bugler to this exercise in law enforcement? Could it be a news guy wanted a story?"

"I put Ed up to it. But not for the story. We were disgusted by what went on." Fassman told them of the slaughter of the snakes, the suspicion that the snakes had been trucked in for the pleasure of killing them.

"I hope it's on your film," Vormund said. "I want a copy for myself."

"It's on it all right," Fassman said. He pointed to his cameraman and soundman. They were holding a sack of film cans. "It's a terrific story."

"Yeah, terrific," Fusaro said. "We got the biggest landowner, the head of the ranchers' association, and every *pezzo grosso* in the county sore at us."

"Joe," Vormund said, "they were hardly our friends before Ed did this. Why not show them we're in this fight seriously? That we intend to fight like wildcats?"

"Wildcats never make it against these people," Fusaro said. "They got us treed, Dan, *treed.* You don't get anywhere with Essler and his crowd by attacking them in public."

Vormund wavered. Host grasped his arm. "Are you all right?" the young man asked.

A Pima woman herded two bawling children past them. A deputy sheriff followed her, talking in poor Spanish to a mestizo ranch hand with a bandaged head. Vormund was suddenly glad he was part of the courthouse scene. Too often he had sat back, played the timid academician. Ed deserved high marks for his quixotic act. So did Fassman for egging him on.

"I'm exhilarated," he said to Host. "I'm tickled over the way Ed got involved. Can we sit somewhere?"

Host guided him to a bench against the wall.

The paunchy man, Mac Timmons, who had been at Essler's side during the roundup, came out of a conference room and waved at Joe Fusaro. "Hey, Joe. We're all in the district attorney's office. Mr. Essler is awaiting. Hi, Mr. Maybank."

Fusaro and Timmons huddled for a moment. Vormund watched them closely—lawyer's talk, confidences. Odd, how they worked together and rarely showed any passion. Duane Essler would be happy to feed Ed Bugler a steak laced with strychnine, but the lawyers got along charmingly.

"Look, Jack," Fusaro said, turning away from Timmons. "Essler is being reasonable, Mac says. He wants to settle this man-to-man, with no lawmen present. No DAs, no police. All right with you?"

Vormund's clear voice rose from the bench. "They have no right to lock Ed up like that. I'm beginning to get angry. Jack, tell them to let Ed out, or we'll make more trouble for them."

Timmons goggled at the old man. "My gosh, it's Professor Vormund. Hi, Professor."

Vormund ignored the greeting. "Ed Bugler should not be in jail. Who can I talk to? Who's in charge here?"

Host whispered something to Vormund. The old man nodded.

Maybank, Fusaro, and Timmons conferred again. As they did, Duane Essler came out of the room. Fassman saw him and tried to melt into the wall. As he backed away, he found himself against the bench where Host sat with Vormund.

"Hello, Mr. Host."

A bob of his head was all that Host could manage. Fassman was dismissable.

"Have a nice plane ride?" the newsman asked.

"Mr. Vormund enjoyed it."

The old man was on the edge of a bench. His right hand cupped his right ear, trying to pick up what Essler was saying to the others. "What's he up to?" Vormund called. "You can't put Ed Bugler in a cage. Let him out. Jack, tell Mr. Essler to let Ed out."

Host touched Vormund's knee. "It will work out. Don't worry about your friend."

How could he be so sure? Fassman wondered. He was having difficulty with Host and his magazine-cover wife. Something odd there. Great wealth usually imposed dullness, not mystery. The blandest, dumbest people Fassman had ever met were among the very rich. Money blurred them. It turned them into wrinkle-free hard-boiled eggs. But there was a brew of some kind bubbling inside Ray Host's terra-cotta façade. Why the interest in Vormund? Looking for a father, friend? As so many of us are? Fassman asked.

There were more smiles. A laugh from Joe Fusaro. Essler detached himself from the group and skipped over to where Vormund was seated with Host. He smiled at Vormund and then addressed the young man. "Have we met . . . you did business once . . . ?"

"I don't recall."

Vormund did not introduce him. "I want Mr. Bugler out of jail. You tell the sheriff to let him go. This is uncivilized."

"Professor, I recall with great pleasure the speech you gave to the Kiwanis. You sure kidded the pants off us. No more roads, no more condominiums, no more grazing on public lands. Had us in stitches."

"I was never more serious in my life."

"But that's what makes a horse race, doesn't it? You serious, me convinced you're kidding."

A uniformed attendant whispered something in Essler's ear. The rancher nodded, then spoke to Fusaro. A state trooper held a door open. The parties to the dispute followed Essler into the room.

Vormund got up and trailed them. "Jack," he called. "Jack, tell them to release Ed."

Host and Fassman followed. They lingered at the threshold of the room. The others had taken seats around a table.

"Should I close the door, Mr. Essler?" the trooper asked.

The rancher's upside-down head darted a look at Fassman and Host. "Friends of the professor? Oh, the media fellow from Los Angeles. Let 'em in. No cameras of course. But no secrets either."

Host and Fassman stood against the wall under framed photographs of Washington, Lincoln, and Barry Goldwater.

"There's nothing to discuss," Vormund said. "Let Mr. Bugler out, then we can listen to your complaint against him."

"It doesn't work that way, Dan," Maybank said.

"Dan, we're working on it," Fusaro added.

"Not fast enough to suit me."

Vormund folded his arms. Too much air conditioning. He was cold. But happy with himself. The new assertiveness, discovered in this ninth decade of his life, was surprising and invigorating. Had he caught some of it from Raymond Host, that blunt young man who flew jets and built cities?

"Mr. Essler, tell us what you want done," Fusaro said. "We'll see if we can't arrange something."

"I'm not interested in what he wants done," Vormund said. "I want Ed out."

"Easy, Dan," Fusaro said.

Essler spoke sincerely. No, he did not want to press charges against Bugler. He was willing to drop the affair. But the Desert Research Institute had to stop persecuting him. It was ridiculous, catching them three times on his property, taking photographs, and worst of all, freeing a killer lion. Bugler was breaking laws. Men had been shot for less in Arizona. And the topper was that stunt at the snake roundup.

"You have a point," Maybank said.

"Jack, I knew you'd see it my way. Give me your word you'll stay off my land, and I'll drop charges."

Maybank looked at Fusaro. "Okay, Joe?"

"Sounds good to me. Mr. Timmons and I discussed it outside. I don't see why the Institute and the ranchers can't get together."

Vormund's cracked lips parted once, twice. He had trouble summoning up the words. Fassman watched him, grieving for him.

"One thing more," Essler said, "now that we're agreed. The film."

"Yeah," Fusaro said. "Mac mentioned that."

Fassman thought: Essler's honeyed words, the laughter, were build-up. He had no real battle with Maybank's people, at least a battle he was not bound to win. But the intrusive media were something else. Fassman, from whom some word was now expected, observed Ballstead's First Law: *silence.*

"That man put Bugler up to it," Essler said. He pointed a finger at Fassman. "I don't know who he is and I don't care. But he's the one egged Bugler on. We have witnesses."

Vormund turned his frail head and in a loud classroom voice, called: "Well done, Alan."

"I'm sorry to see the professor encourages that kind of behavior," Essler said. "That would seem to prove it was a plot and maybe Vormund was part of it—"

"I wasn't, but I wish I had been."

"A nice business," Essler went on, reddening. "Reporter from Los Angeles raises a fuss, fakes the film, makes us look like murderers on the television."

Maybank put a hand over his eyes. "You're not entirely right, Duane. I had no idea Bugler was going out to that event. I just met Fassman a few days ago. I had no idea he brought a cameraman out there."

Timmons smacked the table. "Jack, they worked hand in glove. If it wasn't so nasty to Mr. Essler, it would be laughable."

Vormund's cracked voice stilled the room. "Jack, why aren't we sticking up for Ed? Why aren't we challenging this man?"

"Lay off, Dan," Maybank muttered.

"Why should I? If Mr. Essler and his colleagues are so proud of the mass butchery of snakes, why don't they want it on television? What are they ashamed of?"

Essler's face went a shade redder. He whispered something to Timmons.

"Mr. Essler says he's sorry to hear you talk like that, because he respects you," Timmons said. "You know as well as we do there is no harm in thinning the snake population. It's a public service."

"This is hardly the place for a lecture on ecology," Vormund said, "but you're all wet. Kill snakes and you can't control rodents. Poison rodents and the insects run wild. Destroy the insects and the plants won't pollinate. Soon you won't be able to grow wheat."

"Professor, you're right," Essler said. "This is the last place in the world to debate the eco-system. You're the last person in Senita I want to argue with."

"I'm disappointed."

Fassman took a step away toward the table. "May I say something?" No one responded. "Those snakes were not native to the area. They were trucked in to be killed."

"We have no business with that man," Mac Timmons said. "He's from the media and he gets his orders from an office in New York."

"But were the snakes brought in?" Vormund asked.

Again Essler and the lawyer whispered behind manicured hands.

"We aren't sure. Maybe a few. What the hell is the difference? It merely means we're helping other counties kill them." Timmons managed the defense badly. Fusaro caught his confusion.

"'Every creature is better alive than dead, men and moose and pine trees, and he who understands it aright will rather preserve its life than destroy it,'" Vormund said. He sounded as if he were addressing a class. He turned to Fassman. "Alan, that film. Don't surrender it. Push has come to shove."

Fusaro was shaking his head. "Dan, a deal's a deal. You want Ed out, you want to stay out of court, we need the film."

"You have no right to make deals for my news film," Fassman said. "Don't try it, and don't ask me again."

"That man is going to make you sorry he ever showed up in Senita," Essler said. "That film is a fake. Bugler was out to make a scene for the cameras. I will pursue this matter to the hilt if he doesn't surrender it. Jack, it will be the Institute that suffers."

"Gonna be hot and heavy for you folks," Timmons chimed in. "We got a lot of charges pending. Joe, you know what I mean."

Maybank turned in his chair. His gentle eyes appealed to Fassman. "Alan, you heard them. Give us a break."

Fassman hesitated. Of what value were lost causes, campaigns that were foredoomed?

"Refuse them," Vormund said. "As for Ed, he will suffer a few nights in jail gladly. He is a man who has slept in badger holes."

"It's more than Ed," Fusaro said.

"Dan, there are wheels inside of wheels," Maybank said.

"Things going on, plans that require good will in the community."

"Good will? Why should we behave nicely? Thoreau was wroth with himself for having behaved too well. Jack, we must make trouble and disrupt. I feel the need of a picket sign."

Host, standing an inch from the wall, arms crossed on his chest, now was convinced that Vormund had been told nothing of the Denkerman inheritance. That, of course, was what Maybank and the lawyer had been referring to obliquely. With Bugler jailed, possibly brought to trial, with Essler and his powerful friends attacking them as lawbreakers, Maybank's organization could be smeared as a fake, people hardly worthy of Denkerman's fifteen million dollars. Host could see his father's lawyers reading every word of a court transcript, using it to prove that the DRI was a collection of irresponsible nature freaks.

"There's an issue of freedom of the press here," Fassman was saying lamely. "Mr. Essler has to understand that."

Essler did not honor Fassman with a glance. "Joe, the offer stands. Give me the film and everything's set. And we'll want your client's written agreement to stay off Essler land."

Something seemed to buzz in Vormund's mind. He leaned forward and clasped his hands on the table. "*Essler* land, you say?"

"You must know I own a great deal of land, Professor."

"*Own?*"

"Well, own a great deal, and lease some."

"Ah. Public land, that you lease from the United States Government, is that right?"

"Yes, I lease land. What has this got to do with anything? Professor, my respect for you may soon be limited to your writing. Can we proceed with the matter of that man's film?"

Timmons put a restraining hand on Essler's arm. The rancher's voice was rising, like the voice of a fundamentalist preacher warming up for the Good News.

Timmons spoke. "Professor, this is no court. Whether Mr. Essler owns or leases land is immaterial. For the purposes of this meeting it's his land."

"Yeah, Dan, drop it," Fusaro said.

Vormund ignored them. "And you use toxicants on your leased public lands, do you not? Great quantities of cyanide and

1080? No one can check up on you. The government doesn't mind if you slaughter every living creature with poisons."

"It's another argument, Dan," Maybank said despairingly.

"No, it isn't," the old man cried. "If the discussion here concerns lawbreaking, let's open it up. You people and the mining interests and the big growers have always told the federal government what to do. And you're still doing it. You break the law by drenching lands owned by the American people with insidious poisons, and then you accuse Mr. Bugler of being a criminal. Those animals and birds you slaughter exist for all the people, not just for you and your friends to murder."

"Joe, you'd better advise Professor Vormund that his attacks on my client are not appreciated," Timmons said.

"He's right, Dan," Fusaro said. "Let's stick to the film."

Vormund had run out of steam. His trembling hand reached for a glass of water. It trickled down his withered chin and corded neck. Fassman felt a deep pity rise in him, a sadness he could not bear. He felt he had to interrupt, take sides, succor his old teacher.

"Will someone ask Mr. Essler how many stock-killing forms he's filed in the last two months?" Fassman asked. "And how many lions he and his employees have killed in that period?"

Timmons and Essler turned their heads and glared at Fassman as if he were a coyote who had just dined on a lamb.

"That man is here through Mr. Essler's courtesy," Timmons shouted. "He'd be well advised to shut up, or get out."

Maybank turned to Fassman. "Back off, Alan. Dan, nothing's gained by making charges about poison, leases, or anything except what happened with Ed. Mr. Essler, I'll give you a letter agreeing to stay off your land."

"And the film," Essler added.

Fusaro and Maybank looked at Fassman. Enervated, dehydrated, the newsman slumped against the wall.

"My answer is a firm nonnegotiable *no*," Fassman said. "That film is mine. If you don't like what you see on television, file a complaint with the Federal Communications Commission."

"Does that man speak for all of you?" Timmons cried.

"Hell, no," Fusaro said. "He's on his own. We didn't invite him here. Alan, give us a break. There's more riding on this than Ed being in the slammer. Believe me."

As if in a comic strip, a light bulb sprouted over Fassman's head. Ray Host had experienced the same revelation earlier. Fassman, in many ways an innocent, had forgotten about the Denkerman will. Of course. A court fight with Essler could wound them, perhaps lead to a breaking of the will. Fusaro was right. A lot more than Ed Bugler was involved.

And Host. Where did he stand? Was he here to spy on the DRI, use this tawdry-comical business of the snake roundup, and Bugler's quixotic gesture, against the conservationists? Who was he to come sneaking after the Institute's money, pretending to worship Vormund, behaving like a long-lost son? Fassman was mortified.

"Give us the film, Alan," Fusaro pleaded. "So the American public will be spared movies of snakes getting their heads chopped off. What's the loss?"

What indeed was the loss? Fassman asked himself. The world would spin on, the desert would be processed and die, and man would move inexorably to mastery of all that lived, and eventually his own extinction. Why not ride with the tide? Outside, the cameraman nursed the five cans of color film. What harm to give them up, liberate Bugler, let Maybank and Fusaro pursue Denkerman's millions?

"Agreed, Alan?" Maybank asked.

"I'm afraid not. It isn't that easy."

"Son," Timmons said, "spare us that freedom of the press speech. We know you folks are in show business. If Cronkite and Chancellor hadn't stirred everything up there'd not have been a Watergate and the country would have been better off."

Vormund's teary eyes looked at Fassman. What does he want of me? the newsman mused. To help him save the snakes and coyotes of the world? And why is he so insistent, forsaking the books and plays and poems he loved, and taught others to love, for this parched place?

"No," Fassman said. "You can't have the film."

Essler got up and hitched his belt. He seemed to be ready to reach for his guns, but in deference to the peaceful palaver, he and Timmons had removed them. "That's your last word?"

"We don't surrender film to presidents or kings or Mafia bosses. Why should you get special treatment?"

Fusaro and Maybank appealed to him with mourning eyes. "Alan, the Institute will suffer," Maybank said.

"I'm not so sure," Vormund said. The long day was too much for him. Beneath the freckles and the tan, his skin was chalky. "The reverse may happen. We will be praised. Let Ed come to trial. Let's air this whole thing. I'm curious about those reports Mr. Essler was supposed to file. I want my day in court. I want to testify."

"Last chance," Essler said.

"The matter is closed. The more I think of those snakeburgers, the more I think we've got a good story for the six o'clock news. I'm sending the film to Los Angeles."

"Oh, shit," Fusaro muttered.

"That young man was my student more than twenty years ago," Vormund said shakily. "I told him when I met him that I did not remember him, and that I made a practice of avoiding former students. But I won't forget him now. I haven't the faintest notion if he ever learned anything about Shelley from me, but he learned other useful things. I'd written them all off as numskulls who failed to absorb my infinite wisdom. I was wrong."

Fassman was smiling: the old Vormund. *To what failings in your own character do you attribute your choices?*

"If I'm not needed," the newsman said, "I'll talk to my crew." He walked past Host's marble chunk of a figure, trying to catch his impersonal eyes.

"I'll wreck your operation," Essler said to Maybank. "I can do it. You're outgunned, Jack."

"I can't control Fassman. He doesn't work for us."

"Professor Vormund could have," Timmons said.

"I had no intention of doing so," Vormund said. "I look forward to meeting you all again in court."

Essler and Timmons conferred again. Essler was smiling. They got to the door, finished with the conference. They were ready to make other plans. They did not seem at all worried. As they tried to leave, Raymond Host blocked their path to the corridor.

"Excuse me," Host said hoarsely. "May I . . . ?"

"Yes?" Essler asked.

"May I speak with you a moment?"

"Who are you?" Timmons asked. "Reporter? You came in here with that other one."

"No. I . . . I'm a friend of Mr. Vormund's."

"With the Institute?" Essler asked.

"No. Actually I'm in the construction business. I happened to be spending the day with the professor and his wife, and I came along."

Timmons and Essler searched the square ruddy face, the flat eyes hiding behind wrap-arounds.

Maybank got up. "I'm sorry. With all this confusion, I didn't make introductions. This is Mr. Ray Host from Los Angeles. Mr. Host—Mr. Essler, Mr. Timmons."

The grin on Essler's face turned to a kind of paralyzed awe. The wide mouth drooped. He ran a hand over his pink scalp, fingered the part in the middle, fussed with the lapis lazuli clasp on his black string tie.

"Raymond Host?" Essler asked. He was breathy, respectful. "James W. Host's boy?"

"Yes."

"Thought you looked familiar. I've met your father many times, and maybe you also."

"I don't recall."

"My goodness, what a fine man your daddy is. How is he? Why didn't you let on you were in Senita? I'd have had us a little whiskey party. Mac, you hear that? James W. Host's son is in town. You could have come to the rattlesnake round—" He stopped. Not a good move. The young man had said he was Vormund's friend and Vormund was pro-snake.

"Mighty pleased, mighty pleased," Timmons kept repeating. "I know your father also, Mr. Host. We sure could use more like him."

Through repeated tributes to his father, Raymond Host stood immobile, his face and neck reddening, his Popeye-like forearms crossed on his chest. Softly, he interrupted the babbling lawyer.

"Mr. Essler, may I speak to you privately for a moment? Just the two of us?" No one in the room missed the authority in the buried voice.

"My privilege, sir."

Timmons opened the door. "There's a small room next to the sheriff's office. I'll run and ask him."

"No need," Host said. "The hall is fine." He barred Timmons with a bob of his head. "Just Mr. Essler." He looked at the others at the table—Vormund, Fusaro, Maybank. "Would you all mind waiting a moment? Professor, I'll take you home as soon as this is over."

Fassman came trudging down the corridor. He had dispatched Apodaca and Downs to the airport with the film. They would ship by air express on the first flight to Los Angeles. To the newsman's surprise, he saw Ray Host and Duane Essler emerge from the room and walk to the door of the men's room. He walked past them.

In the conference room Fassman asked what had happened.

"Beats me," Fusaro said. "Everybody's getting in on the act. Essler went into a trance when that guy Host talked to him."

Maybank bit his lip. "I've known Essler five years and I've never seen him kiss ass like that. People usually do it to him."

"Say, I'm tired and I'm hungry and I want to go home," Vormund said. "Are we getting Ed out or not?"

"In a second, Dan," Maybank said. Clara would read the riot act to him. Dragging Dan out when he should be napping, getting him aroused over Ed's foolishness.

It seemed less than five minutes when Essler and Host returned to the room. Once again Host retreated to the wall. Odd, Fassman thought, how he seems to be standing at attention half the time, with those powerful arms locked on his chest, as if keeping the world away.

"Now what I'm about to do," Essler said, "what I'm about to do is strictly a favor to Mr. Raymond Host and his father."

Timmons lingered in the doorway, listening.

"There are few people I respect more than James W. Host, and I'd like for you, Jack, and your attorney and Mr. Vormund to understand that's why I'm doing what I'm doing, right?" He beamed. "If young Mr. Host wants a favor, if he thinks highly of you people, that is good enough for Duane Essler."

Fusaro said: "Don't keep us in suspense."

"I am instructing the sheriff and the DA to drop the case against Mr. Bugler. Mac, will you start the ball rolling?"

The lawyer saluted and waddled out of the doorway.

"That's pretty decent of you, Duane," Maybank said. He was

vastly relieved. "You want it in writing that we'll stay off your land?"

"Won't be necessary."

"And Mr. Fassman's film?" Vormund asked.

Essler waved a hand at the newsman. "That's between Mr. Fassman and his conscience."

At least, Fassman thought, he has called me by my name. What had Host done to him? Thumb screws? Water torture?

"You see," Essler said, "if the reporter who started this wants to go ahead, I can't stop him. If he wants to make me look like a killer, he can. Mr. Host and I agreed we'll take our chances. If it's distorted, or biased, the way the media tends to be toward us, we'll respond. I doubt many people will choose rattlesnakes over people."

"I do," Vormund said. "But my vote isn't much. I want to go home." He struggled to get up. Maybank helped him move the chair back and rise. Vormund shuffled to Host. "We're in your debt, young man."

Throughout Essler's fawning performance Host seemed reluctant to use his father's name or the company's title. He had acted, Fassman sensed, like a former heavyweight champion forced into a barroom brawl with an inept opponent. From the start, Host knew that one swift combination of punches would end the fight.

"I'd like to see Ed," Vormund said. "I want to be the first to shake his hand. Come along, Mr. Host."

"Thank you."

"Mr. Bugler has many defects of mind and character, but he is as loyal as a tame raccoon. He may get to like you almost as much as he likes turtles. Which way?"

Led by the turnkey, they walked to the lockup at the rear of the courthouse. Vormund was spry, gingery. Fassman could see that the adventure had pleased him. Action, at last. But it was Host, and Host alone, who possessed the power to make Essler bend and to free Ed. Behind him, he could hear Maybank and Fusaro thanking Raymond Host with almost the same obsequiousness Essler had manifested.

Vormund and Fassman found Bugler standing on a bench inside the cell, squinting out of a high window. Like a caged bird, Fassman thought, turning to the light. A Pima Indian with a purple lump on his cheek sprawled at Ed's feet. Two young Chicanos with hair to their shoulders played cards on the floor.

The turnkey jammed the key in the lock.

"You're free, Ed," Vormund called. He was triumphant.

"Hi, Dan. Hello, Alan. This place isn't bad." He indicated the men playing cards. "I knew these guys from Sells. They stole a highway department truck."

"You look no worse for the experience," Fassman said.

"I've been in smaller places."

Despite his assurances, Fassman saw that Ed was not a man who took to confinement. The outdoor world was Ed's habitat. Canyons and mountaintops and scorching deserts were his range. That long loping body could not be imprisoned.

The door swung open. The Pima's eyes stayed frozen. The Chicano boys slapped their cards. "So long, man," one said to Bugler. "Stay loose."

Vormund grabbed Bugler's hand. "You know what Emerson said to Thoreau when he visited him in jail?"

"Ask your former student."

The past again, Fassman thought.

"He said 'Henry, why are you here?'" Fassman said, pumping Bugler's hand, "and Thoreau replied, 'Ralph, why are you *not* here?'"

"Not bad," Bugler said. He stretched. "I hope I didn't make any trouble for anyone. Is Jack sore at me?"

"Sore?" Vormund asked. "He will thank you. This is what the Institute must do. Confront. Challenge. Fight."

Bugler peered over his steel-rimmed glasses. He did not quite believe Vormund.

"It was Raymond Host," Fassman said. "He squared everything."

"A valuable ally," Vormund said. "He did what the rest of us failed to do—got you out and made a pact with Jack Maybank. And Essler will let Alan show the film."

"We need a guy like that around," Ed said.

Who doesn't? Fassman mused. But he could not complete a satisfying picture of what was happening. Host, sent by his father (according to luscious Corinne) to spy on the DRI, beat them out of a fortune, had come to their aid. Vormund had worked some desert magic on him. An old shaman, a peyote eater, putting a spell on the inheritor.

In the lobby Maybank shook Bugler's hand coolly. "Clara called," he said to Vormund. "She'll have my scalp if I keep you five more minutes."

Bugler walked up to Host and thanked him. It seemed to Fassman that Ed was not quite sure what Host had done, or why he had done it, nor did he care much. In jail, out of jail, it did not matter to Bugler so long as he could get back to his badgers and creeping devils. There was some rare mammal called a fish bat he started telling Fassman about. A sure-fire exciting species for a TV show.

"'Twas a famous victory,'" Vormund said to the group.

They stood in the pitiless sun on the courthouse steps. "Jack, I nominate Mr. Host to our Board of Directors, if he's interested. He can have my seat. I'm getting too old for these battles, although today's may have shrunk my prostate and dried my hemorrhoids. At the moment I'm ready for a wheel chair."

Host gathered up his shoulders. The head lowered. "The company discourages it. But I'd like to stay in touch. Know what you're doing."

Yes, you would, Fassman thought. *And so would your father.*

Gently, with a suggestion of affection that shamed Fassman for his churlish thoughts, Host took Vormund's arm and helped him down the courthouse steps.

An hour later Fassman lay on his bed at the motel. He was eager to learn the newsroom's reaction to the story he had put together on the snake roundup. It was damned near perfect—a beginning, a middle, and an end. The brutality parading as beneficence. The quixotic interference of Ed Bugler. The reasonably happy outcome. Snakes died but a point had been scored.

His body ached woefully. His mind was disoriented. He toyed with the idea of calling Wendi. Her actor would answer and insult him. Tomorrow he would sort things out. What puzzled him was Host's equivocal role. An odd duck, Host. Not a man Fassman would want as a friend—as if Host would give him the time of day!—but a man not easily understood.

The phone rang. Half asleep, Fassman picked it up. It was Apodaca. He sounded shaken.

"I'm in the bar, Alan," he said. "Downs and me are tying one on."

"Be my guest. Sign my name."

"We lost the film."

"Lost . . . ?"

"They stole it from us."

"Who? Where?" Fassman sat up in bed and turned on the reading lamp.

"We were walking into the freight terminal with the load. I had it packaged in a shipping bag with the KGDF letters on it . . ."

"Yes . . ."

"These two shit-kickers, guys in denim suits and boots came up. They said they wanted the film. It would make the city look bad. I told them to fuck off."

"What happened?"

"They grabbed it from me. I'm fifty-seven. I can't go fighting cowboys. Downs is even older than me. I called them a few names, wrassled a little for the bag. They spit in my face. I guess we have no story."

"Did they say who they were?"

"Jesus, no. I tried to call a cop or get some airport people, but like everyone else in this town, they sleep a lot."

"I'm glad you weren't hurt. Sign my name for the drinks."

Essler. He would keep his word up to a point. He had been submissive to the power of the Hosts, but he could see no loss in double-crossing the Fassmans of the world. Newsmen to Essler were a variety of vermin. No smarter than coyotes, less brave than a mountain lion.

In the darkened room Fassman thought of his trapped cougar. The elegant tormented head. The way he had looked the beast in her amber eyes and helped Bugler free her. Now in the darkness, lulled by the hum of the air conditioner, Fassman appreciated Vormund's retreat from mankind and his search for kinship with the wilderness.

5

---　✳　---

What did the poet mean when he said, "No man is an island?" A great deal more, I suspect, than is commonly supposed. Not man alone, but all living things survive or die in terms of one another. Obsessed eternally with his own gratification, man risks losing his very existence. Yet the warnings appear to reach no ears.

At dawn Host sat in the living room of the suite, reading Vormund's *Desert Idyll*. The old man's thoughts were clear enough. His essays were variations on a theme—live with nature and respect it or perish. But every now and then Vormund seemed to hedge his bets or at least reduce his demands. The young man liked the phrase "man must learn to set a reasonable limit on his ambitions." That might exonerate Host-Labarre and the others who built highways, pipelines, power plants, high-octane automobiles, devoured the resources, fouled the air, poisoned the water. *Reasonable limits.* But who would decide what was reasonable and what was unreasonable? Already the forces of unreason (by Vormund's lights) were winning.

Host's father in his high-backed chair on the top floor of Century Plaza had seen victory coming. "They're finished. The ones against strip-mining, the save-the-redwoods bunch, the forever-wild fools. When jobs and profits are at stake, they won't amount

to a hill of beans. They're dead and they don't know it. We can cut down every saguaro in the country. And nobody will raise a peep if you tell them it means their livelihood."

Host could recall his father telling this to a meeting of his executives. There had been demonstrations at Bald Indian Power Plant. The smoke-vomiting, earth-devouring fortress had long been a target of conservationists. Pickets were there daily. A rabble of students, long-hairs, Indians, a few old ladies. Host-Labarre had been the key member of the consortium that had built Bald Indian. It was James W. Host's reputation that had convinced state legislatures. *Pop Host is getting in? It can't help but be good. Efficient. Productive. Jobs. Power. Progress!*

Who was right—James W. Host or D. D. Vormund? Ray closed the paperbound book. (He was glad to see, thanks to Corinne's shopping, that many of Vormund's works were in softcover editions. Someone, other than hippies, freaks, and old ladies, must be reading him.)

It was 6 A.M. He had barely slept. He had come back from the courthouse, after helping liberate Bugler, and had found Corinne in a drunken sleep. The bed was disheveled and redolent of perspiration and perfume. She looked more beautiful than he had ever seen her—vulnerable, ripe, a woman born to be loved, used the way Vormund's archetypical man used the earth. She had awakened once, complained of a migraine, gone back to sleep.

Host dressed and walked into the cactus garden of the Senita Inn. It smelled of fresh mountain air, green living things. Behind the inn was a carpet of desert bright with orange flowers. He strolled into the soft sand. Creosote bushes gave off their pleasant disinfectant odor. There was no aroma like it anywhere in the world. The desert after rain—pungent, tantalizing.

Lights winked in Senita. Bowling alleys, Laundromats, fast-food chains. All the water and life and vegetation of the dry world, Vormund's paradise, going to create hamburgers. But that was the way man wanted it. The majority ruled. Were Vormund and his friends snobs of the worst kind, denying the plebs their craving for cars, highways, air conditioning, neon?

Host concluded that Vormund and his friends were fighting a battle that by its very nature was doomed. To reject technology and deny mechanical progress were perhaps sound ideas. Communes. Solar houses. Newspapers and tin cans could be recycled.

(Small stuff, Host knew, but at least a start.) It was the other side of Vormund's coin that seemed to him utterly hopeless. That was his admonition for man to learn to love nature, to delight in kinship with bees and frogs. *What a joke!* Host, in his mind's eye, saw millions of Americans, glassy-eyed from watching football, weary of commuting, worried about the next payment on the Buick, fearful of the blacks across town. In the midst of all this would they stop to admire a dune primrose?

These apparent deceptions that Vormund practiced on himself —how naïve the old man was!—filled Host with a sorrow he could not measure. And yet Vormund had not quit. Host recalled a line from *Dry World.* The desert, Vormund had written, spoke to him not of conquest, but of *endurance.* It endured. And in its capacity to endure, perhaps it would teach man some lessons. A kangaroo rat, storing water, never drinking, might mean more to mankind than the Bald Indian Power Plant, spewing filth and darkness over the land.

"And fifteen million dollars will help also," Host said. He smiled at a gila woodpecker as it circled a saguaro and vanished into a hole in the tough green hide.

Rising early, Fassman phoned the Los Angeles newsroom and reported the theft of the film. Ballstead was not concerned. There had been two mild earthquakes in the valley, walls shivering, plaster falling. Every available film crew was working. The rattlesnake story would probably have been shelved.

"Can't talk, Alan," Ballstead said. "There's a reservoir off Sepulveda getting ready to come apart. Flood all the convalescent homes."

"That's part of what Vormund is talking about. Those reservoirs aren't right. They drain the land. Screwing up the balance of nature."

Ballstead was unimpressed. He wanted a report on the men who had forced Apodaca to surrender the film. They would take it up with their lawyers. It would be raised at the next meeting of the Western States Radio and TV News Directors meeting.

"What did you find out about the Denkerman will?" Fassman asked.

"Far as we can find out nobody's contesting it. Denkerman was a Pasadena crazy. A nut thing, no real story."

"But the Hosts?"

"Their lawyers denied everything."

The writer pleaded for a few more days in Senita. Ballstead agreed.

Driving to the Institute, Fassman wondered if Corinne Host, half bombed, a beautiful head with a mixed-up brain, could have fed him a fake story. Yet she seemed to know a great deal—about the bequest and the orders given her reluctant husband.

Fassman had seen photographs of the senior Host in the society pages of the LA *Times*—a small crisp mustached man, just this side of being a dandy. A pale-eyed, pale-skinned man, self-contained, buttoned-up. He was generous with charities, never failed to lend his name and funds to decent campaigns—symphony orchestras, day-care centers, beautification projects.

Fassman stopped for his coffee and soggy doughnut, thinking of the cheerful breakfast room in his lavish house in Westwood, paid for by his father-in-law in Great Neck, who never let him forget it. "So what does he *do?*" Wendi's mother, nose-clipped, mascara'd, would ask. "He's a journalist, Mother." Fassman's mother-in-law would *hrrmph* and dismiss his career with a gesture reserved for Sisterhood members who criticized her cake sale.

Such memories did not ease the pain of the leaden doughnut. He went to a pay phone and called the Vormunds. Clara sounded annoyed.

"Dan is staying in bed today," she said. "You got him excited, Alan. You and Ed and the others. I'm angry with all of you. He's got a sore throat and a chill. He doesn't get out of bed till I say so."

Apologizing, offering his wishes for Vormund's recovery, Fassman drove out to the Institute.

He found the Maybanks seated under the ramada. They were going over bills. Both looked at him warily.

"Haven't we paid this bill for fencing?" Jenny asked.

"I thought *you* did."

"No way. Gad, eight hundred and forty dollars? What did Ed do? Fence in the south forty?"

Fassman watched them. They were deliberately talking over his head. Fassman entertained a veiled jealousy toward him. He had known D. D. Vormund years ago, before the old man came to the desert. Thus he had some prior tie to him. The Maybanks wanted him all to themselves, their jewel, prize, intellectual guide. Fassman's presence diluted Vormund.

"Did Jack tell you how Raymond Host saved the day yesterday?" Fassman asked Jenny.

"The cavalry to the rescue. Has anyone figured out what went on?"

"Nothing much had to. Rich to rich. You say Host-Labarre to people out here and they faint."

"Whatever he did," she said, "it got Ed free and got us out of a mess."

"Sorry," Fassman said. "I was responsible. Ed and I couldn't take much more of that massacre. Those idiots chopping up snakes. Sidewinder swears that a policeman said he saw them trucked in. They salted the desert with snakes."

Maybank shut his eyes. "Sidewinder says a lot of things. He damn near got us into a lawsuit. I hope you took it easy in that newsreel."

"Essler's goons relieved my cameraman of the film. Threatened to punch his head off if he didn't surrender it. That is commonly called suppression of information."

Jenny looked up from her checkbook. She was writing checks slowly in a private school hand—letters printed and slanted backward, i's dotted with little circles. Years ago Fassman had known wealthy Jewish girls from Central Park West who wrote in such a hand. They wrote him prim letters while they screwed their way through Cornell.

"You must think we're a little crazy," she said.

"No. I'm on your side."

"Because of Dan?"

"I once collected butterflies. Would you believe that one summer I caught a spicebush swallowtail outside of Yankee Stadium? Here's everyone screaming for Mickey Mantle inside, and I'm dodging cars and swinging my shirt at a butterfly."

Jenny flashed her dark eyes at her husband. "Can we tell him? Is it all right?"

"Oh, what the hell."

Fassman's ears seemed to point. The bequest? He knew about it. Host's pursuit of it? He knew about that, too. And maybe they didn't.

"Essler's lawyer called this morning," Jenny said. "They want to sell us the land with the creeping devils for a private nature preserve. Ten thousand acres. We'd maintain it and keep it open to the public on a limited basis."

"After Bugler and Sidewinder have been traipsing over his land?" asked Fassman. "After we set a lion loose?"

Maybank did not reply at once. He studied a letter from the Department of Sanitation complaining about their disposal of solid wastes. Then he said: "Host convinced Essler it would be a nice gesture. Host was interested in our work and wanted to help Professor Vormund. How do you like them apples?"

"Now if only we can afford it," Jenny said. "Ten thousand acres of desert? It can only cost a couple of million bucks."

"You can afford it," Fassman said.

"Really?"

"You're about to get fifteen million dollars from a man named Denkerman who liked what Vormund had to say about chipmunks."

Maybank's small features screwed together around his mouth.

"So that's why you came poking out here," Jenny said.

"Not at all. I read the piece on the coyote hunt in your paper. I thought there was a story in it."

"Then how did you find out—" Maybank's mouth stayed ajar.

"Mrs. Host talked. The Golden Girl. She came out to my motel the other night smashed and told all."

Maybank appealed to his wife's shrewd eyes. "Jen? Do you make any sense out of this? Mrs. Host . . . ?"

"I'm lost."

"You won't be for long. Raymond Host is a second or third cousin of Otto Denkerman. James W. Host sent his only begotten son out here to look the terrain over and get a reading on you. That includes D. D. Vormund. The Hosts are going to break the will."

"I don't believe it," Maybank said. "If he's so rich, what does he want with more?"

"How do you think he got what he has? Not by feeding beetle larva to bobwhites."

Maybank's innocent face was affronted. "But Host never told us. He kept hanging around like some kid waiting for autographs outside a rock concert."

"Why should he have told you?"

"Because it was the decent thing to do," Maybank said.

"And what can he have found out about us that would give him the right to contest us?" asked Jenny. "What have we done bad?"

"He can claim you're fakes," Fassman said. "You run a phony outfit that raises funds but doesn't do anything to rescue ferrets. The country's full of fund-raising frauds."

"*Fund-raising?*" Jenny howled. "Jack and I couldn't get a dime out of United Charities if we tried."

Maybank looked strained. "We'd better tell Joe Fusaro."

"I'd advise you to," Fassman said. "Immediately."

"That nice Mr. Host," Jenny said.

"Another thing the Hosts might do," the newsman said. "They may try to prove Vormund had malign influence over Denkerman. Put a conjure on him. Nothing is impossible."

"I repeat," Jenny said. "That nice Mr. Host."

"He isn't a bad guy," Fassman said. "It's his old man got him to do it. Corinne says Raymond should be head of the company, but Dad wants to toughen him up. This was sort of a dry run. They have a theory, these people, that everything that isn't locked up is theirs. Ever read Damon Runyon?"

They looked at him blankly.

"Runyon had this character Honest John. He was called honest because he would never steal anything that was nailed down provided it had an armed guard walking around it. That's James W. Host's problem. They want it *all*. It offended his aesthetic sensibilities that this outfit landed a bonanza, when his son had a genetic claim."

"But all that fussing over Dan?" Maybank asked. "Coming out here? Taking Dan out yesterday for a flight? I understand he invited him to come to LA and stay at their ranch."

Fassman rested his heat-clogged head on his right palm. He would have to get back to his job. "Vast wealth works in curious ways its wonders to perform," he said.

"Or else he likes Dan," Jenny said.

"If he does, it's a two-way street," Maybank said. "Dan couldn't thank him enough for saving Ed. I was ready to congratulate the sheriff for locking Bugler up."

Raymond Host watched his wife taking a tennis lesson. He sat alone on the patio of the racket club, wondering where all her energy and desire originated. Corinne liked to compete and win, but she hated training, discipline, preparation. She was impossible at chess or bridge. She learned the basics, skimmed a few books, then played recklessly, unable to look ahead or concentrate. Her tennis was the same way. She disdained strategy, planning. The single superb ground stroke, the applause-drawing volley at net, these were all she played for. Meanwhile opponents built up points on her errors.

Today she seemed intent on learning. The pro, putting his hand on her body too often, appeared to be getting across. They laughed a good deal. He hit hard forehands. She pirouetted for the backhand return, bent her marvelous legs, raced to net without once giving evidence that she had been in a drunken stupor the night before.

"Something to drink, Mr. Host?" a waiter asked.

"No thanks. Did you tell the desk I'm here?"

"Yes, sir."

Early that morning Host had phoned Vormund. Clara had asked him not to call again. In fact she was taking the phone off the hook. Dan was tired. Too much running around the last few days. She thanked Host for solving the problem with Mr. Essler and getting Ed out of jail, but Dan could not talk to him or to anyone. She was concerned over his kidneys, his heart, his feet. She was calling the doctor. Host had asked: Can I help? Can I fly in the head of our medical foundation from Los Angeles?

What power in the old woman! Seated in the cool shade, watching Corinne's flashing form, thinking of her as spoiled, selfish, always at him to stand up to his father, Host could not help making the invidious comparison. Corinne was like a beautiful stinging insect, gossamer wings, vivid colors—and a barb in her tail. Which tail, he could not help but notice, the pro was now ogling. He wondered what he was supposed to do. Punch the bastard?

Corinne and the pro stopped to sip Gator-Ade. Her hair flashed in the sun. Ray was glad she was happy, using her body, sweating in the deadly heat. Some good had to come out of this trip. Pop would ream him out, point out to him his failings, his entrapment by conservationists. It was being proven every day that they were cranks. They meant nothing. The administration in Washington had realized it. One show of strength, one rallying of the unions and the business community, and the whole mob of canyon savers, dickey-birders, coyote defenders, would melt away.

On the way back from the courthouse, Vormund and the others had deplored the change in federal regulations. Poisons were flooding the wilderness and deserts again. The ranchers were having their way.

"That's right," Bugler had said. Liberated, he seemed none the worse for his experience in jail. "The whole West is going to become a poisoned waste when they're through."

Host had remained silent. He was not of their faith. But he kept returning to Vormund's books, reading them as if they were revelations, notions not only revolutionary, but negations of all he had been taught.

"Hello, Raymond."

Host looked up and saw his father. "Pop. I didn't expect you." He stood up. The men shook hands.

James W. Host sat down and folded his hands in his lap. He squinted at Corinne as she smashed an overhead. He was wearing a gray suit, a white shirt, a blue-and-gray-striped tie. His shoes and socks were black. In the informal atmosphere of the club he looked like an insurance salesman. Already a few of the members had recognized the neat face, the ginger hair, freckled skin, pencil mustache.

"I thought you were hung up on the Sacramento project."

"A hunch you might need some help. The Denkerman business is complicated. The word's gotten out and all kinds of animal societies, ASPCAs, humane shelters, are preparing to file claims. They're all ridiculous, of course, but I wanted to see how our own mission is getting on."

Ray Host swallowed. He experienced, for the thousandth time, that sense of inadequacy that suffocated him in the presence of his father.

"Not too well."

"I gathered that."

"We may have no case."

"I think otherwise. You are Denkerman's only relative. That money is yours."

"I hadn't seen him since I was six years old. He knew his pet chimps better than he knew me." He held up the copy of *The Spirit of the Desert*. "He knew Daniel D. Vormund better than he knew me."

Host stroked the dudish mustache. An odd touch, his son thought. Not like the old man, so plain, so straightforward. Was the ginger mustache a wistful yearning for adventure? James W. Host was stupendously proper, rigid in habit. He was horrified by scandal. The money he lavished on Lutherans and Baptists (the late Mrs. Host had been devout) was given sincerely.

"Vormund again. I see you've taken to him also."

"He's worth reading."

"I've looked into his writings. He seems an intelligent fellow. But I confess, Raymond, he makes no sense. None at all. He fights technology, opposes progress, is against everything we believe in. That man is more of a menace to us than any socialist, any union activist, any bureaucrat. He strikes at the heart of our society. He wants to stop us from building, from expanding."

"You've read more of him than you admit."

"All that sentimental stuff about saving wild flowers and preserving the coyote's dens. I have nothing against animals. I don't wantonly cut down trees. I went through all of this when I was an Eagle Scout in Michigan. But you have to grow up. Vormund has never gotten over some youthful infatuation with nature. Raymond, any man who'll whisper to a frog that 'we're in this together,' or write eulogies to scorpions—"

"That's what I like about him."

"So he's worked his magic on you?"

"Not magic. *Sense*." Raymond leaned forward. He drew his broad shoulders up around his neck. His eyes stared at Corinne, and he spoke in a clotted voice. "It was as if I was waiting for someone to tell me these things all my life. I know that sounds stupid, but it's how I feel."

"It is not only stupid, it is dangerous. You'll get over it, Raymond. The money is not Vormund's. He would not know what to do with it. It was given to that Institute and I've checked on them. They are trivial people. I concede that Vormund is a man of intellect, a finer man than that organization deserves. But this was a freak. Denkerman liked his words—"

"So do I. He's right. He isn't screaming at the world. He's no crazy prophet in a bearskin. In some ways he's like you—quiet and thoughtful and never raising his voice. And he makes sense."

Host stroked the mustache again. He crossed his birdlike legs. "More than I do?"

"I'm not sure. What you—we—stand for is important. Vormund's got an air conditioner in his car. His wife uses a dishwasher. So he's not against *all* progress. He says . . . let's see if I remember it . . . that progress can't continue forever in an upward line."

"Then we disagree."

"He sounds more reasonable than you. He wants a meeting of minds. A pause so we can examine where we're going."

"*Pause?*" Host asked. "Stop building? If you stop, the structure will start to wobble, then fall. Nature must be brought under control. I look forward to the day when men like us have altered nature so that it serves us in the most efficient, rewarding, healthful way possible."

"That's just what he fears. Not only that, he's convinced that it means nothing but death and destruction. He thinks we're moving closer and closer to permanent overcrowding and eventual starvation."

The elder Host smiled tolerantly. "Host-Labarre cannot accept these wailings from seers who claim that every time we cut down a tree we hasten our doom. He has no idea of the good we accomplish. He's too busy communing with bluebirds."

"Maybe they tell him something."

"I don't doubt that they do. They told St. Francis things. And Thoreau. But I'm afraid the modern world hasn't much use for that message. Put it to a vote and tell me who'll win—proponents of birds or builders of highways?"

"Strange hearing you stick up for majorities. You never had any use for them when they were electing Roosevelt and Truman or agitating for minimum wages."

"Ah. Into politics. Didn't I mention on the phone that I had misgivings about Vormund's background? Wasn't he some kind of radical?"

"No, Pop. He can't stand politics. Last night I was reading

something he said—conservatives are greedy for a few top people, and liberals are greedy for everyone, but both want to use up the earth as fast as they can."

"A brand from the burning, perhaps. You'll get over this undergraduate infatuation. There's nothing wrong with listening to what our critics have to say. It won't stop us and it won't stop progress."

Corinne came up the steps from the courts. She was lithe, sweatless. She kissed her father-in-law's cheek, shook her blond mane, and sat down.

"Fantastic lesson," she said. "He's a terrific teacher. He had me really getting top spin on the forehand. He thinks I should play tournament tennis again."

"I've said so for years, Corinne," James W. Host said. "I've never felt you or Raymond fulfilled your potential at tennis."

"Or a lot of other things," Corinne said. She flashed an ivory smile at her father-in-law. The sarcasm was not lost on him. Host had learned to tolerate his daughter-in-law's flippancy. He knew it stemmed from the humiliations of the shabby genteel world.

"Easy, Corinne," Ray said. "Pop just got here."

Host said: "Have you thought again about resuming your studies? Perhaps a master's degree at UCLA. I could talk to the Los Angeles *Times* about a job."

"I'm fine, Pop. I haven't been drinking that much, have I, Ray?"

"You've been good."

"And are you also intrigued with this man Vormund?" Pop Host asked.

"He's interesting," Corinne answered. "We used his books in college. He's interesting, yes. Ray thinks he's got the answers."

"I don't. But I think he may have raïsed some questions. If you want me to admit it, I envy him a little."

"Admirable," his father said. "I'm sure I'd have nothing but respect for the professor. I've never been a foe of academics. Or conservationists for that matter."

Corinne's eyes narrowed. Something wicked glinted in the pupils. "You could fund him, Pop. Finance his work. Endow the Desert Research Institute. If Ray succeeds in stealing Mr. Denkerman's fortune, they'll be broke again—"

"She was not supposed to know," Host whispered.

Ray Host shook his head in despair. He could not seem to do anything properly any more. He was weary of the game he had been playing. Greed was not his strong suit.

"Pop, I don't want to go through with this charade."

"Fifteen million dollars is not a charade."

"It's senseless. Vormund's friends can do good things with the money."

"Better than we can?"

"Maybe both sides should have a chance to get their ideas across. God knows we've got all the heavy artillery."

Corinne touched her father-in-law's hand. It was a small strong hand, spotted with liver-colored circlets. "Why don't you co-opt the movement, as the kids say? You could make believe you're on Vormund's side, finance the Institute, but keep knocking down mountains and polluting the desert. The way the oil companies keep taking big advertisements saying how they're such sincere conservationists, when all they want to do is eat up the world."

Host pulled his hand away. "I find your manner more abrasive than necessary, Corinne. I'm aware of how certain corporations are riding the ecology train. I know it's a fraud. When push comes to shove, they will strip-mine, dig wells, ruin seashores, kill wildlife, cut down watersheds, despoil wetlands, do anything they have to to keep the machine running. And I approve. What I don't approve of is this hypocritical posture so many are taking. I have never been anything less than straightforward."

"Sorry, Pop," she said. "Just joking."

"I would hope so." Host's pale eyes looked into his son's. "Raymond, are you telling me that you will not pursue the Denkerman bequest?"

"I'm not sure you have a case."

"We will let the lawyers make that judgment."

"It's not fair. Let the Institute have the money. They can put it to good use."

"Cut us off from land, water, resources? Ruin our plans for a better world?"

"Vormund says it's getting worse all the time."

"He is not the last word. Raymond, I will make this a cause of my own if you abandon it."

— 242 —

"You have no claim. I'm the blood relative. You're nothing to Denkerman."

Corinne clapped her hands. Navajo bracelets jingled. "What's Denkerman to him, or he to Denkerman, that he should weep for him?"

"Be still, Corinne," Pop Host said. "I would prefer if you left us."

"Go on, honey," Ray said. "I'll join you in the room." Sooner or later she would enrage Pop with her taunts. "We'll go for a swim in a few minutes."

She left them. Heads turned. White-haired matrons nattered.

"I cannot enforce my will on you, Raymond. You're too old and too intelligent."

"Then don't." Ray Host's eyes sought the blue sky. A few miles from them Vormund sat on his patio, reading, writing, watching hummingbirds. Ray had a desire to see him. To talk to him, hear him reminisce about New York in the thirties and forties. Columbia, writers, or the ingenuity of the kangaroo rat.

What was it Vormund gave him? A kind of peace? A sense of rightness? Fassman felt the same way, he had noticed. If the newsman were around, he would try to talk to him. He wanted to ask him what Vormund was like twenty-five years ago.

"I am sorry you have come to this decision," James W. Host said. "I'm not sure I can take it as a final answer."

"I don't want you getting your investigators after the Desert Research Institute. You may find that they're spying on me, as well as the Maybanks and Vormund."

"You?"

"I may have involved myself."

The elder Host listened—sweatless, his white shirt whiter than sunlit limestone—as Ray told him about rescuing Ed Bugler from jail, prevailing upon Duane Essler to drop charges against him, and to overlook the repeated trespassing on his property.

"I had to throw him bait," Ray said. "I told him if he made a deal with the Institute on some land he owns, Host-Labarre would be interested in his other holdings."

"You committed me to this? You used the corporate name for some useless desert that these eccentrics want?"

"Useless. That's the precise word. Vormund says we divide nature into what we can use and what's useless."

"I would appreciate it, Raymond, if you stopped quoting your guru to me." Host shook his head. For the first time he seemed upset. Up to now their conversation had been low-keyed. Even differences of opinion had been discussed in mild terms. Ray knew why. Vormund did not matter, nor did his friends and his beliefs. They were of no account. The matter involving Essler, on the other hand, could be measured in terms of real wealth.

"You seem upset."

"I wish you had talked to me before making promises to Essler. I know the man. He's a land hoarder. Rich on his wife's money. An adopted westerner, full of gun collections and breeding charts for quarter horses."

"He shouldn't faze you."

"I need him. Essler is heading the ranchers' committee in favor of the new power plants."

"Ah, the inevitable connection."

"I came here to see you, Raymond, but also because there's a hearing the day after tomorrow on the power sites. People like Vormund are on our backs again about Bald Indian. The usual lies. Ruining the sky and the land, using up water. They're parading Indians around to protest this alleged spoliation of ancestral lands. What a farce! The majority of Indians are grateful for the work and the electricity. Essler was organizing the ranchers in support of Bald Indian."

"You don't miss a trick."

"You need not be cavalier. Bald Indian represents an investment of over two hundred million dollars. I will not let a mob of animal lovers put us out of business."

"Or cut our margin of profit?"

"Correct. That's why I regret you made overtures to Essler. I have no interest in his land. But you've committed me. In exchange for his selling off a parcel to Vormund's people, I'm to bid on his next parcel. Raymond, I have never done business that way. I expect no special treatment and I give none. Essler should be advised that you spoke out of turn. I'm beginning to regret I sent you here."

"I've regretted it already. I'm not interested in the Denkerman money."

James W. Host shook his head. "May I ask what is so important about this piece of desert you tried to get Mr. Essler to sell?"

"Cactus."

"Cactus?"

"Some rare plant. Vormund says it's a botanical marvel. It has to be preserved."

"Why?"

"If you don't understand, I can't explain it. You should talk to him."

"There's no time. I have to prepare for the hearings."

They sat for a while, father and son, under the glare of the intolerant sun, each searching for new approaches.

"Will you want me to come to the hearings?" Ray asked.

"It might be a good idea. We may even find ourselves on opposite sides of the argument now, although I doubt it." James W. Host leaned forward. "You see, there is no other side."

"You've bought the state legislators. Is that it?"

"They don't have to be bought. They're always on our side. What's a little smoke in the desert? We are creating *life*. People know it. Your friend Vormund is obsolete. Leave him to his cactus, Raymond."

Back at the Senita Inn, Raymond Host was stopped by the manager. A Mr. Fusaro had called urgently. He wanted the call returned. Pop, overhearing, was curious. The name rang a bell. Ray feigned ignorance. He knew the name. The Maybanks' lawyer, the irritable man whom he had seen at the Institute a few days ago.

In the cottage, Ray placed the call. From the window he could see Corinne sunning herself at the pool—unbearably beautiful, an exotic flower amid the withered blooms of the Senita Inn.

"Jack Maybank asked me to get in touch with you," Fusaro said. "I hate this sort of call, Mr. Host. But we picked up some disquieting information today."

"Yes?"

"I have an obligation to a client. Even if it is a client I represent for costs and a year's supply of cactus seeds."

"Go ahead."

"Alan Fassman learned about it," Fusaro said carefully. "Someone at his office in LA probably looked into the Denkerman will. Fassman says you're out here to get a line on the Maybanks and the Institute so as to break the will. You are related to Otto Denkerman, aren't you?"

"I'm a distant cousin."

"I have to tell you, Mr. Host, we'll fight you to the end. I won't comment for the moment on the propriety of a man like you worming his way into the DRI, acting as if he were an admirer of Dan Vormund, and so on. That's not my business. But you'd better drop the fight. Host-Labarre doesn't own the country. Not yet, anyway."

"It's dropped, Mr. Fusaro."

"Dropped?"

"Finished. We won't pursue it."

"That's a wise move. Is your father aware that you're giving up on the Denkerman money?"

"He will be."

"I asked because I heard he was in town. I figured he was here to give you a hand."

"He came here for something else."

"I see. Well, thank you. We certainly don't want to make an enemy of Host-Labarre. And listen—you can come out to the Institute any time you want. I think."

"Mr. Fusaro," Host said. "Has he told Professor Vormund? Has anyone told him?"

Fusaro had dissembled once already. He knew from the Maybanks that Mrs. Host, the gorgeous boozer, had informed Fassman about her husband's plan. But he was a prudent lawyer and he had no desire to aggravate a family quarrel. It was at least *part* of the truth to say that Fassman had told the Maybanks. Vormund was another matter. Sooner or later Dan would know.

"He doesn't know. We'll try to keep it that way, if you wish."

"I'd prefer to tell him myself. We seem to have developed a good relationship."

"That's in your favor. Dan doesn't make friends easily."

"We're not quite friends." Host hesitated. His voice was wistful. To Fusaro it seemed improper that someone so wealthy could sound so sad. "But maybe we will be someday."

Before dawn the Vormunds rose. In wool bathrobes they sat at the picture window—outside the desert was cold and still—and waited for the birds to arrive. Vormund never saw the first cardinal or wren that he did not rejoice in his decision to leave the East and find a new life in the dry world.

"Dan, that big phainopepla is back," Clara said. "Look at him, so black and glossy. The nerve of him, chasing those quail away. And now he's standing up and flapping his wings."

"I see him. Like a writer."

"*Some* writers."

"I'm thinking what Mencken said about us. 'His overpowering impulse is to gyrate before his fellow men, flapping his wings and emitting defiant yells. This being forbidden by the police of all civilized countries, he takes it out by putting his yells on paper. This is called self-expression.'"

More birds flew into the yard. They chirped, chattered, hopped about, contesting for bits of suet, feed, garbage from Clara's kitchen.

"Thank God for birds, rabbits, and our valetudinarian neighbors," Vormund said. "They can take advantage of your culinary arts. I can't recall a meal I've ever really enjoyed. I must write to the people who manufacture Meritene and thank them for simplifying my dietary obligations."

Side by side, on an old couch they had owned for fifty years (Clara had bought it in S. Klein when they lived in Greenwich Village), they held hands and watched the birds. At moments like this she understood him better than anyone in the world. Go to nature, Dan wrote, observe the joy inherent in her, and be glad that you are part of it. *The teeming life in that part of the world that man has not yet pre-empted.*

"Jack called last night," she said. "It was after nine so I didn't wake you up."

"Did he say what he wanted?"

"I don't like the way he pesters you. It was about the hearings on the Bald Indian place. He wanted you to write a statement for the Institute so he could read it."

"Statement? What does he think I am, an octogenarian? I'll testify. Clara, did you say I was too sick to make an appearance?"

"We agreed you shouldn't be put through it. You looked terrible after coming back from the jail."

"I'll call Jack later. There is no question that I must testify. I'm feeling feisty. Spoiling for a fight."

Santa Teresa was patched with sunlight. The angles and facets of the range caught the first rays and created jagged patterns. The warmth was palpable, the very essence of life. Two long-legged rabbits hopped into the yard, avoided the birds, munched vigorously on chunks of discarded lettuce, yesterday's broccoli. No territorial imperative here, Vormund thought. The rabbits and birds who visited them were conditioned to a life of abundance. There was always a free meal at the Vormunds'.

Free lunches would end soon enough. Man was determined to wipe the competition off the face of the earth. Not just the ranchers, growers, and hunters who had begun the assault, but the noxious, grinding machines of giant industries, the gluttons for water, air, the earth.

Bald Indian was a case in point. He had not seen it. But Maybank had visited it with a committee of conservationists. A belching poisonous demon. Growth for growth's sake. The worst kind of *progress*.

"Why was I out of step so much?" he asked plaintively.

"You were your own man, Dan."

"It didn't help me with the arbiters of taste. I never liked Marx. Or Freud for that matter. They robbed man of self-respect. How could I have survived the twentieth century, rejecting both of them?"

He felt rested but uneasy. Too much had happened in the last week—events that seemed to be the culmination of some regional (if not national) lunacy. The week had started wonderfully, with the sighting of the creeping devil and its miraculous flower. But he had seen the coyote murdered. Ed's trapped lion. The sorry affair of the rattlesnakes. Whatever were the frustrations of the local people (whom he liked) they seemed to feel that their souls could be saved, their bank accounts fattened, their futures secured, through the slaughter of animals. Kill a coyote and ensure your happiness.

The sight of Clara returning from the kitchen with his Postum reminded him of the sheltered, almost sissified, life he had led. Out of the area, attacking the enemy through articles, books, pamphlets. The enemy did not seem to fear him much. Essler and his lawyer wanted to shake his hand.

Vormund looked into the half-light of the desert. The birds and animals were in full assembly. A meeting of the academic senate, he thought, tea and cookies at the faculty club.

"One of these days I'd like to see a coyote show up for breakfast," he said. "Remember our pet?"

"She's long gone, Dan."

"I've got to talk to Ed about the coyote's range. Maybe we can do a study. He says they are getting back to the cities. They have them in Los Angeles."

"Poor beasts. There'll be no place for them to hide."

He followed the flight of a cardinal. "Maybe no place for people like us, either."

"But we had our good times, Dan."

"Better than anyone I know, my love." He kissed her cheek.

Host, with a pilot's eye, was the first to see the smoke stream. Brownish-yellow, it hovered in the distance like a stain in the blue sky.

"That's it," he said. "We're about a hundred and fifty miles south of Bald Indian. Some days you can see it from two hundred miles away if the wind is right."

Vormund took off his sunglasses and squinted through the curved window. He was seated next to Host in the copilot's seat. Maybank was seated behind him. As seemed to be his habit whenever his employer took the controls, the pilot, in vested suit and porkpie, slept in the rear.

"It's much worse than I anticipated," Vormund said.

Host clenched and unclenched his fingers. "Pilots use it as a landmark beacon. You'll see the plume soon. It's unmistakable."

"You know something?" Maybank asked. "I was here six months ago and it looks dirtier now. The whole sky is infected. It looks as if all that gunk just lays in the air. The winds don't seem to dissipate it."

Host smiled—secretive, vaguely mocking. Was he being critical of himself? Of his father's mighty works? "Wait till it's at one hundred per cent capacity. It's only going at about seventy-five right now."

"What a mistake," Vormund said. "This was once the bluest sky on the continent. What happened? Why did we let it happen?"

"Progress," Maybank said.

"People want it," Host said. He dipped a wing and began to lose altitude.

"They've got the means to reduce pollution, but they say it's too costly," Maybank said. "Things like filter bags and scrubbers."

"No one insists on them," Host said.

"There have to be regulations," said Maybank.

"They're vague or not enforced. The laws aren't specific on what pollutants are covered. Nothing is said about sulphur dioxide or nitrogen oxides." Host sounded neutral on the government's laxness.

Bobbing gently, the plane nosed toward the soiled sky. That morning Host had arrived at the Vormund house with Maybank and offered to fly Vormund over the site. Clara protested. Dan was doing too much. His breathing was irregular. Dr. Mark had warned him to slow down. And why was he getting PVCs now and then? Clara asked. She took his pulse. She knew. "My dear," Vormund said, "better premature ventricular contractions than none at all at my age."

She hugged him as if he were seventeen and going off to basic training.

Aloft, Maybank and Vormund both had difficulty analyzing why Host was being so generous to them. It was, in a sense, *his* power plant that was ravaging the desert. Maybank and Vormund and the others who would give testimony were foes. Was he trying to be magnanimous—knowing that he could not lose?

When they had reached cruising altitude, Host revealed to Vormund his involvement in the Denkerman matter. Maybank was nonplussed, shocked into silence. Why did Host do it?

It took the old man a few minutes to sort things out. At first he assumed that the Hosts were *giving* the DRI fifteen million dollars. Then he became cross with Maybank for not telling him about it.

"You've got it wrong, Dan," Maybank said, trying to be tolerant of Vormund's determined inability to comprehend money. "Ray and his company aren't *giving* us the dough. A man named Otto Denkerman, who liked what you wrote about road runners, is giving it. It was in his will."

"But I don't understand. Why is Ray involved? Why is he here?"

"A good question," Host said. He battled his embarrassment. "I was sent here to get a reading on the Institute. I'm Denkerman's second cousin. My father decided the money belonged to us, not to a conservation group."

"I'm still at sea," Vormund said.

"I came out here to take that money away from Jack Maybank, and Ed, and you. I apologize. It wasn't my idea."

"But how could you?" Vormund asked innocently. "If this man left it to the DRI, how could you claim it was yours?"

"We can do anything we want. Or at least, we can try anything we think will work."

"Ray's apologized to me and to Jenny."

"I can't apologize to Professor Vormund, because it would be meaningless," the young man said. His voice barely issued from the ruddy head. His mouth scarcely moved.

"Fifteen million?" Vormund kept asking. "Jack, there isn't that much money in the world. What shall we do? Buy Ed a shirt from Sears? How about a truck for Sidewinder?"

"It's not ours yet."

"But it will be. Now that Ray says he's abandoned this scheme of his father's. Say, I'm glad it was your father put you up to it. You seem such a decent young man."

"It was one of my father's few bad ideas. He assumes that money has to be used, for progress, for building. He couldn't accept a member of our family, even a distant member like Denkerman, *wasting* it that way."

"Listen," Maybank said, from the seat behind Vormund, "now that it's all hanging out, why did you change your mind?" He wondered: *Has he changed his mind?* Is this pursuit of Vormund, this inexplicable conversion, another feint? Maybank hoped not. He found Host one-sided and blunt, but rather appealing.

"I don't know. It didn't seem right."

"How does one receive fifteen million dollars?" Vormund asked. "In a sack? Under armed guard? Or do they open an account in our name? Do you think I can cash my social security check with you now, Jack, without going to the bank?"

"Fusaro says it may be years before we see a nickel. Not just

Mr. Host but a lot of other phony claimants are going to turn up. Sorry, Ray."

The three men looked north. Rising in a brown stream was the thick gritty output of the power station. It emerged from the plant, narrow and concentrated at its base, widening, spreading, a gaseous monument to man's ingenuity.

"A classic example of using the desert, my father says. Technology at its best. The coal was there, the water was there, the land was useless."

"Who says it was useless?" Maybank asked.

"No one lived there," Host said. "A few Indians and they're delighted with the jobs."

Vormund clucked. "I'm glad we can still be friends, Ray. Because if I had seen this, I might have refused to shake your hand."

"I didn't build it personally."

"But you approve?" Maybank asked.

"You can't wind everything down. You can't close up shop because of a little pollution."

The thickening discharge hypnotized them. Invasive, uncontrollable, it commanded the sky for miles around.

Maybank read from his clipboard. "Can you believe this? When one of the space flights came down, the astronauts saw that goddamn thing from one hundred and seventy miles over northern Mexico. A brown streak from Grand Canyon to the middle of Colorado. They couldn't figure out what in hell it was."

The source of the plume soon became visible—six giant smokestacks disgorging toxic wastes.

"The people want it," Host said. "Oil is running out."

"So is time," Vormund said. "You can't kill the earth like this, Ray."

Flying into hell, Vormund thought. The nose of the aircraft was leading them into a sky forever stained brown, full of deadly gases—lifeless, life-destroying, meaningless.

Maybank's droning voice went on: "Sierra Club report says the fallout gets into six national parks and most of Grand Canyon, Lake Powell, and Lake Mead. You can't see Shiprock any more."

The air seemed windless, defeated. Nature had given up

under the incessant discharge of foul gas. Below, the chimneys appeared to be taking some kind of revenge on the desert. Arbitrary, malignant revenge, Vormund thought. Indians killed deer to eat. Modern man murdered nature for the sheer joy of asserting himself.

"Our engineers were cited by four governors for the way they solved the water problem," Host said. "They diverted rivers and made an artificial lake. So we had lots of coal and cheap water, and all we had to do was get rid of a few Indians."

How easily Host and his people got things done! Vormund marveled. He had written about the builders, the boosters, the faithful who believed in unlimited progress, but he had never seen the workings of these minds close at hand. And Host was polite, intelligent, and open-minded. He wanted nothing but greater comforts for men, more goods, more services, more power.

"That must be the mine," Maybank said.

A mountain of gray-black slag bloomed below them. Vormund shook his head at the sight of the wound in the desert. What ingenuity it took to create such ugliness!

"Says here this place discharges two hundred and fifty tons of fly ash a day," Maybank read. "It isn't only dirty, it's poisonous."

"They're trying to clean it up," said Host.

He had switched from *we* to *they*, Vormund noticed.

"Not very hard," Maybank responded.

"It's the price of progress," Host said. "There are mistakes made." He flashed an apologetic smile at Vormund.

"Too high a price," Vormund said. "I'm not ready to pay it."

Maybank read from his board. "The hospitals are admitting twice as many kids with respiratory diseases. Ray, don't you people realize what you're doing? Sulphur dioxide is a poison."

"What can be done?" Vormund asked. "If Ray built it, maybe Ray can knock it down, now that he's our friend."

"Not so easy," the young man said.

"What about controls?" Maybank shouted. He was getting angry as he looked at the murky hell below. "What happened to those filters and scrubbers that were supposed to go in? Why isn't government writing tougher laws?"

Host did not seem insulted. "You'd have to ask my father and his associates."

"I may do that at the hearings," Vormund said.

"It's a mugg's game," Maybank said. He was inured to defeats. A product of the ruling class, he knew how skillful they were. "Yeah, we know who runs the state house, don't we, Host?"

The plane seemed impeded by the choking cloud. Fly ash, pollutants, chemicals, modern man's gift to heaven. Some aerial city of dreadful night was enfolding them.

Host said: "We don't have to buy and sell legislators or governors. They want *us*. They ask us to do these things."

Vormund looked over his shoulder at Maybank. "It sounds as if we're outnumbered."

"I get that feeling."

The old man intoned Latin: *"Hic labor, opus est."*

Host turned to him. "An appropriate quote?"

"Virgil. I've shortened it. 'Easy is the descent to hell, night and day the gates stand open; but to reclimb the slope to the outer air, this is indeed a task.' I'm not sure whose translation I just used."

Chocolate brown, lifeless, Host's artificial lake spread beneath them. It was a fitting companion to the desecrated sky.

"I'll say this for modern man," Vormund said. "He makes the ugliest ruins known. The cliff dwellings are works of art by comparison."

"It's no ruin," Host said. He was under attack, but he seemed ready to accept their dismal appraisal of his father's works.

"It will be," Vormund said.

Maybank read from his report. The facts were depressing. The project was to a great extent a fake. The lake was losing twenty million gallons a day, the water table was sinking at the rate of a hundred feet every thirty years. They were sucking every ounce of life out of the desert to light used-car lots in Burbank. Downstate farms were closing because of salt-water runoff.

"I'd take a single dune primrose in exchange for that misery," Vormund said.

"Power demands double every eight years," Host explained. "There are plans for fifteen more plants like this in the next twenty years."

"Do people understand they are writing death warrants for their grandchildren, by permitting nature to be defiled?"

"It's not our concern. They demand, we build."

d morning, Corinne. Is Raymond awake?"

took the plane out."

n white heads, frizzy blue-rinsed heads, bald heads, to stare at her. She was much too young, exotic, and ul for the inn, where the average age was seventy-three e average net worth twelve million dollars. It gratified , as she sat down, insolently crossed her legs, and lit a e, that her father-in-law's fortune was in excess of that of r guests combined.

vas wearing an aquamarine halter and shorts, a costume en in the dining room. But she knew that no manager, no ould dare reprimand a Host. Perhaps later discreet men- ht be made, but never in front of James W.

nt heads bobbed and whispered. Her rich tan flesh was a r that money had limits.

ipped his tea. He ate very little, did not smoke or drink. approve of your attire," he said.

, Pop."

manager will have something to say."

Host. We wear what we want to."

W. Host turned his head away from a filigree of ciga- oke. "We are respected here because we are polite and te. Raymond's late mother was a favorite of Mr. Edger- never raised her voice, not even to a chambermaid."

respected here because you are very, very rich. We ck chickens in the room and stuff garbage in the toilets d still respect us."

s unkind, Corinne. I'm sorry you never knew my wife. he fineness might have rubbed off."

od." She looked at the stout plain waitress. Mr. Edger- y recruited them from Maine, whence originated his niture and chintz prints. "Just coffee, please."

is Raymond off to in the plane? I never approved of e took up flying."

vned. "Up north. With the professor. He wanted to Bald Indian."

izing with the enemy. I hear Vormund will testify . Odd, how Raymond cultivates the old man. If I were sor, I'd be suspicious."

"This thing doesn't only foul the ai
up water, it doesn't even *work*."

"Of course it does."

"More than fifty per cent of the el
in transmission. People would be be
tors. It was built not to supply servic
coal, free water, and empty land, an

Vormund cried: "*Progress for pro*
been better advised to have spent
jelly beans!"

"I'm not familiar with the output

"You don't have to be," Vormun
ther and his people practice is *rel*
Like all rituals, it has nothing to d
people. It will not make rain or gr
masses and keep the priests in busi

"It makes money not only for tl
people."

Vormund touched his knee. "The
the Bald Indian Power Plant. Myt

The plane knifed through the e
distance, Vormund now saw ragge
kind of blue that inspired Perugin
Ray Host's scheme, the sky woul
people wanted *blue,* they would h
at a Perugino. And go to museum
two things he had loved more tl
would be obliterated. He looke
was eager to testify. *Something e
note may yet be done. . . .*

As Corinne entered the dining
Wayland Host was in the process
firmly—to two clergymen. Minist

"Gentlemen," Host was sayin
foundation. If they have merit,
day."

Corinne waited till the clerg
were youngish liberal men) ar
table. James W. always got a se

"Go
"He
Silke
turned
beautif
and th
Corinn
cigarett
all othe
She
forbidd
clerk, w
tion mi
Ancie
reminde
Host
"I don't
"Sorry
"The
"I'm a
James
rette sm
consider
ton. She
"We're
could pl
and they
"That
Some of
"Oh, G
ton surel
maple fu
"Where
the way
She ya
show him
"Fraten
against us
the profes

"Vormund isn't the suspicious type. He doesn't care much for anyone. He reserves his respect for woodpeckers and lizards."

"So I've heard. I rather like the idea of having so worthy an opponent."

"He's more than an opponent."

"Really?"

"He's your mortal enemy."

"That implies he possesses some kind of equal footing in the contest. We will be building bigger power plants, more cities, more dams and airports and highways, when Vormund's name is forgotten. An interesting man, but trivial."

She cocked her head. Sunlight touched off small fires in the thick golden hair. "What if Ray decides he won't play your game?"

"Ridiculous. What else can he do?"

"He can take sides with Vormund."

Host shook his head slowly. Corinne was fascinated by the tan lower face, and the stark white forehead and pate, the areas covered by his hard-hat. "You misread him. Ray is proud of his work."

"*Your* work."

"You pretend to have contempt for what I do. Somehow you consider yourself finer, more moral, more attuned to the aesthetic world. Yet you want so badly for me to give Ray the corporation. Would you be as contemptuous of Host Labarre if I let Ray run it? And you would be the wife of a board chairman?"

"Ray deserves it."

"You have not answered me."

"What's the difference how I feel? I want him to be on his own. He's smarter than any of those hotshots who fill your offices in Century Plaza. Maybe one reason he's after Vormund and wants his approval is that he's never gotten yours."

"That is unkind. But you've always had a streak of cruelty in you. I am aware of Raymond's talents. But I am critical of his insularity and his moodiness. Too often he refuses to communicate. Ours is a business of communication as well as *doing*. I have visions of Ray at a meeting with government officials suddenly lapsing into one of those brooding silences." Host leaned back and put his freckled hands on the table. "There's a challenge for a loving wife. You have a verbal talent. Work on him."

"He won't be worked on."

"Perhaps. Do you doubt I love him? It wasn't easy, widowed at an early age, raising an only child, a shy boy. I was never cruel to him. It was an effort for me, a trial."

"Especially with seven in help."

The elder Host patted his lips with a starched napkin. "How do you feel about his rebellion on the Denkerman matter? I know he's told you."

"I don't care one way or the other. If he won't go along, that's your fifteen-million-dollar problem."

"Your ambivalence again. You possess the curse of the shabby genteel—craving wealth yet ashamed of it."

"Not at all. I'm not infatuated with Vormund's idealism or those Maybanks with their schemes for saving the desert. The desert will wind up like everything else in this country—in your pocket. Maybe it's a temporary hobby with Ray. Maybe he sees something in Vormund he's missed. No criticism of you intended, Pop. On the other hand, it would be nice if Ray had a cushion of his own, money that wasn't yours."

"Ah. You're neutral."

"I guess so."

"I'm not. I am pursuing the Denkerman matter. I want Ray to have that money. I intend to make sure that bumblers like Vormund are stopped before they bring progress to a halt."

"You'll need Ray's help. You have no claim on Denkerman's estate."

"Raymond will co-operate."

"Bet?"

"I never gamble, Corinne."

She lit a cigarette. So it was a matter of principle with James W. Host. It was part of his bushido. Built into the bones and blood of the man, a genetic code that commanded him: *acquire*.

"I suspect what may be in back of Ray's mind," she said, teasing him. "Even if you force him to steal the inheritance, he'll give it to the bird watchers. Maybe set up a fund in Vormund's name."

"He has not thought it through."

"Don't be sure. He promised to buy land for them the other

day. Some place with a cactus that Vormund fell in love with. Ray's got it all worked out."

"I bought the land yesterday."

"You what?"

"Essler came to me after Ray stupidly talked to him. He was so awed by the Host-Labarre name that he accepted my first offer. That piece of desert is ours."

"*Yours*, Pop."

Host's bleached eyes studied the vista of dry land through the window of the inn. What was it there for, except for man to use? "I bought that land for Raymond's good. He had no right to use our name to settle a quarrel involving Vormund and his friends. Some business about one of them going to jail. An Indian, I believe. I'm a charitable man but I will not let our name get involved in pointless confrontations. I find Essler contemptible but I was obliged to end the matter."

"And you taught Ray a lesson. If he's a good boy and goes along with the Denkerman business, you might let him make a present of the land to Vormund. A reward. A scrap from the table. Isn't that it, Pop?"

"You make it sound cold-blooded. People like you cannot believe that we often operate through unselfish motives."

"I guess I'm misreading you again." She got up. The flash of her bare thighs and calves caused aging heads to swivel. Bad for the angina, bad for the digestion. "I'll be at the tennis court."

"You must give us your support. Raymond and I want you on our side, Corinne. It's a minor affair and I have no doubts about the outcome."

It was the saddest picket line Fassman had ever seen. He had arrived at the state office building with Apodaca and Downs in early afternoon. Senita's downtown center appeared deserted. A town struck by plague or atomic fallout. Only the pickets marched in front of the new sand-colored building.

"Death city," Fassman said to the crew.

Apodaca spat into the gutter as he unloaded his camera. "The heat. They stay inside. They built all these new stores and shopping plazas, but nobody goes out. They eat lunch, work, crap, screw, everything, inside."

"It's a shame," Fassman said.

"All these civic centers are the same. One block away, winos and niggers."

Little fish eat littler fish, Fassman thought. Inured to the noble workingman, he expected no charity from Apodaca, himself a minority of sorts. And the pickets: the most miserable futile collection of protestors he had ever seen. He had asked Apodaca to film them, and the cameraman had snarled, exposed fifty feet of film, walked away.

A gray-haired stork-thin man in a baggy gray suit and a clerical collar led the picket line. He had the sunken face of a slightly mad Lincoln. He carried an American flag. Behind him was an Indian woman lugging two snot-nosed children. Her placard read: JOBS NOT WELFARE FOR INDIANS. Then came a yellowish man with a limp, his face hidden under a sombrero, bearing the legend: NO GRAPES, NO LETTUCE, NO WORK. There was a black woman, enormously fat, bursting a pair of lavender slacks, whose sign demanded LOW COST HOUSING. Bringing up the rear were three young people, long-haired, bearded, shawled, barefoot, with a sign demanding that marijuana be legalized.

Fassman wanted to weep for them. "Reverend," he asked the gaunt man, "why are you here? Are you an organized group?"

"Sort of. We come out whenever any state or federal committee meets in Senita."

"The hearing is on power stations."

"It doesn't matter. The specific issue is unimportant. We want them to know we're around."

"It isn't much of a showing."

"I'm not discouraged. Jesus changed the world with twelve people."

"It looks like you need four or five more than you have."

"We'll get them." The minister turned his face to the door of the state building, crying: "Jobs, not welfare! Low-cost housing! Fair wages for migrants!"

The death of the Left, Fassman decided. The last survivors. What happened to the street corner radicals of his youth? Didn't Norman Thomas get a million votes one year? And wasn't there once a New Deal that fed and housed people?

The newsman trudged up the baking stone steps. Maybe Vormund was right. He'd forsworn politics, economics, the affairs of men, and turned to the sun, the earth, the wild creatures. But there was the chance of grave error in such a choice. Who would keep the supremely greedy from grabbing everything if people swooned over birds?

He wondered if he had sold Ballstead a bill of goods, convincing him to let him film the hearings. "Go on, go on," Ballstead growled. "They'll build a hundred of those plants and poison everyone, and people will choke to death, grateful that the dishwasher is working. You and Vormund are on the losing team, kid."

Fassman took a seat at a table marked PRESS inside the icy air-conditioned hearing room. The contrast between the blazing dry heat outside and the frigidity within made him sneeze. Apodaca and Downs set up their camera and sound gear at the rear next to a local crew.

Fassman chatted with a man from the Associated Press and a girl from the Senita *Pantagraph*. The committee entered. It was actually a small subcommittee. There were two state senators, one from each party, the Democrat serving as chairman, and a committee counsel, a friendly man named Smales. All seemed to Fassman to be decent, intelligent men.

The Hosts entered and the room came alive. Corinne was a flaming presence in a scarlet shirt-waist dress and gold sandals. She was too gaudy, like a cardinal in a flock of dun-colored sparrows. Ray Host sat there, stonelike, hands locked between his thighs. He was hiding behind wrap-around glasses, enigmatic, motionless. The birdlike dandyish man next to him had to be James Wayland Host—dark blue suit, white shirt, sparse ginger hair, and pencil-line ginger mustache. When he crossed his legs, Fassman saw black silk socks, gleaming black shoes, and feet and ankles as delicate as those of a wren. Around the Hosts were six men in dark suits, threshing through papers, reports, booklets. Lawyers, obviously. They looked to Fassman like former varsity tennis players from USC. A few rows behind them, Fassman saw Essler, and a blond Juno in a tailored green suit. Obviously Mrs. Essler, the sharpshooting Labelle.

On the other side of the room Fassman saw Vormund. He looked relaxed and was laughing and joking with the Maybanks and Clara. He had just told some story and the Maybanks were chuckling. Jenny was holding his hand. Clara was seated on his other side. She had brought a mammoth blue plastic cooler into which she peeked every now and then. Once she offered Vormund a hard-boiled egg, but he held his hand up and refused. A minute later she forced a plastic cup of Meritene on him.

They had not brought Bugler. Maybe Ed was an embarrassment after his scuffle with the law. Ed was happier back at the Institute feeding his masked bobwhites. But there were other allies present—a few Friends of the Earth, a woman from the Sierra Club, a young attorney from Defenders of Wildlife. Fassman found it encouraging that they looked every bit as solid, dignified, and competent as Host's lawyers. *So we are not alone,* the newsman thought. *Be careful we don't infect your kids and your grandchildren, Mr. James Wayland Host.*

The audience was sparse. Some students, a few bearded young men (one, Fassman learned, was the biology teacher who raised money with recycling drives), and some older people with the look of retirees, who had wandered in out of boredom.

The room went dark, and the committee counsel, Smales, began to show slides of the Bald Indian site.

"These are the smokestacks," the counsel said. Against a yellow-brown sky—a murky color never featured in any issue of *Arizona Highways*—six ropes of billowing brown gas poured upward.

"The open pit mine," the counsel said. The audience looked in silence at the black gouges in the earth.

"A wider view."

The slide changed. The sky seemed heavy with some sickness.

After a dozen more photographs James W. Host was called and sworn. Both state senators shook hands with him. They seemed sheepish, servile. Mr. Host was there out of his own generosity. He did not need to volunteer to represent the consortium. But he was that kind of man. Slow to take credit, quick to assume responsibility.

"May I make a prefatory statement?" he asked.

"Of course, sir," the chairman said.

"I won't argue with the slides the counsel showed us. Any such installation can be made to look bad. It does destroy a limited part of the environment. But I think it might have been fairer to us, and the people of the Southwest—"

"*Some* people," Fassman muttered.

"—if counsel had also shown the millions of homes now properly lit, with power for appliances, heat, entertainment, education, cultural activities. I do wish we were not always depicted as monsters. We make no claim to being charitable institutions, but we supply needed services, and the overwhelming majority of people appreciate what we do."

He spoke in a near-whisper, sitting erect, the same rigidity that his son manifested.

Questioning commenced. Fassman felt that it was perfunctory, wandering. They used kid gloves on James Wayland Host. He was no tyrant, no briber of public officials, a private, discreet, honorable man. Are you aware, sir, he was asked, that Bald Indian pumps two hundred and fifty tons of fly ash into the sky every day? Meaningless figures, Host replied politely, because the area is uninhabited.

Smales pressed on. The single plant at Bald Indian produces *twice* as much particulate matter as all—*all!*—sources of pollution in the city of Los Angeles. Was Mr. Host aware of that? Host stroked his dude's mustache. He was not surprised. Bald Indian produced power for a region far larger than Los Angeles. (Why don't they ask him, Fassman wondered, whether he's talking about a geographical area or population? Wouldn't that make a difference?)

We alter the environment, James W. Host conceded, but that is a small price for progress. The senators and the counsel appeared to be nodding their heads. The ritual continued. A tribal dance, Fassman sensed, in which everyone knew who the shaman was, where the juju resided.

The counsel tried again. "Mr. Host, do you and your associates keep informed as to the nature of invisible toxic gases emitted at Bald Indian Power Plant?"

"I am a builder. Not a chemist."

"I think Mr. Host has been interrogated long enough," the Republican member said. "He came here voluntarily. The facts brought out are not new."

"I agree," said the Democrat.

"Tweedledum and Tweedledee," Fassman muttered to Apodaca. "In a second he drops his pants and they kiss his ass."

"Let me add," Host said, "that in our northern neighbor Utah, people have voted overwhelmingly for five new power plants.

The state needs jobs, a tax base, power. No one opposes these enterprises except for a few misguided enemies of progress."

Did he glance at Dan Vormund as he stepped down? Fassman was not sure. Ray Host shifted in his seat, lowered his head inside his shirt. What was he uneasy about? Fassman wondered. His father had told the truth.

Maybank was called next. In a rumpled seersucker suit and a frazzled Princeton tie, he was too eastern, too casual. But he made a good witness—low-keyed, the information at his fingertips.

The counsel told him to read his opening statement.

"I hope I won't bore the committee with cold scientific data," Maybank said. "I wish counsel had gone a bit further in talking about sulphur dioxide and nitrogen oxide poisoning. SO_2 attacks vegetation. It combines with water and becomes sulphuric acid. Nitrogen oxide becomes nitrogen dioxide, a devastating plant poison and the main ingredient in photochemical smog.

"But it's not only plant and animal life that is affected. Between 1965 and 1971, hospital admissions of children suffering from respiratory ailments have doubled. This, in a nongeriatric, nonsmoking group. The areas are losing population but cases of lung and heart ailments are rising. . . ."

Fassman told Apodaca to resume filming. Then he strolled around the room and looked at Vormund. The old man looked angry. Clara seemed to be holding him back, her hand on his right forearm. What could he say? How could he change things around? More than ever he seemed to Fassman a lonely prophet. The lords of the earth respected him and knew he was a high-class old gentleman. But he did not have to be taken seriously and certainly not feared. Not when nearly everyone in Utah wanted power plants and to hell with the vermilion cliffs, the iridescent buttes and mesas, the haunted canyons and flowering meadows.

Fassman wondered: What is the old man thinking? Where can he turn? He had abandoned man for nature, but could not escape man's noxious works.

Maybank looked up from his notes. "I heard Mr. Host say that everyone in Utah wants those power sites. Maybe so. But is the price worth it? To destroy some of the nation's most precious natural terrain, so somebody can pop toast in San Diego? Which brings me to another point. Despite promises, Bald Indian was equipped with the most primitive of pollution controls. Why? Who let this happen?"

The senators looked at one another as if Maybank's charge was either false, or new to them, or irrelevant.

"Plant efficiency is a poor sixty-five per cent. When it operates at capacity, this goes down to sixty per cent. Forty per cent is lost in transmission to that fellow popping toast in San Diego. I am also informed projections for new plants may be phony. Nobody knows what the power needs for California will be. Everyone has different figures. Why ruin vast natural areas on speculation?"

If Maybank's accusations were directed at the Hosts, it did not seem to bother them. The elder Host smiled and joked with his lawyers. Raymond Host was frozen into a pink and blond chunk. His wife was unreachable. To Fassman they had the look of absolute monarchs, people to whom fly ash and sulphur dioxide were as inconsequential as a wrong number.

Maybank was asking that better controls be installed. The counsel reminded him that there were no federal or state regulations covering many pollutants.

"Then there should be. This committee should see to it that they're on the books."

The Republican yawned. "It would raise costs, Mr. Maybank. Mr. Host will vouch for that. Consumers have rights also."

"They do," Jack conceded, "but there are other rights." He told of the runoff of saline waters from Host's lake, and the poisoning of farms. The earth was taking its revenge. And he quoted Vormund: *If we do not permit the earth to produce beauty and joy, in the long run it will not produce food either. . . .*

Mannerly, low-voiced, Maybank had made a good impression. There were handshakes and smiles as he stepped down. And no questions.

"Professor Daniel D. Vormund," the counsel said.

Vormund patted Jenny's hand and walked with surprising briskness to the chair. He raised his right hand. It was trembling. Blinking under the lights, he was sworn.

The chairman beamed at him. "Before you begin, sir, it's a pleasure to hear you again. When you first moved to Arizona, I was privileged to hear a lecture you gave on Shakespeare's contemporaries. I used one of your books at Arizona State."

"Thank you, sir," Vormund said.

The old Kentucky charm, Fassman noted. The accent was a bit thicker, the drawl more prolonged.

"May I add, Mr. Chairman," Vormund continued, "that the text you mention is still available at college bookstores at the bargain price of two dollars and twenty-five cents, of which I get twenty-two and one-half cents. Every little bit helps."

Everyone laughed.

"We're proud you chose Senita as your home."

"I love it here. That's why I do not want to see it destroyed."

"You may be more pessimistic than the facts warrant."

"I think not. The facts are appalling. Gentlemen, machines are in control. They are determined, with man's prodding, to destroy the natural world unless we learn to accept nature."

"We know your philosophy, Professor," Smales said gently. "But we can't deal in abstractions. We want evidence."

"I have it. Through the kindness of Mr. Raymond Host, I flew over Bald Indian Power Plant yesterday, to prepare me for this hearing. . . ."

The room hummed. Heads came together. There was marked confusion on the chairman's face. He looked puzzled at first, then pleased. Of course! Reasonable men getting together! Vormund, the local guru, treated royally by the people he was attacking—the potent Hosts.

"What I saw horrified me," Vormund went on. "I had read reports on how this temple of progress was poisoning everything from here to beyond Grand Canyon, but I was not prepared for the devastation it has wreaked. I'm advised by Mr. Maybank that this is only a beginning, a sample of what the West can expect. Fifteen more of these diabolical engines, spitting filth into our skies? Today Bald Indian and five sister plants emit three thousand tons of poisonous gases daily. *Daily.*

"Gentlemen, what will this part of the country look like when there are twenty plants belching forth gases? Forty? Why not make all of the Southwest one smoking power plant, covering us with a permanent mantle of brown grit, turning the land into a waste in which no rabbit will run, no flower bloom? We could then all retreat to enclosed oxygen tanks, eat our culture-grown pastes, and watch the world on television. Hell beckons, gentlemen, but we insist it is progress."

"They've promised to use controls," the counsel said gently. "We intend to enforce it. There won't be another Bald Indian without safeguards. The desert will get a chance to revive."

"I'm not convinced. I differ with my friend Mr. Maybank, and with you. Controls are merely more technology. The demand will be for more machines to correct what previous machines have ruined. It won't work. The animals will die, the land will grow cracked and bare. We are trapped by our own mechanical genius.

"Conservation is not enough. Forgive me for sounding quixotic, but there are worse attitudes for a man past eighty. Man must not only conserve, he must redefine his concept of himself. He must not try to use, dominate, and change nature, but accept the fact that he is part of it. It's not only one world in terms of nations and races, it is one natural world. If we fail to admit that we live on this earth along with bluebirds and wolves, then we are doomed.

"You don't believe me? There are signs that I'm right. On a Pacific Island they had to reintroduce wasps and worms to pollinate the crops. They'd killed them all with chemicals, and the vegetation died. How we scheme and plot to make the earth do our bidding! But it's short-term, gentlemen. The land you pollute with chemicals, the water you turn to brine, will serve no one.

"Would it not be better to participate in nature's social union? I'm not being romantic or a moralist, although critics have accused me of being both. If I've learned one thing, it is that no matter how obscure a form of life is, it bears on us. Nature's first law is interdependence and we violate it every day. No amount of proper land usage, reforestation, restocking of streams, will help. No matter how scientifically we plunder the earth, it is plunder. The day will come when the last river turns to salt, and the last pasture refuses to grow grass."

"You are a gloomy prophet," the chairman said. "You have no hope for us?"

Vormund's fluttering hand went to his right temple and rested there. "I am asking my fellow Americans to try to look at the light of common day a bit more carefully. To try to see a universe that is worth seeing. Not just the parts that man has created. That's not a tall order, and it may not save us, but I have always believed in modest beginnings.

"Thoreau said that 'this curious world which we inhabit is more wonderful than it is convenient, more beautiful than it is useful, it is more to be admired than it is to be used.' Look at Bald Indian, gentlemen, and see what *use* does to the world."

"He sounds great," Fassman whispered to his cameraman. "Keep rolling."

"I saw Bald Indian as the classic example of what Thoreau called the business of joint stock companies and spades. The engineer calls all aboard, there's a mad rush for the station, and before the train gets under way, there's a terrible accident. Aristotle told us the purpose of a city is to make the Good Life possible, and that a happy city should be large. What would Aristotle say today, set down in Chicago, or New York, or even our beloved Senita? Garbage piled high, the air a gritty haze, anger simmering below the smiles."

"You underestimate our power to change things," the chairman said.

"It will be a change to more of the same. I beg your indulgence for returning to Thoreau, but he also wrote . . ."

A pause. Fassman saw him: Vormund getting ready to read from a book, pacing the classroom, his eyes seeking the corners of the ceiling.

"'. . . in youth, before I lost any of my sense, I can remember that I was still alive.' Today, under the incessant poundings of technology, we are losing our senses increasingly. With each passing year we are less alive. Our children, hypnotized by television, raised on additives and chemicals, are small machines. We flip switches, shift gears, recharge batteries, but we diminish our humanity."

Tears filled Fassman's eyes. Ah, when his world was younger. In the hopeful fifties. People studied Elizabethan playwrights. And Vormund's words rang across the classroom. The past washed over Fassman like a warm wave on a tropical beach.

"I have not much more to say," Vormund said. "If the chairman will indulge an old English teacher, I would like to call on

Wordsworth as a friendly witness, even though I was never keen on nineteenth-century poetry. He wrote:

'There was a time when meadow, grove, and stream,
    'The earth, and every common sight,
        'To me did seem
    'Apparelled in celestial light,
'The glory and the freshness of a dream.'

"But in his case as in Thoreau's, it was *once* and not now that they had seen a universe worth seeing, full of hope and light, and that they had looked upon a world that might inspire the muses of Homer and Shakespeare—"

Good, good, Fassman thought. He never left them.

"Thoreau and Wordsworth, Mr. Chairman, were men enough to admit that when they could no longer see beauty in the world, it was because of something lacking in *them,* not something lacking in nature. It is my fear that if we keep destroying the earth, no child will ever experience the joy of seeing a world apparelled in celestial light. The glory and the dream will vanish as the smokestacks rise, the trees and meadows leveled, the lions killed. No man will be able to walk through meadows, groves, or streams without being repelled by the stench of machines.

"I have little else to say. My views have been published, and I've talked to many people here in my adopted city. I'm no technician, and I can't tell you how and where to build your power plants, because 1 don't want them built at all."

Vormund breathed deeply. He raised his head. The eyes were piercing, but full of kindness. A peaceful man, he had sought to persuade, realized he was outnumbered, and had chosen to be mannerly and civil to the end.

"God looked at the world and saw that it was good," Vormund said. "I ask only that man be given the same chance."

He got up, haltingly. Jenny Maybank got up and came to him. The room was silent. No one applauded. No one moved.

"I thank Professor Vormund for a beautiful presentation," the chairman said. "Those were lovely thoughts, beautifully expressed. This has been an honor for the committee. Maybe we can have a meeting of minds, a sort of golden mean. Maybe we can do our job well enough to satisfy the majority that needs power and wants progress, and the few like yourself who want the desert to stay as it is."

Vormund winked at Jenny as they came up the aisle. "Charming fellow. The right hand taketh away what the left hand giveth."

Fassman waited on the steps of the state building. He told Apodaca and Downs to stand by before driving to the airport.

Shading his moist eyes, Fassman saw Duane Essler, his formidable wife, and the attorney Mac Timmons come out. A party of booted men were behind them.

To lynch me, Fassman shuddered, *barbecue my kosher body.* "Do you see the guys who stole the film?" he asked Apodaca.

Apodaca scanned the group. "They were shit-kickers. Red hands, dirty jeans. These guys are bankers and lawyers."

"Mr. Essler," Fassman called.

"Ah, the media man," Essler laughed. He dug Timmons in the side, touched his wife's arm. "Labelle, that's the chap I told you about. He's the one turned the lion loose on our property, he and Bugler."

"Mr. Essler, two of your hired guns stole my film a few days ago. They attacked my cameraman at the airport. I want that film."

"I have no idea what you're talking about. You know what he means, Mac? Labelle?"

Mrs. Essler looked the other way. The scum! The filth that sneaked in from Los Angeles!

"You're making accusations again, Fassman," Timmons said. "You're heading for trouble."

"The trouble won't be anything like yours, when KGDF's lawyers go to work on you. My station has a floor full of lawyers just waiting for a case like this. You can let me have that film in an hour, before we leave, or you can start answering subpoenas."

"The boy's sun-struck," Timmons said to Essler.

"New York, I bet," Labelle sniffed.

"No, ma'am, Los Angeles. Say, when you shot at me were you trying to kill me or just shake me up? And is it harder to pop an eagle or a man from a plane?"

"Don't respond, Labelle," Essler said. "His kind isn't worth it."

A protective semicircle formed around Essler and his wife, tall men in sharp suits, cowboy hats, gleaming boots. The late afternoon sun sparkled on tie clips, rings, buckles. They would blind Fassman with their metallic adornments, then stomp him to death the way the ranch boss had dispatched the coyote.

Essler said: "I'm surprised at Vormund having truck with his sort. Let's go."

Clack-clacking on the stone steps, they walked off.

Odd, Fassman thought. They respect Vormund. They can't be all bad. They recognized quality in a horse or a man. He was old, learned, polite, and above all, *harmless*. All his fine words and the poetry and the philosophy would not stop overgrazing and land development.

Fassman told his crew to go to the airport and thanked them. He would fly back to Los Angeles that afternoon. The station wagon took off. Minutes later Vormund, resting on Jenny's arm, came down the steps. He looked frailer, more feathery, than Fassman had ever seen him. Carla would be furious, Fassman knew. The hearings had gone right into his nap time.

"I enjoyed your testimony," Fassman said. "Let's hope it does some good. They might think twice before they build those other plants."

"Thank you, Alan. I worried that I was getting too literary. It was rather like a dull Freshman Humanities class, although the chairman seemed a bright enough fellow."

"He was impressed."

"I suppose so. I'm sorry there were no fireworks for the television. Your superiors may not be moved by a shaky old man, looking as if he's just had his prostate removed, mumbling over Thoreau."

"The story isn't over. We may use it for an hour documentary on the desert. I may be back."

Vormund came forward and shook Fassman's hand. Then, almost with embarrassment, he put his left arm around the newsman's shoulders. "The story's over for me, Alan. Clara is right. This is, as Robert W. Service said, the kid's last fight. I'll restrict myself to watching birds in the morning. I could barely get out of that damned witness chair."

He descended, a step at a time, on cautious feet, the Maybanks on either side of him. His pants and shirt, Fassman noticed, with desperate sorrow, hung on his feeble frame. Were they also dependable Sears items, like Ed's?

Fassman detached Maybank from the group. "Let me know what happens. Bald Indian, the Denkerman money, but mostly the money. I can help."

"Sure, Alan." He squinted at the portals of the building. "The movers and shakers. We better beat it."

The Hosts, father and son, followed by Corinne and the Host lawyers, were emerging. They looked sweatless, wrinkle-free.

Fassman felt obliged to come to Maybank's help. It seemed an unfair fight. "If I hear anything I'll call you," he said. "I'm supposed to be unbiased, but what the hell. Maybe I can talk them into doing an hour special."

Maybank waved good-by to him. Fassman could not help staring at the Hosts. The secret and not-so-secret masters. But they were not bad people. They meant well. They moved with the confident step of people who did things better, got their way.

He could hear James W. Host talking to his son. "Vormund was impressive," he said.

"I knew he would be," said Ray. "A lot of that was from his books. You should read him."

"I may. A man like that is worth listening to. Perhaps we can get together someday."

And why not? Fassman thought. You can dump all over him any time you want. The newsman waited until they had walked past him, ignoring him, obliterating him from the hot steps.

"Maybe I can introduce you now," Ray Host was saying. "Maybe he's free for lunch. . . ."

"I've arranged for lunch at the club."

Lunches. Clubs. And the $800,000 profits they turned down once for someone's *good will.* More, and he would faint, Fassman sensed.

Vormund was hunched forward in the station wagon. Ray Host detached himself from his father, his wife, and the lawyers and ran to the car as Jenny backed away from the curb.

"Professor Vormund," he called. "A beautiful statement. I want to thank you."

James W. Host was bobbing his small head, talking to Corinne. "Lovely sentiments. I have no argument with a man like that."

The station wagon moved away.

"No, you don't," Fassman muttered. "Because you can't lose."

James Wayland Host had reserved a private dining room in the Senita Tower, which he had built. He forbade Corinne to drink. But she was too cunning for him. Pleading an upset stomach, she went to the ladies' room, through the fake Old English dining room, washed her hands, then sneaked into the bar where she drank two double vodka gimlets. When she returned, her breath did not betray her, although her eyes were sparkling and her voice was a shade louder.

"I have just told Raymond what I told you yesterday," Host said.

"About the land? Where those people want to save a cactus?"

"That's right. Essler's land."

Ray Host kneaded his knuckles; they made a red block of joints, hard bones. "What good is that land to us? Why'd you buy it?"

"Trade goods."

"I'm sorry, Pop. I don't understand."

Corinne winked at her husband. "Pop is after the Denkerman money. He hasn't quit."

"The Denkerman . . . ?" The younger Host looked stunned. "But we agreed . . . I said the other day . . . I have no desire to pursue it. I don't want to antagonize Vormund."

"Raymond, the world is a wonderful varied place, as your professor pointed out this morning. But it isn't all eagles and cacti. In our hands the money will do a great deal more for mankind. We will get that money and we will put it to work. The lawyers have advised me that we have an excellent case. There is an argument to be made that Denkerman was not in his right mind. We are getting medical files on him."

"You can't win on that count," Ray Host said, almost pleased at the prospect. "Maybank says Denkerman's own lawyers will swear he was sane."

"Those tunes can be changed."

"Pop, let it alone. It's only money."

"Money that does not belong with people standing in the way of our work. I am not giving up."

Ray inhaled, held the breath a second in his massive chest, let the air out slowly. "But I am."

"Are you?"

"I told you I was. I won't pursue it. You need me to go after the bequest. You have no claim on that fifteen million."

James W. Host waved the waiter away. "Raymond, such defiant innocence will not serve you well in this world. I am tempted to call you impertinent."

Corinne broke in. "Yes, impertinent. Go on, Ray, be impertinent, and insolent and impudent and everything else you never are. Talk back."

"Can it, Corinne," Ray said.

"I don't understand you, Raymond. This infatuation with the worst of the conservation crowd. They're troublemakers, cranks." He stroked his mustache, greeted a banker. "I thought you were up to something when you told Essler you might buy his land. But I wasn't sure what."

"I wanted to get Ed Bugler out of jail. All Essler understands is money and power."

"But didn't you see what a splendid advantage that gave us? If those Institute people see that the battle for the will is going our way, they may accept the land as a bit of charity. We can publicize it. Talk about our desire to save that cactus."

Ray Host said: "Vormund saw it in flower. I wish I had been with him."

"We'll let a dozen flowers bloom—"

"A hundred flowers, Mao Tse-tung said," Corinne interrupted sarcastically.

"—and he and his friends can go look at them. The land will be our contribution to their work."

A purple flush was staining Ray Host's columnar neck, creeping up ears and cheeks. It seemed as if stage lighting had been turned on the taurine head. Someone was changing gels—purple, crimson. "This isn't fair to Vormund and what he stands for."

"But what is fair?" Host asked. "Who is better equipped to dispense that money?"

"I'm not sure."

"Then let your father persuade you. Join me in this. You won't regret it."

"Pop, I can't."

"But you must."

"No. You'll need my co-operation to break that will. You'll need my signatures. I won't give them."

"Attaboy, Ray," Corinne said. "Hang in there." She grasped his hand.

"You must give them. As soon as we are in Los Angeles, we'll meet with the attorneys. You can be of inestimable help to them. You've learned a great deal out here. That business at the courthouse. Those people are not much better than common criminals. We won't give them a minute's peace. They'll be glad to surrender their claim."

"Their *claim?*" Corinne cried. "*It's theirs.* It was willed to them."

"By an irrational old man who was talked into it."

Ray Host's head moved from side to side. He was like a trapped animal. She had heard about Bugler and the newsman freeing the lion. Ray had that look now—caught, in torment. She needed more than an Ed Bugler to pry open the steel jaws.

"Ray, tell him *again*," she pleaded. "You won't go along. Host-Labarre doesn't have to own everything in the world."

"Be quiet, Corinne," Host said. "This is not a matter of greed, but a matter of principle."

"Ray, tell him he's wrong."

James W. Host ignored her. "You can sign a formal letter of agreement—"

"A letter of *what?*" Corinne hooted. "This is too much!"

"We'll meet tomorrow at the office," Raymond's father continued. "I want you to tell the lawyers what you learned about that organization. And I have some tidbits about your friend Vormund's past. Ray, are you aware that he once wrote for something called *The New Republic?*"

"Jesus, this is awful," Corinne said.

"I warn you to be silent, Corinne. I know you sneaked into the bar. Raymond will make up his own mind." He glared at her. His pale eyes, bloodless skin, light hair, appeared to have been overexposed. "You have been urging me, Corinne, to have Raymond named board chairman. You have been persistent and unsubtle in your demands. Now how in heaven's name can I do that, when the board will learn that he turned away from fifteen million dollars that was his? Worse, that he took the side of people who came by it in some underhand way?"

He was twisting facts, but his basic argument was a sound one. J. W. Host was no diabolical plotter. He followed his instincts the way Ed Bugler's badgers dug holes.

Corinne claimed that her stomach was bothering her. She promised Pop and Ray she would not drink again, that her insides were spinning. Too much heat. Too much tension. Please, she had to go to the ladies' room.

"Raymond, go after her."

"I trust her. Right, baby?"

Corinne kissed his cheek and walked off.

"Well, Raymond?"

She did not hear his answer. Corinne took the elevator to the basement garage of the Senita Tower. An attendant brought the Lincoln. The top was down. She gave him a dollar and blasted out of the underground chamber into the blinding sunlight.

"You proud of our achievement?" Bugler asked.

Sidewinder, on his knees, looked through fogged lenses at the six spotted quail chicks. They skittered about the desert floor, fluffy, round, cheeping and squabbling for the orange beetle larvae Bugler tossed to them.

"They're okay," the Hopi said.

"The return of the masked bobwhite quail. And we had a part in it."

"Until the ranchers kill this bunch."

"Not if we can buy land for them or persuade the Bureau of Land Management to protect them."

Sidewinder covered his rotten teeth and laughed into his palm. "The way the Bureau of Indian Affairs protects Indians, huh?"

"One thing I can't stand is a cynical Hopi. Be proud of our accomplishment. I can't wait till Dan gets a look at them. How many people can say they revived a species?"

"They're gonna graze cattle right over the nests, like before."

"You're a big help. Worse pessimist than Dan." A bit of survival, that was all Ed Bugler asked. He did not romanticize his love for animals and birds the way Vormund did, but he felt it as deeply.

Bugler kept herding the scurrying chicks toward one another. He had left the parents—rare survivors that some Papago had brought to them in a carton—in their pen. They were oddities, the last of the curious bobwhites distinguished by a black "mask," a hood over eyes and throats, showing none of the white patches of the standard bobwhite. A man could work a lifetime and not achieve as much. Dan had promised to do an article on it. "Welcome Back the Masked Bobwhite . . ."

"I'd like to see them breeding all over the range again," Ed said.

"You could get lucky, but I don't think so."

Bugler picked up two chicks. "Maybe Alan Fassman could come out and do one of those TV programs about them."

"You could be famous. John Wayne could play you."

Bugler gathered up the chicks. They quivered with life in his arms. They ruffled their feathers, pushed out their spotted chests. A miracle: something the naturalists had written off. "Funny about Fassman. A city guy, as clumsy as Dan. But he had that sense of the desert. You should have been there the day we set the lion free."

"You was both loco. I don't go near a trapped cat. I'd of shot him."

"You always were a sentimental type."

Sidewinder put the chicks in their crate. Both men started across the desert to the Institute. The bobwhites whistled feebly. The Hopi stopped. "Lincoln Continental."

"I thought you specialized in pickups."

Both heard the hum of a motor from the winding road. They stopped a moment and listened. They remembered the huge white car.

"I bet it's the same one."

"That I'd like to believe. How come you're so sure of cars?"

"Listened for the cavalry in the old days. Could tell a squad from a platoon, heavy armed or side arms."

"You lie, Sidewinder. You aren't that old."

They trudged toward the adobe buildings. Bugler thought how dingy they were. They needed plastering, paint, roofing. Sidewinder pointed to the state road.

They saw the white car careening, at much too fast a rate of speed, weaving, rising. The top was down. Golden hair flashed.

A bright red dress. The automobile was swerving from one side to the other, up and down the deceptive dips. Once the car struck a sandy shoulder and bounced along the bumpy track for about twenty yards before righting itself. Like a flash of white fire the car was gone, turning the corner beyond the Institute's sign, vanishing into a trough.

"That lady," the Hopi said.

"The one came out here for lunch with her husband. They were after Jack for something. The guy helped get me out of the jug." In Bugler's mind the Hosts barely had names. Snakes and birds had names. People were just people.

"Made believe they was lost. They was after something."

"She sure looks lost right now. Wonder where she's headed?"

"It don't matter. She's drunk."

Bugler shook his head. Nothing humans did surprised him any more. He was a man of moderate habits who had enjoyed his four wives, but had found them no match for fish, bats or mangrove oysters, or *Crotalus crotalus*. He had no understanding, no sympathy for people who needed booze and big cars.

As they walked into the parking lot, they heard the sirens scissoring the still air. In seconds they saw the flashing beacon of the black-and-white sheriff's car.

"Never catch her," Sidewinder said. "Not if she floors it."

"Wonder what's eating her."

"You ought to be able to guess after four wives."

"That didn't make me an expert. I hope she keeps out of trouble."

Bugler scratched his roached hair. A schoolmasterish frown creased his forehead. Bad business, tearing around desert roads. Dips and curves were unpredictable. Arroyos, canyons.

"She had a snootful," Sidewinder said. "They drink."

"I heard Jack say she could put it away." Ed squinted at the Hopi. "Maybe the sheriff'll need help. Let's take off. We know who she is. I owe her husband something."

"I keep out of trouble."

"You're all heart. Big Chief Charity. Come on, we'll take the jeep."

"I don't norm'lly help sheriffs."

"It's the lady we're helping."

"It's *you* he got out of jail, not me."

Vormund was right. The desert pleaded for contemplation, peace, silence.

Now she was climbing, pushing the car into a tableland of rough grass, mesquite, scrub oak. There was less cactus, less of the sparse desert that Vormund praised so enthusiastically. *It speaks to me of endurance and courage, and the simple truth that scarcity may be a blessing. . . .*

Thoughts jumbled in her head. The gentle ease induced by alcohol vanished. Now there was a pressing pain at her temples. Punishment, penance. Like the saints who sat on columns. She was condemned to suffer in a ten-thousand-dollar car. But if she could keep driving forever, racing over desert, up and down mountains, to the cold blue sea, she would recover. She would go back to Ray and Pop. They would live out their years, Ray as a revered captain of industry, she a distinguished California matron, endowing museums and supporting the symphony. The Denkerman money could be used to elevate Chicanos. Perhaps fund a school of modern dance.

Furious, she jammed her foot against the accelerator. The car responded violently. It was like goading a tiger. She was now rising rapidly, the wind screaming around her, on the winding road to Grace Canyon.

A tourist trailer shuddered to a rubber-burning screeching halt as she fishtailed on a curve. She missed it narrowly, crunched into a guard rail, righted the car, resumed her aimless flight. A truckload of brown-faced Papago children screamed at her. The driver blasted her horn, missed her by inches. Once more she bounced against the low metal rail, ripped chunks of white enamel from the flanks of the car.

The machine burst onto a straight stretch of the state road. It rose again, a ribbon of asphalt on which she could cruise comfortably at eighty-five miles an hour. A road runner tried to race the front wheel, glared at the rubber competitor with a cynical yellow eye, skittered to the safety of a creosote bush.

Now the road followed the canyon, bending sharply to the right, soaring into the red-stone walls. Vermilion rocks of fantastic wind-carved shapes loomed on either side of her. Sunlight intensified the bright greens of junipers. Spring flowers struggled from crevices—daubings of yellow, orange, scarlet.

She saw the black-and-yellow warning sign a fraction of a sec-

"You work for me, more or less. Get rid of the bobwhites and we'll grab the jeep."

Sidewinder smiled crookedly. Because they were so rich. He understood.

The gimlets, imbibed as swiftly as cool water, rendered her legs rubbery, infused her with casual self-assurance. She could drive forever under the burning sun. A witless wonder at the wheel. All the way to the ocean. Right off the Santa Monica pier into the Pacific. Was it still there? In college she and Ray had eaten cotton candy there, screamed on the rides. (Ray screamed discreetly.) She recalled the sunlit scene—surfers with dyed blond curls, coffee-brown bodies, grunion runs, beach picnics.

Muddled and unfocused as her mind was, she felt at peace with herself. It was comforting to surrender to the warm alcoholic semistupor, succumbing to that disembodied state. Her arms and legs were capable of wondrous loose movements, joints ingeniously oiled, the body free of pain. In the Senita Tower she had left Ray and her father-in-law making their peace. She knew what the terms of the agreement would be. Some small protest from Ray, some acknowledgment from Pop that he had a point, unconditional surrender by Ray.

She ended up conceding that James W. Host was smarter than either of them. Get Ray to the top of the corporation and perhaps he would brood less, be less prone to silences, enjoy life more. Let him go after the Denkerman money, exhibit his cunning and his persistence. Vormund? A fine man, James W. admitted. But he was a vestigial organ, a prophet without an audience. He had not the vaguest notion as to how the country functioned, who made decisions, what the mass of people wanted. If the world followed Vormund, people would be back in caves, grubbing for roots.

The desert raced by her, enclosing her in hot dusty air. The land was a blur of gray-greens, browns, yellows. The colors blended into savage abstraction, the work of a sun-mad *fauviste*. She felt vaguely guilty for the intrusive car. Speed and power were inimical to the desert. It set its own slow unmeasurable pace. Saguaros lived for two hundred years and grew at a rate that was the despair of anyone who planted a seed for posterity ond too late. Corinne realized the road almost turned on itself, a turn as bad as any she and Ray had ever negotiated in the Swiss alps. Violently, washed by fear, she swung the wheel to the right. The tires shrieked in protest. Too much was asked of them. The muscular power of the enormous engine was beyond her control. It yanked the body of the car away from the road, over the double white line, toward the guard rail. The nose of the car barely missed the warning sign. The automobile skidded but did not slow down sufficiently for her to change direction.

The low railing appeared pitifully frail, not enough to slow down her headlong surge. But she did not care. Below, at the bottom of the redwall, she could hear the rushing of the canyon stream. For a fraction of a second she thought she recalled something Ray had quoted from one of Vormund's books—modern man trapped in a giant car, speeding at eighty miles an hour, incapable of a single creative or contemplative moment because he was enslaved to the monster. No love, no joy, no understanding.

How wise the old man was. She felt relaxed, optimistic, as if at the end of a long illness, or the way she had felt finishing a term paper. Over the iron rails the hood rose like a white shark, hovered a moment, plunged with echoing metallic clangor into the canyon.

Sidewinder and Bugler got to the Grace Canyon turn five minutes after the sheriff. They saw his Ford parked at the roadside. The flasher was whirling, the doors open. A dispatcher's voice crackled over the radio, but the deputy was not in sight.

"Down there," Sidewinder said. "Lookit the skid marks. Went off like a bird." He pointed to the twisted metal.

Bugler loped down the rocky incline. The Indian trailed him. Time enough, Sidewinder thought. She wasn't going anywhere. They saw the Lincoln first. The nose was smashed into a monumental outcropping of redwall. The abutment had broken the downward plunge of the car, smashed the mighty engine into a pile of junk, as if it had been distressed by a giant hammor. But the body of the car, apart from gouges and dents, was almost intact.

The sheriff was struggling with Corinne's seat belt. The door had crumpled against it. Jagged metal locked her in. She lay with her golden head on the leather headrest. Her arms were

limp in her lap. The scarlet dress was hiked above her knees.
There was a bloody gash on her forehead, rills of blood running
into her dazed eyes. Her knees were skinned and bleeding.

"Give us a hand," the sheriff said.

Bugler knew him. A graduate of the state university. Once he
had come around to meet Dan and was disappointed that the old
man was in bed, wheezing with asthma.

"Is she okay?" Ed asked.

Both men struggled with the jammed door. Like the lion trap,
Ed thought. He jammed a stick into the crack and began to pry
it open.

"I can't tell," the deputy said. "It's a miracle she's breathing.
Don't move, ma'am. Bleeding like hell. I clocked her at ninety-
five below Pima Springs."

"We saw her from the Institute," Ed said. He was on one
knee, putting pressure on the door. "Look at that engine."

A rear wheel, a foot off the ground, was still spinning. Bugler
and Sidewinder shoved the door open. The deputy cut the seat
belt. The three men helped her out of the wreck. As she moved,
the blood flowed rapidly down her forehead, flooding over her
nose and mouth.

"You all right, lady?" the sheriff asked. "Can you hear me?"

Corinne nodded. If only they could do something about the
sun, she thought. Too much light. She needed darkness.

"I'll carry her up to the road. I called for an ambulance. You
fellows mind standing by and giving me a hand if I need it?"

"Sure," said Bugler. He stared at the tanned face. Too much
of everything. The Hosts were people he could not fathom. "We
know her kind of. She's Mrs. Host."

"Who?"

"Lady from California. I'm with the Desert Research Institute.
She and her husband visited our place a few days back. They're
in Senita."

"You know where they're staying?"

"The Senita Inn, I think. Her father-in-law was in town also.
You know, the Hosts, the building people."

The sheriff bore her like a treasure, avoiding clumps of cactus,
the grasping limbs of junipers. "Host-Labarre?"

"That's the family."

"God Almighty. And damned near killed herself. You'd think people like that would know better. All they have to live for."

Bugler said no more. He'd given up on people. A few were okay—Dan, Clara, Sidewinder, even the snake-spooked Noreen. Mrs. Host looked as if she'd make it. Blood was only blood and Bugler had seen a lot of it. She was breathing, and her eyes were open. Maybe there was a special God that looked after the likes of the Hosts. Not only rich but lucky.

"You coming, Sidewinder?"

"Better check that there engine," the Hopi said. He saw gasoline dripping from the tank. What a pile of junk that car made! Sidewinder reached inside the left front door and turned off the ignition. Some deputy, he thought. A kid out of college. And maybe there were some wires he should cut. But the hood was a jumble of crumpled scrap. Nobody could get at that engine without an acetylene torch. The Indian tried to get the lever into park, just to be safe, but it was useless. Everything was knocked to squash, scrap for the junk lot.

On the blacktop, the police car radio sputtered. An ambulance was speeding out from Senita. A heavy wrecker was coming for the car. They were seeking the woman's family. They'd all be here, Sidewinder thought. Call out the marines for that kind of woman. The car—who cared? They could buy twenty like it.

Sidewinder sat on a red rock and squinted into Grace Canyon. Not a bad place if you liked canyons. He preferred Second Mesa, up north. He could see at the summit of the redwall the stone pinnacles the Hualapais called the chief and his wife. Some stuff about looking back. Hualapais were okay but they believed too much. Years ago Sidewinder and his brother had sold them grain alcohol cut with tea.

Sighing, he rested on one elbow, and thought briefly about his wife and five kids at Second Mesa. He guessed they were all right. He looked over the tips of his boots to the red towers. Now he knew. It was the place where Essler's wife took shots at Ed and that guy from Los Angeles. Shoot them down as if they were coyotes. Sidewinder felt nothing one way or the other, although he would have been sorry if Ed had been shot. Whoever was stronger, richer, meaner, did what he wanted, and nobody cared.

A bird flew over the canyon wall, darted about, glided over the rushing creek, in and out of the narrowleaf cottonwoods. Red breast. Green wings. Sidewinder watched as it disappeared into the cottonwoods, flew out again, circled, settled on a branch. He sat up and cupped his right ear.

Kowm, kowm, kowm, kowm . . .

A low noise like drumming. Ed had told him how it sounded, but they'd never really heard it. Almost nobody ever did. You could live a whole life in the desert and the mountains and never see one. A bird with a crazy name, one Sidewinder thought he saw once. And they'd promised Dan they'd find for him. *Old Vormund wants to see that bird as bad as I want a pickup truck.*

The bird took wing once more, glossy green wings, reflecting the gold of the sun. The bright red breast flashed past Sidewinder. The smooth shiny feathers were like a red flower.

"Set down once more so I can see you."

As if responding, the bird found a bare branch on a cottonwood and perched. Its tiny feet (something funny about them, the Hopi thought) grasped the limb. It sat there, erect, proud, bursting with life.

Kowm, kowm, kowm . . .

"I heard better bird songs," the Hopi said, "but Ed and Dan think you're hot stuff."

He no longer doubted it. It was the bird Ed promised the old man he'd show him. Green head and wings, and a white collar on the throat and a bright red breast, and a funny name. Maybe an Indian name, or a Mexican name, where the bird was supposed to come from.

The bird made its drumming noise again. The pleasant sound grew fainter in Sidewinder's ears, then was drowned by the *wah-wah-wah* of an ambulance Klaxon. As if frightened by the wails the trogon flew off. It disappeared into the cottonwoods, emerged once more, and then soared higher and higher toward the canyon wall.

"Maybe you could come back," the Hopi said. "Maybe once for the old man."

He heard Bugler shouting to give them a hand, got up, and tramped up the incline, past the wreckage of the car.

6

※

"Are you comfortable, Dan?" Bugler asked.

"As General MacArthur once said—at least I think he did—I am splendid in every way. Or as Johnson said to Garrick, 'Sir, we are a nest of singing birds.'"

"There's only one bird I want to hear sing today."

The two men sat on folding chairs inside Bugler's homemade blind—an irregularly shaped tent constructed of camouflage netting draped on aluminum poles. They were in Grace Canyon.

"We shall be rewarded," Vormund said.

"I hope so. If you get tired, or cold, I can drive you home. My ears are still ringing from the blast Clara gave me. You heard her, Dan. This is the last trip I can take you on."

"I haven't felt better in weeks." The old man raised his right hand. "Observe. My hand is steady and I haven't even had my Meritene."

"Yeah, but it's cold. If I hear you sneeze, we go back."

"Clara lives to exploit my ailments. Not that I don't have them. I've never had a day in my life when I've felt entirely well. I wonder how it feels—supremely healthy people like yourself, or that young Mr. Host, people who never feel weak or run-down."

"You get other worries." Bugler scanned the lightening sky with his binoculars. "Don't see much. Ravens. Bluebirds. I heard what sounded like a thrasher before, but I don't see him. You're the thrasher expert." He thought of the day they discovered the cactus. "Clara could have come along."

"Three are too many in the blind. She'd rather stay home and prepare medications for my glorious return. What's that bird over there? On the gambel oak."

Bugler peered through the dawn mists. Both men were silent a moment.

"Not ours. The conformation is different. They say the trogon has a fluttering flight. So few people have seen the darn thing, I can't be sure. Maybe Sidewinder was full of peyote when he saw it. But I showed him the color drawing in Peterson's guide and he swore on his ancestors' graves that it was the bird."

"Then we shall wait and we shall be rewarded."

Vormund settled into his layers of clothing. An army blanket covered all. Beneath it he wore a heavy tweed coat, two wool sweaters, corduroy trousers, a flannel shirt from L. L. Bean's that Clara had bought him for his eightieth birthday, and long wool underwear. Tight on his head, pulled almost over his eyes, was an OD army surplus cap.

They had driven out from Senita City at four-thirty that morning in the cold thin air, determined to see the trogon. "I feel it in my ancient bones," Vormund said to Ed. "As surely as I have ever felt anything in my life."

Several days had passed since Corinne Host had wrecked her car, fifty yards above the part of the canyon where the two men now sat. Miraculously she had not been severely injured, the damage being more cosmetic than organic. After emergency treatment for shock, bruises, and contusions at Senita Jewish Hospital, she was discharged. A day later the Hosts flew to Los Angeles. Corinne and Raymond flew in one plane, Pop Host in another. Like nations, they owned airlines. They departed without any further contact with the DRI people.

The next day Jack Maybank called a meeting of the Board of Directors of the Institute and announced the details of the Denkerman inheritance. Vormund, who already knew in general terms about the bequest, and the other board members, largely bankers, educators, and businessmen, were ecstatic. It would mean (assuming claimants failed to break the will) that the Institute would be self-supporting, capable of launching new campaigns, publishing more, influencing legislators, buying land.

Vormund at once raised several matters, much to Maybank's annoyance. First, Ed Bugler was to get a raise. The other directors, unaware of Maybank's despair at Ed's inefficiency, applauded the suggestion. Secondly, the first major expenditure of funds should be for the purchase of the Essler tract where the creeping devils grew. To Vormund's chagrin, one of the bankers said he had heard that the land had been sold—at least some of Essler's land—to an unknown purchaser. It disturbed both Vormund and Maybank and both had their suspicions.

On this cold, clear, bright morning, however, Vormund felt blissfully at peace with the world. *Lord, now lettest thy servant depart in peace.* This was the way he enjoyed nature—restful, quiet, seated with Ed (that most natural of men), sipping water from a canteen, munching a saltine. The struggles of the past week did not concern him. (It all began, he felt, when he lifted the rock and threatened the man with the dogs. Unlike him, utterly unlike him. And Ed and the lion. And Ed going to jail. Too much at once. As if the people out West were infected with the dancing sickness, a public lunacy in which every living creature had to be killed, and killed quickly.)

If the trogon appeared, something might be reaffirmed, some reminder of other truths, other options. The lovely canyon buoyed his spirits—redwall, junipers, bright sky. Even if they did not sight the bird, the day would revive him. The world to which they now surrendered themselves had nothing to do with man. No computer could have created the ragged silhouette of the tree line, the shifting mysterious red hues of the rocks, the hissing waters below. Man craved credit for everything. Vormund was contemptuous of his presumption, delighted to find joy and beauty in creatures, inanimate objects, natural formations that derived from the hand of another power.

"How far is this from where you freed the lion?"

"Half a mile. The traps were set all the way up the canyon. Essler's people know how to do it, too." Bugler cocked an ear. "Sounds like a mountain bluebird. You hear it?"

"I hear something. But I'm still not as good as I should be on western birds. They know it, and they taunt me. Ah, now."

Both men listened.

Chur, chur, chur, chur . . .

"As if for our benefit," Vormund said.

"There he goes. On the cottonwood. There'll be a flock of them before long."

"A splendid dumpy round-shouldered bird," Vormund said admiringly. He opened his log and made an entry—*bird, song, time, place.*

Somewhere in Thoreau there was a passage about the author spending twelve years looking for a rare night warbler. No, not Thoreau. In Emerson's biographical note on Thoreau. Emerson and Thoreau on a stroll, identifying redstarts and grosbeaks, but never the elusive warbler. And Emerson warning the naturalist to beware of finding it, *lest life should have nothing more to show him.*

He told the story to Bugler. Ed contemplated Emerson's advice. "What'd Thoreau say to that?"

"Oh, he said that you look for something in vain half your life, and when you find it, you become its *prey.*"

"I don't know I agree with either of them. If I see the trogon, there's lots more birds I've never seen. I sure won't become its prey. It'll be part of me, that's all."

Vormund huddled inside the blanket. Will I see the trogon and find life empty afterward? He doubted it. He was by no means written out. There was Clara. The Institute. Good friends.

"You'd have done better with a bird man, Dan," Bugler said. "You know me. Snakes first. What was that about the trogon's toes?"

"A peculiarity. The first and second toes turn backward. What the ornithologists call heterodactylus. And did you know that our trogon is related to the quetzal of Guatemala, the Mayans' holy bird?"

"Distinguished family. I feel religious."

Morning light changed the colors of the canyon wall from a dark dull red, almost blood-colored, to bright vermilion, then to orange. The sheer red slopes looked inviting and warm. In the crevices and caves and cracks, life teemed. Trees in a dozen shades of green poked from the rim, from the ledges. To Vormund the variations of greens seemed like gradations on a color chart, only infinitely brighter and more imaginative. *Learn for the ancients a just esteem, to copy nature is to copy them.* Neither ancient man nor modern man could improve on nature. Perhaps man, in some warped jealous way, was intent on altering nature for that very reason. Inferior to God's world, he would malform it, perhaps destroy it.

"Steady, Dan. I saw a newcomer."

"Where?"

"Ducked into that big juniper. It doesn't look like any bird we've spotted yet."

They raised binoculars. "Don't lose him," said Vormund.

"He's in there, the son of a gun," Bugler whispered.

Someone had once written, Vormund recalled, that to be a bird was to be *alive* more intensely than any other living creature, man included. Birds had hotter blood, brighter colors, stronger emotions. More of the pathetic fallacy?

"There he is, Dan."

"I don't see him yet. My eyes aren't as sharp as yours."

"Go up a little. Third big branch from the top on the left side of the tree. Dammit, he ducked back in."

A low throbbing noise drifted toward them. *Kowm, kowm, kowm* . . .

"That's him," Bugler said. "Now he's got to come out."

Thoreau's lost animals—hound, horse, turtledove, Vormund thought. And the travelers he had met who were as anxious to recover them as he was. Why was he now pursuing this bird? Was it with the poignant hope that the trogon would restore lost innocence? The capacity to see the world fresher and brighter? *Apparelled in celestial light* . . .

"I'm as nervous as a bride, Ed."

"Be patient. I promised you you'd see the trogon. I'm nervous too. Forgot to get a light reading. Look, I'll handle the color photos, and you do the black-and-white."

Again they heard the distinctive low call. *Kowm, kowm, kowm* . . .

The shy caller fluttered out of the juniper, circled the tree, then perched on a branch.

Vormund focused the binoculars on him. Unmistakable. As the bird had been described: a quiet erect posture and the oddly arranged toes. It was a male. The head, chest, and upper parts of the body were a dark glossy green. Across the upper breast was a snowy band resembling a white bib. The plump breast was geranium red, much brighter than a robin's, more intense than a cardinal. The long tail was square-tipped, and the inner tail feathers were oyster white. There was, to Vormund, something almost parrotlike about the trogon's conformation—stubby bill, short neck, round head, a kind of arrogance and self-confidence that he found altogether delightful. An elitist among forest birds.

"Behold," he whispered, as Ed clicked off pictures. "Behold, *Trogon elegans,* a secretive forest bird, first cousin of the quetzal of the Mayans. The only member of his estimable family to visit the United States. Ed, this is an epiphany."

"I don't know what that is, but I believe you."

"A spectacular bird. A patrician bird. Look at the colors and their arrangement. Tell me when an abstract artist ever achieved such perfection."

Bugler changed lenses swiftly and took more photographs. "I got a hunch he's nesting. There's a mate somewhere. He's probably gathering food."

The trogon turned its head as if acknowledging the praise. Its clear eye seemed to pierce the netting, advising them it appreciated their laudatory words. Then it took wing.

"Oh, baby," Bugler said. "I got him. I got him the second he took off. Did you, Dan?"

"I've failed. I didn't take a picture. Too nervous. Too exalted. I'm sorry."

"Doesn't matter."

They watched the bird circle the tree again, in an erratic fluttering way, glimpsing the red breast, green wings, white throat. Then it soared higher, rising from the junipers to the cottonwoods and then toward the red-stone walls, higher and higher, into Grace Canyon.

"Gone," Vormund sighed. "He's gone."

"Once in a lifetime. Let's see—five minutes after six. Don't forget to log it, Dan."

Vormund shivered inside the blanket. Now fatigue would set in. The thrill of the hunt was over. "Every time I meet a new bird, I'm sorry I don't know more of them. Someone once called them spokesmen for all of God's creatures."

"Steady, Dan. You sound like you're ready to fly."

"I wish I could. What joy, what life, in him. Ed, you made it possible. We saw the trogon."

Bugler began to pack his binoculars and cameras and clean up the remains of their breakfast. "I better get you back to Senita. Clara will have the cops out looking for us. Are you okay?"

"I have never felt better. Mr. Bugler, we have seen the trogon at dawn. Master Shallow, we have heard the chimes at midnight."

"I can find birds and snakes, but I don't know those fancy quotations. Give me a hand with the net, and we'll get going."

Vormund looked toward the canyon for a last time. "Do you think he'll come back, Ed?"

"He might. He might not. He's his own boss."

The men trudged up the incline. Bugler carried the chairs, the netting, the canteen, the cameras. Vormund walked a pace ahead of him. His feet groped for firm earth, rocks on which to get a purchase. It seemed steeper than he remembered. Halfway up the slope they passed some shards of broken glass and chunks of twisted metal glinting in the morning sun.

"The Host car," Ed said.

"Dreadful. Someone should clean that garbage up."

"Sidewinder saw what's left of the car in a lot downtown. They were selling it for the parts. He says the insurance company took it over."

Vormund paused and wiped his forehead. The Hosts. The beautiful woman and the handsome young man. How would it feel to have so much money, to do anything one wanted to do? He was too old to ever know, nor did he care. He had seen the trogon.

"Never figured them out," Ed was saying. "All that money and they wanted more. Money you'd gotten for us."

"I forgive them. I'm in a forgiving mood this morning. It was Host's father put him up to it. The young fellow knew better. People like that gravitate toward loose money, to land, to riches. It's built into their genetic code. Host's father went after those millions the way a red-tailed hawk pounces on a mouse."

"I'll never understand those people. I've never owned more than two hundred bucks at one time in my life."

Vormund steadied himself against a red boulder, then resumed the climb. It was light now. Grays and browns were magically transformed into reds, greens, yellows. The sun was invasive, prevailing. Vormund took off the wool cap and wiped his face. Both men rested under the last stand of cottonwoods. Above them, on the state road, trucks and cars rumbled to and from Senita City.

"You getting tired, Dan?"

"A bit. Clara packed some Meritene in the valise we left in the jeep. An infusion, and I'll be full of ginger."

"We can rest, if you're tired. We have all day to snooze."

Bugler was also weary. But his powerful body paced itself. He knew when to rest, when to move. Before the sun got any hotter, he wanted the old man in the jeep, refreshed, on his way home to Clara's peevish attentions. He wondered should he tell Vormund that they had not contacted Essler about the trip. He scanned the skies, wondering if fast-shooting Labelle was observing them.

Bugler shaded his eyes and looked down to the banks of the stream. From the angle and elevation at which he now stood he could see the rushing waters and the sandy banks clearly. Something drew his attention and he looked through his binoculars.

"What do you see, Ed?" Vormund was seated on the roots of the cottonwoods. He was fanning his face with his cap.

"I'm not sure." He tried to get more of the bank into his field of vision. But the jutting rocks prevented him. "I'm going down to have a look. You don't mind resting a couple or three minutes, do you? I'll leave the gear with you. Maybe you'll see the trogon again."

"I doubt it. A man is allowed only one such vision in a lifetime."

Bugler stacked the chairs and netting alongside Vormund. It tickled Bugler. Dan looking like a desert rat, an old prospector, sitting amid the stuff.

Sections of the slope were wet and slippery with spring runoff. Bugler's heavy boots trod cautiously. He walked past the ledge where they had seen the trogon, past an old rockfall, down toward the rushing water.

Once more Bugler looked through his binoculars. What was that stuff sticking out? Junk left by campers? He saw them clearly now: two metal cylinders jammed into the soil at the edges of the stream. Projecting three inches above the ground, they looked to be about an inch in diameter. They had the appearance of nozzles or rusted metal tubing.

"If they're what I think they are," Ed said, "I hate seeing them anywhere, but especially here."

He skidded down the stream-dampened rocks, stumbled a few yards, and loped toward the sandy cove. Two yards from the metal projections he got on his haunches and studied the black rods.

"Haven't seen these in a long time," Bugler said sadly. "The homemade kind."

The upper part of each black cylinder had a piece of gray cloth tied around it. Bugler's nose twitched. He knew the stink. "Soaked in coyote urine. Cut the bladders out of the coyotes and use the urine for bait."

Querulous, with a tremor in his voice, Vormund was calling to him. "Ed? Are you all right?"

"Fine, Dan. I'll be right up."

Bugler took some photographs of the metal rods with the peculiar woolen wicks. The stuff looked like heavy flannel. He tried recalling the most recent regulations on poisons; in all likelihood the offensive metal rods were permissible. But rules had been changed so often nobody knew for sure. Legal or illegal, the mechanisms offended Bugler. Grace Canyon was too lovely, too pure, to tolerate such brutal devices. It was the place where he and Dan had seen the trogon. It was a crime to defile it with these wicked contraptions.

Bugler had never seen the old kind of coyote-getter pop, even from a distance. He knew how they worked. Attracted by the urine, the animal bit at the cloth wick. A cartridge went off, and the cyanide exploded into the beast's mouth. And didn't always kill them that fast. The coyote went into convulsions, ran in circles, died in agony. Ranchers claimed the modern guns, the M-44s, were more humane. Knocked the coyote off as fast as he bit at the wick. Maybe. They also killed domestic dogs, ferrets, foxes, badgers, any living thing unlucky enough to catch a blast of cyanide in the mouth.

Bugler decided he would remove them or at least set the charges off. He had always been curious about the cyanide guns. It would be a challenge to Essler or whoever had staked out the coyote-getters. *Bugler was here.* A little response to the people who put the burned pup in his jeep.

Setting his camera down, Ed found two long branches. He knelt on one knee and reached out with the sticks, trying to grip on the cloth wick. He was too far away and could get no leverage. He moved closer. The terrain sloped, the rocks were slippery, and he had trouble finding a place where he could grasp the flannel safely and set the charge off. Once more he knelt and tried to raise the wick with the sticks. It was tied to the metal pipe more strongly than he had imagined. The coyote had to give it a forceful tug to trigger the pellet. Fiddling around with branches would not set it off.

Bugler studied the problem. Why not his hand? Why not? The charge went upward, straight into the coyote's mouth. But if he gripped the urine-soaked cloth with his right hand, cupping it around the pipe, the cyanide would rise vertically and harmlessly, through the opening in his encircling fist. Nothing would hit him, because no part of his hand would be above the shooting poison.

This time he walked into the stream, feeling the cold water rush into his boots. Again he kneeled. Like plucking a snake out of its cage. You had to grab it firmly and quickly, and you could not get hurt (although Clara claimed he had been bitten more times than he would ever admit). And this was even easier. The metal cylinder could not strike at him.

He reached out, his huge hand open, ready to encircle the gray cloth and yank at it. All he had to do was avoid the top of the metal rod. As he moved forward, his knee slipped on the wet rocks. His right leg went out from under him. Extended, ready to grasp the cloth, Bugler's hand came down on top of the black pipe.

Vormund heard the explosion. It was a single *crack!* Like a shot fired by a small-bore rifle. The squirrel guns the children owned when he was a boy in Lexington. Then he heard Ed's outraged shout.

"Godammit, the thing went off."

The old man struggled to his feet. "Ed? What happened? Ed, are you all right?"

"This thing went off in my hand. Dan, stay there. I'll come up."

There was something in Bugler's voice he had never heard before. Surely the most confident of men in the desert, Ed sounded frightened.

Bugler struggled along the stream bank. Vormund, stumbling down the hill, saw his gray-clad figure. Ed was bent double, his hands pressed between his calves. Once he released his right hand and began to shake it, then wring it with the left hand, as if trying to squeeze something out of it.

"Oh boy," Bugler was saying. "Oh boy, that thing hurts."

"Ed! What was it?"

"Coyote-getter. One of those old things. A piece of pipe. It went off."

Vormund began to descend the slope to the stream. "Ed, how did it happen?" He could see Bugler kneeling under a juniper, squeezing his right hand as if to force blood out of it. He was wincing. It was not like Ed.

"I tried to set it off. The damned thing offended me."

"I'll be right there," Vormund said. "Don't move. Why do you have to look for trouble?"

Grabbing at branches for support, Vormund was at Bugler's side in minutes. Horrified, he saw how mangled Bugler's hand was. Something, a bullet or an explosive charge, had blasted into the soft part of the palm below the thumb. There was a bloody, diagonal wound in the flesh. Bugler kept pressing his left thumb against the edge of the wound.

"I'm getting dizzy."

"I'll help you up. You need a doctor. We'll get you to Senita."

"Damn. Why am I so weak? I can stand more poison than anyone in Doble County." He drew his breath in, drawing strength from the air. "Sodium cyanide. There's a 38-caliber bullet somewhere around here. It hit me, filled me full of the stuff. Christ, it hurts worse than snake bite."

"Give me your arm."

"I can manage." Bugler started to climb the hill. Abruptly he doubled over in agony. "No wind. My head isn't on straight."

"Put your left arm around my shoulder."

"No. I can make it. Like a fire in my hand."

"Listen to me, Ed. I'll get you up the hill. Give me your arm."

Vormund looked at Bugler's weather-toughened face. The hard lines had gone slack. The ruddy glow was fading. A sickly patina covered his features and he was sweating. Jaw taut, teeth exposed, he was breathing heavily.

"Getting it in spasms now. I know what it feels like to be a coyote and catch that stuff in the mouth. Jee-*sus*."

Vormund steadied himself. He was having trouble on the slope. His feet were shaking. "You listen to me. One of your failings is your insistence on doing everything yourself in the outdoors. You need help and I'm going to get you up that hill." He tried to sound commanding—an effort for him. Rude students had terrified him.

"All our stuff, you carry it, Dan. The blinds, the chairs . . ."

"Sidewinder will come back for them. Put your arm around me. I'll have you at the hospital in a half hour."

He watched Bugler grimacing, putting pressure on the wounded hand. The blood had stopped flowing, but the hand was angry red and swollen. Suddenly Bugler bent over, leaned against a cottonwood, and began to vomit in heavy spasms. His throat and mouth strained with the effort and his eyes were flooded with tears. "Better . . . *better* . . ." He straightened up, was gripped by convulsions once more, and began to heave again, bringing up nothing but a string of spittle that depended from the corner of his mouth. "Come on, Dan. I can make it. Can't be worse than getting bit by a coral snake."

A rush of strength encouraged Vormund. He would save Ed, get him back to Senita. Clara would fill him with nourishing soups. She would have someone else to nurse, to feed vitamins, dose with drops and pills. He slung Bugler's left arm over his shoulder and they started to ascend the hill to the blacktop.

"Dan, this is crazy. I can make it . . ."

"You can't. I see how weak you are."

"It's the dizziness. The ground is spinning. If I have to heave again, I'll warn you."

An endless climb, Vormund thought. His legs trembled. Virgil was right. Getting in was no problem. Getting out could be troublesome. He could smell the sweat on Ed's gray shirt. He could feel Ed's iron arm and hardwood torso against his. *A frail man I am*, thought Vormund, *and I have no right helping the likes of Ed, who can outwalk and outclimb anyone I ever knew.* After five minutes of arduous ascent, he could feel Bugler's body going slack. The muscles seemed to lose resiliency, tension.

"Stop and take a rest, Dan."

"No. I'm doing better than I expected."

He'd never been strong. A bookish, skinny youngster. In Lexington, he had run from fights, hidden in the attic, read Dickens, Smollett, Fielding, all of Grandma Dean's books that she had brought from Scotland. Or he would wander with his nature books in the woods outside the city, identifying birds and butterflies, weathering the scorn and fists of town toughs. Sister Mary. Four Eyes. Danny Boy. All his life he had envied those with strength, co-ordination, speed, endurance. Is this some test I am being given? Vormund wondered. A chance to prove that I can use my feeble body, overcome the years of asthma and fatigue and colds and headaches and bad stomachs? Exhausted, he plodded on, one foot following the other. He was practically dragging Ed. And the weight had grown heavier. Ed could do less and less with his own legs.

"What possessed you to try to set that thing off?" he asked petulantly. The words were punctuated with gasps.

"It offended me."

"Lots of things offend me, but I don't go sticking my head into trouble, looking to be poisoned."

"I slipped. I could have blown them right off, if I hadn't lost my footing."

Vormund shuddered. Ed sounded distant, ghostly. And he was in agony. Never a complainer, Bugler had clenched his teeth, occasionally emitting a grunt or a moan. Vormund wondered if Ed would make it to the jeep. Perhaps they would do better to flag a car. A truck driver might have a two-way radio. A police car would be even better. But it was not yet seven in the morning. There was virtually no traffic on the road.

"Hold it, Dan. I got to heave again."

Once more the spasms bent him in half. His body trembled. "Damn thing burns . . . like fire." Mouth stretched open, spittle dribbling, Bugler fell to the ground. He clawed at the earth, got on all fours, and tried to vomit again.

"Ed, get up. I'll help you. Give me your left arm."

Bugler rolled over. His face was smeared with sand. "Dammit, this is embarrassing. It's up my arm now, into the shoulder."

"You listen to me. Get on your feet. When I drag on your arm, come up with me. Ready? One, two, three!"

In agonized movements, Bugler got to his feet. "Maybe you better leave me. Get a doctor out here."

"I'm getting you back."

They continued their climb. The sun struck Vormund's face and revived him. "If I were stronger I'd carry you on my shoulders," Vormund wheezed. "You recall the story in the *Aeneid?*"

"Dan, I'm not one of your students." He groaned again.

Vormund told himself: This man cannot die, not Ed Bugler who has been bitten twenty times, who helped the badger dig his way to freedom.

"When they left Troy, Aeneas carried his father Anchises on his shoulders, because he was too weak to walk. A lovely story."

"Keep talking, Dan. It distracts me. The worst thing is I'm ashamed of myself."

"A bit further, Ed." Vormund's legs felt the strain. What had gone wrong with his knees? He felt the need of a strong young body, potent arms and legs, someone like Raymond Host.

"Consider the ant, Ed. He makes us look like weaklings, the way he lugs around weights twenty times his own. Who said we are God's finest work? No ant would agree."

"I can't keep my eyes open. Burning. Dan, drop me . . ."

"Your eyes are fine." The old man chattered on. It was like amusing a class of drowsy freshmen, teaching humanities when he was a young instructor. "You are the man who sighted the trogon."

"First-aid kit in the jeep . . ."

"I know. Try harder. Move your legs."

"Damned if I know what . . . what . . . what . . . burning me up . . . antidote for sodium cyanide . . ."

Pushing off his left foot, pressing the rubber sole against sand, pebbles, rocks, Vormund moved ahead. He seemed to be using someone else's body. His own, surely, was finished, a shell. He gulped for air.

"Iodine . . ." Bugler gasped.

"Yes, I'll take care of you." He stopped to catch his breath. Literature might help. Some recollection to keep his mind off the dread weakness in his legs, Ed's terrible weight on his shoulders.

"No, you're not Anchises. How could you be? I'm old enough to be your father. Old enough to be anyone's father. You're Achates. *Fidus Achates,* the faithful friend."

"Dan, I can't make it."

"A bit more, fidus Achates."

Vormund heard the rumble of a truck above them. He could see a section of the metal guard rail, the twisted stretch where the Host car had careened into the canyon. They had but fifty feet to go to the jeep. Bugler's right leg had gone dead, dragging, clinging to cactus spines.

"A few more steps, Ed."

Vormund did not understand how they had reached the railing, but they were there. The scaling of Everest, he thought, the moon landing. He was supporting almost all of Bugler's weight. He tottered, then stood erect at the rail. "Get your legs over the railing. We're safe, Ed."

"No strength. Burning all over."

Vormund half-lifted him by the chest. Something seemed to snap, change his breathing, his composure. Perhaps, he thought, just the creaking of old bones that had never been too strong. Triumphant, he was dragging Ed to the jeep.

"As I often have said, you have many defects of mind and numerous failings of character," Vormund said, "but you know how to find trogons and *orugas* and water holes. Get into the jeep. One leg at a time."

Bugler, as if in a trance, staggered to the side of the jeep. He rested against the battered metal hood.

"This is undignified, but it works. You've shoved my buttocks up many a mountain, so I can return the favor. A pity I'm not a brilliant young novelist. I'd find vast homosexual symbolism in all of this. Up you go."

Bugler collapsed onto the front seat. "Iodine, Dan . . ."

Vormund reached beneath the seat and found the first-aid box. He unscrewed the cap from the flannel-covered canteen and poured water into Bugler's Sierra cup, then gave him six aspirins. Immediately Bugler retched.

"Can't hold anything."

"Give me your hand."

Vormund doused the red gouge and the bloated hand with iodine, then tied a bandage over it.

"Would a tourniquet help?" Vormund asked.

Bugler's head lolled against the seat. His eyes were unfocused and tearing. "Poison's all over me, Dan. I'm dizzy as hell. Can't see too good."

"We'll try it." He found a clothesline in the back of the jeep and tied it around Ed's forearm. Shaking, his hands had trouble making the knot. He cursed his age, his frailty, his dependence on Clara for everything. He had run from fights, avoided the cruel pain-inducing aspects of life. No dune primrose could teach you to save a man poisoned by cyanide.

"I'll drive you back."

"Better . . . signal . . . police car . . ."

"Nonsense. Every second we waste, you could be under medical care."

Flexing his hands, Vormund sat at the wheel. For the past ten years Clara had chauffeured him around. He hated cars.

"Stick a white rag on the antenna . . . I can't talk . . . can't think . . ."

"I am capable of driving. Clara insisted I was too ill to drive. Now how do you start this thing?"

"Key. Turn clockwise. Pump gas. It's a shift . . . four speeds . . . you know how?"

"Of course. I had a Model T Ford when I was a college student in Lexington. There we go."

The engine exploded with a gratifying rattle. The jeep shook as if trying to dislodge its occupants. The noise roused two ravens from a gambel oak. They scolded Vormund with angry croaks, circled the jeep for a while before soaring into the canyon. The ancients called it a bird of ill omen. Vormund preferred not to think so. He had always regarded the raven's squawks as friendly, an avian salute. He wanted to assure Ed that the raven's farewell was a good sign. But Ed was half asleep, his arms loose in his lap. The massive hands looked lifeless.

The jeep roared into the parking lot at the emergency entrance to Senita Jewish Hospital. Vormund called for help and two Hispanic orderlies came running out.

"Poisoned," Vormund said. "A coyote gun. Get him at once."

The men wrestled Ed from the seat. Each took an arm and helped him to a seat in the emergency room. Bugler sat there, a big, heavy-boned man, clutching the wounded hand, breathing noisily, wincing with intractable pain.

A middle-aged blond nurse in a starched pants-suit asked for Bugler's hospitalization card, his address, his next of kin.

"The man has been shot by a cyanide gun," Vormund said. "He needs immediate attention. I am Professor Vormund of the Desert Research Institute."

"Are you a relative?"

"No. Will you take care of this man or shall I find a physician myself?"

"A relative must sign for him. I have to insist on his hospitalization papers. That is a rule."

Vormund stiffened. "Madam, you will attend to this man, or I will have you arrested and indicted. One more word about relatives or documents, and I will throw a chair. This man may die. He may be paralyzed. I will hold you and everyone in this hospital responsible. I am a bad man to antagonize."

"How dare you . . . you just sit down . . ."

"Your days are numbered, Madam." Vormund spun about and spoke to the two Chicanos in white uniforms. "My friends, I appeal to you. Take this man to a physician at once."

They obeyed him. Bugler, half conscious, saw what had happened. In Bugler's pain-deadened mind, he could recall the Mexicans in Baja, the Indians at Casagrande, looking at Dan, knowing in their primitive wise way that he had *quality*.

The men lifted Ed and carried him into a treatment room. At once Vormund, staring icily past the nurse, picked up a telephone and dialed the Institute. He spoke to Jack Maybank, told him of Ed's accident, and asked him to come to the hospital at once. What did Jack know about coyote-getters, the old homemade guns?

Vormund hung up and shuffled down the hall to the room where Ed lay on an operating table. His flesh was gray. His shirt was drenched. A resident physician was holding a broken capsule of amyl nitrate under his nose.

"Sodium cyanide, Doc," Bugler murmured. "In the right hand, off like a gun . . ."

"Be still, don't talk," the doctor said. "Had a case like this about a year ago. Rancher hit by his own cyanide gun."

A nurse jammed a needle into Bugler's left arm. "Some

Demerol," she said gaily. The arm looked like the limb of an oak. "The pain should subside," the resident said. "Now we'll neutralize that gunk in your system."

"How do you feel, Ed?" Vormund asked.

"It's no party. Always wanted to know how the animal felt who got the shot in the mouth."

The resident shook his head. "You Institute people. Mr. Bugler, you're going to get pumped full of sodium nitrites and thiosulphates. That should take care of the cyanide. The tourniquet was a good idea. Good first aid, Professor Vormund."

"Thank you. I always felt I could manage this sort of thing, if only my wife would give me a chance."

"My hand . . . burning . . ."

Vormund put a hand on Bugler's shoulder. "Another miraculous escape by Edward Earle Bugler."

The nurse wheeled a table covered with operating instruments alongside the physician. He picked up a scalpel.

"Can I help, Doctor?" Vormund asked.

The resident smiled at the cross-hatched face. He had heard Vormund lecture on Thoreau some years ago. "No thanks, Professor. We'll fill him full of antidotes and give him oxygen."

"Ed, you want me to stay?"

"Don't have to, Dan. Sleepy."

"I'll wait outside."

Once more something seemed out of kilter in his system. What? A dullness, an oppressive pain in his head, a sense of having been phased out, going from a positive state to a negative state. It was more than weakness, more than his usual run of headaches, shortness of breath. But Ed's life mattered now. Not his own incessant ailments.

The Maybanks arrived and found Vormund seated in the anteroom. He looked wasted, half asleep, the keenness gone from his blue eyes. His back was straight and his hands were on his knees. His appearance was almost trancelike. Jenny noticed that his lower jaw hung loosely. The lips were parted as if the facial muscles had lost strength. But he revived when he saw them and told them about Ed's wounding and the ride back to Senita.

"Is he okay?" Maybank asked. As he asked the question, he grew increasingly concerned about Vormund's appearance. The old man's eyes seemed to have retreated into the aged wrinkled skin. Fear? Shock?

"The doctor was optimistic. He seemed to know what he was doing."

"Poor Ed. That foolish man." Jenny shook her head. "What got into him?"

"Nothing. He behaved in true Buglerian fashion." Vormund drew his breath in. "I'm worn out myself. A little faint. But what a glorious day it was. We saw the trogon."

"That son of a bitch Essler putting those things out," Jenny said. She felt that by unleashing anger, she could contain her fears. Something was profoundly wrong with Dan. Bugler would probably recover; he handled poisons the way other men got over indigestion. But Dan?

"Easy, Jen," Jack said. "Everyone's using those things. But those old rigs with the bullet. It's a wonder Ed's alive."

"I want to go home," Vormund said. He sounded petulant, neglected. "Clara will be furious. She'll say I encouraged Ed to set that thing off. I didn't. It was his idea."

They could barely hear him. His lips had difficulty meeting. Dread thoughts germinated in Maybank's mind. He looked warily at his wife.

The resident came out of the emergency room. In his hand was a glass dish containing a wad of gray flannel about an inch square. It was stained dark red with Bugler's blood.

"This is what went into him," the doctor said. "That powder blast really sends it up."

"What in God's name?" Jenny cried.

"The wadding," Maybank said. "Sidewinder showed me one once. They stick it between the cartridge and the cyanide powder. How did Ed manage to get that into his hand? He's supposed to be smarter than a coyote."

"He's luckier," the doctor said. "I don't think he caught the full charge of poison, just the stuff stuck to the wad. Otherwise he'd be dead by now. It was a good thing the professor got him here in a hurry. Another half hour and he'd have been finished."

In a lost thin voice Vormund asked: "Will he recover? No impairment . . . ?" The voice trickled into nothingness.

"I'm pretty sure. He's asleep. We put him on pure oxygen to counter the toxic effects."

Jenny, trying not to think about Vormund's appalling pallor, his severe palsy, his slurred voice, tried to joke. "Mr. Bugler is a walking witches' brew, Doctor. He's been bitten by everything. Maybe he has an immunity."

"Not to cyanide. He's lucky. And he can thank Professor Vormund."

Jenny helped him out of the station wagon. His gait was different, dragging, hesitant. It seemed an eternity before they got to the kitchen door. Clara was waiting.

"You've been gone too long," she said. "And look at you. You're sick, I can tell."

On the ride from the hospital he had complained of a headache—a deep ache, unlike anything he had ever experienced.

"Inside and into bed," Clara said. "Jenny, take him in and I'll bring the Meritene and a hot-water bottle. Freezing out there in the morning, when we can see all the birds we want from our window."

"But not a trogon, my love."

Vormund stopped, as if unable to walk any farther. He lowered himself into the abraded leather chair from which he was able to look at the desert and the mountains. "Jenny, stay here," he whispered. "She'll be furious. I disobeyed her once too often. And when she hears what happened to Ed . . ."

"Forget about Ed. You need a doctor. I'll call."

"No, she'll begin to worry."

Clara entered. "Get into bed, Dan. I'll put something over on you."

The same old joke, Vormund thought. But she had not intended it as a joke. It had convulsed Ed, Jack, and the others on the camping trip in the Huachucas. But he was too old to camp out any longer. A morning of bird watching exhausted him. And that damnable ache in his forehead.

"What is it?" she asked. She lifted his feet to a hassock. "Worn out? Racing around the desert, cold in the morning, hot in the afternoon? Your skin is the color of a beet. Your head is hot."

Vormund shut his eyes and waved away the Meritene.

Jenny told Clara about the misadventure in Grace Canyon—Ed struck by the poison, the ride back, the hospital. But neither

— 304 —

pursued (as if reluctant to face some dread truth) Vormund's state. He was breathing noisily.

"Dan carried Ed up a hill? And drove back?"

"No choice, my dear. Ed would have died."

Clara began to weep softly. "You foolish man. Look at you. So exhausted you can't move. Jenny, what is wrong with him? I take such care of him, hot-water bags, ice packs, and look what he does."

"He'll rest, and he'll be better. Clara, they saw the trogon today."

"Indeed we did. Jenny, Sidewinder should go back there and get our gear. The bird log. Some other things."

"So tired he can't move, and he's worried about the bird log," his wife said.

"I'll take my nap. Clara, don't chastise me any more. I'll be splendid in the morning. If both of you will help me to the bedroom."

The women lifted him and helped him to the bedroom. Again, Vormund sensed some deep biological change in his body. Lax, unresponsive, a sensation of falling, evanescing. Was this an epiphany? A mortal one, as opposed to the divine revelation of the trogon?

"You look bad, Dan," Clara said.

He sat on the edge of the bed, holding his head in his hands. "Some aspirin. Or something stronger."

Jenny saw that his left hand was lifeless. When they had walked from the living room to the bedroom, he had dragged his left leg. "I think we should call Dr. Mark at once," she said.

Clara agreed. More than Meritene and aspirin were indicated.

In the living room, Jenny phoned Dr. Mark. He prescribed a sedative and promised to leave his office at once. The Vormunds were old friends.

Vormund took the sedative and fell to the pillow. His bedroom was small, crammed with his desk, bookshelves, folders, filing cabinets, boxes of photographs. Jenny smiled at him. He appeared to have shrunk, the substance of the man shriveling under the skin. The noble face appeared to have suffered some mysterious trauma. The eyes were less sharp, the mouth drooped. Only the high serene forehead was unaffected.

"I'm not asleep yet," he said, "so don't start talking about me. Jenny, about all that money we're getting."

"Yes, Dan."

"Ed is not to be fired. As I have said many times, he has many failings of character, but he is a rare person. Give him a raise. Tell Jack I said so. And it would be nice if someone bought Sidewinder a truck."

"Will you stop talking, please?" Clara said. Her voice was distorted.

"I have a few things to say before that pill starts to work. Jenny, are you paying attention?"

She dabbed at her eyes. "I am, Dan."

"As the most eminent nonsalaried member of the Board of Directors, I carry a bit of weight. After all, it was my immortal prose that hooked the late Denkerman."

Clara sat on the side of the bed and leaned over him. She kissed his cheek and embraced him. "You be quiet. Go to sleep. The nerve of you, climbing mountains. And when did you last drive a car?"

"It was in a good cause. If you had seen the trogon, Clara. More beautiful, more spectacular, than I imagined. Coppery green and geranium red, with a sassy white collar. God's artistry manifest in one happy bird. When I awaken, I want a report on Ed."

"The doctor said Ed will be fine," Jenny said. "Worry about yourself, will you, Dan?" She left the two old people. Clara was holding him in her arms.

The women sat in the living room watching the afternoon sun flood the desert with gold. Vormund had written that he could never get enough sun. It was the glow of eternity.

"His speech," Clara said. "It isn't clear. I know what happened."

"Don't, Clara."

"And the way he dragged a leg. And the arm limp. I know, I know."

"He's tired."

"Not just tired. Oh, my Dan." She sighed. "I knew if I left him alone, something like this would happen. But I don't blame Ed."

"Clara, you couldn't be with him every second."

"He was my child, my poor weak child. Those cold winters in

New York, sick every day, colds, coughs, headaches. One year Dan saw the desert and he felt better in an hour. These were the best years we ever had. He loved the desert because it was open and pure and beautiful, and it prolonged his life."

Jenny took her hand. "I know, Clara. And both of you have given us so much."

She shook her head, as if Vormund were present and she were reprimanding him. "That man. You know, in New York he was so shy, so withdrawn. Except for a few old friends like Tyler Merritt, he didn't warm up to people. But after a few months here, he was a regular westerner, slapping cowboys on the back, joking with Indians."

The phone rang. It was Jack, calling from the hospital. Bugler would live. His leathery body was overcoming the toxic dose he had taken. Jack had called Essler. Essler professed ignorance of the coyote-getters. Yes, they used the government-approved M-44s, and they posted warnings, but . . .

Jenny interrupted to tell him about Vormund. Shocked, Maybank said he would drive to the house at once.

"I'm glad Ed is all right," Clara said. "That will cheer Dan up. He can't stand anyone suffering pain. And you know how he loves Ed."

The women watched the hummingbirds spinning their wings, hovering, needlelike beaks poking into the vials of water. They would return, Clara thought, sip at the water, enliven and beautify the land, long after Dan was gone. She told herself that this would surely occur to him. *If man vanishes,* he had written, *rabbits may still run, and robins fly. . . .*

"Someone hurt Dan when he was very young," she said. "Before I knew him. I don't know the story. Hoodlums, some mean person. That was why he could not abide cruelty to anyone. He was even embarrassed when he got the traveling scholarship to Europe, when he was a graduate student. He was sorry that Tyler hadn't gotten it, they were both so brilliant. Dan walked across the campus on 116th Street in tears. He ran into Tyler, and can you guess what?"

Jenny had heard the story but she shook her head.

"Tyler had gotten the *same* scholarship. It was the first time they had ever given out two, because the boys were so bright. And what a time we had. The four of us lived in Paris near the

Luxembourg Gardens. I would make soup for us, because we didn't have much money, and we had fresh bread twice a day. We were so happy."

Maybank and Dr. Mark arrived within five minutes of one another. The physician was a tall long-jawed man in his forties, laconic, utterly devoted to Vormund. He spent twenty minutes in the bedroom, then came out, the stethoscope around his neck. He sat down next to Clara.

"He's had what we call a cerebrovascular accident," Dr. Mark said.

"A stroke?" Maybank asked.

"I suspected it," Clara said.

"Maybe not," the physician said. "But there does appear to be brain damage. I can't tell how extensive. It could be minor. His speech is slightly slurred and he was a little fuzzy about my name."

"And his leg," Clara said. "Dragging it."

"Possibly. Or maybe he's just fatigued. I heard about what happened in Grace Canyon. I doubt it's a hemorrhage. My guess would be a thrombosis or an embolism. It's serious, but people recover. A piece of the interior wall of a blood vessel breaks off and interrupts the flow of blood."

"But will he recover?" Clara asked. "If Dan is to be an invalid like that . . . not remembering things . . . not able to speak . . . his whole life was words."

"I can't guarantee anything. Dan's past eighty and he's no tower of strength. All we can do is make him rest and give him the proper medications."

"Shouldn't he be in the hospital?" Maybank asked. "Monitoring, nurses?"

"I was getting around to that," Dr. Mark said. "But maybe we can wait a day. He may need diagnostic tests, but I'm not too sure about giving them to him until he's stronger. A nurse in the house might be a good idea." He reached for the phone.

Clara stopped him. "No, you don't. I nursed him all these years and I'll do it now."

"Suit yourself, Clara. I forgot you were in the profession. Nobody knows him the way you do."

"I'm going to make that husband of mine well again. Give

Jack the prescriptions, and I'm going right in and look after him. He's not only my husband, he's my patient."

And always has been, Jenny thought.

Raymond Host sat through an interminable meeting with the corporation lawyers. They were discussing plans for the newly acquired Essler property. It was an important purchase and would open up a vast area of the desert to development. The planners envisioned a complex of retirement homes, dude ranches, tennis courts, condominiums, a junior college. The financial arrangements eluded young Host. His father had bought the land from Essler under some complex arrangement whereby both parties could save great sums in taxes.

Ray Host started to say something about the land. Was it not supposed to contain some rare botanical specimens? He had heard the Institute people discussing it. A cactus unlike any ever seen in the United States? Vormund and Bugler had talked about it as if the plants were tax-free bonds, growth stocks. Young Host wanted the matter looked into. Could they be saved? Could they build around them? Offer land to the DRI?

Answers were vague, noncommittal. Pop was not at the meeting. He wanted Ray to develop the Essler purchase. "I don't see why a *few* of these things can't be left standing," a lawyer said. And another: "Sure. Work them into the landscaping." But that was not what Vormund had in mind. He had preached the gospel of wildness, the earth and its wonders left as God had created them. But Vormund's views did not seem relevant in a board room.

And the Denkerman matter would not die. It remained on the agenda. Ray squirmed and gazed out the window. They were locating old medical records on Denkerman, getting affidavits. How could he be sane, keeping lions in the house, leaving a fortune to bird watchers?

Ray brooded and pulled his head into his massive shoulders. He could not find words to defend Vormund and his people. A sense of something lost, a friendship never consummated, a loyalty killed before it could enrich his life, embittered him. In the brief time he had known Vormund, he had been exposed to a mind so different, a set of values so rare, a challenge so unexpected, as to demand his attention, concentrate his thoughts, inspirit and delight him. Vormund heard different drummers, saw the world through a rare prism, lived his life with no regard for commerce, money, progress, all the things that the Hosts regarded as the be-all and end-all of existence. Looking at the scrubbed faces of lawyers and planners, all the vested scented men, he longed to see the spare sharp-eyed old man, hear his emphatic voice, the perfect sentences, the anecdotes that ranged from Marlowe to mud turtles.

"Denkerman couldn't have done this on an impulse," a lawyer was saying. "Someone got to him . . ."

"We have to look into that early stuff Vormund wrote . . . a lot of left-wing drivel . . ."

Host turned his back and dialed his home. He was concerned about Corinne. The doctors had warned her to rest, to let her bruises and scars heal. But she was insistent on playing tennis, hobbling around the court, her knees bandaged, a patch on her forehead. And she was drinking more recklessly. The maid answered. Mrs. Host was not at home. She was in the quarter-finals at the club.

The attorney who had looked into Vormund's writings held up a sheaf of Xerox'd clippings. "If Vormund was a political lefto of some kind, it might be useful in court," he said.

"How?" Host asked softly.

"Show that he was erratic, unreliable. First revolution, then saving coyotes. Not the sort of man whose writings were dependable. We could claim that Denkerman was misled by him."

Host's voice turned hoarse with anger. "That is the damnedest nonsense I ever heard. I met one of his former students at Senita. Vormund had no political ties, and he hated communism before it became fashionable to hate it. What did that fellow tell me?" Host shut his eyes. "Vormund couldn't stand Marx or Freud because they robbed man of his dignity."

The aromatic faces looked at him blankly.

"From what I'm hearing here now," Host said, "I wonder if a lack of dignity isn't characteristic of certain people in the free enterprise system."

"Just a suggestion," the lawyer said. He put the Xerox'd papers back.

"I don't want to hear anything about Vormund's politics

again," Host said. "If you have any secret data, any nasty stuff on how he stood on Shakespeare, let me know."

No one responded. Chastised, they awaited his next words. Was this Raymond Host?

What was it like, Raymond Host wondered, to sit in Vormund's classroom twenty-five years ago and hear him read from Homer or reminisce about Dreiser?

They heard him calling for Clara. It was dusk. He had eaten nothing, taken only weak tea. The doctor had given him blood thinners. Clara went in and stood at the side of the bed. The room looked smaller—too many books, folders, boxes.

"I'd appreciate something, dear," Vormund said.

"You want to know how Ed is. I've told you twice that he is fine."

"No, not that. Damnation, I can't keep my thoughts straight. It's those drugs the doctor gave me."

The words were imprecise. His speech was blurred. She sat beside him. "Don't talk too much. Tell me what you want."

"I can't remember now. You set me off with that reference to Ed. The photographs of the trogon. I must see them. Jack can have them developed."

"Everything will be done, Dan."

"Now I know what I wanted. Could you or Jenny move some of our plants outside the bedroom window? Put them on top of the potting shed so I can see them. The fishhook cactus and that young ocotillo you were nursing. This room never gave me much of a look at the desert. I wonder if Dr. Mark would let me stay in the living room? I'll miss the birds tomorrow morning."

"I'm sure he will."

Vormund closed his eyes. He had no pain, just a sense of absolute weakness, as if his body had surrendered. He knew that his speech was not right. The words came too slowly, the emphasis was wrong. And he had been the clearest of lecturers. *In my youth, before I lost any of my sense, I can remember that I was still alive.* He had done rather well, he felt. Losing one's senses at eighty-one was in the category of permissible failures.

He opened his eyes. "I suppose I'm dying."

"You are not. Dr. Mark says you will start showing improvement in a few days."

"I won't be fooled or humored. I am man enough to face up to it. That's the advantage of a peaceful life. You can be courageous at a time like this. It makes up for all the fights you avoided."

"I won't sit with you if you keep talking that way."

Vormund smiled. "Ready or not, here I come. That's what we used to say when we were children in Lexington. They may not be ready for me, but I'm coming anyway."

She began to weep. "Stop that, Dan."

"Listen to me, my love. I don't want them pumping me full of embalming fluid, all those wires and tubes running into me, trying to keep me going. I won't tolerate it. I refuse to die two or three or four times. I've never been a notably heroic man and I want no heroic measures. Let nature do its worst. Or I should say, its best."

"You are not going to die."

"It's not as bad as I imagined. It has a certain logic. And it is fitting that I die here, a place I loved more than any we ever lived in. What I absolutely refuse to do is to make a mess, and to keep bothering people, to have nurses and doctors hovering around me day and night."

"I'll be your nurse."

"I heard Jack and the doctor talking about the hospital. I won't go there. I'll go out like an old coyote or a wounded lion, without medical benefits. If you stay with me and listen to me talk, it won't be nearly as dreadful as they say it is."

"Dan, please . . ."

"Not exactly a Rabelaisian feast, but manageable."

The Maybanks were standing in the doorway.

"Want anything, Dan?" Jack asked.

"Not a thing. Clara is all I need."

"I spoke to Essler again. He says he'll clear those contraptions off his land."

"Jack, don't excite him," Jenny said.

"I want to hear about our small victories. I keep worrying that we lose all the big battles. That fellow Host, the older man, was right. Everyone wants power. They'll welcome the stench, the smoke, the filth, the poison."

"Is that anything to aggravate yourself over?" Clara chided.

"The battle has to go on."

The Maybanks left. They would move some of Dan's plants to the window. Especially the ocotillo—the long wands, waving in the faintest breeze. *The essence of life,* Vormund had called them.

"I'm glad the Institute's getting that fortune," he said. "Good things sometimes happen—if for the wrong reasons."

Jenny Maybank was in the doorway again. "Your writing did it, Dan."

"A fortuitous accident. In that great nature preserve in the sky, I hope to meet Mr. Denkerman and shake his hand."

Clara shook her head. "He is impossible."

"Have I ever told you the story of the old monk who was dying?"

"We don't want to hear it," his wife said.

"I do." Jenny smiled at him.

"The old fellow was breathing his last. The other monks stood around the bed and prayed. 'I pray for Brother Anthony's charity,' one said. 'I pray for his gentleness,' a second said. A third said, 'I pray for his holiness.' At which point Anthony sat up in bed and exclaimed, 'Don't forget my *humility.*'"

Jenny laughed. "Dan, what a story."

"It isn't much but it evoked polite laughter in Freshman Humanities. At least they were less hostile to me when I told jokes. There's the one about the old Orthodox Jewish gentleman who was dying . . ."

"I won't hear any more," Clara said.

In the living room Dr. Mark was telephoning a cardiologist. The specialist would try to get to the Vormund house in an hour. Hearing Mark's description of the symptoms, he suggested that Vormund be taken to the hospital at once.

"They won't permit it," Maybank said.

"It may save him," the physician said.

"This house and that view of the desert means too much to Dan. He's convinced he's dying and he'll die here."

"He's got a chance . . ."

Maybank shook his head. "If it means he'll be bedridden, with his senses impaired, forget it. I know Dan. Seeing the world clear and plain means too much to him."

Later, he slept fitfully, awakened, called for Clara.

"Clara, where did I have that attack of migraine that damn near blinded me? And you chasing after ice for my head? Was it in Vienne?"

"Orange, Dan."

"Of course. A Roman amphitheater. How can I ever thank you for the good care you gave me? You should have submitted a bill for medical services."

"You sound silly. You must be feeling better."

Turning his head, he looked at the spiked green plants outside his window. *I have loved the desert because it suggests to me endurance, courage, variation, that what seems to be scarcity is actually abundance. . . .*

"It's appropriate that I die first," he said. "Were you to die first, I could not manage. You were the only person who understood that I was not only a hypochondriac but also a very ill man. So it's good that we approach this matter, as the Bible says, decently and in good order."

"You will be running around the desert in a week, you and Ed."

"Listen to me. I want no myths arising about Vormund's last lines . . ."

"Please don't talk so much, Dan." She wept.

"I have made my livelihood with words. Why stop now? Clara, you must not cry. As you know, they started all sorts of myths about Thoreau's last words. That business of 'one world at a time' and the quote about never having quarreled with God. Not so. His last words were *moose* and *Indians.*"

"You must be getting better if your memory is so good."

"I had marvelous dreams before. The desert was flaming with flowers—rose-red beaver tails, pink fishhook blossoms, white saguaros, the pincushions' bright orange. I never saw so many flowers."

"It's a sign you're recovering."

He shook his head. "More likely those drugs the doctor gave me." He moved forward from the pillow. "No weeping, no services, no clergy. Cremate me. Give my ashes to the desert. I may help a saguaro reach maturity."

Jenny entered the room. "The cardiologist is coming. Dan, they insist you'd be better off in the hospital."

"Over my dead body. Which will present no problem very shortly."

Jenny stroked the silken white hairs on his head. "I heard Clara. You'll be climbing down Grace Canyon soon."

"It really isn't that frightening." He closed his eyes. "Odd, how Tennyson keeps popping into my head. I never cared much for him, but there's a certain funerary quality to his verse." He began to recite in the resonant voice of the great teacher:

"'It may be we shall touch the Happy Isles,
'And see the great Achilles, whom we knew . . .'"

"Think of something more cheerful," Clara said.

"Tennyson suits me in my current mood. He may be the pre-eminent figure in mortuary verse, a man born to write inscriptions for gravestones."

"It's useless," his wife said. "He keeps talking that way."

Vormund lifted himself on one elbow and again looked out the window to the enduring desert plants.

"Clara, wasn't that a grand day? The day you and I and Ed and Sidewinder found the *orugas?* And do you remember that incredible flower?"

"They were all grand days, Dan."

At eight-thirty every morning Fassman's tour of duty as over-night news editor ended. But because he was conscientious and could not sleep in his sunny apartment, he usually remained in the newsroom for an hour or two, discussing the news log with the day staff. Once, after his return from Arizona, he had called Wendi. She had cried a little. Fassman assumed the tears were for him until she informed him that her actor had moved out and stolen her twelve-hundred-dollar stereo. She would not let Alan talk to the boys. It was no use. She was still seeking her identity.

Sipping lukewarm coffee from a cardboard cup, Fassman began to read regional copy from the Associated Press. When he saw the short notice he blinked, read it again, then rested his head in his hands and did not talk to anyone for several minutes.

"Oh, dear," Fassman said. "He's gone."

Senita City, Ariz., April 29—(AP)—Daniel Dean Vormund, naturalist and writer, died early this morning at his home in Senita City. He was 81 years old. Death was due to a stroke.

Mr. Vormund was a leading conservationist and was in the forefront of the fight to save the American desert. He was the author of more than twenty books on nature and conservation, as well as works on literary subjects. Prior to coming to Arizona in the fifties, he had been a professor of English literature at Columbia University. He had been an editor and a critic for several scholarly journals.

Since 1969 Mr. Vormund served on the Board of Directors of the Desert Research Institute in Senita. He was active in helping preserve large areas of the Arizona desert.

He is survived by his widow, Clara Pandolfo Vormund. Services will be private.

"He deserved better than that," Fassman said, annoyed with the cold newspaper prose. "What about *Desert Idyll*, or *Journeys with Thoreau?*" But he could not be wroth with the obituary writer. He had never sat on a spring morning in Vormund's lecture hall and heard him extol Sheridan, read from a Congreve play, recite Dryden.

Fassman assured himself that his teacher had died peacefully. Understanding nature the way few men did, he must have accepted death as inevitable, a link in the mysterious chain, immutable, predestined, as appropriate as the blooming of a cactus flower or the digging of a badger. He had lived a long time, written a great deal, meant a great deal to many people. Above all, he had been his own man. A giant before the flood.

A copy boy dumped a Los Angeles *Times* on his desk. A news writer was shouting at the operator to get him the LA fire department. The clamor seemed irrelevant, frenzied. No, Fassman thought, I can't force his standards on anyone, or even myself Better to think of Vormund in his prime. No enemy of words or man's achievements, a man with a foot in both worlds.

Fassman could see Ballstead scowling at the layers of morning smog outside his office. They had discussed a possible program with D. D. Vormund, letting the old man sit on his patio and talk. Now it would never happen. People would have to go to libraries and bookstores to share his wisdom.

Impulsively Fassman reached for the phone and asked the operator to get him Mr. Raymond Host at Host-Labarre. With some difficulty the newsman got through to a secretary.

"Mr. Host is in a meeting," the woman said.

"This is rather important." It was unlikely Host knew. The Associated Press had just moved the story. Radio newscasts would hardly consider Vormund's death worthy of mention. The hills above Malibu were burning again, and there had been a triple murder in Redondo Beach.

"What is your name?" she asked.

"Alan Fassman. I'm with station KGDF."

"Does Mr. Host know you?"

"We met in Senita City a few days ago. I'm a journalist."

"I'll give him your name but I doubt he'll call back. He's in meetings all day."

Processing the desert, Fassman thought. "I see. Could you tell him—"

"Can I help you? Can you tell me what it is you want?"

"Tell him Professor Vormund died today."

"Who?"

"Daniel Vormund. He'll know."

"Spell it, please. Where does Mr. Host know him from?"

"They met in Senita City."

"Why should Mr. Host be interested?"

"That's a good question. Maybe you could ask him."

Two hours later in drugged sleep in his studio apartment, Fassman was awakened by the phone. It was Ray Host.

Again, the cautious voice. "Mr. Fassman? Raymond Host. You say Vormund died?"

"It was on the AP report. There weren't any details. Just that he had a stroke and died early today."

"I see. Did you call? Talk to his wife?"

"I'm going to call the Institute in a little while and talk to the Maybanks or Bugler."

There was no response. Fassman could see the blocklike ruddy face, the blond curls, the aura of health, power, wealth, success, breeding, an ultimate Californian. "I suppose I should call even though I didn't know him that well. Are you going to the funeral?"

"I think so. It says services are private but maybe Mrs. Vormund won't mind."

"Right." The buried voice seemed to be struggling. "If you decide to go, call me. I'll be glad to give you a lift in the company plane."

"Thank you. But I work such screwy hours. I'm not sure when I can leave. I'll have to squeeze in a visit when I can."

Fassman, naked except for his jockey shorts, sat up in bed. He wondered what Host's bedroom looked like. Did the man ever suffer insomnia? Was he ever depressed, lonely, constipated?

Fassman dialed the Desert Research Institute and spoke to Jenny Maybank. She told him what had happened—the trip to Grace Canyon, Bugler wounded by the cyanide gun, Vormund bringing him to the hospital. And dying of a stroke two days later. If Fassman wanted to come to the service, it would be all right. He would be the only one of Vormund's former students present.

Lime-green, gleaming in the sun, the pickup truck was parked at the edge of the Institute's lot. Fassman drove his rented car into the space next to it. The truck, a new Ford, looked as if it had been driven off the Detroit assembly line a few hours ago. By contrast the yellow buildings looked dingier than ever. The newsman scanned the horizon and the hazed mountains. Hot, hot.

Sidewinder and Bugler came out of the adobe office. In the background, Fassman heard the squeals and grunts of the peccaries. They were aroused by the sight and smell of their keepers.

"Hi, Sidewinder. Hello, Ed. Out of the hospital so soon?"

Bugler greeted Fassman with a bandaged right hand. "Take more than a dose of cyanide to kill me." He frowned. "Thanks to Dan. What a dumb stunt I tried and getting Dan involved. I hope Clara isn't sore at me."

"She ain't," the Hopi said.

"About Vormund," Fassman said. "He . . ." What could he say about him, that these two did not already know?

"We'll sure miss him," Bugler said. "Only Dan could look at a lizard and find you a poem to go with it." He shook his head. "All that money will come in and the Maybanks will put up a research building. But it'll never be the same. Dan gave the place meaning."

"I know, Ed."

They walked to the green pickup. Bugler held the door open for Fassman. Sidewinder climbed in and settled into the driver's seat, as if he had been born to handle Ford pickups.

"Did the Institute buy this?" Fassman asked. "The Denkerman money so soon . . . ?"

"It's mine," Sidewinder said. "Miz Vormund bought it for me." His clouded eyes studied the bright dashboard with the same intensity with which his ancestors read peyote buttons.

"Mrs. Vormund did?"

"Got a cruising gear and four-wheeled drive."

Bugler was smiling. The pickup's tire dug into the sand, bounced onto the blacktop.

"It was Dan's idea," Bugler said. "Couple or three hours before he died, he called Clara in. His mind was clear and the sentences were perfect right to the end. He says, 'Clara, the banks are still open, so there'll be no problem. Go to our bank and take out enough cash to buy Sidewinder a pickup truck. If we wait I'll be dead and I know how these estates get tied up. I would like to know while I'm still breathing that Sidewinder has it, because he's given me so much pleasure.' Clara went right out and got the money and our friend here owns a truck."

"Yeah," the Hopi said. "Dan was okay. Dan understood."

Fassman wiped hot tears from his eyes. Too much dust, too much heat. "What did he understand, Sidewinder?"

"Whole lot of things."

At the fifth road past the Pima Trading Post the Hopi bounced the truck over an irrigation ditch onto a cattle path. They rode through a cattle guard. After less than a mile, they could see a half-dozen vehicles parked beneath the saguaros.

"It's Clara's idea," Bugler said. "She wanted to go out to where we found the creeping devils, but it's too much of a trip. This is close enough."

About twenty people had gathered around the automobiles. Fassman saw the Maybanks, and the students who worked at the Institute, some elegant elderly ladies (perhaps the beneficiaries of Clara's nourishing soups) and the bearded biology teacher.

Clara Vormund was standing with the Maybanks. Her round strong face was very much in command. She would see to it that Dan's last rites were exactly as he wanted them, just as she had seen to it that the Meritene was always ready and the ice bag good and cold.

"I'm so sorry, Mrs. Vormund," Fassman said. "I hope it's all right for me to be here."

"I am glad you are here, Alan." She gazed about her. "This is Dan's favorite kind of desert—ocotillo, saguaro, lots of bare sand."

Fassman looked at a gray-haired man with the face of a Roman senator. He was resting on a cane. "Professor Merritt," Fassman said. "You taught me the nineteenth-century novel over twenty years ago."

Clara introduced Fassman to Tyler Merritt. "I don't remember you, but I'll take your word," Merritt said. "Do you live here?"

"Los Angeles. I visited Professor Vormund recently."

"It's fitting that at least one former student be present. Someone who remembers Ben Jonson and Wimpy."

"I never forgot."

The Maybanks greeted him. Fassman sensed that he had not intruded. Jenny Maybank pointed to a white Mercedes that had just parked at the rear of the other cars. Raymond Host got out. He wore a dark blue suit, a white shirt, a dark blue tie. He walked toward Clara hesitantly, as if trying to minimize his strength and his youth and his wealth, stopping once to talk to Ed and Sidewinder at the green pickup.

As Host approached Clara, Fassman stepped back. Fassman's claim on Vormund and Vormund's memory was easily understood—a former student seeking assurances, good sense, guidance, from an old teacher. But what had Raymond Host been seeking?

Host, standing stiffly, was expressing his condolences to Clara. She introduced him to Merritt. The young man stood with the two old people, rigid, polite, nodding his head.

Joe Fusaro walked up to Fassman. "How well do you know that dude? I mean, the two of you being from LA and all."

"Out of my league. Nobody knows the Hosts except the people *they* want to know."

"Crazy, his coming back. First time out, he's casing us to see how he can break the Denkerman will. And now he's here for Dan's funeral."

"Maybe he's taking pictures with a hidden camera," Fassman

said. "The way the FBI does when they bury a Mafia boss." Saying it, Fassman was immediately ashamed of himself.

"Who knows?" Fusaro asked. "Maybe Dan got to him. Dan had that effect on some people." The lawyer scowled at the desert floor. "Still, I can't figure all the angles. The estate lawyer phoned me yesterday. The rumor is the Hosts are still after the Denkerman money. And here's Junior among the mourners."

"Look who else," Fassman said. He pointed to a Cadillac that had arrived. Duane Essler, Mac Timmons, and some of the "posse" got out.

"That crowd," Fusaro said. "They respected Vormund. What he preached would have them out of business, but they figured he couldn't hurt them, because no one cared."

"They could be wrong," Fassman said.

Bugler was striding toward them. "You guys won't believe this, but guess who's flying the plane."

"Plane?" Fassman asked.

Bugler explained that it was Vormund's wish that his ashes be strewn over the desert. Clara decided that the site where they had seen the creeping devils would have pleased him. "Mrs. Essler's at the controls," Bugler said. "Alan, remember her? The dame who blasted us when we set the lion loose?"

"How could I forget? Maybe she wants to make sure Vormund doesn't rise from the dead and haunt them."

"No," Fusaro said sadly. "They didn't agree with a thing he said, but they respected him. They knew he was high class."

Bugler folded his arms. Still in the faded Sears work shirt, Fassman noticed, but with a black tie. "I'll never forget how Dan threw his arms out that day when we saw those cacti," Ed said. "Like he wanted to embrace them."

Fassman wondered about the appearance of people like the Esslers, and for that matter, Raymond Host. They were the vigorous *users* of the earth and Vormund had opposed them. But they honored him, regarded him as a worthy adversary. What did it mean? That his warnings would go unheeded, or be distorted? Were his prophesies as flimsy and wind-borne as his remains would soon be? Fassman did not know.

He looked at Ray Host's blocklike figure. There was a strange one, a brooder. He had seen some vision on a dusty road to Damascus, Arizona. Would he ever be the same? Again Fassman had no answers. Perhaps all Host had sought was someone who talked, thought, and behaved differently from the lords of the earth among whom he moved.

The Maybanks were asking people to come closer and form a circle around Professor Merritt. At Clara's request Merritt would say a few words. Fassman battled tears again. There was no use weeping over the past. He was delighted Merritt had come—an elegant reminder of better times. He had stuck it out on Morningside Heights well past retirement age.

"Mr. Vormund wanted no eulogies," Merritt said, "but Clara tells me that this is one time we can disobey him. He was a forceful man in his quiet way but not an easy man to know. He influenced so many of us and in so many ways. How could he not help but do so? He loved life on this earth as few men do. Not just his own, but the lives of all creatures in God's scheme. And he spent the last quarter century of his life defending them from those men who, out of ignorance or greed, would wipe them out."

Fassman glanced at Host and at the Essler party. They seemed subdued. But surely they made no identification with Vormund's enemies. How could they? All they sought was progress.

"Dan was ill a great deal. We who knew him for sixty years joked about his ailments, and paid tribute to Clara's devotions as his nurse. Yet the truth was he was always ill—in pain, exhausted, despondent. But he did not let these handicaps deter him from a life of achievement that might have furnished material for a dozen lifetimes. What a man he was! How many rich lives he led! Writer, teacher, biographer, editor, naturalist, philosopher . . . I have probably left a few out. He told me not long ago that he would settle for being remembered as an inspector of wild flowers.

"How many times have we turned to Daniel Vormund to remind us that life is rich, rewarding, joyful, and that the harmonious madness of the skylark is around us every day if only we seek it out! But he was more than a naturalist, a mere observer of nature. Dan was a prophet in the desert, warning us to stop destroying God's domain lest we bring on our own destruction. Withal, he was a cheerful prophet, ready to praise the goodness of mice, exalting the beauty of a hawk's flight. Dan taught us the lesson that life was never ugly except to those indifferent to it, or to those who despised it and destroyed it.

"Good-by, Dan. All of us who knew you as friends, students, readers, all of us who listened to your wise voice salute you. For my own part, I can truly say, 'We have heard the chimes at midnight, Master Shallow.'"

For a while no one moved. No one spoke.

Bugler wiped his eyeglasses and whispered to Fassman: "Dan pulled that line on me the other day. When we saw the trogon. I guess he and Tyler used it before."

"I guess so, Ed."

Fassman saw Host walking away—stiff, solitary, ignoring the greetings from Essler's people.

The monoplane hummed toward the funeral party. It flew low, a growing mote in the burning sky. Soon the engine's noise was surprisingly loud, cutting the silence. Lower and lower the plane flew, circling the people in the clearing, then making a wide turn and pointing its nose toward Vormund's beloved *orugas*.

They squinted and shaded their eyes and tried to see the final act.

Fassman saw it, and so did Bugler, and they nodded to one another as a thin streak appeared in the sky and then diffused to settle invisibly on the dry land.